Shall We Dance?

MAGGIE
ALDERSON

PENGUIN BOOKS

PENGUIN BOOKS

Published by the Penguin Group
Penguin Group (Australia)
250 Camberwell Road, Camberwell, Victoria 3124, Australia
(a division of Pearson Australia Group Pty Ltd)
Penguin Group (USA) Inc.
375 Hudson Street, New York, New York 10014, USA
Penguin Group (Canada)
90 Eglinton Avenue East, Suite 700, Toronto, Canada ON M4P 2Y3
(a division of Pearson Penguin Canada Inc.)
Penguin Books Ltd
80 Strand, London WC2R 0RL England
Penguin Ireland
25 St Stephen's Green, Dublin 2, Ireland
(a division of Penguin Books Ltd)
Penguin Books India Pvt Ltd
11 Community Centre, Panchsheel Park, New Delhi – 110 017, India
Penguin Group (NZ)
67 Apollo Drive, Rosedale, North Shore 0632, New Zealand
(a division of Pearson New Zealand Ltd)
Penguin Books (South Africa) (Pty) Ltd
24 Sturdee Avenue, Rosebank, Johannesburg 2196, South Africa

Penguin Books Ltd, Registered Offices: 80 Strand, London, WC2R 0RL, England

First published by Penguin Group Australia Ltd, 2010
This edition published by Penguin Group (Australia), 2011

1 3 5 7 9 10 8 6 4 2

Cover design by Emily O'Neill © Penguin Group (Australia)
Text design by Kirby Armstrong © Penguin Group (Australia)
Cover photograph by Michele Aboud
Stylist Amanda Moore
Hair and make-up by Michael Wolf
The Vintage Clothing Shop blouse and skirt
Bally shoes
Diva ring

Typeset in Fairfield and Serifa by Post Pre-Press Group, Brisbane, Queensland
Printed and bound in Australia by McPherson's Printing Group, Maryborough, Victoria

National Library of Australia
Cataloguing-in-Publication data:

Alderson, Maggie
Shall We Dance?/Maggie Alderson
9780143205609 (pbk)

A823.3

penguin.com.au

For Victoria Killay

Author's note

This book is set in the lovely London 'village' of Primrose Hill, in a house around the corner from where I used to live. I still have such a sense of ownership of the neighbourhood that I've allowed myself free licence with the architecture, setting my heroine's shop in a row of houses at the eastern end of Regent's Park Road, which is strictly residential. I wanted her to have a terrace. I gave her one.

I

Loulou

'I don't know why you're so hung up about this stupid birthday anyway,' said my daughter, Theo, from the damningly casual perspective of a twenty-one-year-old. 'You're only going to be forty-nine. Isn't it fifty you're supposed to worry about?' You know, the big "Five Oh"'

She made those annoying inverted commas signs with her fingers as she said it, simultaneously pulling a pained old person face and bending over as though she had a hump. Charming.

'No,' I said, throwing the wretched harem pants I'd been trying on down onto the changing room floor in disgust. They made me look stunted. Stunted and incontinent. 'That is a common fallacy,' I continued, reaching for a rather lovely floral chiffon dress which Theo had brought in. She did have a good eye, I thought. Maybe there was something in genetics, after all. Shame she didn't use it more productively.

'Everyone gets so hung up about the big "0" birthdays,' I continued. 'But the nines are actually much worse. For a whole year everyone thinks you're lying about your age.'

'Aren't you?' said Theo.

'No,' I said crossly, my voice muffled by the dress which was now stuck somewhere between my shoulder blades and my upper arms, half on and half off. 'But I'm going to start – from now on I'll tell everyone I'm fifty-eight and then they can all say how marvellous I look.'

Then as I finally got my head out of the dress and into daylight again, I realised that Theo wasn't even listening. She was too busy admiring herself in the blasted harem pants, while simultaneously sending someone a text.

'Can I have these, Mum?' she asked, when she saw me looking at her.

'Sure,' I said, starting to put all the garments she had dropped on to the changing room floor back on their hangers. As the proprietor of a dress shop myself I had a lot more respect for the merch than she did. 'You're an adult. You can spend your money on whatever you like.'

'But Muu-uuu-uuum,' she said in a very non-adult wheedly tone guaranteed to lock my wallet tightly closed. 'I haven't got any money . . .'

'Well, you'll have to save up then, won't you? And what have you done with it all? I thought your father paid your allowance at the beginning of each month – it's only the fifth of May.'

She looked sheepish.

'Have you spent it already?' I asked, incredulous.

She nodded.

'On . . .?' I persisted.

'I'm having all the hair lasered off under my arms and on my bikini line. It's really expensive, but it's for life. Ariadne had it done and it's amazing. You've always told me how important grooming is . . .'

I picked up the harem pants and pretended to cuff her around the head with them.

'Well, I suppose that is an investment of sorts,' I said, slightly relieved she hadn't spent the lot in one splurge on throwaway clothes in Primark, which she was more than capable of doing.

'I will buy you these trousers, because they do look great on you, but please try and budget better, because now I'll be subsidising you for the rest of this month. The one thing your father is good for is money, but you still need to learn how to make it work for you. I had to.'

She put her head on my shoulder and looked up at me with her most appealing smile. It was hard to resist. She was exceptionally pretty, which I could say without embarrassment, because she looked a lot more like her handsome bastard father than she did me. I knew I was striking rather than beautiful and I was used to that. I'd been told often enough I was a 'style icon' not to be hung up about it, but Theo was properly gorgeous.

'Thank you lovely Mummy,' she said.

'You work me like a whore sometimes,' I said, shaking my head. 'Go and pay. I'll see you at the bottom of the escalators.'

I handed her my wallet and she skipped off as happily as a six-year-old heading for the swings. I stayed behind, grateful to be getting back into my own clothes, which I was happy to see still looked as good as they had when I got dressed that morning.

There was a reason I was a bit of a legend in the London fashion scene, I reminded myself, even if I was too old to carry off chain-store tat. Then I put everything back on the hangers and braced myself for the heaving melee that was the sales floor of Top Shop Oxford Circus.

The craziness nearly swept me away before I even got out there. The corridor in the changing area seemed to be full of young women with very little on, dashing between cubicles, squealing and waving clothes in the air. A pair of pointy pink bosoms bounced past at eye level and a round black bottom in a bright white g-string appeared between the curtains of another changing room, as someone bent over to pull up some jeans. It was all a bit much.

I remembered with a shudder the communal changing rooms in Miss Selfridge, which had been the big thing when I was Theo's age. Had we skipped about happily half-naked like this? I didn't think so. My abiding memories were the smell of other people's feet recently released from cheap shoes and the constant fear your handbag was going to be nicked.

Those changing rooms were one of the many reasons that even as a teenager I had preferred vintage clothes. I'd always thought browsing in charity shops, flea markets and jumble sales was far preferable to fighting for your life in hard-edged mass market hell-holes like this.

But for Theo and her friends, I knew this was shopping Shangri-la and that's why I checked it out every few weeks, with her as my eager escort. As a fashion retailer myself, I had to stay up with the game.

I handed our pile of unwanted clothes to the girl at the changing rooms entrance, who seemed amazed they were back on the hangers, and then made a break for it. The shop seemed even more crowded than it had when we'd come in and my head whirled with the music, the crush of people and the crammed racks of clothes.

Despite the sensory overload I couldn't help noticing, as I made my way through, a shiny black PVC trench coat with a very full skirt, a blouse in a printed sheer with interesting high puffed sleeves, and a terrific blue-and-white stripe seersucker boyfriend jacket.

But then spotting the one fabulous garment among great piles of tat was my special talent. My eye was as finely trained as a wildlife photographer looking for a particular kind of ant in a rainforest, to finding exquisite old clothes in the wild. I'd always been able to do it, which is why I'd ended up rather prominent in my particular world, as a dealer in the finest vintage clothing.

When I was fifteen I'd found a Balenciaga couture coat at a jumble sale in the affluent Cheshire town where I grew up. Something about the fabric had caught my eye and once I'd grabbed it and had a proper look, I'd known immediately the coat was something special. Although in those pre-Google days, it had taken a trip in to the big library in Manchester to find out what the name on the label meant.

Not long after, when I bought a Savile Row dinner jacket for 20p in an Oxfam Shop and sold it to a friend's boyfriend for £2, my future was decided. As I would say to the fashion journalists who often rang me for quotes, I was dealing in vintage long before they came up with a fancy name for it.

Needless to say, Theo wasn't at the bottom of the escalators when I got there. I hung around for a few minutes, getting more and more impatient, because I had to get back to the shop before my assistant left, and then called her.

'Where the hell are you?' I asked, exasperated.

'Coming!' she said brightly and rang off.

Five minutes later she finally appeared, smiling and pink of cheek, toting a bulging carrier bag.

'What the bloody hell is all that?' I asked.

She grinned at me in a way I was clearly supposed to find winning, but it made her look so like her father at the same age it had the opposite effect. My heart turned to granite.

I grabbed the carrier and opened it to see that the harem pants I had agreed to had been joined by several other items. The floral dress was in there and a glimpse of striped fabric told me she'd spotted the seersucker jacket too. Fortunately, I could also see the receipt.

'Can I have my wallet, please, Theo?' I asked with all the control I could muster and once she handed it over, I headed determinedly towards the row of tills. I wasn't going to let her get away with this outrageous behaviour. I was going to return it all.

'Muu-uuu-uum!' she said, trotting along beside me. 'What are you doing? I'll pay you back . . .'

'Then you won't have any money in June, either, Theo,' I said, getting really exasperated. 'The bank took your credit card away because you were so irresponsible with it and now you're just using mine. It has to stop.'

She looked defeated, but not for long.

'Can I just have the boyfriend jacket?' she tried. 'It's so great on me . . .'

'You know, Theo,' I said, turning to look at her as I took my place in the queue, 'if I wasn't obsessed with clothes myself I would think you were actually deranged, but I had to learn how to manage my money when I was your age and I'm going to make you do the same if it kills me.'

'But your dad was really rich,' she said petulantly.

'He was well off,' I qualified. 'But he didn't start that way. He made every penny himself and made damn sure we kids understood the value of it. Your dad's not short of a few bucks either, but wherever it comes from, you've still got to learn to manage it. This is all going back.'

'Even the harem pants?' she said, sounding wretched.

I sighed.

'OK, you can have those,' I said, my resolve crumbling, as the genuine disappointment in her voice reminded me painfully of the adorable little girl she used to be. I knew I should be tougher, but somehow Theo always found a chink in my defences. And, I told myself, knowing it was pathetic self-justification even as I thought it, if I couldn't wear them, at least she could.

'I will buy you those,' I continued. 'Because I already said I would, but here's the deal: you have to show your gratitude by promising at least to make an effort to live within your monthly budget. You're so lucky to have a bloody allowance. My dad made me work for mine doing boring filing, but you just have the money dropped into your lap. You really have to start being responsible about it. Most people your age are supporting themselves, you know . . .'

But I was wasting my breath. She was already texting again. I might have had the chance to continue the lecture more calmly on the way home, but she mumbled something about meeting a friend, so I kissed her goodbye at Oxford Circus and headed off.

All the way along Upper Regent Street, past Broadcasting House, over Marylebone Road, and on into Regent's Park, I beat myself up for being weak with Theo about the stupid trousers, which then developed into a more general anxiety about her refusal to adopt any level of adult behaviour. What was wrong with her? And was it my fault?

Her father hadn't helped, of course, abandoning us both when she was barely a year old, and it certainly hadn't been easy being a single mum, trying to make a family out of just two people, but I'd done my best. Clearly, though, it wasn't enough.

At Theo's age, I reflected, as I paused to look up at a beautiful chestnut tree already in full leaf, I'd already had my own business for two years, based in my own house. The one where we still lived in Primrose Hill, with the wrought iron sign saying 'Loulou Land' in curly letters hanging over the door.

I'd put down the deposit on the five-storey house, with a shop on the ground floor, with the money my dad had given me when I'd announced I wasn't going to take up my place to read history at university, but wanted to start a business instead. He'd been delighted.

'That's my girl,' he'd said, beaming at me across the family dinner table. 'Ditch the books and make some brass.'

I smiled at the memory, but tears also filled my eyes, as I wished yet again that he hadn't died before seeing what how well I'd done with his capital. He would have loved it. But if he hadn't had that fatal heart attack all those years ago, shouting at someone in his board room, whatever would he have made of my slacker daughter?

All she'd achieved since leaving school was a dismal gap year working in a café along Regent's Park Road from our house, before cruising through her art college foundation year with minimum effort, still living at home.

She hadn't even bothered to do anything about applying to other colleges for the next stage, so I'd had to do it all for her.

My first instinct was the fashion design degree at St Martins. It seemed a no-brainer for a girl who'd been dandled as a toddler on Jean Paul Gaultier's knee and had a princess dress made specially for her fourth birthday party by Jasper Conran – they were both long-time clients and friends – but she'd thrown such a wobbler at the suggestion, I quickly gave that idea up.

I'd thought she was finally on her way when I got her into Manchester Art College to do illustration, which made sense for someone who had been drawing fashion dollies since she could hold a wax crayon.

Away from me – which was clearly what she needed – but back to my north England heartland, where my sister and brother and all Theo's cousins still lived, it had seemed ideal. But, no, she'd dropped out in the second term, turning up in the shop one afternoon, declaring illustration to be 'kiddie art for retards' and Manchester and everyone in it to be 'desperate and naff'.

Since then, for over a year, she'd just been cruising. Living off me and her absent father, who assuaged his guilt about leaving by paying her a generous allowance which, as a very successful commercials director based in Los Angeles, he could easily afford.

As I reached the perimeter of London Zoo at the top of the park, I was reminded all too poignantly of taking Theo to that spot when she was still a little girl. In those days you'd been able to see right into the wolf enclosure through the fence and she'd been fascinated by them.

It had become a daily ritual for the two of us to walk down there to say hello to the 'wooves' before I opened the shop each morning, with a round trip back via the playground in Primrose Hill park, and a snack as we sat on one of the benches on the top of the hill, which we came to consider our own. We still did.

I glanced at my watch as I waited to cross Prince Albert Road, thinking how much I would have liked to continue my walk right up the hill to spend a while sitting on that bench, with its wonderful views over London. But I had barely ten minutes to get back to the shop before my assistant was due to leave for the day.

So no time to be maudlin now. I had a business to run. Time for Loulou Landers to make some brass.

Theo

Diary date: Wednesday, Why-nes-day?

Went on a Top Shop raid with Loulou Zulu Lala the mad mother who is still trying to be down with the kids. Tragique c'est chic – PAS. Got wicked harem pants which look genius on me.

Wanted a boyfriend jacket and other stuff as well but Zulu Lala got all Northern on me and said I was lucky to be getting anything snore snore snore and how she'd been sent up chimneys to earn her crust. Her father sounds like a right old nightmare. Not like I exactly love mine puke sick vomit but at least he hands over the cash without any fuss. Squeeze that guilt gland. Oh yeah. Pay up daddy dearest. Nonghead.

Lala is still obsessing on her stupid yawny birthday which is so madmadmad. Who does she think cares how old she is? Think I will buy her that dress I want as her present ha ha ha. In my size.

Have horrible spot on my nose. Thought spots were strictly for teenagers and supposed to disappear once you are 20. Feel cheated of promised adult advantage.

Had coffee with Tattie who went on and on and on and on about the work experience she's supposed to be doing at Dover Street Market. Bore RING. Couldn't even be bothered to tell her that most of the designers for sale in there are my mother's regular clients. Bunch of fashion vampires. It's all just so dull to me.

I love clothes the more the better gimme gimme gimme but

I don't have to micro-analyse them for god's sake. Make it all into some kind of draggy homework. I just want to wear them. Look at me!!!!! I'm faaaabulous!!!!! I don't need to talk about them. Listened to way too much of that when I was a kid. Spent all my formative years surrounded by hags and poofs ranting on about divine plackets – give me an enormously massive break.

Tattie said she and Ari are going to some new bar opening in Hackney tonight and I should go with but can't be bothered. Too pustular. Want to play dressing up with new harem pants plus have selection of freshly downloaded black-and-white movies to work through and latest *Heat!* mag. Perfect night really.

Also have house to self as Lala the Mad has gone out to see Keith the Teeth. Lucky her – so not. I told her the only thing worse than a tragic fag hag was a tragic *old* fag hag but she didn't seem to think it was funny.

Picked spot now has 3D crust. Like my life. I am so bored. When will it ever start?

2

Loulou

I was early to meet Keith – an unfortunate habit of mine, considering that everyone in London seems to run pathologically late – and settled into our usual table in the cocktail bar at Claridges where we often met for drinks. Well, most Wednesdays actually. Keith and I both liked a bit of a routine. It was one of the many things we had in common and which made our friendship so mutually pleasing.

This meeting was the first for several weeks, though. We'd both been very busy travelling for work and hadn't been able to make our Wednesday cocktail date, so I was particularly looking forward to seeing him.

The maitre d' greeted me like the regular I was, and as he led me over to the corner table I smiled at two young women who had clearly recognised me. It was my Northern upbringing. A cool Londoner would have studiedly ignored them, but I thought that was rude.

I still found it flattering to be spotted by total strangers who clearly knew I was Loulou Landers, 'Queen of Vintage', as I had been dubbed – and not for the first time – in *Vogue* that month. It still tickled me that I had achieved some kind of minor celebrity status just by doing what I loved since I was nineteen years old.

And considering I was wearing a tight-waisted bright yellow floral 1950s dress with crazy sticky-out petticoats and a veiled cocktail hat, with my current season Louis Vuitton shoes, which had three-inch platforms, I could hardly expect people not to notice me.

The girls smiled back, and apart from doing my bit to promote Northern friendliness, I suspected I'd see them in the shop fairly soon, now they knew they were likely to get a warm welcome. I'd never been able to understand the idea of making a shop so snobby people were scared to come in. Everyone was welcome in mine.

Keith arrived five minutes before our agreed time.

'Still didn't get here before you, dammit,' he said, swooping down from his great height to kiss my cheeks. 'I keep trying . . .'

I didn't get up to greet him. Even in those shoes, I'd only come up to his chest. He put one of his catcher's mitt hands delicately on my shoulder and manoeuvred himself surprisingly nimbly into the chair next to me. I was always relieved it didn't collapse beneath him. Not that Keith was fat, far from it, he was just huge, built on a bigger scale than anyone else I knew, which he said was a result of having steak for breakfast every day, growing up on a farm in country New South Wales.

The waiter came over with the cocktail list and went through the pantomime of handing it to Keith, who turned to me.

'What would you like, Loulou?' he asked, as though I ever changed my order.

'A terrifyingly strong vodka martini with an olive,' I said.

'I'll have the same with a twist, please, Gianni,' said Keith happily, as tickled as I always was by the unchanging ritual of our Wednesday night cocktail hour.

Keith reached out and took my hand in his, and for a few moments we just sat smiling at each other. It was a typical gesture of his. He was a very physical person, and although it had taken me a while to get over my English reserve about it, I had grown to love the comfort of Keith's big warm body.

We would often walk along the street together holding hands. At home, or even out at a party, I'd sit on his knee, which was big enough for me to curl up on. I was sure we looked like some kind of odd couple to the outside world, but it didn't bother me. Keith and I made each other happy, without any of the complications involved in a romantic liaison.

'So how's the fascinating world of insurance?' I asked him, breaking the silence with a longstanding line of teasing.

'Fascinating to those of us involved in it,' said Keith.

After more than twenty years of friendship, his role as an executive with one of the world's biggest insurance companies was still a novelty to me. I didn't know anyone else with such a sensible job. He was a qualified actuary, an expert in risk assessment who spent his days looking at spreadsheets, but his more reckless side had other outlets, mainly in his private life.

'How is the fascinating world of old nana knickers?' he asked me.

'Fabulous, darling,' I replied in my best fashionista tones.

'And how is my utterly dreadful goddaughter?'

I grimaced.

'She's pretty bloody appalling, actually,' I said, sighing, but relieved I could share my anxiety with somebody who knew all the details and still loved Theo, despite her increasingly unreasonable behaviour.

'Still no sign of her going back to college, getting a job, helping in the shop, using her considerable artistic talent, or even being consistently nice to her loving mother?'

I shook my head.

'Does she have a fabulously busy social life to take up her time?' he asked.

'Nope,' I said. 'Her girlfriends from schooldays are always inviting her to fun things, but she never seems to want to go. For someone who claims it's impossible to live outside London, she doesn't get out in it much. Apart from to the shopping fleshpots of Oxford Street.'

'So what does she do with herself?' asked Keith, shaking his head in exasperation.

'Nothing useful,' I said. 'She's holed up in her room most of the time, glued to her laptop, trying on her latest haul of crappy chain store clothes and reading magazines well below her intelligence level.'

Keith took a sip of his martini and looked thoughtful.

'No boyfriend on the horizon, I suppose?'

I shook my head and picked the olive out of my drink. Theo's lack of boyfriends was another ongoing mystery. She'd never really had a proper one – and not for want of them trying. Walking down the street with her was quite entertaining, as you watched men's heads snap round on reflex for a second look. On a good day it was like a Mexican wave.

'No boyfriend,' I said. 'I'd think she was a lesbian, if she wasn't permanently obsessed with random male actors and musicians. Her latest discovery is Humphrey Bogart and when I dared to suggest that he died quite a while ago, she told me I didn't understand and flounced out, slamming the door. Twenty-one going on thirteen, my daughter. The original kidult.'

'Hmmm,' said Keith, turning his canny blue eyes on me. 'So that makes both of you man-free zones, then? Must be a getting up a powerful head of oestrogen around your place.'

I slumped in my seat, dreading this line of conversation.

'You know what I'm saying, Loulou, don't you?' he persisted. 'Maybe little girl lost needs mama to take the lead and show her how to have a boyfriend?'

'You know how I feel about that . . .' I said.

'Look,' said Keith gently, leaning towards me. 'I understood why you didn't want to run a constant stream of overnight uncles past Theo when she was little. I admired you for it – it's not like you didn't have plenty of offers – but she's twenty-one now. Quite old enough to see Mummy holding someone's hand – apart from mine.

It's just not healthy, the two of you living in some kind of weird self-imposed purdah. It's a long time since Rob left now . . .'

'Nineteen years,' I butted in. 'Eight months, two weeks, three days and . . .'

'That's what I mean, Loulou,' said Keith, interrupting me before I could get to the hours. I could have done the minutes. 'It's really time you let all that go. About nineteen years overdue actually. Just because he was a total bastard it doesn't mean every straight man on earth is. It's no reason to live like some kind of fashion nun.'

'I haven't taken a vow of chastity, Keith,' I said. 'You know I've had plenty of liaisons over the years, I just didn't ever want to parade it in front of Theo. She'd already been brutally abandoned by one man; I didn't want her to get attached to someone else and be hurt again if it didn't work out between me and him.'

'Like I said,' he responded, getting a bit impatient. 'That did all make sense when she was little, but now I think you might be damaging her with your self-isolation policy. You've got to set an example for her.'

I sighed and took a deep sip of my drink. I suspected there was more than a kernel of truth in what he was saying and that was what made it so hard to take. The thought that I might be playing an active part in making Theo such a hopeless case was unbearable, but before I could get really upset, Keith clearly understood he'd pushed it as far as he usefully could this time, and patted me on the knee.

'Anyway,' he said. 'Enough of that, lecture over, we've got other things to talk about, like your birthday, in just over two months' time.'

I pulled a face. That subject was almost as bad.

'Really, Keith,' I said. 'I'm very touched that you care, but I really don't need to celebrate my forty-ninth birthday. If you want to send me a card, that would be lovely, but that is enough. Really.'

'Too late,' he said brightly and started fiddling around in his attaché case – it still made me smile that he carried one of those around with him. 'It's all organised.'

He found what he was looking for and handed me an envelope.

'Open it,' he said, smiling broadly.

I pulled out the contents gingerly. It seemed to be tickets to something, although I couldn't quite make out what. I squinted a bit longer and then felt Keith pressing something cold and hard into my free hand. It was a pair of wire-framed glasses with very small lenses, like something a stern headmaster would wear.

'Put them on,' he said. 'You'll find everything strangely easier to read.'

I couldn't be bothered to argue and found he was right as the tiny print on the tickets now seemed to be completely legible. It said "Big Chill", and the dates below the title neatly encompassed my birthday at the beginning of August.

'What is it?' I asked, bewildered but not wanting to be grossly rude. I scanned the ticket again but it didn't tell me much apart from the fact that it would be taking place in Herefordshire. Even putting aside the issue of not wanting to celebrate my birthday, I was already sure it wasn't my kind of thing, whatever it was. But then, as I studied the hologram artwork and fluorescent bubble writing, it dawned on me.

'Is it some kind of music festival thing?' I asked, trying to hide my alarm as I took off the specs and handed them back to him.

'It's a lot more than that,' said Keith, putting the glasses back into a tiny little case with a pen clip, which he slipped into the front pocket of his suit jacket like the big nerd he was. 'It's got the amazing atmosphere of Glastonbury, but without the massive crowds, or the yobbos.'

Glastonbury! My face clearly signalled the extreme horror that was now dawning on me. It wasn't the music side of things I was worried about, I loved music as much as anyone else, it was all the other stuff that went with it.

'And yes, we are camping,' said Keith. 'Leave it all to me, we're going to have a wonderful time.'

'Who is the "we"?' I asked, trying to count the tickets as he reached out to take them back. I'd got to four, before he snatched the envelope away from me.

'You, me and dear little Theo, for starters,' he says. 'Everything else will be revealed nearer the time.'

I groaned and put my head in my hands.

'Another drink, darling?' asked Keith, clearly highly amused by it all.

I nodded, lost for words at the nightmare unfolding before me. The only thing I could think of that was worse than a forty-ninth birthday party was spending it in a tent. With Theo. It was hard enough living in a five-storey house with her. And no doubt when we weren't huddled under canvas, we would be tramping around in vast fields of mud. How was I supposed to do that in heels? I certainly wasn't going out in public in wellington boots.

Keith had really done it this time.

To my great surprise, when I got home, Theo already knew all about his plans for the music festival and seemed surprisingly enthusiastic about it.

'He's told you, has he?' she said smirking, but not moving her eyes from whatever rubbish she was watching on the big TV in the sitting room, happily stretched out on my sea-green velvet sofa with a bowl of chocolate ice cream balanced on her chest. She was spooning it into her mouth without raising her head. I hoped none of it had missed.

'I think it's going to be hilarious,' she continued between mouthfuls. 'I've been wanting to go to a festival for ages, but not something boringly obvious and I've heard the Chill is really cool.'

She smirked again. 'I can't wait to watch you and Keith trying to put up a tent.'

'Perhaps you'll help us,' I suggested.

'You must be joking,' she said. 'It's your treat and it was his idea. I'm just coming to do my duty, although it should be a laugh. I'm going to need a whole new festival wardrobe. I think I'll go classic Kate Moss Glasto, in really short cut-offs and wellies. They've got some great ones in New Look with big stars on them.'

Reminded of the nightmare wellington boot scenario, I groaned and slumped down on an armchair, kicking off my painful shoes and massaging my right foot. The joint of my big toe was really hurting. I'd have to ask my yoga teacher about it. Maybe I was overdoing it when she told us to spread our toes out wide. As I rubbed it, the joint suddenly clicked painfully.

'Ow!' I squealed.

'Bunions hurting, Mum?' asked Theo brightly, glancing over at me.

'I haven't got bunions,' I said.

'Be a miracle if you didn't with those stupid shoes you wear,' she said, with the smugness of someone who never stepped out in anything more challenging than a ballerina pump. With her long slender legs she didn't need to. Mine needed every bit of limb elongation they could get.

I looked down at my foot. With a dawning sense of dread, I realised the joint did look a bit enlarged. Did my mum have bunions? She'd died only a couple of years after Dad and it all seemed so long ago now, I really couldn't remember.

For the second time that day, tears filled my eyes at the thought of my lost parents. Why did they both have to die before I was thirty? It was so unfair. I knew people years older than me who still had both their parents and poor Theo had never known any of her grandparents. I'd have to ask my big sister Jane if she remembered Mum having bunions – and if she had them too. I'd read somewhere that the tendency to bunion-isation was genetic and as she was fifty-two, she'd probably have them by now if she was going to.

I looked down at my feet again. The big toe joint on the left foot looked a little bit swollen too, although not as bad as the right. Bunions! What a nightmare. I wouldn't be able to wear high heels and they were essential for looking good in vintage clothes. You couldn't mix vintage with flats unless you were Theo's age – it was one of the golden rules I always quoted to magazines when they rang me for 'How to Wear Vintage' articles.

'So, how about the camping, Mum?' said Theo, clearly warming to her theme, a new thing to wind me up about. 'Are you looking forward to it? I'll ask Tattie for some tips. She's been to millions of festivals. She says there are communal showers, built from plywood and open to the sky, and the loos are truly vile . . .'

I groaned.

'He can't make me go, Theo,' I said. 'There are limits, even to my friendship.'

'You wouldn't dare say no to Keith the Teeth,' she replied.

'Oh, don't call him that,' I said, irritated.

Partly because it was true. Keith did have very big, very white teeth, but everything about him was big. The perfect product of that animal protein-fuelled Australian country upbringing. Well, the gay aspect hadn't gone down so well with his farmer father, but his robust physique had been fully appreciated on his arrival in London twenty-plus years previously.

I'd met him at a party thrown by one of my clients who was also an Aussie. We'd bonded instantly over some silly joke and been friends ever since.

But beyond the usual fun and jollifications of a straight woman/gay man friendship, when my husband had left me and Theo so suddenly and moved to LA with a younger woman – quite an achievement considering I hadn't quite been thirty at the time – Keith had been a caring and sensitive supporter to us both, always there with a hug when I really needed one – and to whirl Theo around and provide some crucial male energy when she needed it. She used to call him the BFG when she was little, I remembered. The Big Friendly Giant.

On top of all that, he was also the ideal human handbag for those formal occasions when I needed a male companion. He could fit in anywhere – and he looked very fine in a dinner jacket. He would, I realised, cut a similar dash in wellington boots. So it was just me who was going to look like a hobbit at the festival. Happy Birthday Loulou.

Theo

Weed-nez-day night

The harem pants are definitely coming Chilling with me. They look real sweet with just a bikini top and my leather flip-flops. A very small bikini top. I've cut my old cut offs off (off off ha ha) so high you can see my lower arse cheek crease. Seriously hot pants. Loving it.

But I will need more new festival gear so lucky I conned Dad into increasing my allowance/guilt payoff/hush money. Told him Mum had put my 'rent' up and I needed photographic books for a 'course' I am starting in September. He thinks I'm going to 'take after the old man' as he said in his smarmy email. It's such a joke that he thinks he's still a 'photographer' when he's just a vile advertising leech.

'Now photography is something I can really help my little girl with . . .' he said.

Yeah? So why don't you just shut the shut up and hand over the CASH?

Of course I have no intention of being a photographer arsehole like he was before he became an even bigger advertising arsehole. He is so easy to con it's hardly even fun.

I can have my whole legs lasered now. Apart from the harem pant scenario my festival look is going to be entirely leg centred so it's clearly necessary. If it's cold I'll go all moochy and waify in my over-size cotton jumper and that big scarf I've liberated from Loulou Lala but I'll keep the legs out. Oh yeah.

Tattie and Ari are going to be there too with loads of their college friends so I'm going to ditch the olds on day one and just hang with my peeps. No way am I going to be seen in public with some old gayer with teeth you could use to pave your back garden who will be parading around with my trag hag mother like they are some kind of creepy couple. It makes my flesh crawl the way those two carry on. Sometimes they HOLD HANDS in public. Gak.

When he rang to tell me about his 'Big Chill party plan' forfucksake he was spouting some crap about me only getting to go if I 'behaved myself' whatever that's supposed to mean. He said I had to 'show more respect to my mother'. What? Salute? Curtsey? Walk out of the room backwards? I reckon I'm showing plenty respect just by living with her.

If it wasn't for me she'd be all alone with just a load of stinky old clothes to keep her company. Poor little Lala. I do feel sorry for her sometimes. When she's not being a total cow to me about 'budgeting'.

Tattie says some of the boys she knows who are going to the Chill are really hot but I know what that means. Hoxton haircuts pointy white shoes and stupid lame drainpipe jeans. Why doesn't she just buy her friends from a catalogue? They're all so mass produced what's the point?

I don't mind a great big rack of identical Primark tops. So comforting to know they're all there waiting for me if I need them my little chain store babies. But when it comes to men I'd like something a little more . . . oh I dunno. A one off. I want couture manhood not something off the peg.

I wanna meet someone who is going to show me something I haven't already seen on a million other tossers who can't believe they're not in the Arctic Monkeys. Ooh look. I'm wearing a trilby. I'm so arty and edgy. Yeah right maybe in Guildford.

Someone who would wear a double-breasted suit with turn-ups to a festival and sleep in it and everything. That would be worth talking to. Humphrey Bogart does the Chill. Sweet.

Going back to Topshop tomorrow for that stripy jacket. Tattie's going to lend me the cash. Will hide it until the Chill and then Lala mads won't even remember. Her memory is so on the blink. Early Alzheimer's. Very handy sometimes.

3
Loulou

I had another surprise about the festival the next morning, when I was sitting on the terrace at the front of the shop drinking fresh mint tea with my other best friend, Chard. He was really called Richard, everyone else called him Ritchie, but he was always Chard to me. Dear old Chard. I adored him.

'I hear you're going down to the Big Chill,' he said, blowing smoke out of the side of his mouth and over his shoulder as only a forty-a-day career rock star could. 'Should be a blast. I'm going too.'

'Really?' I asked, so surprised it didn't occur to ask how he knew I was. 'How come?'

'Performing,' he said, taking another big pull on his full-tar ciggie. Chard was the most unreformed smoker I knew. Which was the reason we always had to sit outside. Couldn't have that stink in the shop. I hated it, but it was part of him, so I'd learned to endure it. He'd made smoking into something of a personal art form.

'I didn't think it was that big a festival,' I said.

'Not the whole band, babe,' he laugh/coughed. 'They couldn't afford us. Just me. For fun. I'm going to do an acoustic set – some classics and some of the new stuff I'm working on for the next album. A sort of work-in-progress scene to keep the fans excited and I'll accidentally get some of it "illegally" recorded and slipped onto the interweb . . .'

He chuckled to himself. He loved playing the game of his industry, which was probably why he was still so successful in it after so many years.

'That sounds great, Chard,' I said, genuinely enthusiastic. I was mostly dreading the festival, but now at least I had one thing to look forward to. I really loved seeing Chard up on stage.

He was an actual proper real rock giant and had been since the early 1970s, when he'd first started filling stadiums as lead guitarist in his band Icarus High. Their style of 'intelligent' rock – they'd formed in the sixth form of a private school, as the pretentious name might indicate – had been totally out of fashion in the punk era when I was a teenager, but I'd always loved their music.

My older brother was a big fan, so I'd grown up listening to it, but I still hadn't recognised Chard when he walked into my shop one afternoon, not long after I'd opened. Which was probably one of the reasons we immediately hit it off. He found the whole starfucker scene very hard to take, so being treated as a 'civilian', as he called it, meant a lot to him.

By the time I'd realised who he was, we'd already connected, and his fame was never an issue between us. And as he lived just round the corner, in Chalcot Square, he'd started dropping in whenever he was at a loose end. Over time and many cups of fresh mint tea – a novel concept back then, which he'd introduced me to after a trip to Marrakesh – we had become very good friends. Thirty years and counting.

Over those years, the Ickies – to use the customary abbreviation – had been rehabilitated back into cool after they'd played at Live Aid and now had their rightful place in the rock 'n' roll pantheon. But while I knew they had one of his guitars on prominent display in the Hard Rock Café, I still tended to forget what a legend Chard was. He was just my funny old mate, so it always rather thrilled me when I got the chance to see him in his rock god incarnation.

And I did think of him as another person when I saw him up

on stage. He was so cool, strutting around, hair flying, owning the crowd, making wonderful music. He was amazing. Then the real man would lope into my shop and, while he was still handsome in his lanky, craggy-faced way, I'd just see him as my pal again.

'Where are you going to stay at the festival?' I asked, as it suddenly struck me that being such a legend, he might have a room in the fabulous stately home at the Big Chill site, which Theo had shown me on her laptop. A room with access to a bath and a real loo. A room where I could sleep on the floor.

'In my yurt,' he replied, and my hopes were dashed.

I took a sip of tea, trying to put the camping side of the festival out of my head again, when something else occurred to me.

'By the way, Chard – how did you know I'm going to the Big Chill? Did Keith tell you?'

He shook his head while taking a deep draw on his ciggie, scattering fag ash everywhere, sunlight bouncing off the enormous gold ram's head ring on his right hand.

'Bumped into Theo in the park yesterday,' he replied. 'I was walking Dogbreath, and she was coming back from town. Keith had just rung her, and she told me all about it. She seems quite excited. For her.'

I laughed. Chard knew Theo as well as Keith did.

'Yes,' I said. 'I was quite surprised that she was looking forward to doing anything with me, beyond exercising my credit cards in Oxford Street.'

'Don't be like that,' he said. 'She loves you really. She's just a bit of a superannuated tricky teenager. Like me.'

As he spoke, he leaned over to pat my shoulder, just as he would Dogbreath, the beautiful afghan hound asleep at his feet. That pat was a very typical gesture for Chard and summed up our relationship. The length of our platonic friendship was probably worthy of the *Guinness Book of Records*, I thought, as I took a sip of my tea, but it had just never seemed right for it to develop into anything more.

I'd still been with Theo's father, Rob, when we'd met, then too broken-hearted and busy with a tiny child and a business to think of romance with anyone. Then once I had emerged from the worst of that, Chard was established in the only proper relationship he'd had in all the time I'd known him, married to a well-known model.

By the time that ended, ten years later – very sadly, after her third miscarriage – our friendship was so firmly bedded in, anything closer was just never on the agenda. And judging by the string of lovely young things he went out with I was clearly too old for him now anyway. Although I loved to tease him that the age prejudice worked both ways.

'Vintage clothes are one thing, but some women just don't go for the vintage man, Chard,' I reminded him, after he'd re-started the conversation to complain that the last beautiful girl he'd tried to pick up in my shop still hadn't phoned, texted, Facebooked, Twittered, emailed or faxed him.

It was quite unusual. Probably not surprisingly considering his fame, income and charisma, he had a pretty good success rate with his dolly birds, but they were never anything more than short-lived flings. Some of them had lasted a few weeks, but he hadn't had what you could call a partner since his wife. We were as hopeless as each other in that regard.

This time he was particularly peeved because the card he'd given the girl in question was a new one, featuring his band's most iconic album cover: a black-and-white photo of a naked baby sitting on the top of a Sherman tank. It was one of the great rock 'n' roll images, he told me.

'Her grandfather might have a copy of *Inexplicable*,' I added. 'She's probably more into Kanye West.'

'He sampled one of my riffs on his last album,' said Chard, a large plume of noxious smoke now veiling his face, which was already well hidden behind mirrored aviator shades. 'Getting royalties. Sweet.'

'Maybe you should put his artwork on your calling card then, love,' I said, flicking his ear, as I got up to follow a customer who had just walked past us and entered the shop.

It still looked almost exactly the same in there as it had all those years ago, when Chard had first strolled in, I reflected, as I took my customary non-intrusive place behind the counter, while the customer flicked through the rails.

He had loved the shop immediately and started bringing in his girlfriends to buy them antique kimonos, chiffon lingerie and 1930s evening gowns. As pretty much all of them were models who would subsequently wear their vintage treasures to magazine shoots, London's key fashion editors started coming in to check the shop out, which had really helped put Loulou Land on the map, so I seriously owed him.

But while that had been very handy, the simple reason I had become such good friends with Chard was because I loved his company. He made me laugh, introduced me to new ideas and stimulated my brain, which I had particularly appreciated when Theo was little and my world threatened to shrink down to the size of a Sylvanian Family. One without a daddy badger.

And, just as with Keith, when I found myself the suddenly single mother of a tiny little girl, I had really appreciated having a supportive male friend who was happy to leave our relationship at that.

Thinking about those early days, I was still covertly monitoring the customer, and I could tell by the expression on her face that she was shifting quickly from hopeful anticipation to panicky defeat and needed my help, so I went into long-practised action. Pretending to be sorting out a basket of silk scarves, I edged close enough to make conversation seem natural, rather than the intrusion of a pushy saleswoman.

'Are you looking for anything in particular?' I asked, smiling encouragingly. 'It's just that I have a lot of new stock in the store room that I haven't put out yet and there might be something perfect in there . . .'

It was all nonsense. I never had unsorted stock. It might only have been a frock shop, but I ran Loulou Land with the same rigour my father had brought to his empire making obscure widgets for fork-lift trucks. I'd spun that line to maintain her sense of possibility. Once a customer felt it was hopeless, that there was nothing for them in your shop, you'd lost them whether it was true or not. You had to keep the dream alive for them.

It wasn't that I wanted to trap her into buying something; my aim was for every woman who came into Loulou Land to have a delicious time there. And if she was holding one of my signature corset-pink and gold carrier bags when she left, so much the better.

I'd clearly made the right call with this customer, as she sighed with relief at my intervention.

'It's for a wedding,' she said, her brow knitting up again. 'The bride wants everyone to wear vintage tea dresses . . . It's all right for her, she's tiny, but I really don't think something so unstructured will work for me.'

I could see her point. I'd already discreetly checked her out and she was quite short and a bit, well, puddingy. I never judged my customers for their bodies – my own shape was average enough for me to have sympathy with everyone – but I was realistic about them. That was how I could help people find the perfect outfit.

Floaty tea dresses were definitely not the obvious look for this lady, but it didn't worry me. I knew I could dress her.

'Is it Tanya Herschowitz's wedding?' I asked.

'Yes,' she said, surprised. I wasn't – Tanya was a good customer and we'd discussed her dress code before she printed the invitations. She was one of my select clientele who got the full personal service in my private studio upstairs, a privilege I bestowed only on the very well know, who needed the privacy, or the ridiculously wealthy, who demanded it.

'Thought so. I've had quite a few guests in looking for outfits and I've dressed the bride, actually . . . so I know the kind of thing you're looking for. Have a seat, I'll get you a cup of tea and show you some possibilities. Would you like mint tea, or regular?'

'Mint, please,' she said, sitting down on my grey velvet chaise longue and looking mightily relieved.

I nipped into the back room and buzzed on the intercom. A grumpy voice answered from upstairs.

'What?'

'Guess who, darling?' I said brightly.

'Give up,' said my lovely daughter.

'Very funny, Theo,' I said, losing patience. 'I've got one of Tanya's guests down here. It's going to take me a while to sort her out and Chard's on his own out the front. Can you come down and keep the old boy company?'

'Muu-uuu-uuum!' she groaned.

'Don't Mum me, he's been very good to you and the least you can do is entertain a lonely old rock star for a few minutes. It's not like you have a lot else to do . . .'

An edge I had hoped to keep out had crept into my voice and she hung up on me, slamming the handset back onto the wall so hard I could hear it through the ceiling. Immediately afterwards, though, I heard heavy footsteps trudging down the stairs. At least she was dressed, I thought. That was one positive point and, I had to admit, they were becoming few and far between with Theo these days.

I ducked outside to get the tea for my customer and to tell Chard what was going on. His face lit up when I said Theo was coming down. He'd known her all her life and was like some kind of doting uncle, probably because he didn't have any children of his own.

All the other guys in the band seemed to have hordes of kids, by various baby mamas, but it was the strain of the repeated miscarriages – one of them at a horribly late stage – that had ended Chard's marriage.

I remembered all too well the terrible day he had turned up at the shop, trembling with shock, after coming home from a recording session to find his wife had left him.

Her farewell note had blamed him and his 'toxic sperm' for the lost babies. It was heartbreaking to see him so shattered and, not surprisingly, it had taken him a very long time to get over it. We'd been the love wars walking wounded for a while there together. No wonder we understood each other so well.

That was when Chard had started dating much younger women – and keeping it all super light. It was as though he was actively avoiding any situation where a baby might feature and I'd always suspected that was why he had such a soft spot for Theo. She was the closest thing he'd had to a child of his own.

For a couple of lean years in the early Nineties recession, when vintage was out of favour and her father was being difficult about her maintenance, Chard had even paid her school fees. In return I'd made him her honorary godfather, a title he relished.

Theo had adored him in return when she was little, but as she got older and began to despise 'grown-ups' as a concept, his affection was less obviously returned, but he didn't seem to mind. He was such a sap around any female.

Theo appeared just as I was about to go inside again, dressed head to toe in clashing fluorescent jersey sportswear. It was very Eighties, but I knew none of it was more than a few days old. Theo never wore vintage. Of course she didn't.

I'd long ago given up trying to get her into things from the shop, although she would have been the perfect house model. It was another argument I just couldn't be bothered to have with her any more, and I let her get on with her chain store obsession – just as long as it wasn't my money she spent on it.

'Whoa,' I said, recoiling from the lurid colours. 'Let me put some shades on.'

She curled her lip in reply.

'It's a gas, babe,' said Chard, nodding like an old tortoise – with a lot of shaggy hair – wearing head-to-toe faded denim. 'Bright lights big city . . .'

Theo rolled her eyes and then grimaced again at the sight of the Moroccan teapot I always got out for Chard's visits.

'Ugh! I'm not drinking that vile mint cack,' she said. 'Toothpaste tea, no thanks. Can we go and get some real coffee, Ritchie? Skinny latte mio caro?'

Her voice took on that familiar wheedling tone as she said it, which sent me quickly back in through the front door. I couldn't stand that voice, but Chard was a sucker for a sulky girl.

'Of course, baby angel,' I heard him saying, followed by an aside to me. 'See you later, Loulou-by . . .'

I was relieved when I heard the garden gate slam – Theo never closed it properly using the latch, despite twenty years of nagging from me – then I remembered I hadn't reminded her that I would need her back before lunch. I had to get ready for one of my most important clients, who was coming that afternoon, and I needed her to mind the shop while I did it. My part-time assistant, Shelley, was away for a few days, so I was relying on Theo. I made a mental note to send her a text when I'd finished looking after my customer.

It didn't take me long. Fifteen minutes later she was admiring herself happily in a mid-calf bias-cut dress in a simple white-on-grey floral print – not too large a scale – on matte silk satin, rather than the less forgiving chiffon.

But the key thing which made the outfit perfect for her was the matching jacket falling to just below the waist, with a very flattering flared peplum and peaked shoulders. Plus a pair of the bust-to-booty support knickers I always kept in stock, because everyone but the most bullet-bellied needs them under bias cuts.

The outfit was an original 1970s Biba take on a 1930s style, which she had agreed was a very witty solution to the bride's rather unforgiving dress code. I'd put it aside ready for just such a customer and had a couple of other variations on the theme lined up just in case.

She left smiling and I stapled her business card into my filing system, along with a few case notes, knowing she would be back.

Theo

Turdsday

Loulou Lala mad as always. Fully meno and grumpy. Buzzes me while I was re-reading *Polo* which canNOT be interrupted – and forces me to go out for coffee with old Ritchie perve head. Gagolaroid. She should pay me to 'entertain' him as she so creepily put it.

I know he only wears those stupid mirrored shades so he can look at people's tits without anyone seeing. Not mine obviously that would be way paedo and sick but any other woman going past. He's such a throwback. I don't know why she likes him. Probably because he paid my school fees ha ha ha. Sucker.

All the time I was with him he kept checking his Blackberry and his iPhone – tell me, who has both? – because so many people were 'hassling' him about his Big Chill gig. Puhleeeeease. Does he really think anyone will notice he's there?

Blagged a couple of lattes off him and then legged it into the park. Needed some time up on my own personal bench on my own personal hill in my own personal park in my own personal city. He tried to follow but I put a spurt on and lost him but the bloody dog kept up with me so I had to take it back to him.

Really annoying and embarrassing to be seen in public holding lead of dog breed which belongs in a museum. Dogbreath would be a good name for its owner actually. He smokes so much his breath could give you cancer at 50 yards. Maybe I'll call him Deathbreath. Ha ha ha.

He was trying to persuade me to have lunch with him at Lemonia like it was a big treat. I've only been eating there since I was born and it was totally fucking boring then but then brilliant luck happened. Tattie rang me in total panic about her big final college project and I had the perfect excuse to escape.

Bye Deathbreath! And you too, puppy!

4
Loulou

After the wedding customer left I was desperately hoping to have a quiet morning so I could finish getting ready for my appointment that afternoon. It was with Paris-based British fashion designer Stevie Palumbo, and required immaculate preparation. He was one of the elite I showed for in my private studio upstairs, so I needed to get everything ready, displaying the special pieces I had picked out for him to their best advantage. I always had fun doing it, deciding which things to keep back for crucial 'How about this . . .?' shazam! moments, and which to 'hide' so he would think he had discovered them himself.

I had been known to stuff some of the best pieces into bin liners with a lot of random tat. Then I'd pretend it had just arrived and I hadn't had time to go through it yet; he'd tip it out on to the floor and leap upon exactly the items I'd known he would love. Then I'd act all surprised and amazed.

It was shamelessly manipulative, but I knew it greatly increased Stevie's enjoyment of the process. If he'd still had time, he would much rather have trawled charity shops and markets for hidden treasure himself, as he used to, but it wasn't possible for a man responsible for four major collections a year, so I tried to re-create something of that feeling for him in my studio.

He usually had a rootle around in the shop as well – adding an extra frisson for any customers who recognised him – and I planted little finds for him there too. I didn't feel guilty about any of this contrivance, because I knew the thrill of serendipity helped to inspire him in a way that a rack of pre-sorted fabulous things never could.

I was so absorbed setting up for him, I forgot to wonder where Theo had got to. She was supposed to be manning the shop while I did this, I thought crossly. I'd sent her the reminder text, but she'd clearly still forgotten – or more likely, just decided she couldn't be bothered. She hadn't even deigned to answer it.

It was pure luck there hadn't been any more customers that morning who needed much attention, just a few browsers and a pair of Japanese girls who had bought a diamante clip each, probably just to get one of my distinctive carrier bags as shopping trophies. They asked me to sign them, which was very sweet.

I was used to being a stop on London's fashion tourist trail and I wrapped their choices in my special tissue printed with 'Loulou Land' in the same curly writing as the shop sign, and popped in a couple of little extras – a lace-edged hankie for one, an ostrich feather for the other. It cost me practically nothing and would, I hoped, make their day. And bring them back when they were older and richer.

I also agreed to have my photo taken with them outside the shop under my sign, another request I was well used to. One of them told me shyly in halting English that she had based her hairstyle on my signature bob – and I pointed to the framed photo of Louise Brooks, which had been on the wall since the day the shop opened, to show her where I'd got the idea from. Also my name, but they didn't need to know that. I had actually been christened Elizabeth, but that was my little secret. I'd left that name behind forever when I'd moved to London.

Shortly before Stevie was due to arrive – i.e. an hour after the agreed time, he was always horrendously late – Theo still hadn't shown up. I didn't want customers coming in when I was mid-presentation, or even the interruption of her finally showing up, so I realised I'd just have to close the bloody shop.

Very irritated, I texted her:

> Where the hell are you? It's too late now.
> Wherever you are please stay there.

I got a typical one-word reply:

> Huh?

I sighed as I read it. When had my relationship with my precious daughter descended into this permanent state of stand-off? Perhaps as a single mother and only child unit we'd been unhealthily close for too long and this was her reaction. But if she found me so irritating, I asked myself for the umpteenth time, why did she continue to live with me? It wasn't that I wanted her to go – she was still my baby, however foul she was to me – but she was twenty-one years old and it was time for her to be living her own life. I knew that.

I thought again about her refusal even to give Manchester and the art college a proper chance. I'd been gutted for so many reasons. Mostly because she was prodigiously talented and seemed to put no value on it, but also because I'd loved the idea of her connecting with my Northern roots.

As a result of my dad's success, I'd grown up outside Manchester in well-heeled Wilmslow, in Cheshire, but my entire family – my brother, my sister and Theo's six cousins – were all back in our home city now. She'd loved going up to see them when she was a lonely only child, but at twenty she'd reacted like some kind of hideous London snob, saying Manchester and everyone in it were 'not on her radar'. It was mortifying for me. I was still fiercely proud to call myself a northerner, even if I had lived in London since I was nineteen.

Admittedly the private convent school had knocked the edges off my accent even before I moved away, but I knew I still had a trace of it and if I was in the company of anyone who had been born north of Birmingham, I was broad within seconds. And of course I supported Man U with an inelegant fervour. Theo found all of that grotesque – the precise word she used whenever it came up.

'For fuck's sake,' she'd say, flicking her hair out of her eyes. 'You're an international fashion legend and you try and make out you're some kind of clog-dancing tripe-eating Mancunian. It's grotesque. Accept it, Mum – you're a middle-class Londoner. You didn't even grow up in the proper north, you're from *Cheshire*. No-one in Manchester wants you. Give us all a massive break and let it go.'

If she was feeling really vicious she would then burst into a mocking rendition of 'Matchstalk Men and Matchstalk Cats and Dogs'.

I might be a Londoner by default, I thought, as I turned my shop sign to 'closed' and locked the door, but my darling daughter was a Londoner to her core – and in all the worst ways. Unless it involved an aeroplane and a foreign destination it was practically impossible to get her to leave the confines of the M25. Even south of the river was a challenge and Hampstead was as far north as she felt comfortable.

She'd find her way, I told myself yet again. I just had to give her the space and time to do it. But why all the abuse? Was I really as risible and ridiculous as she seemed to think?

I sighed and went into the main changing room – a lavish arrangement with a huge old mirror, a deep armchair and a kidney-shaped dressing table complete with bottles of scent for customers to use – to put on fresh lipstick ready for Stevie.

I applied the dark plum shade I had worn, with matching nails, since I was a teenager, and smoothed my bob. I'd had the same look for over thirty years. Was it boring of me? Theo was always telling me it was, but I felt comfortable like that. I didn't care whether it was in fashion or not, it was my style.

With my deep-set brown eyes, retroussé nose, and rather

out-of-proportion full lips, somehow a small cap of shiny hair – darkened to an ultra-deep brunette – seemed to make the best of them. Sort of joined it all together. I'd worked that out when I was seventeen and stuck to it.

It was the same thing with clothes. I was never fat, but my body type had been a nightmare when I was young. In the mid-Seventies, you were supposed to be shaped like a piece of bendy linguine, but mine was more like Betty Boop's. I had firm high boobs, which was good, but not the right look at all when matched with a small waist and a big, round, sticky-out bottom. And my legs were a total disaster. Short and stumpy, shaped like something sawn off a Victorian table.

With that body shape, I'd never been able to wear jeans, which had been a serious trauma in my youth, but then I'd discovered that I could really carry off a classic 1950s dress, with a full skirt and belted waist, which were still widely available in charity shops in those days. So I'd started wearing vintage in my teens almost out of necessity and it had quickly become my style – and my livelihood.

I surveyed that day's outfit: a navy-on-red jacquard silk polka dot 1980s pussy-bow blouse, with short puff sleeves and huge shoulder pads; navy-blue 1970s Saint Laurent high-waist sailor-style button-front wide-leg pants; and current season Balenciaga platform shoes. It worked for me – and I'd been featured often enough in magazines, so I must be doing something right, whatever Theo said.

I had just stacked both arms with assorted chunky bangles from a selection I had displayed in a big glass bowl when I heard the door bell tinkle. Stevie had arrived.

'OMIGOD!' he screamed when he saw me. 'Nancy Cunard guests on *Dynasty*! It's perfect!'

And we were off.

Theo

Ran practically all the way to Leon in Carnaby Street where I found Tattie sobbing all over her superfoods salad which was heinously embarrassing. Had to give her my headband to blow her nose on. Lucky I was never going to wear it again anyway.

Couldn't see what her problem was. All she had to do was mock up a fashion magazine but she's left it way too late to organise any shoots and she'd just found out that everyone else had been using real models who needed the test shots and nearly real photographers and had practically actual magazines to hand in. One rich kid had even got her dad to pay to have loads properly printed on glossy paper and was selling them in shops in Hoxton. Bitch.

I got Tattie to stop wailing by threatening to leave and then told her to just do it with paper dress-up dolls and like it was all through the eyes of a child. But make the dolls' clothes badly drawn copies of new-season Lanvin etc and then to photograph the paper dolls in settings using doll's house furniture and stuff. Then stick it all on to small pages with kiddie writing. I said she could call it *Baby Doll.*

It wasn't exactly rocket science but she looked like she had just won the Lottery. I drew the doll prototype for her. Took about ten seconds on a napkin and she carried it off like it was a holy artefact. I do love Tattie but she is a bit thick sometimes.

I've agreed to go out with her on Sunday to meet some of the peeps/creeps who are coming to the Chill. She told me to 'do one of your looks' because there are some really hot boys going to be there. Yeah right.

The prospect bores me so much I think I might wear my pyjamas in case I want to take a nap. But I do want to have some new best friends set up for El Chillo to keep my Lala and Teeth escape options maxi-ed up. Now it seems I will have Deathbreath to avoid as well. Will die a death of a million cringes if anyone finds out I know him.

Loulou Mads sent me a really insania text while I was with Tattie asking where I was and then telling me to stay there. So I did. Spent the rest of the afternoon cruising Oxford Street considering my next purchases. It really was bonkersly nuts that text so I turned my phone off in case she sent any more and I got frightened. She weirds me out when she really mads it up like that.

Got the New Look wellies and went to drop them off to Tattie at college so she can keep them until I am ready to smuggle them in at home. Ended up going back to hers to work on her project some more.

Her mother is still running some major bank or country or something like when we were all at school so the housekeeper made us dinner. It was so cool. I wish we had staff.

Her brother was there. He's OK as males go I suppose. Didn't stare at me too much. Read the paper while he ate his food and then left the table. Best you can expect. He's doing some kind of vomitingly dreary degree in politics or some cack like that so will end up as desiccated as his mother. Tats is a bit of a miracle in that family really. Being human and everything.

We worked on *Baby Doll* until after midnight because she said her mother's 'evening driver' would take me home. Really who has an evening driver? Tattie's mum does that's who.

Actually now I think about it Tattie had a morning nanny an afternoon nanny and a night nanny when we were at school. Her mum clearly likes to organise her staff strictly according to the 24 hour clock. No wonder the dad shipped out. Probably couldn't handle the shifts.

Anyway that all went bung when she found out the evening driver had the evening off. So brother Marc drove me home which was OK of him considering it was pretty late by then.

He told me he had to drop something off to some friend in Hampstead anyway which so didn't interest me and I tried to keep conversation to a minimum by immediately plugging my iPod into the dock in the car.

He started saying he likes the New York Dolls too so I quickly changed it to Noel Coward and he pretended to like that as well. So then I gave up and just let him twat on about music while I actually listened to it. Sarah Vaughan.

Anyway it was cool of him to drive me home but Tattie still so owes me. And I will have my kilo of flesh. Medium rare.

5
Loulou

Stevie bought so much from me – including everything I was wearing, apart from the Balenciaga shoes, which he recoiled from in mock horror, hissing the word 'competition' – that I had to spend the whole evening re-stocking the shop.

I was glad to have something to keep me occupied, as Theo didn't come home for dinner and didn't reply to any of the texts I sent, and by eleven I was beginning to feel a bit worried. I couldn't help it. I just didn't like having no idea where she was, so I kept working to keep my mind off it.

I knew, with the rational side of my brain, that if she were a normal twenty-one-year-old and living away from home, whether at college, with friends, or a partner, I wouldn't know where she was every night. But as she chose to live with me, in what had been her childhood home, I couldn't let go of the feeling that if I didn't know where she was, there was something to worry about. It was impossible to let go of that mother hen instinct. She still felt like my freshly hatched chick. Like so much in our relationship, it was very confusing.

It was nearly one in the morning, and I was standing up a ladder, arranging a display of 1950s cocktail hats on a high shelf, when I heard a key in the door. Theo walked into the shop – it was the only entrance to the house – and straight past me without even saying hello.

'Hello?' I called after her.

'Hi,' she said flatly, carrying on up the stairs, as the door swung shut behind her.

I was about to climb down my ladder and go after her, when I realised there was someone else in the shop.

'Do you want me to help you down from there?' said a distinctly male voice, which had the immediate effect of making me nearly fall off my precarious perch, I was so surprised.

I was saved by the firm grasp of a young male hand on my upper arm. I looked from the hand – after noticing it had rather elegant fingers – and across to the head. Thick dark blond hair, fine features, a rather wide curly mouth, which was smiling shyly at me, and golden-brown eyes which didn't look shy at all.

A young man! Above averagely attractive! With Theo! It was lucky I was now at the bottom of the ladder, or I would have done a nose dive with the shock.

'Hi!' I said in a strangulated squeak.

'Hi,' he said, taking his hand off my arm and putting it out to shake mine.

I looked at it for a split second before realising what I was supposed to do. I was a bit preoccupied trying to slip my feet back into my shoes in an unobtrusive way. I took the hand. It was warm and smooth and had a very firm grip.

'I'm Marc Thorssen,' he said, apparently not noticing I had just grown six inches. 'Tatiana's brother . . .'

I must have been looking blank as he immediately added: 'Theo's friend, Tattie . . . Tats?'

'Oh, yes, Marc,' I said, vaguely remembering an older brother at Tattie's childhood parties. 'Gosh, I'm so sorry, I didn't recognise you.'

'Well, I was probably in school shorts the last time you saw me.'

I laughed, slightly hysterically, as I wondered what to do next. Theo had finally brought a boy home – a very nice one too, it seemed – and she seemed to have dumped him at the threshold.

Was the romance over already? I glanced towards the door up to the house.

'Shall I take you up to Theo?' I said, hoping she had just rushed ahead out of embarrassment and was putting the kettle on, lighting scented candles and plumping cushions. She had probably been expecting to slip him in while I was asleep and was mortified to find me still up.

'Oh, no, it's fine,' said Marc. 'I just brought her home, because she worked really late with Tatiana and we didn't want her to get the Tube. I just wanted to make sure she got in OK and then you were here, so . . .'

'Ah,' I said, trying to hide my crushing disappointment that he wasn't Theo's boyfriend, combined with intense shame at my daughter's rudeness. She hadn't even said goodbye to him. 'Well, thank you so much for bringing her back, Marc. I'm sure she meant to say thank you herself . . .'

'That's fine,' he said. 'She's a very good friend to my sister. I was delighted to help.'

He glanced around the room.

'Beautiful shop you have here, Mrs Landers,' he said. 'I've heard Tattie talking about it, but I had no idea it was like this. It's amazing.'

'Loulou,' I said. 'Please call me Loulou – and thank you. I've just been re-arranging the displays. Had a big customer in today. Stevie Palumbo – the designer? He's based in Paris. He bought practically everything. That's why I'm up so late, re-stocking.'

I was babbling, I realised. Babbling because I didn't know what to say to this charming young man who was in my shop at nearly one in the morning. And wasn't dating my daughter. I was thrilled she even knew him, delighted he thought she was a good friend to his sister – any good news about Theo was a bonus – but gutted that was all there was to it. All of that swirling around together was addling my brain somewhat.

'Come back sometime, when we're open,' I said, picking up one of my cards from the counter and handing it to him. 'Bring your girlfriend. We'll give her family discount.'

He smiled at me again. The same way as before, with the eyes much more knowing than the rather boyish mouth.

'I don't have a girlfriend,' he said.

'Well, a friend, whatever . . .' I gabbled.

'Thanks, Mrs, er, Loulou,' he said. 'I'll do that. Well, I better be going.'

'Yes, yes,' I said. 'Thanks so much. Drive carefully.'

'I will,' he said, with that disconcerting smile. 'All the way to Hampstead. OK, then. Say goodbye to Theo for me.'

'Will do,' I said moronically, leading him to the door and standing in it while he walked down the path. 'Bye, Marc.'

'Bye Loulou,' he said, closing the gate carefully behind him.

For a moment, I carried on standing in the doorway like I was in some kind of trance, watching him walk to his car, until he turned round and raised his arm to wave to me. Mortified he had seen I was still standing there, I pulled myself together and shut the door.

How embarrassing. I'd been so gauche with him. It was all Theo's fault. He was the first boy, apart from a few platonic (ie gay) pals, she'd ever brought home. How was I supposed to know how to behave? Especially as she hadn't actually been bringing him home in that way – he'd driven her home and she hadn't even thanked him. I was still in shock that she could be so bloody rude.

Suddenly a flame of anger ignited somewhere in my belly. On top of everything else, it was just too much. She'd completely failed to help me in the shop that afternoon, she'd disappeared for the whole day without any contact, she'd ignored all my texts apart from one rude 'Huh?' and now she couldn't even greet me pleasantly, or thank the person who'd very kindly brought her home.

I'd had enough. It was time for me and Princess Pouty to have a little discussion about her behaviour.

I locked the shop door and kicked a hat block that nearly tripped me up out of the way in frustration. My instinct was to storm up the stairs, demanding an apology, but I made myself pause for a moment at the bottom to take a few breaths.

If I lost my rag, that would just give Theo grounds to sulk and although I was absolutely furious with her, I knew what was really needed was a proper talk, not a flaming row. It wouldn't vent my rage in the same way, but it might have more chance of helping our situation.

Reminding myself of one of my dad's favourite sayings – 'Think about the loaf, not the baking' – I walked slowly up the stairs, determined to hold on to my dignity and make this confrontation productive.

The problem was, I couldn't find her. She wasn't in the kitchen, where I thought she might be raiding the freezer for her nightly ice-cream fix and she wasn't in the sitting room watching telly. She didn't answer when I knocked on her bedroom door, so I went in and she wasn't there either. Then I heard the taps running.

She was in the bathroom – my bathroom. She had her own, but mine had a bigger bath. Another lick of anger flared in my stomach. How dare she use my bathroom without asking! Loaf, I told myself, taking another deep breath. Think about the loaf.

I tapped on the door.

'Theo,' I said. 'Please come out here and talk to me.'

'I'm in the bath,' she said.

'Well, could you please get out of the bath?'

'No.'

'Theo,' I said, still holding on valiantly to my self-control, 'can you please get out of the bath just for a moment and come and talk to me? You can have your bath afterwards.'

'I'm having it now. It will be cold if I get out and I'll drip all over your precious seagrass flooring. We can talk after.'

'I want to talk to you now!' I said, my voice rising despite my efforts.

'I told you – later,' she said and I was sure I could hear that smirk in her voice.

'Get – out – here – this – minute!' I intoned, like a strangulated robot. The best I could do without shouting.

'You know you really are being unreasonable, Mum,' she said. 'Go and take some HRT and calm down.'

And that did it. I blew my top.

'How dare you speak to me like that, you ill-mannered little brat!' I screamed through the door, all precious dignity and loaf thinking destroyed in an instant. And once I'd started, I couldn't stop.

'And I don't need HRT,' I yelled. 'I might be middle-aged, but I'm not menopausal yet! I've had just about enough of your sulking, your rudeness, your complete lack of respect for me and my friends – people who have been very good to you. You didn't even say thank you to that nice young man who brought you home just now. How could you be so bloody rude? I was mortified.'

'I'll bake him a cake,' she said sarcastically.

That was it. My anger, which had been hot and fiery, turned to something cold and hard. Something I had never thought I could feel in relation to my beloved only child.

'You completely let me down today, Theo,' I said, my voice low and oddly calm. 'And you didn't even apologise. You didn't reply to my texts, you didn't let me know where you were tonight and then when you did come in, you didn't even say hello. You've gone too far.

'So, I've got news for you, young lady. You're not a child anymore, you're twenty-one years old and if your attitude doesn't improve, if you don't start helping in the shop regularly, or get a proper job of some kind, I will throw you out of this house and I'll tell your father to stop your allowance. Then you'll find out what real life is all about. I'm deadly serious. Got it?'

There was a moment's silence and then she started laughing. Not nervously, but real laughter, like it was the funniest thing she had ever heard. That made me so angry I kicked the bathroom door very hard and made a big dent in it. In those shoes it was amazing my foot didn't go right through.

I could still hear her laughing as I stomped back down to the shop and locked the door to the house behind me. I wasn't ready to talk to her yet, even if she did come to try and apologise. I needed some time to think.

I looked round the room full of old clothes which occupied so much of my thoughts and energy and took a deep breath. I'd finish re-stocking and give the whole place a mini-makeover and spring clean at the same time, I decided. I'd funnel the angry energy that was still coursing through my veins into my beautiful shop, which gave me a lot more back than my own daughter did these days.

Retail is detail I reminded myself, as I gathered the cleaning gear from the basement, and upkeep is particularly crucial, if you are dealing in old gear. Everything about the environment had to be exquisite, or it all just became a stinky heap of old clothes. Then customers might start to get funny about the price tags.

I kept going until past three in the morning and it looked absolutely beautiful when I'd finished, but hard graft didn't make me feel better the way it normally did. By the time I went up to bed, I was feeling lower than I had for years. I was terribly hurt by Theo's behaviour, but I was also upset with myself for losing it like that. It wasn't going to help improve things between us if I behaved like the monster she already seemed to think I was.

As I walked past her bedroom door, I stopped out of long habit and turned the handle, only to find it was locked. I didn't even know there was a working lock on it. She must have put one on. That made me feel even worse. It seemed such a symbol of the loss of trust between us. I'd only wanted to look at her sleeping.

I still did that, as I had since she was a tiny baby. There was something about seeing her in that peaceful, vulnerable state that made me able to reconnect with the relationship we used to have.

When she used to press her cheek urgently against mine and tell me I was her best friend.

After that additional blow, I went to bed and cried myself to sleep, something I hadn't done since the dark days after her father had first left.

Theo

How do you get someone sectioned? Lala has finally really lost it. She completely flipped her wig tonight yelling and screaming at me. She even tried to kick the bathroom door down which was pretty scary in the Frankenstein shoes she wears. If it hadn't been so hilarious I would have been frightened trapped in a house with a violent mad woman. With appalling taste in footwear.

I told her to take some HRT and calm down and that made her worse. She says she's not menopausal. Duh! Everyone knows women go bonkers when they turn fifty. It's a medical fact. I'm just glad that by the time I'm her age they will have invented a cure.

I don't see what she's so upset about. Something about me not saying hello when I came in tonight. I mean – what's that to get all psycho about? I was just walking into the house like any normal person. Do I have to make a big entrance with page boys and trumpeters? Get the town crier?

And I hadn't said 'thank you' to Marc. Well I did actually. In the car. I nodded at him. So I don't see what that's all about either. I didn't know he was going to follow me into the house like some creepy stalker. Why does she care?

And she was furious I hadn't come back to 'help' when she'd sent me a text telling me NOT to come back. And help with what? That's what I mean about her being actually mad. At least I've got proof of that now. I'm glad I didn't delete that text.

Then there was all the usual crap about getting a job. Why? It doesn't cost her anything to have me in her house. She'd be living here anyway and it's not like I eat much. She can spare a few crusts for me. And I get the money I need for other stuff from 'dad'. Rhymes with 'dickhead'.

He's loaded and she's not exactly short of funds – she doesn't even have a mortgage anymore. I've looked through her paperwork. She's got loads of shares and stuff and she paid the house off years ago when her mum croaked. That means everything she makes in the shop is play money – so why do I have to work?

Why should I take a job that someone else actually needs so they can eat and stuff? And a room in some scummy share house that might be the only place on earth some other poor bastard could ever afford to live in? She wants me to make poor people unemployed and homeless. Nice. Not.

I know I'm lucky and I don't see why I should take jobs and homes from people who aren't. I talked to Deathbreath about that when we were having coffee today and he actually got it. He said that's why he's a rock star. Wasn't fair of him to take a proper job from someone who needed it when he could make a living just tooling about on his guitar.

Just because Lala's got some tragic throwback northern work ethic she seems to think I should have it too. Well I haven't. I don't want to work for the sake of it. It would be all right if I could earn money doing something I like and that I'm really good at and would do anyway like Chard does but until I can think what that is I'm just going to hang out and enjoy myself.

Other career options include:

a) I win the lottery (might help if I ever entered it).

b) My father dies and I get all his money.

And Lala can finally get rid of me as she so clearly wants to. Until then I've locked my door so she can't get in while I'm sleeping and smother me with a pillow.

6

Loulou

When I woke up the next morning, the drama of the night before flooded back into my consciousness like a tsunami and for a moment I wondered if I could get out of bed. I felt completely flattened by the whole thing and I almost dreaded seeing Theo, in case we had another row. Or worse – she was as cold towards me as that locked door had felt.

I lay there for a couple of minutes wondering yet again what was making her so hostile to me – and the world in general. I knew it wasn't exactly ideal for her general emotional equilibrium that her father had abandoned her when she was tiny, but why would that make her so angry with me?

Did she blame me for it in some deep, twisted Freudian way? For pushing Daddy away? But if that was the case, why was she so reluctant to leave the safety of my nest? It wasn't like I hadn't lovingly encouraged her to do it.

Mulling the same old thoughts over and over with no progress was starting to make me feel crazy, and I longed to pull the covers over my head and block it all out, but a glance at the clock told me I had missed my yoga class and it was already getting close to shop opening time. That was all it took to get me to my feet.

I was exhausted from lack of sleep and the emotional turmoil of the night before, but I had a business to run. Buried somewhere inside me was a core of steel where that was concerned – the legacy of my father, which I valued far more than the money he had left me when he died. My relationship with my daughter might be crumbling around me, but I wouldn't let Loulou Land go down with it.

I knew there wasn't any chance Theo would open up for me – if only – and my assistant Shelley was still away, so I did a quick sun salutation and assumed my Loulou Landers, Vintage Queen persona. I picked out a severe black crepe 1940s dress – very Mrs Danvers, which seemed appropriate – and some ropes of jet beads. It took me a while to do my eyes, the full number with smoky shadow, liquid liner and loads of mascara, but then with a shake of my bob, a swipe of my dark red lipstick, and a quick spray of Mitsouko, I was ready.

There was no sign of Theo anywhere when I emerged. Her bedroom door was unlocked, which was something, but she wasn't in there. I was almost relieved. I needed a bit more time to gather myself before I saw her and I badly needed tea. Strong builders' tea.

I was so groggy from my late night, it wasn't until I'd drunk my second cup that I realised it was pouring with rain. That meant Chard was unlikely to make his morning visit and it would probably also be very quiet in the shop. After all the work I'd done the night before, even a perfectionist like me couldn't find much to do to make it look better, and I walked round from room to room, twitching hangers into ever more exquisite alignment and wishing I had Shelley there to chat to.

I was just wondering whether it would be too neurotic to start changing the displays again, when inspiration struck. I picked up the phone and pressed the quick dial for my big sister Jane.

'Lizwas!' she said, when she heard my voice. None of that Loulou nonsense for her; her nickname for me was her comment on that pretension, although she usually called me Lizzie. 'How are you, love?'

'Oh, all right,' I said, smiling to myself as my vowels spontaneously flattened. 'Can't complain . . . How are all of you?'

'We're all grand, but you don't sound too special, chuck. What's up? Tell your big sis.'

Good old Jane. This was exactly why I'd rung her. She'd been to the same private school as I had, but she'd never lost her northern soul.

'It's Theo . . .' I started and before I could say anything else, the sobbing started.

'Nothing's happened to her?' asked Jane quickly.

'No, no,' I said, quickly walking over to the door and turning the shop sign to closed. I couldn't have anyone seeing me in this state. I probably had mascara all down my face.

'Well, stop weeping and tell me what the little madam has done now.'

I was glad Jane had first-hand experience of how bad Theo could be.

'She's just so horrible to me, Jane,' I said. 'She treats me with no respect. She never helps in the shop, just spends all of her time wasting her unearned money on rubbish clothes and watching telly. She's done nothing about getting a job. She seems to think it's fine to sit on her arse all day and do nothing. I'm at the end of my tether and last night we had a terrible row about it and . . .' The sobs started up again with a vengeance as I remembered. 'She locked her bedroom door to keep me out.'

'The little bitch,' said Jane, the only person I could take such a blunt comment about Theo from. 'I'd suggest you send her up here so I could knock some sense into her, but we tried that. I blame her dad, of course. It's all because he left her like that. It's nothing you've done, love. You've been a wonderful mother to that girl.'

'It's hard to hold on to that when you're constantly being told you're old and stupid. Last night she told me I was menopausal and needed HRT.'

'Are you?'

'No! I'm not even fifty yet . . .'

'Some women start long before that.'

'Not helping,' I said and she started laughing, then I joined in and couldn't stop in that slightly hysterical way that can happen when you've recently been crying, until I had happy tears running down my cheeks where the sad ones had been.

I dried my eyes with a lace-edged hankie from a display and it came away covered in soggy shadow, mascara and liner. I'd have to do all my make-up again, but I didn't care. Jane had got me out of my funk as she always did.

'Actually,' I continued, still dabbing my eyes. 'You've reminded me of something else I wanted to ask you.'

'What?'

'Did Mum have bunions?'

Jane laughed. 'No, love, she had beautiful feet. Dainty, like yours.'

'Oh, that's a relief.'

'Dad had them though . . .'

'Dad! I didn't know men could have them. I thought it was all to do with high heels.'

'Well, daft shoes like you wear don't help, but it's a genetic tendency, bunions. I've got them, they're killing. Are you getting them?'

'I think I might be . . .'

'Anyway, stop changing the subject, I want to talk more about your Theo. Has she got a boyfriend yet?'

'No,' I said, my voice getting slightly higher. Not that again. I'd already done that subject once that week and couldn't face it again. Especially not after last night.

'I've told you before, Lizzie,' said Jane. 'It's not normal, a girl like that; she's absolutely stunning and she's never had a boyfriend. Loads of lads asked her out when she was up here, but she just laughed at them. I know you think she's not a lezzer, so there's got to be a reason and I reckon it's her dad again. She's very mixed up about men. She feels let down by them and you don't bloody help, you never have a boyfriend either – well, not so anyone would know. There was that bloke in Paris and that other one you had in New York, but she never sees you with a man, apart from Keith and Ritchie, who are lovely, but not exactly normal, let's face it, so how does she know how to do it? You need to set an example for her.'

'Funny you should mention that,' I said. 'Keith was saying exactly the same thing the other night.'

'Well, there you are then. He's got a good head on those girder shoulders of his, has Keith. You should listen to him, if you won't bloody listen to me.'

She laughed again. A deep hearty laugh so like our mum's it gave me a pang.

'I am listening to you, Jane. But like I always tell Keith, I'm not avoiding having a boyfriend. I'd love to have a partner, but you just don't meet many available men at my age – especially in my business. Theo practically has to beat them off with a stick every time she leaves the house, but she seems to think they're all stupid.'

'Well, she's quite right in one way,' said Jane. 'I don't like to think of her picking up some stranger on the street. I think you need to set things up for her. Get pro-active, introduce her to the right kind of blokes.'

'Pro-active? How on earth would I do that?' I said, bewildered.

'Do you remember reading Jane Austen at school?'

'Vaguely,' I said, stretching out on my chaise longue and flicking its pompom trim.

'Well, have you seen any of the films or on the telly, you know, them ones Colin Firth was in?'

'Oh yes,' I said with much more enthusiasm.

'Well, you've got to think like one of those mums. Set up parties for them to meet and that.'

'Are you serious?' I said, laughing. 'Quadrilles?' I thought it was one of Jane's jokes.

'I'm dead serious,' she said. 'All my friends are doing it now. That strangers in the night nonsense, it just doesn't work, does it? Waiting to meet "the one" by fate, too many girls these days are ending up single. It's too risky. I want grandchildren, Lizzie, and a big wedding, and a son-in-law who can really be part of our family. Because if they do meet someone by their selves half the time they turn out to be rubbish. Look at your Rob! He seemed like the biggest dreamboat and he was a total ranking bastard, so we've decided to go back to good old-fashioned match-making. We've had some Indian friends of mine over to tell us how they do it. It's fascinating.'

I was speechless.

'Are you still there, love?' said Jane.

'Yes. Well, I think so. I'm just taking it all in. It seems a bit radical. If not actually insane. Do the girls know you're doing it?'

She laughed heartily.

'Not exactly. No. You know they'd hate it. They've seen too many rom coms. They all think they're going to meet Mr Right tripping over his dog in a lift.'

'Have you had any successes?'

'You bloody bet! I've got five weddings this summer – all those hats, I might have to come in your boutique . . .'

She laughed again. Jane thought secondhand clothes were appalling. She still couldn't believe I made a living out of it and thought of my emporium as some kind of tricked-up Oxfam shop with ridiculous price tags.

'And you know what?' she continued. 'Our Becky is going out with a lovely young bloke she met at the one of the parties. He's a surveyor. Nice-looking lad too. They've been on three dates and the beauty of it is, I've already met both his parents and they're super people. And you do want in-laws you can like, as well, don't you? Do you remember Rob's parents at your wedding? They were like the bloody Addams Family, but not so friendly.'

'Don't remind me!' I said.

The wedding had been the first time I'd met them. I shuddered at the memory. I should have known then it was going to end badly. Actually, I should have known earlier, but I'd been too blinded by lust to notice it was peculiar that he had never introduced me to his parents. The only upside was that they had shown no interest in seeing me – or Theo – since. I didn't even know if they were still alive. Or care.

'Anyway,' I added. 'I don't want to think about him or them. How on earth do you do this arranged marriage thing? It sounds like something out of *Yentl*.'

'It's not arranged marriage, Lizwas,' said Jane. 'It's more like helping them along. We just take out some of the random variables without them knowing, and it's been proved that marriages last better if both sides come from families with similar values. It's obvious really.'

'But what do you actually do?'

'We get together in groups of mums with kids the same age – just like when they were all toddlers at play group, but now the age range is twenty-one to twenty-nine. We have coffee mornings and everyone in the group has to bring at least one other mum she knows with a single child that age to increase the pool of people. We all have pictures of our kids with us – some of them bring CVs but I think that's going a bit far – and we just chat and get to know each other and suss out who's nice and might have a child suitable for our own little darling.'

'So it's kind of like a Tupperware party for marrying off your children?' I said, still feeling quite dazed at the prospect.

'Yes, that's it,' said Jane, happily. 'Then when we've got the numbers – and we have to be careful we get a good balance of male and female candidates, remember – one of us has a proper party, at night; all the kids come, we introduce them and sometimes it pays off. Often enough to keep us at it.'

It sounded appalling. There was a sinister Stepford Wife

social engineering feeling about the whole thing. Or maybe I was just picturing Jane's immaculate executive home filled with other expensively dressed women who, like her, thought that anything 'secondhand' was nasty. But I had to admit that beyond those prejudices of mine, there was a certain crazy logic to it.

The idea that we would all somehow meet the perfect partner by fluke was a bit nuts when you thought about it. No one expects to find the right house, school, dentist, or even hairdresser simply by luck, so why had we collectively decided to leave the most important decision of our lives to chance?

'Perhaps I could ring the mothers of some of the girls Theo went to school with . . .' I said, thinking out loud. Anything was worth a try.

'That's right,' said Jane, encouragingly. 'You want to start with the ones with brothers. Try it. What have you got to lose? You can't let her carry on like this, Lizzie. She needs a man in her life. And the worst that can happen is that you'll meet some nice new people yourself.'

On that note, we said our goodbyes and, feeling much better, I quickly re-applied my make-up and opened the shop again. Then I sat behind the counter and started going through my card file to see if I still had any numbers for the parents of Theo's school friends.

Tatiana was an obvious choice, I thought, as I flicked through. Jane had said to go for the ones with brothers and I already knew she had a lovely one; perhaps he would have some friends who might be right for Theo, even if he wasn't. Although I still really couldn't understand why any young woman would dismiss someone as nice – and cute-looking – as Marc, the way my daughter had the night before.

I sighed as I remembered her foul behaviour and that awful row again. Talking to Jane had taken my mind off it for all too brief a time, and now I wondered yet again how I was going to put things right between us. Especially as I didn't even know where she was.

I reached for my phone to send an enquiring text, but thought better of it. I didn't know if I'd be able to handle it if she ignored another one. Better to leave her alone now and wait until she came back of her own volition. Then I would have to apologise for losing my temper – at the same time as trying to make her understand that she'd given me very good grounds to do so.

I went back to my card files trying to find a number for Tatiana's mother. Otherwise I'd have to come up with an excuse to ask Theo for it and I didn't want to do anything that could arouse her suspicions. If I was going to try Jane's crazy matchmaking idea, it would have to be done with the utmost delicacy.

Mind you, I couldn't imagine what kind of a party I could get Theo to come to, but I wasn't going to let myself get bogged down at this stage in reasons why it wouldn't work. I had to try anything I could to get my daughter out of this funk she was in.

I couldn't find anything under Tatiana, Tattie, or Thorssen, which was frustrating – although I didn't really relish the idea of ringing their mother up anyway. Even when the girls were tiny – they'd been at school together right through, from nursery – she'd been very aloof, on the few occasions we other mums saw her. It was usually one of the nannies who'd brought Tatiana to parties. Still, they'd been best friends so long, I should have had a number for her.

As I flicked back and forth through the card boxes, in case it had been misfiled, something Keith had said to me once came into my head – it really was time I got my database onto a computer. He was right. This was ridiculous. I did have a computer, a chic white thing Theo had chosen for me, but I'd never used it. I felt so threatened and freaked out by the whole thing, I'd just put up a mental wall and refused to have anything to do with it.

Theo had that laptop now and if I needed to book a train ticket to Manchester or a flight to New York, or research an obscure 1950s couturier, I got her to do it for me and print out the results. She'd even organised a domain name for me years earlier as a school IT project, but I'd never used it.

I'd enthusiastically embraced texting, so I could see that email and all the rest of it was the next stage, but I'd done such a good job of convincing myself I could get along without it, I hadn't bothered. But deep down, the business side of my brain understood that Loulou Land really needed a website and possibly even a blog, whatever that actually was.

Then it struck me like a heaven-sent thunderbolt – I could get Theo to set it all up for me. That could be just the project to give some structure to her life. She'd always been brilliant with computers and with her artistic ability she'd be able to design a fabulous website for me. And perhaps working on a joint project could bring us closer again. I allowed myself to feel quite optimistic.

I couldn't wait to talk to her about it, but when she finally turned up late that afternoon, there were a couple of very full-on American women in the shop. They'd been in before and I knew the level of attention they expected. It was really annoying, because I'd been on my own all morning and I was worried that if I didn't get things immediately on the right track with Theo, it could all get even worse, so I was delighted when she came right over and kissed me on the cheek.

'Hi Mum,' she said, smiling with what appeared to be a sincerely contrite expression. 'Sorry about last night. I wasn't very nice.'

'Neither was I,' I whispered. 'I'm sorry too.'

But before either of us could say more, one of the customers emerged from the main changing room backwards, the zip hanging open on a strapless 1950s chiffon dress I had tactfully tried to tell her would never fit her.

'I think your zipper's broken,' she said in accusatory tones.

Theo caught my eye, but before I could say anything the other customer was waving a 1980s parachute silk jumpsuit round the side of the lacquer screen she was changing behind and demanding one with 'a size two fanny . . .'

'Would you like some help, Mum?' asked Theo, raising one eyebrow.

And rendered speechless for the second time that day, all I could do was nod.

Theo

Fried-day

Woke up weirdly early feeling all woofy and wonky. Lala was really unbelievably horrible to me last night and I gave it right back to her of course but for some reason I felt funny and bad about it this morning.

I suppose it's coz even though she drives me crazy with all that northern work ethic ay oop my-granddad-was-a-miner bullshit she is still my mum. My parent. The other one being an invertebrate. She can't help it if I'm a hardass London girl. Well she could. She could have had me somewhere else but she had me here and brought me up here but . . . Oh I don't know. Blah.

Maybe I should have said hello to her when I came in last night. I don't know why I didn't. I just feel so cross all the time. At least she was there. Tattie's always telling me how lucky I am to have a mother I actually see as a living human. She says she sees her mum more on *Newsnight* than she does at home.

I would like to have housekeepers and chauffeurs like they do but at least La is a laugh. She looks like Ronald McDonald's less well-balanced little sister most of the time the way she dresses in those hideous old clothes and trannie shoes but at least she has a sense of humour. The few times I have met Tattie's mum I felt like I was being interviewed for a job. A really boring job. You can be too grown-up.

So I don't really know why I'm so horrible to La. It's my dad I'm really mad with. I do know that. I don't need to page Dr Freud on that one. But because he lives in Californication he never sees it because I'm always sending him creepy crawly emails to get money. Plus it amuses me to make him think I like him because if I actually saw him I'd probably kick him in the knob. With Elsa Kleb's shoes on.

Tever.

So anyway I got up really early and went out to get some croissants as a peace offering for Lala – plus I was starving ha ha ha – and then I just had to go up on to my hill to my bench so I could look over London and breathe. And while I was on my way there I bumped into Deathbreath and Dogbreath and Old Daddy Deathbreath – who I hadn't seen for ages. He's more like a collapsed soufflé than ever. Makes Homer Simpson's dad look like Zac Efron.

Deathbreath Junior was pushing him over to the park in his wheelchair poor old sod and that made me feel even worse about being horrid to La La because Deathbreath is even older than her and he still lives with his parents. Well – they live next door to him with a wall knocked through – and he's so flipping nice to them.

I've known his nearly dead dad all my life which is weird really. He used to be really funny. He'd slip me extra strong mints when La wasn't looking because she didn't let me have sweets. I didn't like them much actually – bit mouth blistering – but I forced myself. Anything was better than the carob-covered raisins La La bought me as a treat. If you like eating rabbit turds.

Anyway Old Daddy Deathbreath had no idea who I was. D-breath Jnr kept saying 'It's Theo, Daddy. Loulou's little girl . . . you remember Loulou . . .' and ODD thought he was talking about the loo and kept saying or more like shouting 'I don't want the lavatory Richard. Please stop asking me about the lavatory. It's humiliating.'

I found it really hard not to laugh so I pushed D-breath out of the way and grabbed the wheelchair and I ran the old bloke right up the hill and down again really fast and he seemed to enjoy it. He was shouting cabbage crates over the briny as we came down. D-breath nearly had a stroke trying to keep up with a fag hanging out of his mouth.

Then it suddenly started pouring down because this is crap England so we ran back to Regent's Park Road to escape and have coffee. Well I ran with ODD who was singing some kind of filthy song and D-breath sort of crippled along behind us with his sunglasses all crooked. Where's a paparazzo when you need one?

So I scammed my usual two lattes and ODD was rambling on with Danish pastry crumbs all over his face about his plane and bombing Germany and pranks he'd played on the chaps in the mess. He was quite hilarious actually not Lady Gaga at all just really deaf so when DB Jnr invited me to go back to theirs for lunch I thought: why not? I can shout.

It was all right actually. Old Mummy Deathbreath's not so great. She stays in bed and doesn't seem to know who anyone is but in a nice way and ODD and son were really sweet to her. DB Jnr still calls her Mummy. That made me feel a bit teary and weird.

I gave her a kiss because they both did and she said 'Hello Gloria have you done the bed baths?' I said I'd started but then had to stop because of the air raid and that went down well. She told me to watch out for the ARP warden who had 'wandering hands'. It's lucky I watch *Foyle's War*.

No wonder D-Breath spends so much time at our place.

Which was probably why I was nice to Lala when I got back. She looked so pathetically pleased when I said hello I went a bit overboard and offered to help with some spectacularly spoiled cows who were in there.

It wasn't too bad really. I took the skinny bitch and left the fat bastard to Lala. I knew I would just tell her to come back when she had dropped two stone – off each of her arses.

I flogged mine a hilarious snakeskin leather hotpants jumpsuit object telling her she was the only customer who had ever been able to fit into it and I could see Lala was thrilled. Fatty got some kind of heinous old nightie but seemed ecstatic about it.

I was quite enjoying the freak show and was willing to stick around to watch some more but then Lala suddenly pushed me out of the shop. More weirdness. But I was glad to get up here for a chilling. It was quite a lot of action for me for one day.

7
Loulou

Theo really couldn't have chosen a better time to be nice and helpful as, unusually for me, I was actually struggling with those customers when she came in and had thought I was about to see a lot of money walk right out of my shop door.

The women in question were two of my more demanding clients. They lived in LA and always came in when they were visiting London – and always together. This presented particular difficulties, as they were both former models, but while one of them was still eating-disorder tiny, her friend had total body dysmorphia and refused to accept that she was now a size 18. I always thought of them as Little and Large. In fact they were listed as that in my card index.

So that was a challenge, made excruciatingly worse by the fact that they knew my ex-husband. With his usual arrogance he'd told them about the shop – and, of course, implied that he had pretty much set the whole thing up in the first place. And from what they'd said the first time they'd come in, a couple of years before, it was clear he'd also told them to 'mention his name' to get a fat discount.

The cheek of it! It wasn't the money that bothered me, they spent so much I would have given them ten per cent off anyway, it was just his arrogance – that after all this time and what he'd done to me and Theo, he could still make assumptions like that. I was furious at the idea he would even casually mention me to someone. I didn't want to exist anywhere in his world. I hated the idea of my name in his mouth, between his perfectly sculpted lips.

It was all very well Keith telling me to get over him, but how could I when twenty years after he left us – and from a range of 10 000 miles – he could still be so appallingly intrusive and high-handed?

'Robbie says hi,' Little had said this time, after the usual air-kissing greetings.

'Yeah,' joined in Large. 'We told him we always come by when we're in London and that you always look after us so nicely . . . He's such a honey, isn't he? Ooh, I love that pink strapless dress. It's so Norma Jean, can I try it?'

I was intensely relieved that their ability to focus on anything other than themselves was so blessedly limited, although I knew my next challenge would be to distract Large from attempting to get her fat back into a fragile dress four sizes too small. So Theo's entrance – and amazing offer to help – couldn't have been better timed.

She took over Little and I watched out of the corner of my eye in thrilled amazement as she found and sold her one of the most expensive pieces in the shop. It was a snakeskin hotpants jumpsuit by Ossie Clarke that I'd nearly passed on when I found it in a market up in Leeds, because I thought no one would pay the £3000 it was worth for something so impractical.

'Omigod!' Theo had gushed, when Little had appeared from behind the screen in it, her legs looking like tiny little pipe cleaners poking out of the shorts. 'You are like so totally Kate Moss in that. And I mean Kate Moss, like, five years ago. It's amazing, because no one else has fit that. I tried it on and I looked like a python who'd just eaten a cow . . .'

It was masterful stuff and for once her tendency to slip into terrible cod Valley Girl patois was an advantage. Little had beamed at the Kate Moss reference and when Theo grabbed a white silk square and knotted it around Little's neck as the perfect finishing touch, I knew that my takings for the week had just been deliciously boosted.

Mind you, it meant I had my work cut out not to lose Large, who I could see was seething with jealousy, while pretending to squeal with delight about her friend's amazing 'find'. I had to get busy.

'I'm so glad you came in,' I said, pushing her back into the main changing room, so she wouldn't be able to see Little preening skinnily in the main shop, and simultaneously whisking the pink chiffon dress out of her sight before it got shredded.

'It's amazing, because I was thinking about you just the other day – I've found something perfect for you. Much better for your gorgeous skin tone than that vulgar pink . . .'

What I'd found was the rail I kept on permanent emergency standby for bigger girls. Shelley called it Hefty Hideaways – although not to clients' faces. I flicked through it at high speed and swept back into the changing room with a few options over one arm to give the impression of plenty of choices, holding up a really beautiful black silk petticoat with the other.

It was a lovely thing, French, 1950s, with hand-rolled seams and exquisite lace trim, and in perfect condition – I didn't think it had ever been worn – and I knew it would suit Large beautifully. Although she was big, her skin was tanned and firm like a luscious frankfurter, and she had very splendid self-supporting boobs. I reckoned she could show off acreage of her ample flesh to great effect, like Anita Ekberg in *La Dolce Vita*, and I was right. She looked amazing in it. Like Helena Christensen's fatter sister. Not flabby, but ripe.

As soon as I saw the self-satisfied smile appear on her beautiful botoxed face, I jumped in with a splendid Art Deco rhinestone clip, which I snapped on the décolletage to draw attention to the cleavage which I was sure had helped her to get ahead in Hollywood.

After that there was no stopping her. I was thrilled I had

re-stocked the shop the night before, as she went into an accessories orgy – as big girls so often did. Handbags, bracelets, necklaces, scarves, stoles and hats always fit.

Between the two of them, they had racked up nearly £6,000 and I was delighted, until I suddenly noticed Large had come to a standstill in the main shop and was looking at Theo with her eyes narrowed and her head on one side.

At that very moment, my daughter turned round and flashed her a smile that made her look so like her father, my heart did a weird little bungee jump. It was partly the memory of the stupidly handsome young dude who had swept me off my feet when I'd met him at the Camden Palace in 1983, but it was more the horror that Large had just made the connection between the girl in the shop and Rob.

Large turned to me with a questioning look on her face and as her lips parted, I knew exactly what she was about to say. I practically ninja-leapt over to Theo, putting my arm round her in an act of pure animal maternal instinct. I had to protect my cub.

'Thanks so much, darling,' I whispered. 'You've been amazing, but you've done enough. Go upstairs and have a rest. I'll see you after.'

Then I pretty much pushed her through the door into the house and closed it. Actually, I locked it. Extreme events require extreme responses. Then I turned back to Large, smiling like Sybil Fawlty.

'Anything else I can help you with?' I asked. 'Would you like some tea?'

'I've just realised,' she said. 'That's Rob's daughter . . .'

'Ah, yes,' I said, laughing gaily. 'Yes, that's my daughter Theo.'

'I *thought* she was beautiful,' said Little, joining in. 'She looks so like him when you know. She's totally gorgeous. She should model . . .'

I was having problems keeping my smile pasted on.

'Crazy things, those genes,' I said. 'Now, fresh mint tea or regular?'

'It's such a shame she left before we could say hi,' persisted Large, despite my efforts to change the subject. 'Rob's told us all about her. It's great she's going to be a photographer like him. He says she's really talented. You must be so proud. It's beautiful they have such a good relationship. He said she's coming out to visit soon, so we'll be able to see her again, that'll be fun. I'll throw a party for her . . .'

For a moment I just stood there frozen. Photographer? Good relationship? Visiting? I felt like I had slipped through a wrinkle in the space-time continuum and had landed in a parallel universe. What cock had Rob been telling these women? Or, much more worryingly, was there something Theo hadn't been telling me?

Whatever was going on, this wasn't the moment to find out. My only option was to keep the Loulou Land show going now and to investigate later. That was when Chard walked in. I'd never been so glad to see anyone.

'Hey babe,' he said, kissing me warmly on the cheek and handing me a box of Primrose Bakery cupcakes. 'The sun's finally come out, so I thought I'd see if we could have some late tea, but if you're busy . . .'

Before I could answer, Large had started squealing.

'Ritchie!' she said and threw herself at him.

Little realised who he was at the same time and launched herself at him from the other side.

'Hey, ladies,' he said, clearly having no idea who they were. He was sometimes assaulted by fans like this, but it didn't happen often in my shop. He made sure he didn't go to 'uncool' places where it was likely. He looked at me desperately over his aviator shades, too much of a gentleman to just tell them to get lost.

I looked down at their black Amex cards to see if I could find first names to help him out, but it just said Mrs David Blombeck on one, Mrs Ruben Lussack on the other. Made sense. With their husbands' names akin to Open Sesame in LA – studio executives so powerful even I knew who they were – why would it say anything else?

'Ritchie, it's Carol,' said Large. 'You know, I used to date Steven Tyler . . . and you remember Romaine, she was with Don Henley.'

'Oh Carol, Romaine, hi,' said Chard, clearly none the wiser, but happy to have something he could hang on to. 'How is Stevie?'

Large/Carol laughed.

'Ask his manager . . . But how are you? You look great. What are you doing here?'

'Visiting Loulou. I come most days. She's my best friend.'

Both women glanced at me with new respect. I'd clearly just gone up several notches according to the rules of their particular game. Having a legendary rock star as a friend clearly took you straight up to the next level in Super Mario Super Groupie.

'We haven't seen you for so long,' Large was saying, her focus already back on the prize. I could see how she'd finally bagged her super-alpha male. Shameless persistence. Immoveable tenacity. 'Why don't you come and have dinner with us? We're staying at Claridges. It's so fun in the bar there.'

As she spoke she linked her arm through his and, as if on an unspoken signal, Little did the same on the other side, chumming up and smiling at him. Large even ran her hand over Chard's head, as you would with a dear little dog. It was outrageous, but quite an education to watch them in action. They knew exactly how to get their man. Or, in this instance, someone I felt was slightly my man.

It was horrible when they started pawing him like an exclusive handbag they wanted to add to their collections, but my indignation was tempered by relief that Chard's arrival had distracted them from Theo – and her relationship to their darling friend Rob. So while I was sure Chard wanted me to rescue him, I just couldn't.

So much had happened that day, I needed to digest it. I had to work out what to say to Theo about Rob and the visit. Ugh! Just remembering that comment made me shudder. Plus I had to decide how I was going to present the computer idea to her. Then there was what Jane had told me about the matchmaking parties. I needed to think about everything. I needed to go to an ashram.

'Do you want to come with us, Loulou?' he asked, tipping his aviators further down his nose and opening his eyes wide.

'I'd love to,' I said, my fingers crossed beneath the counter. 'But I'm afraid I just can't. I'm sorry, Chard, I've got so much to do here . . .'

Large didn't look in the slightest bit bothered.

'Oh well, great to see you, Loulou,' she said, air-kissing me again as I handed back her credit card. 'Thanks for all the great stuff. We'll say hi to Rob from you and Theo, and we'll see you next time. And don't worry, we'll take good care of Ritchie.'

She laughed her throaty laugh again – it was very sexy, I had to admit, clearly part of her man-eating armoury – then they swept out, each with an arm still linked through Ritchie's, presumably so he couldn't escape, leaving the carrier bags behind. I knew better than to say anything. The driver would be in for them in a moment.

Chard's appearance and subsequent kidnap had been a welcome distraction, but as soon as they left, I felt quite flattened again. What a day it had been. And it was only six o'clock. I'd woken up feeling desolate after the horrible row with Theo the night before, we'd made it up so nicely, but now I had all this other crazy stuff to take on board – particularly the latest doozy: Theo's possible visit to Rob.

Why did that have to come up? I thought as I turned the shop sign to 'closed' and locked the door. Just when Theo had started being nice to me again, another obstacle appeared.

Maybe that was why she was suddenly being nice, it occurred to me, like a punch to the stomach. Maybe she'd decided to go and live with him in LA and was working up to telling me. I felt physically ill at the thought of it. That had always been one of the worst aspects of it for me over the past twenty plus years, that he might try some kind of custody claim.

He had pulled a bit of a stunt during the Easter holidays when she was seven, appearing in London on a mission to 'get to know' his daughter. She had been whisked off her feet by treats from this handsome, smiling creature with the magical name 'Daddy' attached to him, but when he had casually suggested at the end of a week's orgy of shopping trips, matinees and ice cream sundaes that she should go back to LA to spend a 'trial term' living with him, she had flatly refused.

Theo and I had both been so traumatised by the idea, I'd let her sleep in my bed for several weeks afterwards. I could still remember one of those nights, when she couldn't go to sleep unless I was holding her in my arms. She would look up at me with those big brown eyes open wide and whisper: 'You're my world, Mummy. I could never live away from you. Promise me I'll never have to.'

Then I'd cross my fingers and cross both our hearts, saying I promised.

I sighed at the memory. So bitterly sweet and ironic, considering that it seemed that she still really couldn't live away from me – just not in a good way. Looking back, those words seemed like some kind of curse from a fairy story, where the princess gets her wish and then can never properly grow up and leave the castle to marry the prince.

But perhaps this was it. Maybe she had finally decided to make the break and Rob was her ticket out. Of course now she was over eighteen, she could do whatever she liked and she really did need to leave home, I knew that. I just fervently hoped it wouldn't be to live with him.

Rob had stolen my heart and my youth. He couldn't have my daughter too.

Theo

Later: Was going to try and be nice to Lala some more tonight but just when I was about to go down and find her I heard Keith the Teeth shrieking through the intercom and hid in my room.

I do seem to be having Be Nice To Old People week but I draw the line at him. His teeth frighten me.

Staying in room to re-watch first series of *Glee* followed by my *Summer High* DVDs. I think spending too much time with Tats has put me in some kind of weird school mode. Hoping this will sweat it out. Then I've got *St Trinians* (original b&w not that rubbish re-make featuring worst offender of male skinny jean crimes) and of course *Grease.*

My life may be a featureless void, but there will be no shortage of entertainment in it. No there will be not.

Just realised they will be down there right now swilling down their dental rinse cocktail. Imagining the horror teeth with a tinge of pink. Eek.

Might have to watch *Carrie* as well.

8
Loulou

I didn't get my chance to talk to Theo because just when I was about to go up and ask her to come and have a drink with me, Keith dropped round unexpectedly.

He walked in waving printouts of possible tent arrangements to show me, but it turned out his main reason for showing up unannounced like that was actually much more worrying.

'This is lovely, Keith,' I said, sitting down at the kitchen table and saluting him with my 'Gin and It'.

That was another little thing we always did. At Claridges it was vodka martinis, but when we went to each other's houses we always had gin with 'Italian' – meaning sweet red vermouth. It was a very old-fashioned drink, which is exactly why we had taken it up years before, when everyone else was discovering vodka and cranberry, just to be different, and it had become another of our shared habits.

My life was made up of a series of these little bourgeois rituals, I realised, as I put the customary bowl of Cheddars on the table between us. I wondered whether it was entirely healthy.

'Up yours,' said Keith raising his glass and clinking mine. 'So what did you want to see me about?'

I raised my eyebrows. I'd been wondering what he wanted to see me about.

'I don't know,' I said, which didn't really help. 'What did you want to see me about?'

'I don't know either,' said Keith, laughing. 'You texted me.'

'Did I?' I said, starting to feel really bewildered.

'Yes,' said Keith, whipping out his phone. 'Yesterday. I would have come sooner, but I was up in Edinburgh overnight.'

He handed me the phone and then reached back into his jacket pocket and brought out his little case with the specs in it and passed them to me too.

'I'm going to get you some of those,' he said. 'They're only fifteen quid from a pharmacy and they open up a whole new world of seeing for you.'

Reluctantly, I put them on and looked down at the phone – which certainly did seem much easier to read than mine – and there it was. The text I thought I'd sent to Theo:

> Don't forget I'm going to need your help later. Come as soon as you can.

'Oh no,' I groaned, slumping onto the table with my head in my hands, shaking it slowly from side to side.

'Hey, Mrs,' said Keith. 'You're bending my specs. Give them here.'

I handed them back to him without raising my head. I'd bawled Theo out for not responding to a text I'd never actually sent to her, because I'd absentmindedly sent it to my friend instead. And now I really thought about it, had I ever even discussed Stevie's appointment with her? I wasn't sure I had. I'd meant to, which had somehow become I *had*, in my addled brain. Oh dear. Oh dear oh dear oh dear.

I lifted my head and looked at Keith.

'I think I'm finally losing the plot,' I said.

'What plot is that?' he said, holding up his drink playfully. 'I never had one to lose, darls.'

'I'm serious, Keith. That text I sent you was meant for Theo and we had the most terrible row last night because she didn't come back and help me in the shop, when she didn't even know she was supposed to, because I'd sent the bloody text to you.'

'Didn't you realise what you'd done when you got a reply from me?'

'Did I?' I said.

'Yes,' said Keith, nodding. 'Let's have a look here in my sent box . . .'

He fiddled with his phone again, before handing it back to me, with the specs.

I put them on and read it:

> Ten four rubber duck. But am in Edinburgh so will have to wait until tomorrow.

I started laughing. I had received that text. I just hadn't made the connection between it and the one I had just sent – or not – to Theo.

'I thought it was some kind of gay code . . .' I said and then we both got absolutely hysterical.

Keith was slapping the table.

'And that explains your reply to me . . .' he said, when he'd recovered himself a bit. 'I was a bit confused by that at the time . . .'

'What was it?'

He passed the phone again:

> Sounds delicious. Can't wait for more haggis details.

The laughter temporarily took my mind off feeling bad about the misunderstanding with Theo and the subsequent row and the possibility of her going to live with her father and all the other things that were just too much to take on, so in pursuit of more distraction, I happily accepted Keith's invitation to pop out to Lemonia for dinner.

I knocked on Theo's door to see if she wanted to join us and she answered by opening it just a crack. It seemed a bit odd, but at least she was smiling. Smiling was good, I told myself. But why the secrecy? Peeping over her shoulder, I could just make out an enormous pile of clothes on her bed. For a terrible moment, I wondered if she was packing.

'Are you OK, love?' I asked, my voice a bit squeaky.

'Fine, fine,' she said. 'I'm just sorting out some stuff and watching films, you know, what I like to do . . .'

It took all my self-control not to come straight out and screech: 'PLEASE TELL ME YOU'RE NOT GOING TO GO AND LIVE IN AMERICA WITH YOUR ARSEHOLE FATHER!' but I knew I had to approach the whole situation very delicately. And at exactly the right moment. This was not it.

'Keith and I are going to Lemonia,' I said brightly. 'And we wondered if you'd like to join us?'

A horrified expression crossed her face, but she quickly composed herself, which I took as a good sign. At least she'd made that small effort – on recent form she would have just made retching noises and slammed the door in my face – but still she couldn't entirely rise above it.

'No, thanks,' she said. 'I'd hate to be a gooseberry with the happy couple . . .'

'Oh, Theo,' I said, my old irritation flashing back for a moment. I hated the way she was about Keith now. She'd loved her BFG so much when she was little.

'I'm only kidding, Mum. Thanks for asking me, but I'm not really hungry. Catch you later, OK?'

'OK,' I said recovering myself, and kissed her on the cheek. She didn't flinch away, but as I turned and walked down the stairs I distinctly heard the sound of a bolt sliding on the door and it was like a stab in my gut.

Dinner with Keith was as comfortable and familiar as lying on the sofa with a mug of cocoa watching re-runs of *The Good Life*. Maybe Theo did have a point about us being like some freakish old married couple, I thought, as the waiter came over and asked us if we wanted our 'usual', and then headed off to put our order in at the kitchen without us having to do anything more than nod.

We were such regulars there, the *souvlaki* (me) and the *kleftiko* (Keith) were probably on the go the moment we stepped over the threshold. The waiter visit was just a formality. Another ritual, I realised. For a moment I was tempted to wave him back and change my order to something wild and crazy like the stuffed vine leaves, but I didn't. I loved the *souvlaki*.

The food and wine arrived and we chatted happily about this and that. He showed me the tent possibilities, I rejected them all for not having plumbing, hanging space or electric light, and we agreed to leave the subject of festival accommodation alone until I had got my head round the footwear side of things.

Things didn't get more animated until I told him about my conversation that morning with Jane. I still couldn't decide whether her twenty-first-century matchmaking was the most ridiculous idea I'd ever heard, or so nuts it was actually brilliant, and I wanted another opinion.

'I love your sister,' was his immediate response. 'What a fantastic idea; why didn't *we* think of it? I'm furious we didn't. It's inspired. She's absolutely right – why do we expect the most important meeting of our life to happen by chance? It's like driving around with all your possessions in a moving van waiting to stumble across somewhere perfect to live. And so much better to get someone else – ie your mum – to do all the boring groundwork. Once we've fixed Theo up, can you do it for me?'

He opened his attaché case and got out a notebook and pen.

'I'm going to start a list . . .' he said – which was the greatest compliment Keith could pay an idea. He was lists crazy. He wrote 'A Suitable Boy' as the heading and then looked up at me.

'OK,' he said. 'You need to get on to the mums of all her school friends – the nice ones – and I'll see who I know through work who has kids the right age . . . Get that look off your face, Loulou Landers!'

'What look?' I asked with faux innocence.

'The *insurance* horror look. Not everyone I meet through work plays golf and lives in Surrey, OK? And even if they do, they might have some cool kids, so get over yourself – unless you want to end up living with Theo forever in some kind of creepy Grey Gardens NW1 scenario.'

I raised my hands in appeasement, but he was already back to his list.

'Now,' he said, tapping his pen against his teeth in a way I knew sent Theo berserk. Even I thought it wasn't really something he should do in a public place. They were awfully big teeth. I reached over and gently pulled his hand down.

'Mmm?' he responded, distractedly, totally immersed in his number one favourite activity – planning. No wonder he was so good at his job.

'OK,' he said. 'First we have to have the initial meeting of the mums. We can't have a coffee morning, obviously, because it's not 1962 . . . And we can't do anything at your house, because Theo rarely leaves the premises and she mustn't know what we're up to. So how about a seven-till-nine meet-and-mingle bubbles-and-nibbles at mine?'

'Great,' I said, with genuine enthusiasm.

The coffee morning side of it had been seriously putting me off and Keith had a beautiful flat in Bayswater, which would be perfect for the drinks.

Plus, I knew if he was hosting it, the event would be as immaculate as an Embassy ball, from the handsome young chap who would take guests' coats on arrival, to the trays of witty little hors d'oeuvres and flutes of champagne which would be constantly topped up until they left.

I was almost looking forward to it.

Theo

Splatterday

Hello London! Alright? Can you hear me at the back? One two. One Two.

Have woken up feeling pretty damn special. Greatly boosted by my private Skool's Out film and TV festival last night.

I was so cheered up by hilarious *Glee* and *Summer High* I went straight into the prom scene of *Carrie* then lab room *Twilight* (when he still wants to eat her alive grrrrrrr) and big canteen number in *High School Musical 1* leading right into the opening bit in *17 Again* where Zac Efron shows off his marvellous hairy armpits. Such style! Such segue! I am a TV DJ. A genius really.

Also worked on my festival wardrobe which is so starting to rock. Had a long talk to Tats and she said people do this whole fancy dress thing on the Saturday, so think I will need to raid Mum's shop. Obviously my fancy dress has to be better than anyone else's. Obviously.

Lala will love me wanting to wear her stinky old rags and as I am trying to be nicer to her that is good. If I can please the ageing ma and look sensationally cool at The Chill that is what you call a WIN WIN WIN WIN WIN WIN situation. Especially for moi moi moi.

I only hope the clothes don't smell too much. I'll spray loads of her Mitsouko on them. She only wears that cack because it's so strong it hides the stench of dead people in the shop. The ones that the garments have just been prised off ha ha ha.

Tattina also said there is this thing at some festivals called the Dressing Up Box where you can rent mad old wigs and costumes and vintage tat to wear for the weekend. A lot of non-homo blokes strut about in dresses the whole time apparently which would be amusing as long as they didn't keep their skinny jeans on underneath but I'm sure they do because they will basically all be tossers.

If being nice to Lala works out I'll tell her about that too. The dressing-up box thing. We could do a stall and sell off all the crap that she gets in with consignments. I'll keep that ace up my Primark sleeve though.

Only draggy thing last night was fantastically irritating email from Rob the Knob getting pushy about me sending him some of my 'work' for him to look at.

He's also wondering if I should 'consider' doing the BA in photography at UCLA where he has great 'connections'. And I could live with him while I was 'studying'. I'd have my very own 'cabana' apparently looking right over Malibu 'beach'.

I think he should 'consider' jumping into the Pacific 'Ocean' in a lead suit so I scanned in some Mert and Marcus shots from an old copy of *Another Magazine* and sent them to him. I didn't actually say they were mine but if he chooses to make that moronic assumption that's his 'problem'.

Oh look – here's a reply from him now with one of those incrrrrredibly irritating red exclamation marks next to it which is like someone shouting at you in a public place. Delete. Next question?

It's still early. Can't hear the thud of Lala's surgical boots on the stairs so reckon she's still asleep probably dreaming sweetly of Keith's teeth chewing sensuously on a Greek sausage.

Mmmmm food. Not such a bad idea. I think today I really will go out and get us some breakfast having failed yesterday. Give the old trout a treat. Yessir. Indeed I will.

9
Loulou

Saturday morning was one of those miraculous English days in May, when you want to throw open every room in the house and let the soft spring air come flowing in. Which is exactly what I did.

Theo's room was empty again, but at least it wasn't locked. I hadn't heard her go out and she hadn't left a note, but every time her bedroom door was unlocked now, I considered it a bonus. I was just about to open her window to give the room a good airing, when I realised she probably wouldn't like the idea of me having been in there while she was out, so I left it.

Although I didn't go poking through her things – tempting though it was – I was glad to that see the great piles of clothes were no longer on the bed and her suitcases were still safely on top of her wardrobe.

Of course, it did occur to me that the clothes that had been on the bed the night before could now be neatly packed inside the cases up there, ready to leave for the airport, but I put those paranoid ravings aside. Her laptop, I was glad to see, was in its usual place on the bed, right next to where her head would be. As long as that was there I knew she couldn't be far away.

That rectangle of white plastic had such a central place in her life, it was more like a pet – or a boyfriend – than an inanimate object, and I did wonder whether it was healthy how much of her time she spent on it. If she wasn't shopping in Oxford Street, or watching TV in the sitting room, she was glued to the bloody thing.

On the other hand her devotion to all things digital made me feel quite encouraged that she would be willing – perhaps even enthusiastic – to get involved with the online side of the business I was so keen to get going on. I was determined to have that conversation with her as soon as possible. And if that went well, it could lead casually onto the scarier topic of what Rob's LA lady friends had said about her going out there.

Just allowing that thought to play through my head made me feel nauseous again. Really, I would have been less concerned at the idea of her going to live in Antarctica. I knew it was silly, but I couldn't help it. That was how I felt.

Looking out of Theo's bedroom window at the sun spilling down on the urban gardens, I was delighted that my assistant Shelley would be back in the shop today. The first really mellow Saturday of the year, it was going to be manic, as every fashion-conscious woman in London simultaneously realised she couldn't bear to wear her tired old winter weeds one more day.

It was the sort of morning that made you want to dress for the French Riviera – so I did, in a red-and-white striped 1940s dress and vertiginous apple-green espadrille wedges which Stevie Palumbo had sent me as a present from his summer collection. The finishing touch was a chunky Hermès enamel cuff with an anchor motif.

Shelley arrived perfectly on time, as always, fifteen minutes before we opened at ten. It always lifted my spirits just having her in the shop. She was one of those people with the ability to make everyone around her feel as cheery as she always was. Even Theo couldn't help liking Shelley.

'Morning Loulou,' she sing-songed, with her lovely Scottish rolling 'r', as she came through to find me in the store room, where I was sorting out extra sunglasses to maximise the retail opportunities of the sunny day. She gave me her customary smacking double air-kiss greeting, guaranteed not to smudge her lipstick or leave fluorescent pink marks on my cheeks.

'Hi, Loulou, darling,' she said. 'How are you today?'

'I'm great thanks, Shell,' I said, smiling at her rose-print 1950s dress, so tight round the hips I couldn't imagine how she'd sat down on the bus in it. With her customary five pairs of false eyelashes – a mixture of black, bright pink and diamante-tipped – and super-straight long, glossy black hair, she was a perfect walking object lesson in how to wear vintage in a modern way. She had a fetish for 1950s style, but only wore elements of it herself.

'Great dress,' I said.

'Oh, do you like it?' she said, doing a twirl, which was more like a shuffle, it was so tight. 'I got it in a market while I was up in Glasgow.'

'It's fab. How's your family?'

'Oh, they're all fine, the lot of them, and they spoiled me rotten, but now I'm ready to get back to work.'

'Good,' I said. 'Because I think we're going to be very busy today . . .'

Just half an hour later, it was nuts. We had people trying things on right there in the middle of the shop, stripping down to their underwear. At one point I had to lock the door and not allow anyone else in until a few had left. It greatly detracted from the Loulou Land experience when it felt more like a jumble sale than luxury retail – not to mention the risks of clothes getting damaged, and shoplifting, which was always worst on a Saturday anyway.

I knew all of that was why my high-end competitors opened only by appointment, but it wasn't my style. I really loved the energy of the constantly changing parade of people in the shop. And while I was more than grateful for the big spenders, my favourite customers were the ones who saved up to buy one precious piece and then treasured it.

That was how I'd found Shelley – when she'd fallen in love with a pair of rare mint-condition 1950s crocodile-skin stilettos and persuaded me to let her buy them on an instalment plan. I got a real boost from having a shop full of people like her, wildly enthusiastic about the merchandise, so mad days like this were a big part of the buzz.

Chard came cruising in just after eleven and his face lit up when a young woman pulled her T-shirt off right in front of him to try on a dress.

'This is crazy, Loulou,' he said, leaning on the counter and nodding in satisfaction. 'Reminds me of early Biba in here today. You should get some hat stands and feather boas.'

I didn't like to tell him that the reason for my disrobing customer's lack of inhibition was probably that he was so old he hadn't registered on her radar as a male of the species, and subtly shooed him out on to the front terrace before he made a fool of himself.

I brought a stool out for him, as there were already four young women sitting at the table, two to a chair, waiting to get inside, and he spent a couple of happy hours chatting up each new wave of customers.

A tall blonde asked me about him as she paid for two dresses. She had a face like a kitten's, but the eyes of a shark.

'Is that old bloke out there the geezer from that band . . . wotsit . . . The Ickies?'

'Icarus High, yes,' I said. 'That's Ritchie Meredith. He's the lead guitarist.'

'Thought so. My dad used to like them. I thought he was dead.' She laughed harshly. 'Is he married? Or better – has he got a son?'

I smiled coldly at her, tempted to snatch the carrier bag back and eject her from the shop physically, but I restrained myself. Not a good idea in front of so many other customers. But how dare she talk about Chard like that! I was outraged. No wonder he kept his relationships short and casual, I thought. He knew he was a target for big game hunters like this one.

So many women like her had been through my shop in the thirty years it had been open – some starting out like this creature, others making the most of their kills, like Little and Large from LA – I'd heard it all before, but it still appalled me. It made me feel very protective of Chard – and almost made me proud that my own daughter didn't seem to have any interest in men whatsoever.

And then I wondered yet again where she could be. I really could have done with her in there to help me, I thought, locking the shop door again to keep the numbers manageable. Where on earth was she? She'd been gone since before nine that morning.

A couple of times my hand had reached out to my phone to call or text her, but I managed to stop myself. We'd been on good terms the last time I'd seen her the night before and I wanted to keep it that way. I didn't want her to think I was nagging. It was beginning to drive me insane not being able to have that conversation about Rob with her, but I knew I had to wait until all the conditions were perfect.

A bit later, though, when we were enjoying the lunchtime lull, I was glad she wasn't there when the mother of one of her school friends came in.

I hadn't seen her since they all left over two years earlier and she'd been one of the ones I'd always liked. Perhaps I could enlist her for the matchmaking group, I thought. This was my chance to get going on that. I just had to think how to approach it.

She was with her younger daughter, in search of a prom dress. Vintage was suddenly the big trend for proms, so I was used to this scenario and had a whole strategy for it. Sulky fifteen-year-olds looking for dresses with their mothers were probably my trickiest customers – and this one looked particularly attitudinal, with dark hair flopping all over her face.

I was tied up with another client when they came in, so I couldn't go over immediately, but I had a good look at the girl out of the corner of my eye. She had a sweet figure, I could see, despite the fact she was doing her best to hide it under scraggy old jeans and a shapeless plaid shirt.

I knew the big challenge would be getting her to try anything on, and my secret method was to distract the mum – which was handy in this case, as I wanted to talk to her anyway – and then let Shelley take over. Shelley's extraordinary look short-circuited even the sulkiest teenager's attitude, as she had achieved what they all most aspired to, being simultaneously glamorous and cool. I might be London's high fashion 'queen of vintage', but Shelley was my secret weapon for the very young customers.

While her long-suffering mother pulled out beautiful dress after beautiful dress, this little madam kept shaking her head and pulling disgusted faces, until I was quite glad her curtain of hair was covering her entire face. By the time I was free to intervene, Miss Grumpy Prom looked like Joey Ramone on a bad hair day.

'Rachel!' I said, seizing my moment and going over to them. 'How lovely to see you.'

Not for the first time I was glad that I could always put a name to a face. It was a great business advantage which my father had encouraged me to develop as a child. He'd had all kinds of mnemonic tricks for remembering names and had passed them on to me. I'd logged this one in my head as Radiant Rachel, as she'd always had beautiful skin.

'Loulou,' she said, clearly delighted to be recognised. 'Great to see you. I wasn't sure if you'd be here. I hoped you would be. I've brought Iolanthe in to find a prom dress.'

She raised her eyes fleetingly to the ceiling and I nodded to show I understood.

'Let me make this easier for you,' I said, quietly, so the daughter wouldn't hear. 'She won't try anything on, right?'

Rachel nodded. 'How did you know?'

'Don't worry, they're all like that. It's not just you, they won't consider anything I suggest either – too much oldness – so you come over here with me and leave her to it for a bit.'

I led Rachel over to the shoe display, as if I were going to show her something, and watched covertly in the mirror on the wall above as the daughter took in the fact that we were otherwise occupied – or so she thought – and started looking methodically through the racks.

'If we just ignore her,' I said, 'she might find something.'

Rachel laughed.

'I should have brought her here first,' she said. 'I did suggest it last Saturday, but of course she wouldn't listen – because it was my idea. I only got her in here today because we were "passing" en route to David Mankin.'

I smiled at her.

'So how's Jemima doing?' I asked her, referring to the daughter who had been at school with Theo. 'Is she still at college?'

'Yes, she's at Oxford, second year, Classics, Oriel, having a marvellous time, non-stop parties as far as I can tell. I don't know when she ever does any work.'

My heart sank. She didn't sound like a candidate for my matchmaking club. I tried to remember if Rachel had any other kids. I had a feeling there was some complication, but I couldn't quite recall what. I'd done enough conjuring up the name; I couldn't be expected to drag up the family tree as well.

'How's Theo?' she asked me.

'Oh, she's OK,' I said. 'Well, not great, actually. She dropped out of art college and she's back living with me.'

Rachel pulled a sympathetic face.

'Sounds like my oldest,' she said. 'I don't know if you remember Cassandra? She's my daughter from my first marriage. She's twenty-five and still living at home. Did a cordon bleu, gave that up, got a job in the city, gave that up, started at Cirencester, gave that up. She just can't find her way and she doesn't ever seem to have a boyfriend . . . My sister keeps introducing her to my nephew's friends, but nothing ever happens.'

Bingo! I had my first recruit. And I liked the sound of her nephew and his friends too.

'Sounds all too familiar,' I said, with feeling. 'Actually, Rachel, I'm organising something that might interest you. Can I have your number? I'll ring you when I'm less frantic and tell you about it.'

By the time she'd written out her contacts and I'd given her my card, Shelley was just emerging from the changing room holding a beautiful grey shot-silk shift dress. It was an early 1960s French dressmaker piece with a contemporary Lanvin feel about it.

'Your daughter quite likes this dress,' said Shelley to Rachel, whose eyes popped open in amazement. 'But she's not sure and wants to bring her friend in to see it, so I said we could put aside for a couple of days. Is that all right, Loulou?'

I nodded and Rachel hugged me.

'Don't show her how pleased you are,' I whispered into her ear, as I saw Iolanthe emerging from the changing room. 'Show complete indifference and she'll be back for it – trust me.'

Theo finally turned up two hours before closing. We had the late afternoon rush on – last chance to get a new frock for Saturday night – and she had to tap on the locked door so I could let her in.

'Hi Mum,' she said, smiling awkwardly. 'Shit, it's a madhouse in here. I should have been here to help you. I'm really sorry. I was going to help today, but I nipped out to get these . . .'

She held up a brown paper bag that was darkly stained with grease.

'They're croissants,' she said. 'I was getting them for us for breakfast and then . . . Anyway, I'm here to help now.'

'That would be wonderful, darling – and while I've got you, Theo,' I had to restrain myself from grabbing hold of her arms so I could get it out before she disappeared again, 'I was wondering if you would have dinner with me tonight, just the two of us? We can go out. I've got something I want to discuss with you. Does that fit in with your plans?'

A slightly wary look came into her eye, but I could see she was making an effort to stay nice.

'Yeah, great,' she said, pausing before adding: 'Can we have Japanese?'

I pretended to cuff her around the head. That was my daughter. Always looking for the angle.

Theo

Splatterday night

I did actually buy the croissants this morning but when I was walking back with them I couldn't help thinking about Deathbreath at home on his own with Old Daddy Deathbreath and 'Mummy' and as I passed Chalcot Crescent I just found my feet were walking down there and the next thing I knew I was ringing the doorbell.

Some bloke I didn't know answered. Turns out he's Chard's new housekeeper. Bulgarian dude. Seems like everyone's got a housekeeper except us. Maybe Lala could get Shelley to start cooking our meals and making the beds ha ha ha.

Actually I can just see her getting into that. It would fit in with her weird 1950s fixation. All those tight dresses. She could wear a little apron and have a shocking pink feather duster to match her eyelashes. I love Shells but she is a bit of a perve about all that. I can't understand why any 21st-century woman would admire a decade where our forebears were treated like floor-scrubbing whores. I'm in love with the modern world.

Anyway I got a very warm welcome from the old folk. They were all having breakfast together around Mummy's bed. Boiled eggs and Marmite toast soldiers. ODD was very happy to see me and Mummy started calling me Gloria again. I helped to feed her.

Deathbreath gave up on his breakfast and was leaning out of the window smoking a ciggie until Mummy told him off.

'You'll get expelled Richard!' she kept saying.

'I already was Mummy' said Deathbreath. 'Three times.'

Then ODD started spluttering like he was totally about to die and Deathbreath had to wheel him off somewhere so I stayed with Mummy whose real name is Nancy. I asked her. We sat there for a bit after that staring at each other then she asked me the most brilliant question: 'What are the fashions?'

Talk about my subject. I told her it was all about brights with a return to a structured shoulder and unexpected proportions and she nodded and looked quite happy about it. Then I read some of her book to her. It was a Barbara Cartland and after about two minutes she nodded off and I can't say I blamed her. Utter cack. I'm going to get her a decent book.

I found Deathbreath with his dad downstairs looking cross with each other. So I told DB to go out for a stroll and I'd stay with ODD.

DB looked like he was about to burst into tears he was so grateful so I told him to fuck off out of it before I changed my mind which made ODD start laughing. He reminds me of Basil Brush when he gets going.

I wheeled him into the garden to sit in the sun and found Vlad or Nosferatu or whatever his weird eastern European name is and asked him to make us some coffee. If people have staff you've got to keep them busy. It's rude not to. On the way back to the garden I noticed a pack of cards so I took them out and ODD thrashed me at rummy. It was a brilliant laugh.

Then he nodded off so I wheeled him into the shade where his old bald head wouldn't get fried and spent the next couple of hours stretched out enjoying the delights of DB's complete Sky package. Didn't think much of the porno but the Disney Channel is genius. I must force Lala to get Sky. I love Miley Cyrus. I think I'll get a blonde wig for the Big Chill.

I didn't even ask and Nosferatu brought me a plate of smoked salmon sandwiches for lunch. And fruit salad. And sparkling mineral water. He asked if I wanted to have it in the garden and I told him I was quite happy on the sofa. It was absolutely brillo.

When I got back to Lala Land this afternoon it was all nutsy loony with the usual hysterical freaks who love fetid old clothes and I felt a bit bad I hadn't come back sooner.

Lala asked me to have dinner with her which I accepted on the condition it was Japanese. I categorically did not want to find myself in one of her three accepted restaurants where she always has the same thing. It makes me feel like my head is going to turn inside out just at the thought of it. How can she stand living in a box like that?

So we went to this funny little Japanese place in Swiss Cottage which looks like it was made of the leftover bits from a sauna and I've always wanted to try. The food was actually all right with those bits of green plastic pretend grass on the plates which look like something off Teletubbies.

Then two really freaky things happened. One: Lala asked me if it was true I was going to go and see my father.

I was so shocked my miso soup came down my nose which was lucky because I could use the coughing and spluttering as a distraction while my head whirled around like the lottery machine. How the fuck had she got that idea? Had she been reading my emails? Even the deleted ones?

Turns out those monstrous American bitches who were in the shop yesterday live in Los Arse-eles and actually know Knobhead and they told Mum he'd told them I was going over to see him.

Utter utter bollocks and I was pleased I could tell Lala that cos she looked greener than her wasabi paste just talking about it. I actually felt really sorry for her. I think she hates him even more than I do which is hard to imagine.

I didn't tell her that maybe I do butter him up online a bit to get stuff I want like MONEY and it is possible I may have slightly given him the impression I wouldn't possibly mind possibly going to see him one day possibly . . . But I didn't tell her any of that because I have no intention of doing it. No point in making her suffer any more.

So that was freaky number one happening. Freaky numero duo: Loulou wants a website. And she wants me to do it. In fact she wants me to digitise the whole 'business' as she will insist on calling her stinky old shop. Then she said she really needs to have a blog and I said: That's fine. I think they're just downstairs and to the left.

Ha ha ha.

Anyway I told her I needed to think about the digitalis proposal. She looked a bit miffed like she was expecting me to high-five her. Yay! Down wid da kidz! but I said I was really tired and we can talk about it again tomorrow.

So now I am going to lie here and think about exactly which model of serious Apple Mac kit I am going to get out of it.

10
Loulou

A couple of days after she came into the shop, Rachel and I met up in an obscure Café Nero in Holborn – where I was sure no-one I knew could possibly overhear – and I tentatively explained my sister's matchmaking system. To my delight, Rachel was so enthusiastic she immediately started a list of possible recruits.

We went through all the girls who'd been in the same class as Jemima and Theo, and when we got to Tatiana, Rachel had pulled a face which told me she felt exactly as I did about the prospect of ringing her mother to invite her along.

'She'd probably tell us she's already got Tattie's engagement party, wedding and first caesarean section booked into her electronic diary,' said Rachel. 'And the husband in preparation at Harvard Business School.'

'We can have Tattie to the party without involving her mum at this stage,' I suggested. 'We already know she's a very nice girl and I know she's single, because she's one of the few people Theo does still see.'

'Aren't there a couple of useful brothers in that family, as well?' said Rachel.

'I know there's one,' I said. 'And he's absolutely lovely, so we'll get him along and ask him to bring some friends.'

'Do you think that works with the system?' said Rachel. 'If we haven't vetted the mothers of the friends first?'

'Hmm,' I said. 'You're probably right, it would be just like any normal random party then, wouldn't it? But does that really matter? I think I just want to see Theo interacting with the opposite sex. I'm not as bothered as my sister about the colour of the grandparents' eyes, or the contents of their bank accounts.'

We both sipped our coffee and pondered silently for a moment.

'I know what you mean,' said Rachel. 'But if we're going to this much trouble, we might as well really go for it, don't you think? I've often thought how much easier my life would have been if my parents had forbidden me from seeing the boy who became my disastrous first husband – let alone marrying the idiot.'

I raised my cup to her in recognition and agreed that the first party, at least, would run exactly according to my sister's rules – right down to me having to do an introductory speech to the other mothers at the first meet 'n' mingle, explaining it all, a prospect which appalled me.

Two and a half weeks later, that moment had arrived. 'Go on,' said Keith, appearing at my side with a bottle of champagne in his hand at 7.25pm, five minutes before we'd agreed I should address the troops. 'Scull a few more glasses of this and you won't even notice you're doing it.'

I crossed my eyes and held out my flute for a refill. But I needn't have worried. As soon as I tapped my glass with a teaspoon to get everyone's attention, fifteen pairs of attentive maternal eyes fixed on me and I knew I had a captive audience. They were all as eager to help their children as I was.

By the end of the evening all the mothers had enthusiastically signed up to take it on to the next stage. We agreed that we would have another recruiting party in a fortnight's time, to which they would each bring another interested mother, to get the numbers up. Then we reckoned we would have critical mass to move on to the next stage – the proper party with the kids. It seemed like good going.

After they'd all left, Rachel, Keith and I flopped out in his sitting room, finishing the canapés and one last bottle of champagne.

'Well, I think that went brilliantly,' said Rachel. 'Thanks so much for organising it, Keith.'

'You're most welcome,' he said. 'I'm thrilled if we can help all of you, but I'm really doing it for my goddaughter – I want to see her sorted out with a boyfriend just as much as her mum does. Actually, I'd like to see her mum fixed up with a bloke too. Forget about the young studs for a moment – you don't know any single, straight male grown-ups do you, Rachel?'

I picked up my left shoe and threw it at him, although I aimed to miss. I didn't actually want to kill him.

'That's a good point,' said Rachel. 'I'm presuming all the mums who have husbands and partners will be bringing them to the big party, or it would arouse suspicions among the young ones about the exact nature of the event, and if there are a lot of single mums, maybe we will need to ship in some grown-up chaps to even out the numbers a bit. Perhaps I'll put that in my first group email, ask them what they think? What do you reckon, Loulou?'

She looked down at the notepad the ever-organised Keith had supplied for the mothers to put down their contact details.

'What's your email address, Loulou?' she said. 'It's the only one I don't have on my list here.'

Keith snorted with laughter. 'Go on, tell her, Loulou.'

I threw my other shoe at him.

'He wants me to tell you that I don't have an email address,' I said. 'But he's wrong. It's loulou@loulouland.com. OK, Keith?'

'Are you serious?' he said.

'Yes,' I said, giving him a smug smile. 'I have an email address, and you will notice from it that I also have a domain name, and soon I am going to have a website and a blog and a Facebook page and Twitter thingie. Not forgetting a whiz-bang integrated digital database of all my clients, contacts and suppliers.'

'Wow, I'm truly amazed,' said Keith. 'Welcome to the twenty-first century, baby. But what brought this on so suddenly? I've only been nagging you about it for ten, maybe fifteen years . . .'

'Yes, you were quite right, Mr Digital Clever Pants,' I said. 'I should have done it years ago, but I was just too daunted. I felt so left behind I didn't think I could ever catch up, but now I have my own private IT consultant, I'm finally able to get on to it.'

'How come?' said Keith, clearly incredulous I'd been able to achieve this result without him at least contributing a few lists.

'Theo's doing it for me,' I said, this time smiling sincerely.

Keith's mouth fell open – quite a startling effect with his teeth – and I laughed, delighted with myself. I hadn't told him about it deliberately, so I could have the pleasure of springing it on him like this at an opportune moment.

'You've actually got her to do something for you?' he said.

'Well done,' said Rachel, who knew all about Theo's antics now, as I did the times and crimes of her daughter Cassandra, who sounded quite a handful.

Cassandra's problems seemed to stem from over-enthusiastic all-night partying starting in her late teens, moving on to serious cocaine abuse in her twenties. I was sorry to hear about it, but I couldn't help feeling a bit better about Theo by comparison. Drugs might have explained some of her strange antisocial behaviour, but I was fairly sure that wasn't Theo's problem.

'Yes, Keith,' I said. 'She's been amazingly helpful and I'm quite amazed too, but she seems to be really into it. Of course she's conned me into buying her a flashy new computer to do it all on, as well as a chic new laptop for me, but I'm so happy to see her engaged with something – and communicating with me about it – that's a small price to pay. Well, it was quite a big price, but you know what I mean.'

I was really surprised how much I was enjoying playing on the computer myself, now Theo had spent some time showing all the things I could do on it. The joke was on me, as I realised how easy it all actually was. A major development was being able to access all the important fashion auctions online, rather than waiting for catalogues to arrive. There was also a whole new sector of my industry now that was conducted entirely over the web, and I could see I had been really missing out there.

It could also save me a lot of travelling, as my key suppliers could now email me pictures of things they thought I would like. It wasn't the same as touching – and smelling – the fabric and being able to check the quality and condition first-hand, but with the contacts I really trusted it could seriously speed things up. And as there was more and more competition in the vintage world – with less and less good stuff out there – I couldn't afford to lose out on any possible sources.

I was also enjoying checking out fashion blogs and websites and, as a result, I was discovering just how much time you could waste on the internet. It was unbelievable. I'd go on to look up something I really needed to know and an hour later I'd still be tooling around on Style.com or The Sartorialist. (There were quite a few pictures of me on there, I discovered – so that's who the nice man with the camera was . . .)

This virtual voyage of discovery had given me a useful insight into how Theo could spend so much time holed up in her room. Now I understood she wasn't alone in there after all. She'd had the entire world at her fingertips the whole time and I was thrilled that I could now share that with her.

Although I was really tired when I got home from Keith's place, I couldn't resist checking my emails and found I had one from him, which was typical. He would have sent it the minute I left his flat. As well as a few sarcastic remarks welcoming me to the 'Computer Age', it had a link to the Big Chill website which I clicked on to find a big picture of Chard's face looking out at me.

They were clearly very excited about his forthcoming appearance.

> 'New festival highlight!' it said. 'A unique acoustic solo performance by Ickies' guitar legend and songwriter Ritchie Meredith, performing classic tracks and new material for the very first time. Not to be missed!'

I clicked around the Big Chill site and began to feel the first stirrings of anticipation for the whole event – not just Chard's performance. In this spirit, I clicked on Keith's next link which led to the tents section of the Argos catalogue. Up came what looked like a tipi. But made of nylon.

I immediately emailed Keith back: 'You cannot be serious.'

Just a few moments later his reply came back:

> Deadly darls. I've ordered five of them and a huge gazebo. We are going to have us a compound. All you've got to do is sort out your footwear issues.

That was when inspiration struck. I got on to Google and typed in the words: 'Wellington boots high heels' and up they came. Loads of websites devoted to wellies of all shapes, styles and patterns.

I clicked on a few of them and then explored the one with the most appealing graphics. Among the pink Hunters, the Cath Kidston florals and the Thomas the Tank Engine kiddie specials were some fabulously kinky black ones with spiky heels and a French brand, designed by a Russian girl, with chunky heels and platforms. Eureka!

I immediately ordered a pair of each – purple in the platforms – and five pairs of something called 'welly socks' to go inside them, in all kinds of crazy stripes. Suddenly I was really looking forward to my birthday treat.

Theo

Oh how I love the first day of the month as plop into my bank account goes one thousand delicious little poundlings. It used to be just eight hundred so that extra two – my phantom 'rent' ha ha ha – will be most handy. I'm not sure what for yet but I'll think of something. Darling Daddy you have your uses. I won't have you killed yet.

Hmm there's an idea. I wonder what I actually am due to get in his will? Presumably something. No doubt his two subsequent ex-wives will be expecting their due if he doesn't find a way of cheating them out of it. I'm just glad he hasn't had any further children to confuse the picture but he's bound to fit in another wife or two before he carks it. Apart from them I guess it's me or a donkey sanctuary to get the cash.

Actually knowing him he's probably 'bequeathed' it all to a photography museum so they can build a Rob McKnob Memorial Toilet Block or something equally wanky. But perhaps I should check it out. Maybe I should go over to see him to secure my inheritance. Take a little trip through his hard drive while I'm there . . .

Because if I did get all his and all Lala's dough I really would never need to have a job or a husband. Now that would be sweet. And Lala said once she was sure Ritchie would leave me something in his will and when you think about it who else is going to get that? Dogbreath? I might be minted. Watch out Paris Hilton.

At least I won't need any money for computer equipment for a while. I will have to tread a little carefully as Lalina Madina is not completely a dumbass when it comes to £££ but it was just so very easy to persuade her to open a 'business' account for me at the Apple Store.

So much easier if I can just ring up and order things as I explained to her. Rather than having to constantly bother her when I need to get us a new – I don't know – AIRBOOK or something.

You should see it. So beautiful. I've also got a full 36-inch screen mothership up here for me to do the big work on. I did really actually honestly not a word of a lie need it to do the website stuff for her properly but oooh imagine all of what else I will be able to do on that baby. I could launch a space shuttle.

I'll keep my old lappie as my special friend though. That is a deep bond which cannot be broken. We've been through so much together. A large part of the Humphrey Bogart oeuvre among other things. He really did make a lot of shit films as well as the good ones. I now understand that if he's not wearing a seriously cool suit in the opening shot – fling it. That could have saved me from *The Treasure of the Sierra Madre* and *The African Queen* two of the most tedious films I have ever yawned through with terrible wardrobe.

I've already pretty much designed Lala's plebsite. Took me . . . ooh at least a day. I haven't told her that though. I keep giving her tantalising glimpses and she thinks I'm still 'building' it. She loves saying things like that and 'the site'. Makes her feel young and modern. She's always trying to talk to me about her favourite 'pages' and 'Tweeps' like she has just invented the internet.

The other day she said she could now understand how I could spend so much time on my computer. Oh really? Well, whoop ti doo. Am I supposed to be thrilled that she has now discovered the advantages of the wheel? It's not like we didn't try and tell her for the last ten years. Stubborn much?

The website is looking pretty sweet though I must say. I'm quite proud of it. When you log in the shop sign comes up and it looks like it's swaying in the wind. You click on it to get in and as the site loads you hear the sound of the garden gate opening and clanging shut behind you and the click clack of high heels across the terrace up to the door. I recorded Shelley clip clopping along for that.

The only draggy part of this whole project is inputting all the names-addresses-inside-leg-measurements-'wants' and other crap from about five million of Lala's papyrus scrolls or whatever she calls those old file cards which she expects me to do as well. She says it's all part of the gig. I am taking the angle that she and Shelley need to do it as they will know what all the stuff about 'tastes and preferences' means. I can tell you what my preference for the lot is and it intimately involves the recycling centre.

Actually I might spend my spare allowance paying someone else to do the inputting. Someone who needs the money. Division of labour and all that. I was talking to Old Daddy Deathbreath about that the other day. He told me he was a communist when he was 16. Wanted to go and fight in the Spanish Civil War but his dad stopped him. Then he said he grew up and became an Air Marshal and started voting Conservative like everyone else with property to protect.

I told him I didn't believe in voting because they're all crooks and idiots and he ranted and raved at me about how lucky I was to have a vote and how it was my duty to use it and I had to distract him with a game of cards before he choked on his dentures. Luckily he forgot about it very quickly. Very useful aspect of visiting the elderly.

Note to self: do not bring up politics on next visit to Deathbreath Old People's Home. Could cause fatalities.

Nancy was in good form when I saw her yesterday morning. I'm reading her *Polo*. She seems to be enjoying it.

What an attractive man this Rupert Campbell-Black is she keeps saying.

Yeah I said. If you know anyone like that can you introduce me?

Deathbreath is trying to work out how to use the super duper new coffee machine I casually suggested he bought. I'm already an expert of course from my gap year café career where I prided myself on making the tallest cappuccinos in North London. Man can I froth. We had a froth fight yesterday after I put a blob on his chin and told him he looked like Father Christmas but older. I won of course.

Tattie's just been on the phone nagging me to come to her 'pre-Chill drinks' tonight yawn yawn and – did I mention? – yawn.

I blew out the last one. Just couldn't face a load of her twerp friends in a confined space and I was also very busy. It coincided with the day I discovered Robert Mitchum's chin and I had a lot of research to do. Didn't bother trying to explain that to her. So I just said I had period pains. She knew I was lying because that was the excuse we always used to get off games at school. I always had about seven periods a month but nobody seemed to notice.

Don't try the curse trick on me Theo she said. You are turning into a shut in and I am only trying to help you.

I told her if I was a shut in she was a slut in and it quickly descended into our old game of *you* are, no – *you* are, no – *you* are and so on. I do love Tats.

Then she said something bizarre about how her brother Marc was going to be there tonight and he really wanted me to come. Why does he care what I do? And why would I care what he wants?

The last time I saw him at her house he was wearing a PINK Abercrombie & Fitch polo shirt which renders him barely human in my opinion although it was nice of him to drive me home that time. And I use the word 'nice' with every negative connotation implied thereof. Moreover. Notwithstanding. Insomuchas.

Will put my iPod on shuffle at exactly 6pm and the second song which comes on will tell me whether to go or not.

6.05pm Shit shit shit. It was *There She Goes* by The Las. I have to go. DAMMIT. Wish I'd never read the bloody *Dice Man*.

1.20 am Many very great weirdnesses have occurred.

One: I went out. With other people.

Two: I had quite a good time.

Three: Two is true even though every single male there was wearing skinny jeans except one who was wearing chinos. Chinos. Honestly. Couldn't make it up.

Of course the heinous heinos were on Tattie-brother Marc's skinny arse with – wait for it – a baby blue polo shirt on the top. Puhleeeeeeeeeeeeease. I think that is almost worse than the skinny jeans and pointy white shoes combo. And of course he had the collar turned up and his hair all ruffled and sticky uppy. He really thinks he's something special that one. And he would NOT leave me alone.

He kept trying to talk to me about the New York Dolls because I'd played them that time in his car and he clearly thought we had something in common. I told him I'd never heard of them ha ha ha. Then he started asking my why I don't wear vintage clothes because my mum has such 'amazing' stuff in her shop and he thought I would look 'amazing' in it. I told him I was wearing vintage. Vintage Primark. It's officially vintage when it's twenty minutes old. Oh I amused myself.

Managed to escape from him when he went to the bar to get me a drink. Ran off and hid in the loo for the rest of the night with the one really fun bloke there who is a big old fageroo who goes to college with Tats.

Obviously I'm not going to be a tragic hag chick like Lala but Stew really is a laugh. He hates Abercrombie & Fitch too. He says he resents straights colonising a gay aesthetic but I suspect it may also be because he is somewhat porky and has major man boobs. Bigger than mine. About a C cup. He is bloody funny though so I'm very glad he's coming to the Chillski. Unfortunately I think Mr Cup of Chinos is also planning to attend.

I really hate good looking men.

I don't mind them in films and stuff where they belong and no one is pretending it's normal but in real life it's just an affront. Pah.

11

Loulou

Rachel and I were sitting at the dining table in Keith's flat, planning the matchmaking party with a committee of three other mums. He was up at his company's office in Edinburgh again and was letting us use his place as a 'safe house' where none of our offspring could overhear our plotting. We didn't even feel we could discuss it in a restaurant. It was just all too delicate.

'OK, let's get stuck in,' I said, winging my new role as a party committee chairperson. I had been involved with organising a few fashion charity events over the years, so I hoped I could carry it off, trying to remember what had gone on at those meetings. I'd taken a tip from Keith and made a list. The first thing on it was 'Guests'.

'Now, Rachel,' I said, 'can you tell us what the final numbers are?'

'We've got twenty-six mums in total,' she said, peering at her own list through a spare pair of Keith's pharmacy specs, which we'd found in the kitchen. 'With nineteen husbands and partners, and forty-four children. That's eighty-nine in total. We just need to drum up a few more senior males to even things out a bit. Keith says he's going to bring a couple of friends and I'm going to email the mums to see if any of their partners have any adult male single pals who can come along.'

I looked at the next thing on my agenda: Money.

'Have they all paid up?' I asked Fiona, one of the bossier recruits, who we'd appointed treasurer.

'Just three outstanding,' she said. 'I'll chase them tomorrow and tell them if they haven't paid by the end of the week, they're off the guest list . . . Mind you,' she added conspiratorially, 'one of them is Lucy Pugh-Williams and we don't want to lose her – she's got three gorgeous single sons.'

'Hmm,' said Rachel. 'And she was married to that hedge fund bloke, wasn't she? Let's give her a bit longer.'

Everyone laughed because, by coincidence, all of us on the committee had daughters we were trying to fix up. It was funny, but I was always a tad uncomfortable when things got a little too Mrs Bennett like this. I wasn't particularly looking for a single man in possession of a good fortune for Theo – just one in reasonable possession of his wits and quite nice with it.

'How are the numbers balancing for the kids, actually Rachel?' I asked, wanting to move things on. 'Are they remotely even?'

'Even-ish,' she said, running a finger down her columns of names, then looking up at us with a distinct twinkle in her eye. 'Actually, it's a little bit loaded towards the boys . . .'

'Let's make it do then, shall we?' I said and they all laughed again. 'Now, let's see . . . Venue. What have you got for us, Lauren?'

This was the first time I'd met this mother properly. She'd been brought to the last recruiting party by someone I didn't know either, and I hadn't had the chance to speak to her then, but Rachel had been very excited about getting her on to the committee, telling me that she was very well connected.

'Well,' said Lauren, in her appealingly drawly American accent, 'we could have Hurlingham on the date we've chosen, but it's a bit far for some of you north Londoners and I think the kids would think it was a bit "straight".

'So then I looked at Hoxton but decided that was too far for the west Londoners and would make all of us feel really old, so then I thought – why suffer? We need to be straight up central, so I suggest we have it at my house. I live in Fitzrovia, and it's pretty big, and it would just make things a lot easier, as long as you all are comfortable with that . . .'

'Wow,' I said and everyone else made similarly appreciative noises. 'That would be amazing, Lauren, but are you sure? Obviously we would spend the money we'll save on the venue on caterers and waiters and all that, so you won't have to do anything.'

'Yeah, yeah, that's cool. I've worked all that out. I think we can have a much nicer party this way.'

'Having it at your place will really help me with the invites, as well,' said Natalie, the fifth committee member. 'I've been racking my brain how to word them and now we can just put "Lauren Beaney at Home", if that's OK with you, Lauren?'

She nodded and Natalie spread out some sample invitation styles. We all agreed on simple engravers' type in raised ink on bright mauve card.

'So,' I said. 'If you get on with ordering the invites and sending them out, and Lauren finds out exactly how much champagne we can buy with our budget, that leaves just one last thing to decide.'

They all looked at me expectantly.

'How the hell are we going to sell it to the kids?' I asked. 'Is it just me, or will it be very hard to casually suggest to your daughters that they will love to come to a lovely party with loads of people they don't know, including a lot of draggy old parents? The reason I'm doing this crazy thing is because my daughter is so anti-social she hardly ever goes out at night and I honestly don't know how I will convince her to come along to this. I know Rachel has the same problem, so how about the rest of you? Got any ideas?'

Fiona was nodding sympathetically.

'Phoebe isn't exactly thrilled to do anything I suggest,' she said. 'But she was at school with Theo and Cassandra – albeit different years – so we could play the reunion card, couldn't we?'

'Cassie definitely wouldn't come to that,' said Rachel, with a wry laugh.

'What does your sister in Manchester do?' asked Natalie. 'How do they get the kids to come?'

'Good point,' I said. 'But she's no help. She said they just tell their kids there's a lovely party on with lots of free drink and they all happily turn up. I think there's more of a norm in her circle for parties with mixed age groups. She says the kids just go along with it and any who don't are natural wastage. To quote my darling sister: "If they're too bloody mardy to come to a perfectly nice party, I don't want them in my bloody family anyway . . ." So, no help there.'

They all laughed and I turned to Lauren. 'Have you got any ideas?' I asked her. 'If the party's going to be in your house, you'll have to give your daughter a reason for having it, won't you?'

She smiled broadly.

'I think I've got it covered,' she said. 'We've lived in London for fifteen years this year, so I'm going to tell Claudia we're throwing a series of parties to celebrate that – which is true, actually – and this one is for all the lovely people I've met who haven't been to our house yet, which is kind of true as well. And I will add that if she wants to carry on living with us, she has to come to it. No discussions, no excuses.'

I looked at her with admiration.

'That's excellent,' I said. 'But it doesn't really help the rest of us, does it?'

'Well,' said Lauren. 'Perhaps you could say that there is this nice woman that you know from your yoga class and she's having a fabulous party because she's lived in London for fifteen years and she wants everyone coming to bring their kids, so they can meet her kids. Not a word of a lie, except for the yoga detail, but I'm sure you all do yoga . . .'

'Mmmm . . . I'm still not sure how that will go down,' I mumbled, not wanting to be rude but all too clearly imagining Theo replying, 'And what has that got to do with me exactly?', or some other withering remark.

'Well,' said Lauren, 'you could also mention that the woman's husband is the owner of West Wind and the goodie bags are likely to be pretty damn good . . .'

I just stared at her. She was *that* Lauren. No wonder Rachel had expected me to know who she was. And this really was a result, as far as I was concerned. West Wind was one of Theo's favourite chain stores, up there with Topshop, New Look and Primark, in her estimation. I'd even heard her say they did the best handbags on Oxford Street, which was very big praise from her.

'So you're married to Paul Beaney,' I said, stupidly.

'That's right,' said Lauren. 'We met when we both worked for Gap in San Francisco, back in the 80s. I'm a Californian girl, but Paul's a Brit, of course, and we moved back here to launch our own label. Felt there was space in the market here for something with a little more edge to it than in the US. That's how we got the name – we blew in on the wind from the west coast. I'm from LA originally.'

'Wow,' I said, genuinely impressed. As well as being in Theo's top five, West Wind was one of the chains I kept a professional eye on. 'That would most definitely get Theo along to the party. She loves your shops. How about the rest of you?'

I looked at the other three mothers and they were all nodding enthusiastically.

'Phoebe would love it too,' said Fiona. 'But how about the boys? Would that lure work for them?'

'Well, we do a very successful men's range aimed exactly at this age group,' said Lauren. 'And if my two sons are anything to go by their generation of guys are just as vain and fashion-crazy as the girls are.'

'And failing that,' said Rachel, 'as another mother of children of both sexes, I can reliably suggest they'll come if we just tell them loads of hot girls are going to be there . . . Which is not far from the truth if Theo and Phoebe are anything to go by.'

'Great,' I said, delighted that the one thing that had been really worrying me about the whole project was now sorted.

'I've just got a couple more suggestions,' said Natalie. 'How would you feel about us putting the West Wind logo on the invite, Lauren? That would really suck the young ones in, I think. It would seem less like a family party and therefore more appealing to them.'

Lauren nodded. 'That's a great idea – and Paul would love it too. Any opportunity to flog his precious brand . . .' She rolled her eyes. 'And I'll tell Claudia it's only on there so the party can be a tax deduction. You've got be on it all the time with these kids, huh? They're so savvy, it's scary.'

We all nodded in knowing agreement.

'And just one more other thing,' continued Natalie. 'I think we should send a personal invite to each of the kids, so they know they're not just plus-ones with their parents, they are invited in their own right. I think that would also make them more likely to come.'

'I agree,' I said. 'Totally. And if there's a West Wind logo on the invite, Theo will be waiting outside for the door to open.'

By the end of that week I had the proof that Natalie's idea about the logo had paid off brilliantly. Theo came rushing down to the shop to find me, waving a square of mauve card in the air.

'Mum!' she said, with a level of enthusiasm in her voice I hadn't heard for years. 'Look at this, I've been invited to a party by the people who own West Wind! How amazing is that? I think it's at their house. Do you think it's because I'm such a loyal customer?'

I picked up my matching invitation, which was lying on the counter in front of me and held it up. Her face fell ever so slightly and I knew I had to try and surf the wave of her initial excitement, or I'd lose her.

'Well, I think it's actually a lot more exclusive than that,' I said quickly. 'Lauren and Paul Beaney are having a private party to celebrate fifteen years in London and they asked me if we'd both like to come . . .'

'I didn't know you knew them,' snapped Theo, peevishly. 'Why didn't you tell me? I could have been getting discount all this time. I thought all your fashion contacts were at stupid pretentious shops.'

'I don't know them that well,' I said truthfully. I'd met Paul once, for about thirty seconds, when the party committee had its final meeting at the house. 'As I said, they're having this party to celebrate living in London for fifteen years and they have specifically invited people they would like to know better – and that includes kids as well. They've got two sons and a daughter around your age, who seem very nice.'

I could see Theo was zoning out now. She clearly wasn't interested in the family details and I was worried I might have lost her with the risky mention of the kids, but suddenly her attention snapped back to me.

'Do you think we'll get a goodie bag?' she said, her eyes wide.

'I'm sure we will,' I said, sending silent heartfelt thanks to Lauren.

'Excellent!' said Theo, all enthusiasm returned. 'Hmm, what will I wear . . .? Too obvious to wear their stuff, but I wouldn't want to wear the competition either. I'll have to go down to the flagship immediately and seek inspiration.'

I smiled with relief. It was some kind of miracle, but we'd hooked her in.

She smiled back at me, but then her eyes narrowed to her more customary suspicious expression.

'What are you going to wear?' she asked.

'Are you worried I'm going to embarrass you?' I asked, kicking myself mentally as the words came out.

'Depends what you put on your feet,' said Theo, showing that we were drifting dangerously back to our old sparring ways.

'Well, you can advise me on the shoes,' I said quickly. 'I'll let you choose them for me – as long as they're not flats, of course – but as for the rest of the outfit, I am going to seriously dress up. I'm going to have some fun with it.'

'Yeah,' said Theo, nodding. 'Me too. I'm definitely going to have fun with it.'

And with a cackle of laughter she disappeared out of the shop door.

Theo

A miracle has happened. Lala actually knows somebody worthwhile in the fashion biz, not just cross-eyed fashion editors and wankhead designers of many lands. I can't BELIEVE she didn't tell me but she actually knows Paul Beaney of genius West Wind most excellent clothing emporium particularly strong on accessories IMEO (the E is for expert BTW LOL LIGAS).

And we are going to his house for a party – with a goodie goodie bag.

Perhaps it will be something exclusive which will never be on sale in the shops. Or a 100% off lifetime discount card. Whatever it is I don't care because I know I'm going to get it and I'm going to get it first. I plan to stay at the stupid party just precisely until they start doling the goodies out and then I will be out of that door faster than you can say TAXI!

And I may get more than one if I can finesse it. Can I have one for my friend as well? She had to leave early. Period pains. Yeah that should swing it.

So that's all good.

I've nailed my outfit too. I went straight down to the flagship first to scope what's going on right now so I can do something completely different and to say inspiration struck would be an understatement. It got me by the neck and pinned me to the ground.

I really can't wait to see the look on Lala's face when I walk in. Because of course I will be arriving separately. I'm not walking in with her obviously. Whatever shoes she's wearing.

I'll go with Tats because Lala said I was allowed to invite her too which was amazingly great. But then it was weird because she gave me invites for her and for dopey bro Marc with their actual names on them. You won't be allowed in without your invite and I.D. apparently (not the magazine ha ha ha). Presumably something to do with the fabulous exclusiveness of the door gift. Maybe everything will be personalised? This I would like.

So I just gave both invites to Tatarama and said it was up to her if she gave it to him or burned it. On a pyre of polo shirts.

12
Loulou

Nothing ever seemed to go simply and smoothly with Theo, I reflected, as I did my make-up for the party. I was painting on a very thick sweep of liquid black eyeliner to set off my early 1960s Givenchy cocktail frock, which had sheer chiffon sleeves and a wide band of fluffy ostrich feathers round the hem.

Sacrilegiously I had cinched it in at the waist with a wide belt, as the simple shift cut did nothing for my shape, but then 'wearing vintage on my own terms' was what I was known for. I had been quoted to that exact effect in the *Telegraph* magazine just the Saturday before and I felt it was expected of me.

Less characteristically I'd teamed it with a pair of simple black patent court shoes with a silver buckle on the toe and relatively low heels, rather than my usual towering clompers. I felt distinctly stunted and would have preferred to balance that dress with a pair of seriously fierce boots, but I'd decided to wear the pumps, which I'd had to borrow from the shop, as a concession to Theo. I was hoping she might be more relaxed at the party if she wasn't mortified by what I had on my feet – although she hadn't taken up my offer to choose my shoes for me after all.

I was really disappointed because I'd been looking forward to seeing what she would have picked out for me, but even more so because after her initial enthusiasm about the invitation she'd appeared to take great pleasure in telling me that we wouldn't be arriving at the party together.

She had to go and help Tatiana with her outfit, she'd said, or she would look so terrible she wouldn't be able to be seen with her. I felt as if I had been punched in the gut. She cared more about Tatiana than she did about me. For once I was glad when she flounced out of the door without a backwards glance after dropping her bombshell. I didn't want her to see how hurt I was.

Rather pathetically, I had been imagining us getting ready together, having a glass of champagne, advising each other what to wear and which extraneous accessory to take off, swapping lipsticks and all that lovely girly stuff we used to do, which had dwindled away so quickly after she had first gone to college. That was when she'd first started to change.

She'd been a bit of a moody teenager, but nothing beyond the norm; there had still been enough of my little girl there to communicate with. Her sulky guard would drop and she'd snuggle up to me on the sofa while we watched telly. Sunday afternoons with *On the Town*, *High Society* and the like, back to back, with a box of Charbonnel et Walker rose and violet creams to dip into, had been one of our little shared delights. We could sing 'True Love' together with all the harmonies. Theo had always insisted on taking the Bing Crosby part.

Tears pricked my eyes as I hummed it in my head. 'For you and I have a guardian angel, on high with nothing to do . . .' What had happened to that beautiful relationship?

She'd started to close down on me while she was doing her foundation year at Camberwell. That was when she'd first begun coming home, going straight to her room and shutting the door, without even saying hello, and it had just got progressively worse after that, until she'd come back during that second term at Manchester Art College like a cold stone statue of my once-loving daughter.

I hadn't thought anything could hurt me more than when her

father had left us, but Theo shutting her bedroom door in my face for the first time had nearly killed me.

Since we'd started working on the computer project together, things had improved a lot, but she still went out without telling me where she was going, let alone when she would be coming back, so most of the time I still felt more like a flatmate than a mother. Which pretty much summed up the paradox of our situation: at her age, that was exactly the kind of set-up she should have been living in. It wasn't surprising neither of us knew how to behave; there wasn't a script for it.

I still felt stupidly like crying as I blotted my lipstick and sprayed Mitsouko behind my ears, imagining all the other mothers and daughters getting ready together, and was very glad I had co-opted Chard at the last minute to come as my date, so at least I wouldn't have to arrive on my own.

Darling old Chard, he was such a reliable pal – and a handy addition to the senior single male numbers for the party. I'd told him the truth about the real subtext of the party, partly in the hope it would stop him hitting on the girls too enthusiastically, but mainly because I just couldn't lie to him. Not even by omission. We were too close for that. He'd thought the matchmaking concept was hilarious – if slightly sinister – but had promised not to breathe a word to Theo. And I knew I could trust him.

We arrived at Lauren's house, which was just off Tottenham Court Road, but so grand inside it was more like a small country house, a little early, just after seven, so the committee could have a final group hug before the crowds started descending.

As befitted the daughter of a well-known film director, which I'd learned Lauren was, she wasn't at all abashed at having a major rock god showing up at her front door with me and welcomed us both in.

'Hi Loulou,' she said warmly, simultaneously kissing me on both cheeks and handing my wrap to a uniformed maid. 'Come in, come in, you look amazing, as always . . . and you must be Ritchie . . .'

she said, turning to him, without missing a beat and kissing him on both cheeks with a confidence I knew would put him immediately at his ease.

Lauren had the makings of a really good friend, I thought. Every time I saw her I liked her more – but I wasn't so sure about her husband Paul, who headed straight over with an excited gleam in his eye when he recognised Chard.

'Welcome, Mr Meredith,' he said, pumping Chard's hand and completely ignoring me. 'Better be gentle with that right hand, eh? You've probably got it insured at Lloyds. Great to meet you, big fan of the band. Seen the Ickies loads of times. I was at the legendary Wembley gig in '75, an amazing show. Got the bootleg of that one, I'm afraid, so I'd better make it up to you tonight for the lost income.'

He laughed loudly and I could feel Chard tensing next to me. He hated this kind of thing, it defined what he considered 'uncool'. He found simple autograph hunters much less irritating than self-styled Ickies experts and always obliged them with charm. It was the Ickie-ologists, who treated a social encounter like an interview for *Q* magazine, that made him act up. He was happy to talk about the band in the right context, but hated it when people assumed it was the only thing which defined him.

Lauren clearly understood what was going on and signalled a passing waitress to bring us drinks, which immediately diffused the tension.

Then, as Paul was distracted by having his champagne glass filled – 'To the top please, young lady. I paid for it, I wanna bloody drink it . . .' – she linked her arm very naturally through Chard's and took him off on a spurious mission to 'show him round the garden'.

I was left with Paul, wondering whether to remind him he hadn't actually paid for the champagne, but then deciding against it.

'So Ritchie Meredith's a friend of yours, is he?' he said, a distinctively competitive edge in his voice.

He had eyes like a shark's behind his heavy black framed glasses.

He was an impressive-looking man in a thuggy way, with a firm jaw and broad shoulders beneath what I was fairly sure was a bespoke Brioni suit. But with his close-cropped black hair, the specs gave him a menacing look, like Buddy Holly's sociopathic brother.

'Yes,' I said, maintaining a determinedly light tone. 'We've been friends for thirty years. We live very close to each other; he came into my shop one day and we've been mates ever since. He's a great guy.'

'He's a great guitarist,' said Paul, in a completely unnecessary contradictory tone.

He seemed to approach conversation as a combat sport, so I nodded, thinking it was easiest just to humour him.

'You're right there,' I said. 'One of the greats.'

'So,' he said, looking me over like I was a racing greyhound. 'You've got that vintage shop, right? The one in Prim-pose Hill. Is that some of your gear then?'

He gestured at my dress with his glass.

'Yes,' I said, having to make an even bigger effort to keep an edge out of my own voice. 'Givenchy, 1962. Audrey Hepburn had one the same, there's an iconic photo of her wearing it. The shoes are Roger Vivier. The belt's contemporary. Balenciaga.'

'Yeah?' he said, dismissively. 'I don't see the appeal of old ladies' cast-offs myself. I've never understood why anyone would want to wear second-hand shit, but a lot of the young chicks seem to like that clobber.'

I was now speechless at his rudeness and felt like telling him I didn't see the appeal of racks of cheap crap made by children in Bangladesh from intensively farmed cotton which had caused environmental devastation to large parts of Central Asia. But I restrained myself. He didn't.

'Do you make a living from it then?' he said, sniffing loudly and wiping his nose on the back of his hand.

'Yes, thanks,' I said, wondering how someone as nice as Lauren could be married to such an ignorant pig. He did have a reputation in the fashion business as a bit of a hard nut – and you didn't get to be as successful as he was in the ultra-competitive high street sector on charm alone – but I couldn't believe he was quite so awful.

I was relieved when his face suddenly lit up, and I followed his gaze over to where an attractive young woman was walking down the curving marble staircase.

'Here's my girl,' boomed Paul. 'Look at that, that's my Claudia. Isn't she beautiful?'

She was lovely – and fortunate that she seemed to have inherited mostly her mother's genes. She had a very pretty fine-boned face, set off by thick black wavy hair, which was clearly from her father, as Lauren's was blonde and poker-straight. She was wearing a dress with a preposterously short skirt revealing legs nearly as long as Theo's. But not quite, I noticed with satisfaction.

'Come over here, darling, and give your old dad a kiss,' boomed Paul, holding open his arms.

She came over and dutifully submitted to his bear hug, then she put her hand out to me. She clearly had better manners than Daddy dearest.

'Hi,' she said. 'I'm Claudia Beaney.'

I shook her hand.

'Hello Claudia, lovely to meet you. I've heard a lot about you from your mum – all good, of course. I'm Loulou Landers.'

'I know,' said Claudia, with an appealing grin. 'I've seen you in *Vogue*. I love how you dress. Mum's promised to bring me to your shop.'

'Great,' I said, as charmed by her as I was by her mother. 'We've got plenty of stuff that would look wonderful on you.'

Paul was listening keenly.

'You like that vintage tat then, do you, Clauds?' he said.

'Yeah, Dad,' she said, as if he were retarded. 'It's so cool. I love that dress, Loulou, it's Givenchy, isn't it?' She reached down to touch the feathers. 'And are those original Roger Viviers?'

I smiled and nodded.

'You've got a good eye,' I said. 'But the belt is Balenciaga – like your dress . . .'

She grinned and put up her hand to give me a high five. I smacked my palm against hers.

'Is your daughter coming tonight?' she asked. 'Mum said you had one a bit older than me.'

'Yes, Theo's coming,' I said. 'She's really looking forward to it. She's a devoted customer of your father's and wouldn't miss meeting him for anything. She thinks you do the best handbags on Oxford Street, Paul, and she considers herself an expert on that.'

I smiled at him, hoping it didn't look as fake as it felt. As I wanted to be friends with Lauren, I'd already decided the only way to deal with a bully like him was shameless flattery – working from the position that his kind of behaviour was usually a symptom of deep-seated insecurity. On the other hand, he could just be a total bastard, but at this stage I was willing to compromise.

Either way, he grinned with self-satisfied pleasure.

'Yeah, they are fucking good and we love our customers, don't we Clauds? They keep us in the style to which we have become so happily accustomed.'

He laughed coarsely, and she nodded and smiled sheepishly. She'd be a lovely friend for Theo, I thought – and if the brothers were as nice as she was, that could be a very promising connection. If they were like Daddy, less so.

I looked round to see if I could see any of the other committee mums and their daughters, just as Lauren and Chard walked back in. Unfortunately, before I could come to my friend's rescue, Paul had spotted him too.

'Come with me, Clauds,' he said, in a low tone, grabbing her arm and clearly forgetting I existed again. 'Going to introduce you to a very special guest – Ritchie Meredith of Icarus High. Greatest rock guitarist of all time.'

I didn't intervene as I knew the irritation of Paul would be greatly offset for Chard by meeting his beautiful daughter and I was happy to be on my own for a moment to collect my thoughts before the party really kicked off.

I looked round the massive hall with its polished marble floor and huge chandelier, the curved staircase sweeping elegantly down. Lauren hadn't been exaggerating when she'd said they had a big house. For central London, it was palatial, but decorated with restraint I was sure was her taste. I could imagine Paul would have preferred more of a Roberto Cavalli approach. Or perhaps he could have wallpapered it with £50 notes.

I watched him disappear into a room in the corner, with Claudia and Chard – I could only hope it wasn't to view his collection of Ickies' memorabilia – and then Lauren appeared at my side.

'Ritchie's a darling, isn't he?' she said. 'I'm so glad you brought him. I just hope Paul won't bore him to death, but I'll keep an eye on that, don't worry. All the committee girls are here now, so we're going to have a quick pow wow upstairs before everyone else starts arriving, OK?'

I followed her up to a room that seemed to be a combination of a walk-in closet, study, boudoir, library and sitting room, decorated in calming shades of grey. Whatever it was I wanted one. Rachel, Fiona and Natalie were already there.

'Here she is,' said Fiona, jumping up to greet me and nearly losing the contents of her drink down the front of her dress in the process. 'The star of the hour – welcome to the first matchmaking party! Oooh, I'm so excited!'

'Hi everyone,' I said. 'You all look fabulous. I've just met Lauren's lovely Claudia – are all your girls here? I didn't see them downstairs.'

A row of subdued faces looked back at me.

'Freya couldn't decide what to wear,' said Natalie. 'She rang me from a changing room in Selfridges as I was leaving home. She won't be here until well after the shops all shut and as it's Thursday, that will be pretty late.'

'Cassandra was still in the bath when I left,' said Rachel. 'She's coming on later with her brother – who was still in bed the last time I saw him,'

'Phoebe is having a pedicure,' said Fiona, her high spirits visibly dampened. 'She's got new shoes for tonight and said she couldn't possibly wear them until she'd had a total foot makeover. She's coming straight here from that. Is Theo here?'

I couldn't help laughing.

'Oh, I'm sorry to laugh,' I said. 'But I was so miserable when I was getting changed tonight, because Theo has gone to her friend's place to get ready rather than do it with me, and I was imagining all of you having lovely girly times with your daughters and arriving together . . . But it looks like we're all in the same boat with a bunch of recalcitrant brats. Except you, Lauren – Claudia is a delight.'

'You're kidding,' she said over her shoulder from the dressing table, where she was refreshing her lipstick. 'This afternoon she told me categorically she wasn't going to come tonight. It took that ridiculous dress to persuade her. I'm sure she was charming to you and her darling daddy, but she's vile to me.'

I looked at her in amazement.

'Well,' I said. 'It just goes to show. We really need this party, don't we?'

They all raised their glasses in agreement.

Theo

Writing this on iPhone as email to self in bathroom at Tattie's house. Can paste it over to main diary when I get home. Oh brave new world that has such gadgets in it. Imagine being Lala's age. When she was 21 she probably had to write with a quill and send it by carrier pigeon. Or the stage coach.

Mind you ODD and darling crumbling Nancy would have been scratching hieroglyphics into terracotta tablets. Although now I am getting to know Nance I think she would have been too busy trying to cop off with the pharaoh. She's absolutely filthy.

Cop off is one of her expressions. They got up to all sorts in the blackout and I'm hearing it direct from very nearly beyond the grave. They should wheel old birds like her into schools to make history interesting for teenagers. Copping off through the ages.

By the time I have a daughter my age she will just have to think her diary and it will be encrypted in the cyber chip which was implanted in her brain while she was growing in the lab. Actually she will be not a daughter but a clone as no man then necessary in process.

Seriously considering chucking party. Have come in here to decide what to do. Three minutes then it's the third song on shuffle. I want the goodie bag I want to meet Paul Beaney and I want to see their house. Mostly I want the goodie bag – or several – but coming here has reminded me of every reason why I don't go to parties.

First up the door is opened by Marc the Minghead with his stupid hair sticking up so far he could practically paint the ceiling with it. But not in a cool Mohican way more of a 'Oh I just got back from surfing in Cornwall and my hair is SUCH a mess . . . Oh I really LOVE Rick Stein' kind of way.

And he's wearing a dinner jacket. So that means he's coming too. Very very bad.

No black tie by the way or a cool lariat just a white dress shirt open at the neck. So fucking obvious. An idea I'm sure he got from his patron saint Hugh Grant or the Jack Wills catalogue. And he's wearing Converse on his feet with it. Crazy!

And I forgot to mention. He's working in a branch of Jack Wills in his 'yooni vac'. What's that? I said, a new model of Dyson? He'll probably get paid in polo shirts.

So that was a bad start. Then I go into Tattie's room and there are clothes everywhere. It looks like a Tracy Emin installation. All the Clothes I Have Ever Owned. And she is crying because she can't find anything to wear.

Don't worry I said. Auntie Theo is here. I'll find you an outfit.

So I put her in a simple black jersey dress which I ruched up over some silver sequin leggings I had brought with me specially and she starts crying more saying she looks fat.

Well you have got a big arse Tattie. I said. But some men like that.

Then she told me to fuck off and started throwing shoes at my head. So I ducked out and told her I was going to get changed and that I would come back after she had a) stopped her Benjamin Button age regression and b) was ready to be helped.

I got changed in a spare room and when I came out I bumped right into Minging Marc and he was so weird with me. He gave me this psycho look.

What? I asked him. Never seen a pair of pants before?

Are they really pants? he said. Like actual knickers?

And I said: Yes. Do you like them?

Minging: Aren't you going to put anything over the top?

Me: No. I'm dressed. When are you changing?

Then I went back to Tattie and she took one look at me and started crying again.

Me: I don't look that bad do I?

Tattie: Waaaaaaaaaaa

Me: How about if I pull them up a bit higher?

Tattie: Waaaaa you look waaaaaaaa so waaaaaaaaaaa amazing and I'm so waaaaaaaaaaaaaaa faaaaat.

Me: You are not fat. You have a deliciously curvy man-crazing rump like JLo. I have a flat butt like an old lady which is why I'm wearing old lady pants. Come here my little enchilada let me dress you.

So she finally submitted and I convinced her that an arse you could balance your drink on is considered a great asset in many cultures and got her to wear the leggings and the dress after all.

I really did think she looked great by the time I'd evened her out with an armful of bangles and a huge necklace and made her put her hair up in this really enormous 80s look. Tats has the best hair. So much of it I used nearly a whole can of hairspray on it. Then I took the necklace off again which slightly destroyed the hair but it all kind of works.

Anyway she is now doing her make-up and I'm still not sure whether I can stand being trapped in a taxi with Minghead and then spend at least an hour with his creepy ilk who will be at this event before they start handing out the goodie bags.

So about to hit Play then forward two. Here goes.

Brass in Pocket. Shit.

I think that means I've got to go. Gonna make you make you make you notice me and they kind of all are in these pants so I better go for it. Gonna use my arms and most definitely my legs ha ha ha.

13
Loulou

An hour later the joint was jumping. Lauren and Paul's house was so big I had been a bit worried that even ninety or so people would rattle around in it like peas in a barrel, diffusing the party atmosphere, but Lauren deliberately kept the doors to the drawing room and dining room closed to keep us all milling around together in smaller spaces. It worked brilliantly with most of the parents in the hall and most of the kids in the garden, where they could smoke.

I was glad I was in the hall or I would have missed Theo making her entrance. That was the only word for it. It was Eliza Doolittle at the Embassy Ball, Theo-style. Conversation didn't quite come to a stop, but it definitely paused for a beat as she strutted through the door and stopped to lift a glass of champagne from the waiter's tray. She scoped the room, caught my eye and raised the drink to me.

I raised mine back, smiling and shaking my head affectionately. She looked nothing short of amazing, in a faux-fur leopardskin coat I had never seen before, worn open, with the collar turned up, shrugged over a plain white shirt, done up to the neck and tucked into what looked like a pair of old lady's big pants, in black.

She had a fisherman's cap tipped low over one eye, her long hair falling down over one shoulder, but it was what was at the end of her endless smooth bare legs that made me nearly choke on my drink. She was wearing a pair of sky-high Christian Louboutin black suede platform pumps – which belonged to me.

I should have been furious. They were practically new, she hadn't asked if she could borrow them, and considering how rude she was about my taste in footwear, it really was astonishing cheek. I should have been furious, but I was too happy to be upset. She looked sensational. And clearly I wasn't the only one who thought so.

'Holy shit,' said the man I was talking to, the husband of one of the mothers – I wasn't even sure which one. 'Who's that babe?'

'That's my daughter,' I said loudly and everyone who heard turned to look at me. What the hell, I thought. Theo gave me precious few occasions to be proud, so I might as well enjoy it.

'Hi Mum,' she said, arriving at my side and planting a big kiss on my cheek. In the towering shoes, she had to bend down quite a long way and I felt even more truncated in my boringly discreet pumps.

'Hello darling,' I said. 'You look wonderful.'

'You like?' she said.

'I like very much,' I said, nodding. 'But what is all this? That coat's vintage, but it's not one of mine – I wish it was. I could sell that coat five times every day. Where on earth did you get it?'

'Oh,' said Theo, with infuriating nonchalance. 'I borrowed it from a friend. She lent me the pants too. Do you like them?'

'I love them,' I said. 'The whole look totally works. Of course, I particularly love the shoes . . . You cheeky little bugger.'

I play-punched her gently on the shoulder.

'You don't mind, do you, Mum?' she said, smiling at me so sweetly, I couldn't possibly be cross. 'I just totally needed these for my look.'

'It's fine,' I said laughing. 'I'm delighted you've finally given your seal of approval to one pair of my shoes. I've always thought it was such a waste that you hate them so much when we are the same size. Those look better on you than they do on me actually – and I like the shirt too. It's nice and narrow in the cut. Where's that from?'

'John Lewis school uniform department . . .'

We both burst out laughing. I don't know why it was so funny, it was probably just a release of tension, but I was so happy that she was sharing a joke with me for once – rather than making me the butt of one.

'Where's Tattie?' I asked. 'And did Marc come too?'

She rolled her eyes and nodded at the same time, an advanced combo that would have stretched a less expert optical spinner.

'He's paying the taxi and she wanted to come in with him . . .'

'And not with you, presumably?'

'They both think I should put something on over my big knickers,' said Theo. 'I told them to get stuffed, but I think they're still coming to the party anyway.'

She looked round the room.

'Nice gaff,' she said. 'I wonder which bit of marble I've paid for? Where's Paul Beaney? I want to have a look at him. I'm going to tell him his bags are great, but his T-shirts are crap. The fabrics are too light and the cuts are all wrong.'

'He's the speccie four-eyes over there by the fireplace,' I said. 'The one Chard is backing away from . . .'

'Ritchie!' said Theo, in warmer tones than I would have expected. 'I didn't know he was coming. I'll go and talk to him and then I can meet Mr West Wind from a position of strength, under the wing of my world-famous slightly paedo pretendy godfather.'

She kissed me on the cheek again and I watched her sashay across the room with every pair of eyes – male and female – following her. Almost the last person to spot her was Chard who, I noticed, had put his mirrored aviator shades on, presumably so he could nap while Paul droned on about guitar solos he had absolutely no memory of playing.

It almost seemed like slow motion as Paul's eyes practically popped out at Theo's approach and Chard flicked his shades on top of his head in what I took to be a well-honed hot chick reflex. I was pleased to see that when he realised it was Theo, he raised his eyebrows and the shades fell back down on to his nose again.

He put his arm around her in a sweetly protective avuncular manner and introduced her to Paul, who looked as though he was having to make an effort to stop his tongue hanging out. The sooner I got Theo introduced to some young men the better, I thought.

Just at that moment, I felt a touch on my arm and turned round to see Tattie and Marc standing there.

'Hello Mrs Landers,' said Marc. 'Loulou. We just wanted to say thank you so much for the party invitation. It was really kind of you to get us included . . .'

For a moment I just stared back at him. It was partly because it seemed as though my thoughts about needing young men for Theo had been instantly answered in a spooky way. You want young man? Here be young man. But it wasn't only that. He looked so ridiculously handsome in what I immediately clocked as a vintage tuxedo, I was momentarily lost for words.

He had the most marvellously thick hair, which stood up from his scalp in a mad tangle. His jawline was well defined and perfectly symmetrical, like an old school Hollywood film star's, his cheekbones were high and then there were those striking eyes. They were an unusual golden brown with a darker circle around the edge of the irises that made them appear particularly intense.

'Marc, Tattie,' I said, recovering myself. 'How lovely to see you. You're so welcome for the invites. You know how hard it is to get Theo to go out and I thought if you two were here . . . plus I thought you would enjoy it and I wanted to thank you for putting up with her.'

I kissed them both on each cheek.

'You look lovely, Tattie,' I said, taking in her sequinned leggings and the chunky bangles on both arms. She had fabulous thick hair, like her brother, but more auburn. It was all piled up on her head and looked great.

'Theo dressed me,' said Tattie.

'Maybe that's why she forgot to put her own trousers on,' I said, laughing indulgently.

'She can get away with it though, can't she?' said Tattie, with just a trace of envy in her tone.

'With those legs, I don't think she should ever wear trousers,' said Marc.

I was thrilled. If he thought she was attractive, that was fifty per cent of the outcome I was hoping for. Now I just needed her to fancy him – or someone like him – back.

'Where is she?' said Tattie, looking round the room.

I looked over to the fireplace, but she wasn't there any more and neither was Paul. Chard was chatting to Lauren.

'I think she must be out in the garden,' I said. 'That's where most of the young ones are. You go out through that door off to the left over there.'

'We'll go and explore,' said Marc. 'See you later.'

I watched them walk off and noticed that he was wearing yellow Converse with his tux. It was a good look.

As the evening went on, the party just got better and better. At eight-thirty, Lauren threw open the doors to the dining room, revealing a table gloriously laden with food, which I knew had nothing to do with the official party budget. It was a brilliant stroke of social engineering, the perfect way to bring all the kids in from the garden and get everyone mixing.

Everyone except Theo, as far as I could tell. She didn't come and eat until the desserts were brought out and then she snuck off into a corner with Chard, four plates lined up on the side table. Trifle, profiteroles, chocolate mousse and apricot tart with a big dollop of whipped cream on the top. Theo loved her puds.

I was glad she seemed to be feeling better disposed towards Chard these days, but at the same time, the point of this party was not for her to spend quality time with her godfather. She could do that at home. There was a great gaggle of attractive young people on the other side of the dining room and I noticed several of the guys kept glancing over at Theo, clearly longing to talk to her, but intimidated by the rock god at her side. I had to intervene.

'Hi, you two,' I said casually.

'Hey, Looby Lou,' said Ritchie, smiling broadly and slipping his shades up on his head. 'Having a good time?'

'Great actually. You?'

'Cool,' he said, nodding.

'How about you Theo?' I asked, nudging her outstretched leg with my knee.

'Mmmm,' she said, through a mouthful of profiterole. 'I'm still here, aren't I? When do you think they'll put the goodie bags out?'

'When people start to leave,' I said. 'Much *much* later.'

She sighed and picked up a bowl of chocolate mousse.

'I'll just keep eating until then,' she said.

'Do you want some more of anything?' asked Chard.

But before she could reply, I jumped in.

'Actually Chardie,' I said. 'There's someone I really want you to meet. Can I steal you for a moment?'

He ambled to his feet and after patting Theo affectionately on the shoulder followed me out of the room. My ruse had worked perfectly, except now I had no-one to introduce him to, because just about everyone was still in the dining room. Then inspiration struck. The DJ was setting up in the corner of the hall and by luck, I knew his name, because he'd come to Lauren's house to check out the venue the night we'd had a committee meeting there.

'Luke,' I said, walking determinedly towards him. 'Great to see you. Really looking forward to your, er, set. I'd just like to introduce you to my friend Ritchie Meredith. I thought perhaps you two could mix up some interesting sounds together.'

Then I practically ran away. I'd dropped them both in it horribly, but I had to get Theo away from Chard, or the whole point of this elaborately planned evening would be lost. I just hoped Luke knew who Chard was. I tended to presume everyone did, but there was a chance that the Ickies could have passed by a twenty-something DJ who was heavily into dance music.

But I didn't hang around to find out, hurrying back to the dining room and peeping round the door. I wanted to see if my plan had worked without Theo knowing and was delighted that I could hardly see her for the crowd of young men which had gathered around on Chard's exit. Result.

The only problem was what to do with myself now I had sorted her out. I could see Keith deep in conversation with Lauren in another corner of the dining room and thought about joining them, but was worried that if Theo saw me she would have an excuse to escape the young men who were talking to her. So I darted across the room and out into the garden through the French windows.

Once out there, I discovered a light rain was falling and was about to head back inside when I noticed there was a bench off to one side, sheltered under a rose-covered arbour. The vegetation was thick enough to keep the drops off and I sat down wondering how long I would have to remain in isolation before I could safely go inside again. Then reminded myself that the whole point of this party was for Theo to meet people, not for me to have a good time.

It was getting dark and the light coming through the French windows from the dining room made the outdoors seem commensurately darker, so I didn't notice anyone else was in the garden until they were practically on top of me. I squealed with surprise.

'Oh, sorry,' said a male voice. 'I didn't realise anyone else was out here.'

It wasn't until he sat down next to me on the bench that I realised it was Marc.

'Oh, it's you,' I said with relief. 'You gave me quite a shock. Sorry about the squeak.'

'I have that effect on women,' he laughed. 'They squeal with horror when they see me. Mind if I join you?'

'Not at all,' I said, shifting over on the bench. 'I'd be glad of the company.'

We sat there for a moment, the sound of rain getting heavier on the leaves above us.

'Mmm,' said Marc, breathing deeply. 'Smell those roses. It's lovely out here, isn't it?'

'Glorious,' I said. 'And amazing to think we're in walking distance of Oxford Street.'

We sat in silence for a bit longer before Marc spoke again.

'So did you need to escape the throng for a while, like me?' he said.

I hesitated before replying. It would have been easier just to agree, but something about Marc's easy manner made me want to be honest with him.

'I needed to leave Theo alone in there,' I said. 'She was stuck in a corner with her godfather, so I got her away from him and then I had to make myself scarce too, because I want to force her to spend this evening with people her own age. She spends way too much time home alone.'

I couldn't see much in the darkness, but I could make out that his face was turned towards me and something about his attentive silence made me keep talking. It wasn't nervousness, I wanted to tell him. He felt like an ally somehow.

'She does disappear out for quite long periods during the day and I don't have a clue where she is then, but I just feel instinctively that she's not with friends. There's no social buzz around Theo the way there should be at her age. I think your sister might be the only real pal she has these days and I want her to get out more, to be with people. Have fun. Live it up. She's verging on being clinically anti-social.'

He still didn't say anything and I carried on.

'Like that night you very kindly brought her home, Marc. She didn't thank you, or even say goodbye. I was mortified. I'm so sorry about that.'

'It's fine,' said Marc. 'I've known Theo a long time. She's always been a prickly customer and she loves giving me a hard time, but I still like her. She's a one-off. And she's a bloody good friend to Tatiana. Underneath all that private school confidence my sister is a very vulnerable girl and Theo has always been there for her.'

'Well, that's good,' I said, delighted. 'But tell me, honestly, do you think she's anti-social?'

'She does seem to be a bit reluctant to come out and play,' said Marc, choosing his words carefully. 'Tattie is always trying to drag her along with us, but she rarely comes. She came out for drinks a couple of weeks ago but she spent most of the evening holed up in the loo talking to one guy.'

'Really?' I said, my hopes rising. 'Who was the guy?'

'One of Tattie's friends from college. Stew.'

'Is he nice?' I asked.

'Yeah,' said Marc, chuckling. 'Very nice, very funny, very gay.'

'Oh,' I said. 'Had my hopes up for a romance there, not that it matters. I'd be thrilled for her to have a good gay friend. Best friend a single girl can have, and I should know.'

'Are you single then?' said Marc.

'Well, yes,' I said, more than a little taken aback at his bluntness. 'Since Theo's dad left I haven't had another "partner". I didn't want to go there again for lots of reasons. I mean, I have had men in my life, boyfriends or whatever you want to call them, just nothing formal.'

I didn't feel comfortable using the word 'lover' to him, but that's what they'd all been. Exquisite occasional liaisons, usually in a foreign city, with no strings attached. Some of the relationships had gone on for years, but nothing more committed than could be conducted over a restaurant table and in a hotel room.

'Well, you sound better than my mum,' said Marc. 'Her work is her first love. Always has been – that's why my dad left and I don't blame him. No-one wants to come second to the board of directors in their marriage.'

We sat there in silence for a bit. I was surprised by the very personal turn the conversation had taken but something about being in the dark of the garden like that made it feel all right.

'What about you?' I said. 'You told me that night you dropped Theo off that you don't have a girlfriend. Don't you want one?'

He was quiet for a moment before answering.

'I did have a girlfriend in my first year at uni who I was really keen on, but it all went horribly wrong and it's put me off. In second year she went off with my best friend, so I lost both of them and it made my social life stupidly complicated. It seems that everyone likes the happy couple better than the sad reject. It was very boring. I'm sure I'll meet someone eventually, but after that they'd really have to be worth it.'

'That sounds really tough,' I said with feeling. 'I had a similar experience when Rob left. People I'd thought were friends found me a drag as the wronged woman, rather than part of a so-called golden couple, and just dropped me. Sometimes I don't know what I would have done back then without my gay best friend Keith.'

'Maybe I should get one,' said Marc, laughing. 'A nice friendly lesbian to hang out with. Sounds like it's just what I need. Good company, no romantic complications and no strings attached.'

'You wouldn't regret it,' I said, smiling broadly at him in the dark.

The more we talked the more comfortable I felt with him. Maybe it was because I'd known him since he was a child, I thought. I hadn't seen him for years, but as Tattie and Theo had grown up together, he just seemed like someone I could trust. I decided to go out on even more of a limb.

'Can I ask you a favour, Marc?' I said.

'Of course,' he answered.

'Can you help me get Theo to go out more? To meet men? She's never had a boyfriend and I'm beginning to worry it's my fault, not setting an example for her, so I wondered if you had any friends you could introduce her to . . .'

He laughed.

'I can guarantee that any of my friends would be more than delighted to meet Theo – she's one of the most beautiful girls I know – I just don't think the pleasure would be mutual. She doesn't seem very comfortable with men. It doesn't bother me when she's vile to me, because I know her and find it funny, but I think she would terrify most blokes.'

'You don't think she's a lesbian, do you?' I asked. 'Perhaps she could be your gay best friend . . . I don't really think she is, but it would be an explanation. It wouldn't bother me in the slightest, but I would rather know.'

'I asked Tattie that once,' said Marc, laughing. 'And she promised me that's not the issue. She says Theo just doesn't think any of the guys she knows are interesting enough to bother with.'

'I wonder what she thinks is interesting?' I said. 'She's so complicated, that girl of mine . . .'

'I tell you what,' said Marc. 'Why don't I specifically try and find that out for you?'

'That would be so great,' I said, with sincere enthusiasm. 'And I meant what I said that time about discount at the shop. That's a nice vintage tux you're wearing and I really do have some great menswear, so why don't you come in and see if there's anything you like? My way of saying thank you.'

'You really don't have to do that,' he protested.

'But I want to, Marc,' I said. 'Besides, you'll be a good walking advert for the shop – and if your friends start coming in, Theo might meet them.'

'You've got all angles covered, haven't you, Loulou?' he said, laughing.

'I do my best,' I said. 'I'm my father's daughter in that way . . . He was a miner's son who made himself into a millionaire. Considering every possible angle of a deal was one of his golden rules.'

'Well, I'd like to hear more about him, but this rain's getting heavier; shall we go back in before we get drenched?'

'Good idea,' I said, standing up and then just as we were about to leave the shelter of the arbour, I put my hand on his arm. 'And thanks, Marc. It was good to talk to someone Theo's age about all that.'

'No problem, Loulou,' he said. 'Inspector Thorssen is on the case. Operation Theo.'

Theo

In loo on iPhone again. I like this new system. Not blogging but bogging. Welcome to my Bog where I am going to write about how much I hate parties. And people.

Had to come in here for a breather. Bloody Lala left me all on my own in the dining room dragging my Deathbreath security blanket away and all these creepy guys immediately came over. I felt like a dead antelope with the vultures circling.

One of them claimed I'd met him at Tattie's Big Chill drinks a couple of weeks ago and seemed to think that meant I would want to talk to him again. What's that about? I talked to you once now fuck off. I didn't actually say that but I thought it so hard I think he got the message.

I feel sick. Had way too much chocolate mousse but had to do something to pass the time until they put the bloody goodie bags out. I thought I'd be able to grab one and leg it after an hour of this torture but it's been well over two hours now and no sign of anyone leaving.

I couldn't help noticing a glint of turquoise plastic on the floor behind the coat rack where I totally didn't hand over my coat on the way in – it's an intrinsic part of my look even though I am now boiling hot – and I'm pretty sure it was part of a dear little flock of West Wind carrier bags. Just longing to come home with me.

Seriously considering quietly sidling in there and helping myself and then whoosh – gone before anyone sees.

Shit someone just knocked on the door and asked if everything was 'OK' in here. Sure. It's fine in here – it's just out there I get diarrhoea.

I'll have to go out and find another place to hide.

14
Loulou

When Marc and I got back inside, the party had completely changed tempo. The dining room was deserted and it seemed everyone was out in the hall, dancing.

They were really going wild – all ages mixed in together – and I looked over to see Luke and Chard both wearing headphones and leaning over the turntables in great concentration, their heads nodding to the beat in perfect synchronisation.

As I watched them, one track segued perfectly into the next with a bit of cool overlap in the middle and then everyone on the dance floor cheered when they realised what was playing next.

'Woo hoo!' went the crowd, leaping up and punching the air like crazy people. I looked over to see Chard and Luke double high-fiving each other. What had I started?

I stood transfixed on the edge of the mayhem, feeling a little stunned. I couldn't see Theo anywhere among the gyrating bodies and was wondering if I should go and look for her, when suddenly I felt a hand grasp mine and drag me into the heaving crowd. It was Marc.

'Come on, Loulou,' he shouted into my ear. 'We've got to dance!'

So we did. And I jumped up and down like a loony with everyone else, glad that for once I wasn't wearing my usual vertiginous shoes; I could have killed myself – but it would have been worth it.

Something about that crazy jumping made me wildly happy. It made me feel young and free and more alive than I had for years. It was pure uncomplicated fun and the feeling remained as that song blended into the next and then the next, and while they weren't all tracks I immediately recognised I had the rhythm in my bones and got right into it.

After a while a song came on that I did know and love: *Everything Changes But You* by Take That. Something about the beat and the strings took me straight back to the Northern Soul music of my first school discos in the 1970s, and it was one of my all-time favourite tracks to dance to.

For a moment I was amazed to hear it played by such a cool DJ, but then I remembered Chard. I looked over to the decks to see him grinning at me, holding up both thumbs. He knew it was one of my guilty pleasures and had put it on just for me. I blew him a kiss and then got back into my groove.

To my surprise Marc was still dancing next to me. I kept expecting him to melt away into the crowd and leave me to it and I really wouldn't have minded. I was quite happy to dance on my own and was uncomfortably aware that it can't have looked very cool for him to have been getting down with one of the mothers at the party, but he was still by my side and there was just enough catching each other's eyes and smiling for me to know that we were dancing together, but in an easy relaxed way.

Once the Take That song started playing I really expected him to disappear, thinking it must have been seriously naff in his estimation, but to my great surprise he really seemed to be into it. From the occasional smile in passing, somehow we were now dancing closer, eyes meeting, and then, without any signal, our turns spontaneously started to coordinate, until I was laughing out loud at the silliness of it.

I had just executed a double spin – one of my repertoire of trick moves – when I felt him take my hand and without letting go, he threw me out to the side, then pulled me back into him in a tight turn, rocking me in his arms for a couple of beats, before sending me spinning out and then in again.

My brain switched immediately into that blissful dancing automatic pilot when your body moves perfectly without you having to consciously think about it and is always in the right place at the right time. Never missing a beat, Marc turned me under his arm ballroom style and then, still holding hands, we both threw ourselves out to the side and met in the middle. We weren't dancing, we were flying.

From there we eased as smoothly into dancing to the next track – *Rock With You* – as Chard was spinning the discs. He certainly seemed to be enjoying himself. The end of Michael Jackson slid into *The Time of My Life*, which was pretty hilarious. I half expected Marc to lift me up over his head Patrick Swayze-style.

I looked over at Chard, who was grinning back at me. He gave me another thumbs up, then raised his eyebrows questioningly over his shades. I blew him another kiss and he surpassed himself with his next choice.

'More than a woman . . .' trilled the Brothers Gibb. Spin, turn, swoop, clasp, spin, twirl went Marc and I. We never got tangled up or out of step, it was like a higher form of communication and so exhilarating I knew I was grinning at him like an idiot. He was smiling back at me, those golden-brown eyes locked on to mine. Both of us silently sharing the same knowledge: this kind of perfect dancing synchronicity doesn't come along very often.

And maybe because it was such an extraordinary surprise, it didn't seem strange to find that by the end of that song I was in his arms more than out of them and was gazing up at him as the Bee Gees sang, 'Say you'll always be my baby, we can make it shine . . .'

It was the word 'baby' that did it. He was a baby. Was he even twenty-five? He was half my age and I was dancing with him like some moon-eyed teenager. I was more than a woman, I was nearly an old lady and it was cringingly inappropriate for me to be dancing with him like this in public.

My arms dropped to my side and in an instant all the rhythm left my feet. And at that exact moment I looked up to see Theo standing on the stairs staring at us with an expression of absolute horror on her face. She'd seen us. She'd seen me in Marc's arms, gazing at him.

Marc's head turned to follow mine, but Theo was already on her way down the stairs and while he couldn't have missed that leopard-print coat, he hadn't seen the appalled look which had so mortified me.

I glanced around the dance floor to see who else had seen us and to my great relief, no-one seemed to have noticed. Everyone was so into their own dancing, they were oblivious to anyone else. Chard seemed to be fully engrossed flicking through one of Luke's record cases, so while he had certainly seen me dancing with Marc – and had positively encouraged it with his music choices – I didn't think he had seen that final clinch, when I'd been gazing into Marc's eyes.

The only person who caught my panicked glance was Paul Beaney who was looking straight at me with a knowing smile playing around his mouth. He raised one eyebrow just perceptibly behind his heavy spectacles and slightly inclined his head. That tiny gesture said it all: I saw you, you naughty girl. And now I've got one over on you.

I already disliked him for his rudeness and arrogance, and in that moment I found him almost sinister, but I couldn't worry about him then. I had to activate damage limitation with Theo.

'Thanks for dancing with me, Marc,' I said breathlessly, partly from exertion, mainly pure panic. 'It was great, but I think I need a break.'

And I fled the dance floor towards the direction Theo had been heading, which I realised was the front door. There was no sign of her so I opened it and ran out just in time to see a flash of leopard-skin disappear around the corner.

'Theo!' I called out, but I knew it was no good. She wouldn't have stopped even if she'd heard me and what was I going to do now, start screeching in the street like someone off *Eastenders*?

For a moment I just stood there and felt all the joyous fizz of the evening seeping out of my body. It had been such a great night until then, a terrific success on every front, and now it had gone horribly wrong, just because of a moment's lack of propriety on my part.

But was it really so bad, what I'd done? I'd enjoyed dancing with an attractive young man who seemed to enjoy dancing with me. I hadn't tongue-kissed him, or even wanted to, I'd just loved dancing with him. And it had happened completely spontaneously. I hadn't pursued him – or him me.

No one would have looked twice if Chard had been flinging Tatiana or Claudia around the dance floor – and I knew his intentions would have been a lot less innocent than mine. But because I was an older woman and Marc was a younger man, it was somehow wrong.

What really disturbed me was that while I could just about understand it seeming unacceptable to Theo, who was ridiculously touchy about most things and seemed to have some kind of additional weird problem with Marc, creepy Paul had also picked up on my discomfort. And that was the worst thing of all: seeing how it looked through their eyes, it also felt wrong to me.

I wondered what to do. Should I go straight home and try to sort it out with Theo? It seemed as if I should, but the memory of the last falling-out we'd had – also tangentially involving Marc, I realised with a sick feeling – was still too vivid. I really couldn't face having another ding dong with her so soon. Better to let her go home to sleep, I thought, and we'd talk about it calmly in the fresh light of morning. Everything always seemed more dramatic and disastrous in the dark of the night.

So I didn't want to go home, but I didn't really feel like going back into the party either. I didn't want to see Paul, I didn't want to see Marc and I didn't want to see anyone else who might have seen us nearly smooching.

But while I hated the idea of going back in, I knew I had to. If I left early the other mums on the committee would wonder why and I was sure plonker Paul would be all too happy to fill them in.

Taking a couple of deep breaths of the summer night air, which was pleasantly fresh after the downpour, I lifted my chin and turned round, determined to walk back into the party looking perfectly composed. But before I could get to the door it was flung open and Keith was standing there.

'There you are!' he said. 'I've been looking everywhere for you and Paul told me you were out here. Quick! They're playing our song.'

I walked in to the unmistakeable strains of Lily Allen singing *Fag Hag* and, as Keith grabbed my hand and pulled me on to the dance floor, things suddenly didn't seem quite so bad.

I ended up enjoying the rest of the party a lot more than I should have, considering it had been an utter disaster as far as Theo was concerned, and she'd been the point of organising it in the first place. But I just couldn't help having a good time dancing with Keith and Lauren and a constantly shifting random group of happy people, getting down with wild abandon to Chard and Luke's crazy mixes.

Chard even hit the dance floor himself at one point. He was a pretty good mover, as you'd expect for a man with music in his blood, and he twirled me round in some nifty rock-and-roll turns. It wasn't the instant Fred and Ginger communion I'd had with Marc, but like everything with Chard, it was easy and great fun. And being seen contact dancing with someone else – someone more appropriate – made me feel a bit better about what had happened earlier. It evened it out a bit in my head.

I didn't dance with Marc again, of course – or even anywhere near him, I made sure of that – but he waved at me across the floor, in a casual way that made me a little more at ease about the situation. He clearly felt exactly the same way about it as I did: that we'd found by chance that we had that rare perfect dance partner compatibility and we'd had a good time enjoying it. Theo's reaction had been completely over the top and I would tell her so when I saw her the next morning.

Creepy Paul clearly thought it had more mileage in it, though. At nearly two in the morning, when everyone but the hardcore organisers had left, we were sitting at the kitchen table having a post-party post-mortem, with coffee and smoked salmon bagels, thoughtfully laid on by the marvellous Lauren.

'You were having a good time dancing, Loulou,' he said, slouched down in his chair like a big slob and looking at me through arrogant half-closed eyes.

'Oh yes, I love to dance,' I said, smiling radiantly and deciding I had to put an end to his malevolent little campaign right there.

'Hey, Keith,' I continued, turning my attention to him. 'Did you see me dancing with Marc Thorssen? Tatiana's brother? He's only twenty-four or something and the most heavenly dancer since John Travolta. I tell you, you've got competition as my number one favourite dancing partner.'

'I stand defeated,' said Keith. 'Beauty before age.'

'What about me?' said Chard.

'Well, obviously you and Keith will always be my special favourites,' I said, keeping up my playful tone. 'But Marc really is a champion twirler.'

'I kept putting tracks on to keep you two going actually,' said Chard. 'I just loved watching you.'

'You looked ready to do a bit more than twirl with him,' said Paul, abandoning subtlety in the face of defeat.

I laughed, as though I thought it was the wittiest remark I'd ever heard.

'Well, he is gorgeous, Paul, you've got to admit. Those amazing eyes . . . I'm only human and why should the young girls have all the fun? Maybe I'll go cougar – what do you think, girls? Keith? Chard? You both like them young, don't you? I see where you're coming from now. Actually, I think twenty-four is too old. I'll see if he has a younger brother.'

They all laughed uproariously and I knew my ruse had worked perfectly. I looked at Paul with wide eyes while taking a big bite out of my bagel. It was 'fuck you' with everything but the finger and he knew it. He looked back at me without blinking, behind his heavy framed glasses.

You've won this one, bitch, his look seemed to say. But it's not over yet.

Theo

Eeeeeeeeeeeeuuuuuuuuuuurrrrrrrrrrrggggggggggggggggghhhhh. Spew sick and vomit. Bleeeeuuuuccccggggh. Gag. Splutter.

No other way to express how I feel. I have just seen something so repulsive and wrong I really don't have words to describe it. I can't even bear to write down what I witnessed as it would be like living the moment again. Eugh. Sound of small amount of sick coming up and being swallowed.

I am writing this on my phone on a bus. Wish people would stop staring at me. Yes I am wearing BIG PANTS. Next question.

This isn't really a public transport outfit but no choice as no money and can't even walk in these STUPID shoes that STUPIDLY belong to a STUPID person. Got on through back door to avoid paying. May have to make like Blanche Dubois and rely on the kindness of strangers if driver notices.

Now there was a man. Marlon in *Streetcar* with his filthy T-shirt stretched across his sweaty chest. Not a pair of skinny jeans or cutesy Converse sneaker in sight. That's the kind of T-shirts stupid West Wind need to do. Jersey with a lot of jerzing in it so it really clings where it curves. Thicker would work better than flimsy. I know these things. I just do.

Best thing that happened tonight was explaining to Paul Beaney why his T-shirts are crap. He appeared to listen. I've got a lot more to tell him about his shop if he wants to hear it. He asked for my number so maybe he does.

Considering my next move. Can't go home. No way. Possibly ever. Can't go to Tattie's house like I was going to for obvious reasons. Don'tthinkaboutit. Don'tthinkaboutit. Egidugdhfkjdh nearly thought about it. Shit! I did. Gag. Will just have to find somewhere else to lay my weary little head.

Oh yeah and I didn't even get my stupid bloody goodie bag. BOL-LOCKS. Bet it was crap anyway. Everything is crap.

15
Loulou

The next morning I did not feel so great. Not for the first time I was more than relieved it was a Friday and darling Shelley would open up for me. I was so confident I could rely on her, I hadn't set the alarm, and it was after ten when I eventually woke up.

It would have been very easy to go back to sleep after necking several glasses of water and a couple of headache pills, but I knew I had to get up to talk to Theo. The sooner the better. I urgently wanted to make her see that there was absolutely nothing wrong about me dancing with Marc – and to make her acknowledge that her reaction to it had been quite unwarranted.

I also wanted to find out whether she'd got anything at all out of the party before that incident. As a sweetener, I'd brought her one of the goodie bags she'd been so excited about, as they hadn't started giving them out before she'd fled and I knew she would be furious at missing out. Lauren had slipped a couple of extra things into it, specially for Theo, so I was sure it would help mollify any ongoing sulks.

I usually got completely dressed, with hair and make-up all done, before I left my room, even to go down and make a cup of tea. It was part of my ritual of staying on top of things, but that morning I decided to go straight down to see Theo. I thought the informality of me sitting on her bed in my nightie might help the conversation to go more easily.

But when I opened the door to her room there was absolutely no sign of her. The bed didn't look slept in and I couldn't see the leopardskin coat – or my black suede Louboutins – anywhere. She clearly hadn't come home. In other circs, I would have been thrilled because it might have meant she'd met someone she liked at the party and gone home with him, but I knew she'd fled into the night alone. I'd seen her go. And in the circumstances it was unlikely she'd have gone back to Tatiana's. So where the hell was she? I really couldn't imagine.

I sat down on the edge of her bed and put my head in my hands. The painkillers hadn't kicked in yet and it was really throbbing, but it was more than that. I felt desolate. Just when things had seemed to be getting better between me and Theo – with us doing the computer project together, and then her agreeing to come to the party relatively good-naturedly – we'd hit another problem. Were we ever going to get our relationship back on to an even keel?

I lay back on the bed and turned to bury my head in Theo's pillow, trying to latch on to a trace of her, remembering how I used to smell her dear vulnerable neck when she was little. How I longed for even a taste of the closeness we used to have. It was making me feel so lonely. Having her physically there, but emotionally absent was worse than when she had briefly left home, because it was a constant reminder of how things used to be. No matter how many cosy chats I had with Chard, and jolly drinks and dinners with Keith, nothing made up for the yawning hole where Theo had been.

Sighing deeply and telling myself to snap out of it, I opened one eye and just as I was about to sit up, I caught sight of an old photo of us together hanging in a frame on the wall over her bedside table.

It had been taken on a trip to Disneyland when she was nine and we were standing with our arms round each other, with the Haunted House in the background. It had been her favourite ride and she'd made me go on it five times in a row. We were grinning at the camera – which my sister Jane had been holding – doing rabbit's ears with our fingers behind each other's heads.

I knew she hadn't put the picture up recently – I remembered knocking that nail into the wall myself all those years before – she'd just never taken it down again. But seeing how happy and close we looked pushed me over the edge I had been clinging on to and I just couldn't keep the tears back any longer. They came out in a torrent, just as they had on the night of our big argument.

I don't know how long I sobbed for, but as I finally came back to normal consciousness, and was able to take some shaky deep breaths to calm myself, I began to wonder how much more of this I could take. It was really starting to affect me. Although I could hardly bear to acknowledge it, between overeagerly working on the website with Theo and secretly organising the matchmaking party, I hadn't been on top of the business to my normal standards for weeks.

Just that Tuesday I'd missed a really important auction. I'd looked at it online, made a note of the things that interested me – and then completely forgotten to go along. Even in the dark time when Rob had first left I'd never been that slack and it was so out of character, the woman who owned the auction house had called me the next day to make sure I was OK. That had been seriously embarrassing. I'd had to fluff up some lame excuse about being overstocked, but I knew she hadn't believed me.

Galvanised by the need to get down to work, I sat up and just as I swung my legs over the side of the bed to stand, I heard the intercom from the shop buzz. I rushed over to answer it on the landing outside Theo's room, immediately in a fluster that it was something to do with her unexplained absence. Were the police down there?

'Hi Loulou,' said Shelley, in her usual tweeting lovebird tones. 'Just calling up to let you know I'm here.'

'Oh, thank you, Shell,' I said. 'I knew you'd be there. You never let me down.'

As I spoke, I could hear how thick and choked my voice sounded. So could she.

'Are you all right Loulou?' she asked, sounding really concerned.

I let out a wobbly sigh.

'Not really, Shell,' I said.

'Wait there,' said Shelley and hung up.

I sat down at the top of the stairs, leaning against the wall. I felt absolutely humiliated at the thought of her seeing me like this, in my nightie, not a trace of make-up, hair a mess, no shoes, but between the hangover, the upset and the worry, I just didn't have a speck of energy left to do anything about it.

From my semi-foetal position, I heard the door from the shop open and close, and then after running footsteps, Shelley's concerned face appeared.

'Loulou,' she was saying. 'Whatever's wrong? Is Theo OK?'

That was all it took to set me off again and the tears were flooding out as she down next to me on the top step and put her arm around me.

'I don't know whether she's all right or not,' I choked out. 'I don't even know where she is. She didn't come home last night. She just left the party in a huff without even saying goodbye and I have no idea where she went . . .'

'Oh, that's no good,' said Shelley. 'That's very silly of her. I'm sure she's fine, she's probably at a friend's house, but of course you're worried. Why don't we go down to the kitchen and have a nice cup of tea and then we'll make a few phone calls, OK?'

I nodded feebly and she helped me to my feet. I felt quite limp from the emotional outpourings and happily leaned on her for the flight of stairs down to the kitchen. When we got there, I slumped in a chair while Shelley put the kettle on.

'Who was the last person you saw her talking to?' she asked.

I had to think.

'Well, of people I know, Chard, so that doesn't help. She was talking to some young guys after that, but I don't know any of them and anyway, I know she left on her own, because I saw her go.'

Shelley was looking at me with one eyebrow raised.

'We had a kind of a . . . misunderstanding,' I said, reluctant to go into any further detail. 'She was very angry with me and stormed out.'

'Who's her best friend these days?' said Shelley.

'Still Tatiana,' I said, sighing deeply.

'Do you think you should phone her?'

I just stared at Shelley stupidly for a moment. It was the logical thing to do and I couldn't possibly explain why it was pointless, so I decided I might as well do it. Maybe there was a chance Tattie would know where else Theo might have gone. I didn't have Tattie's mobile number, I realised, but I did have the number of the family house now – we'd found it filed under 'T' for Theo, when we'd digitalised my contacts, a thought that stabbed me in the heart yet again as I dialled. That renewed closeness had been so brief.

Marc answered.

'Marc Thorssen,' he said, in a cool and authoritative voice.

Shit. I was so befuddled with misery and anxiety that him answering hadn't even crossed my mind as a possibility. I almost dropped the phone in shock.

'Oh! Marc!' I squealed in such an uncharacteristic way, Shelley's head whipped round to look at me, from where she was pouring the tea into mugs. 'It's, um, Loulou, Theo's mum . . .'

'Hey, Loulou,' he replied, in much warmer tones. 'Great to hear from you? How are you today? That was a truly great party. I've got a bit of a headache this morning and my feet hurt like I was dancing all night. Do you think I was . . .?'

I laughed stupidly. 'Haha, yes, so have I, yes, and you were, feet, ha ha, but the thing is, Marc, is, er, Tattie there?'

'Tattie?' he said, sounding surprised – and a bit disappointed.

'No, she's gone into college. She's putting together her final degree presentation and it all happens next week, so the pressure's on. Anything I can help with?'

I sighed involuntarily.

'No,' I said. 'It's just I'm trying to find Theo and I thought she might have stayed with you guys last night.'

'No, she didn't,' said Marc. 'Sorry, can't help you with that and I didn't see much of Theo at the party in the end. I was all ready to get going on our project, but I couldn't find her anywhere.'

I didn't want to go into any more details with him, in case he worked out why Theo might have left early, so I forced myself to tighten my voice into something that sounded more like the patronising mother of a friend. Like his mother.

'Never mind, Marc,' I said. 'She's probably just gone out early this morning. Thanks for coming last night. It was lovely to see you. Give my regards to your mother. Goodbye.'

And I hung up before he could say anything else.

Shelley put a large mug of extra strong builders' tea in front of me and then opened the fridge.

'I'm going to make you a piece and bacon,' she said. 'That's a bacon sandwich to you. With lots of ketchup. You need some fat and carbs for energy. You're very tired and you've had a shock.'

I didn't argue. The throbbing in my head was lessening, but I had a queasy gnawing feeling in my stomach, which I thought a bacon sandwich might just help. I smiled at her.

'Thanks, Shell,' I said weakly. 'That sounds wonderful. Although actually I'd call it a bacon butty . . .'

'Would you like a fried egg in it, as well?' she asked and I nodded as enthusiastically as I could manage.

An hour later, much fortified by Shelley's fatty snack, I was bathed, dressed, made up, shod and – relatively – ready for normal action, but it was still bugging the heck out of me that I didn't know where Theo was.

I had tried calling her, of course, but her phone hadn't even gone to messages. It just rang out. I started writing a text, but deleted it, because I couldn't think of anything to say which didn't sound all wrong before we'd had a chance to talk through the stupid Marc misunderstanding.

I tried to tell myself that it was ridiculous to be so anxious. If she'd been living away from home, like a normal young woman of her age, I wouldn't have had the foggiest idea if she didn't sleep in her own bed for nights on end – and as it was I never knew where she was when she went out during the day.

It was just coming on top of the stupid thing with Marc that her latest vanishing act was getting to me. It had even crossed my mind that she might have done something terrible, but I quickly pushed those thoughts away.

Back in the kitchen with another mug of strong tea in front of me – plus a plate of 'emergency' chocolate biscuits brought up by Shelley, who had a Glaswegian's belief in the healing power of sugar – I called Keith for some moral support. Even though I knew it was pretty much a waste of time, because I couldn't tell him the real reason I was spooked.

I'd done such a good job of making light of dancing with Marc when we'd been chatting in Lauren's kitchen after the party, I couldn't now reveal how mortifying it had been when Theo had 'caught' us. Especially as, somewhere deep inside, I still felt a bit uncomfortable about it. Theo's reaction had been unfair, but something about the scenario did niggle at me.

'Result, Loula,' was Keith's reaction, when I told him the edited version of events – just that Theo hadn't come home the night before. 'You must be thrilled. She must have got lucky with one of those gorgeous guys in the dining room. Did you see them? It was like an Abercrombie & Fitch catalogue in there. Lauren had to fan me. Not that I'm surprised they were all over Theo, she looked bloody amazing last night, definitely the belle of the ball. But which one do you think it was? I liked the blond with the scar on his lip, but that's just my personal cup of tequila. But, I'm wondering, Louls, are the girls allowed to put out on the first date according to your sister's system? Aren't they supposed to wait until the dowry's been agreed?'

He laughed and I joined in as best I could, letting him chatter on.

'I think the whole thing went really well, don't you?' he was saying. 'I've spoken to all the committee girls this morning and every one of their daughters was asked for their number by at least one bloke last night. How great is that? Sounds like Theo was too, eh? More than her number by the sound of it . . . Rachel and I have decided we need to have a big AGM of all the mums sometime soon to get the group feedback whether we should do another one. She's sending out the email today, but I reckon it was a soaraway success, don't you? I mean, even apart from all that, it was a great party and you were inspired putting Ritchie on the decks. We nearly wore that floor out dancing. I told him he's got a whole new career as a club DJ and I think he took it seriously. Hilarious.'

He carried on in this vein, telling me who he had chatted to and which sons – and which fathers – he thought were hot and I just let it flow over me. I found Keith's motormouthing relaxing. It was always entertaining and I could put my brain in neutral while he rattled on.

Finally, he said he had to go – like I'd been keeping him, a quirk of his I'd got used to over twenty years – and there I was again, alone, distraction gone, drumming my fingers on the kitchen table, not knowing where my beloved daughter was.

I felt bad leaving Shelley to it downstairs, as Friday was always a busy day and I could hear the shop bell jangling repeatedly as customers came in, so it was probably heaving in there. But she would have to cope, because while I had managed to get some kind of a look together, I really wasn't feeling up to being Loulou Landers, style icon.

In the end I decided I just had to get out of the house. So I swept through the shop without stopping, although I noticed a few heads snap round to watch me as I passed. It meant a few fashion tourists weren't going to get the full Loulou Land experience, which was against all my normal principles, but this was no ordinary day and I knew Shelley would do her best to make it special for them in my absence.

I felt better once I got outside into the soft air of a balmy July day. The trees along Regent's Park Road were heavy with leaves, and the yummy mummies were out in force, casually dressed down – at great expense – fully made up and pushing adorable toddlers in designer buggies.

I wandered along my street, feeling slightly unreal. Every inch of that road was as familiar as my own palm, but it was so odd to be out among it in the middle of a working day – especially a Friday – I felt quite disoriented.

I was still too full of Shelley's supersonic tea to have coffee, so I checked out a new shop – another emporium of reproduction French furniture, scented candles, Marseilles soap and bunting, which I was sure would flourish – and then spent a while browsing in Primrose Hill Books. After that I headed back towards home, intent on taking over from Shelley, but then on impulse I turned right towards Chard's house. I very rarely went to see him there, because I needed to be in the shop all day, so we'd got into a habit of him visiting me, and it seemed like a fun idea to surprise him.

But the person who got the surprise was me. Theo answered the door. And then promptly closed it again.

Theo

Oh lordie what a palaver. I don't know which of us was more horrified when I opened the door – Blah Blah or me.

I thought it was the postman bringing the DVDs I had thoughtfully ordered to flesh out Deathbreath's frankly patchy collection or I never would have gone near it. Front door opening is Vlad's job and he's very thingie about it. He's very thingie about everything.

Anyway so I open the bloody door and there she is looking like a goth Lucille Ball in a bright blue bog-roll-cover frock and surgical boots – but not in a GOOD way – so what could I do? I shut it again. I shut it and ran upstairs and hid in Nancy's closet.

'Air raid!' I called out to her and she pulled the covers over her head.

The next thing I knew Blah Blah was hammering on the front door like a crazy person and worse – shouting. I could hear her even behind Nancy's fur coats.

'Theo!' she was screaming. 'Open that door immediately or I will call the police!'

It would have been hilarious if it hadn't been so utterly pathet.

'Is it the MPs Gloria?' Nancy was whispering more loudly than her normal voice. 'Have they found out we're hiding Richard? He's my son! They can't have him. They've had my brother and my father. I won't give him up. They can take me but they can't have him.'

Poor Nancy. Her dad was killed in the First World War and her darling brother died in Burma in the second one and she's not letting them have her son. It doesn't matter how many times I tell her the war has been over for sixty years and they wouldn't want Deathbreath anyway because he's practically a cripple from smoking. Plus nearly of pensionable age. She's still convinced every knock on the door is the Press Gang and Blah Blah screeching like a pikey tipped her over the edge.

'I'll take a cyanide pill before they take my boy!' she was shouting.

'Have you got one?' I asked coming out of the closet.

No dear she said. Calming down in an instant that way she does. But I'd take it if I had it.

I'd take it if you had it I said and kissed her on the forehead. I'll get you a nice cup of tea and a biscuit instead and then I'll paint your toenails.

I don't want any of those nasty garibaldis she said. Italian squashed flies.

Then I went down on the stairlift laughing at the idea of Italian flies. Bum freezer suits – suede shoes – yellow socks on their six little feet – Persol shades – riding Vespas without helmets smoking cigars. Tee hee hee.

Essential to enter laughing to deal with who I knew would be down there. I had to see the vile old pervert eventually and after the initial shock of finding her on the doorstep like a trick or treater – but not so well dressed – I reckoned I might as well do it on my turf.

Sure enough there she was at the kitchen table and Vlad the sycophant was making her a cup of tea. She was sniffing like she was trying to stop crying and I watched through a crack in the door and saw him give her a box of tissues. I felt a bit bad when I saw that. A bit. But I just had to think of that VILE thing I had witnessed the night before and my heart hardened right up again. Gag. In public! She did it in public!

Vlad was talking. I am Stravko – Mr Ritchie's housekeeper – and you are Miss Theo's mother is that right? he was saying which shows how often she visits Chateau Deathbreath. Nice kind of a friend she is.

Blah nodded and snotted into a tissue.

Lala: That's right and I'm so sorry about all that fuss just now Stravko. It's very nice to meet you and I'm really sorry I'm in such a state. But it was just such a shock when my daughter opened the door and then she shut it again in my face and I'm afraid I rather lost it.

I watched in fascination as Vlad sat down opposite her. Bloody cheek! He's staff.

Vlad: In this country I think kids very bad to parents.

What? Who was he calling a kid? But there was more Third World sycophancy to come.

Vlad: In my country is more respect. And gratitude. I send most of wages back to parents. Here I think children spoiled brats.

That was it. I swanned into the kitchen.

Moi: Mrs Meredith would like a cup of tea and a plate of biscuits thanks Vlad. She says she'd like it hot if you can possibly manage it and none of those nasty squashed fly biscuits you keep giving her either. They're giving her bad dreams.

Then I started to make myself a cup of coffee which I happen to think is a perfectly reasonable thing to do at 12 noon.

I was vaguely aware of my ho mother saying something but managed to block it out with extra enthusiastic milk frothing. Then I felt the jug being forcibly removed from my hand. I yanked it back but Vlad was stronger.

I will make drinks Miss Theo he said eyeballing me like the mad vampire he is. You go and talk to mother. Now.

For mother he said 'Mudda'. Not a bad name for her. Now the frother was off I could hear Mudda carrying on. She was shouting again.

Mudda: Theo! Stop it! Stop being such a nightmare! It's one thing being rude to me but talking to Stravko like that is totally unacceptable.

I glanced over and she looked like a squashed fly herself crammed behind the table in her stupid panto dress waving her fists around like some mad little puppet. It would have been funny if it wasn't so creepy.

Madda madda Mudda.

I just looked at her as though I had never seen her before and turned on my heel. I headed straight out of the kitchen door and that's when the real trouble started. I walked smack into Deathbreath pushing ODD in his wheelchair. There wasn't room to get round them.

Ah Theo said ODD clapping his claws with glee. I've just had a good report from the quack and now I am ready to thrrrrrrash you at cards. Prepare yourself.

Hi Theo said Deathbreath. I heard you stayed over.

And then he was on to me. I knew I was in trouble when he flipped his shades onto his head. He was staring right into my eyes and his own were all narrowed and squinty. And not just because he's half blind.

What gives, baby girl? he said and literally pushed me backwards into the kitchen.

Shit.

16

Loulou

It was Chard who saved the day. I don't know why it hadn't occurred to me until that crazy moment in his kitchen, but all his years of dating women under twenty-five had actually made him a world expert in the species and – of all my friends – he was actually the one best equipped to help me with my out-of-control daughter.

I was still too much in shock to speak when he forced her back into the kitchen, using his father in his wheelchair like a human battering ram. He kicked the door closed behind him with one cowboy-booted foot and leaned against it, indicating with a nod of his head for Stravko to cover the French windows that led into the garden. Suddenly Theo had nowhere to run.

She stood in the middle of the kitchen like a cornered deer. Her endless legs – she was still wearing the old-lady knickers and white shirt combo from the night before – made her look like the vulnerable child she really was under all that outrageous rudeness.

'So, can someone tell me what's going down here?' said Chard.

Theo started rolling her eyes, stamping a foot – still wearing my shoes as well, I noticed – and harrumphing, trying to assume her former snarky attitude, but she couldn't make it convincing and she knew it.

'Oh, for god's sake Deathbreath,' she started saying. 'I was just heading out . . .'

'Head on over to the table and sit down,' said Chard with unusual authority and it worked. With one last roll of her eyes, she slumped into the chair farthest from mine and stared up at the ceiling, presumably to save herself from accidentally catching sight of me.

With another flick of his head, Chard signalled for Stravko to come and take over on the wheelchair. Years of communicating with roadies and techies while playing electric guitar at five million decibels had made him a master of non-verbal communication.

'What?' said Air Marshal Meredith. 'Where are you taking me? I want to play cards with Theo and I haven't even said hello to Loulou. How are you my dear girl?'

I nodded and waved as enthusiastically as I could muster. I still wasn't ready to speak. I really didn't know what would come out if I opened my mouth. Possibly a banshee wail.

'That's all going to happen later, Daddy,' said Chard, patting his shoulder affectionately. 'Loulou and I just need to have a chat with Theo. Go up and see Mummy for a bit and then I'll come and get you.'

'Well, don't forget,' said the Air Marshal. 'OK, Stravko, we've had our orders. Chocks away. Off we go.'

Chard waited for them to leave and after shutting the door again came over and joined us at the table. He said nothing, just fired up a full-tar with his trusty old Zippo lighter and leaned back in his chair, looking at us both and nodding silently as he blew out plume after plume of smoke.

Even through the vile tobacco smog, it was very effective, all that nodding, somehow keeping Chard in charge of the situation without having to say a word. He seemed very still in the mystic moment communing with his ciggie, a kind of guru aura around him.

I still didn't say anything, because I didn't know what to say. I wasn't working a silent number like Chard – or Theo, for that matter – I just felt like I had been struck mute. It was all too much. Eventually it was Theo who broke the standoff.

'Oh for fuck's sake,' she said. 'Am I a prisoner here? Or am I allowed to leave?'

'You can leave when you tell me what's going on,' said Chard in very measured tones.

'What's going on is I want to go – now,' said Theo, sounding like a sulky child.

'Go where?' said Chard.

'Oh, I dunno,' said Theo, getting uncharacteristically flustered. 'Home, I suppose.'

'And where is that, exactly?' said Chard, keeping his voice at the same level.

'Oh, come off it Deathbreath,' said Theo. 'You know where I live, you come there every bloody day.'

'I do go along Regent's Park Road most mornings, it's true, Theodora. To see my best friend – your mother – at her house, where you live. Is that where you mean by home?'

'Yeah . . .' said Theo, resorting to some more eye rolling. It was getting less and less effective and I suspected she knew it.

'Well, I think you need to have a little think about that,' continued Chard. 'Because I know you stayed here last night – without asking me if it was OK – and I'm wondering if you told your mum where you were? And if you didn't, I think that was very bad manners, because you are living in her house and you owe her that respect – and a whole lot more besides, which I don't really see you giving her these days. I haven't said anything up to now, but I've been watching and I have to say, Theo, I think you're being uncool.'

It was Chard's most damning criticism and we all knew it. I watched Theo's face turn from shock to amazement to fury. Her chest started lifting and falling as her breaths got deeper. It was a physical expression of rage I recognised, because my dad used to get angry in exactly the same way. Those wacky old genetics. Just when you think things can't get any weirder, up they pop.

'Well, I'll tell you what's uncool, Mr Deathbreath Not My

Friend,' she shouted, her face getting red, just like my dad's used to. 'It's very uncool when you're at a party with a load of total strangers and you see your tragic middle-aged mother getting it on in public with a guy young enough to be your brother, practically humping him on the dance floor in front of everyone. That is seriously uncool and that is what *she* . . .' she pointed at me, 'that is what *she* did last night.'

Chard burst out laughing, which turned into coughing, but didn't stop him talking.

'What? That dude your mum was dancing with? Tattie's brother? They were having a ball. Did you see how they danced together? They were like poetry in motion. I kept putting on really cheesy tracks to keep them going. I wish I could dance like that. It was magic. And isn't he your friend's brother? He's a cool kid. He knows your mum. What exactly is your problem?'

I still couldn't speak. I was looking from one to the other, slightly hoping they had forgotten I was there.

'What's my problem?' said Theo. 'It was disgusting. She was practically tonguing him.'

'Actually she wasn't, Theo. She was dancing with him – I was there, remember? And if she had been tonguing him, so what? They're both adults, they're both single. Once everyone's legal it's open season for tonguing.'

'Well, we all know you like dating foetuses,' said Theo viciously. 'But that doesn't mean I want to watch my mother practically shagging my best friend's heinous brother in public. It was the most pathetic thing I've ever seen.'

Chard leaned forward in his chair and spoke very quietly.

'You know what I think is a lot more pathetic than a beautiful woman dancing with a younger guy who is clearly very attracted to her? And that's seeing a gorgeous young girl, looking better than anyone else at the party, snapping the head off every young dude who tries to talk to her and not even getting her arse on the dance floor once. Now that's sad. So if you want to check out what's pathetic, Theo, go look in a mirror.'

He'd done it. He'd shut her up and as I watched the colour drain from her face, I realised he'd shocked her too. He didn't take his eyes away from hers, wanting his words to have maximum impact – and it worked. She burst into tears.

'Over to you, Loulou,' he said, standing up and tossing his lighter in the air and catching it before putting it in his jeans pocket. 'I'm going up to see to my folks. I'll see you later.'

And after blowing me a kiss, he left us alone.

For a moment, I didn't know what to do. Between that and being struck dumb most of the morning I had rarely felt so useless. At any other moment of Theo's life, her bursting into tears would have had the immediate effect of making me rush to put my arms around her, but she was clearly so angry with me I really didn't think she would want me to do that.

She had her head down on her arms on the kitchen table and was howling on to them. Gently I pulled the nearest hand towards me and stroked it.

'Theo, my darling,' I said gently. 'It's all right. Let it all out.'

As I feared, she didn't react well, yanking her hand roughly out of mine.

'Get off me!' she said, sitting up and looking at me with furious red-rimmed eyes. 'Just because I'm crying doesn't mean I've forgiven you. I'm crying because the one so-called "adult" I thought was a true friend and really understood me has turned out to be as big a fuckwit as the rest of you.'

At that moment, I decided that as things couldn't get any worse, I was just going to jump in and tell her the truth.

'Well,' I started. 'If absolutely everybody is giving you a hard time – even someone as laidback, loving and non-judgemental as Chard – perhaps we have a point? Have you ever considered that?'

'No,' said Theo, blowing her nose on the tissues Stravko had put on the table for me. 'Because it's complete bollocks. Like everything you say.'

'OK,' I said, a hum of anger starting up deep in my belly and snapping me out of my shocked state. 'So absolutely everyone in the world is wrong except you. Especially me. Fine. I can't be bothered to argue with you any more, Theo, and do you know why? Your behaviour is starting to remind of someone I don't care to be reminded of. Can you guess who that might be?'

She shrugged and pulled a why-would-I-care?-but-you-might-as-well-tell-me-anyway-arsehole face.

'Your father,' I said.

I knew it was a low blow, but that was what she'd driven me to. Then I stood up and walked out of the kitchen. I'd had enough. If Theo wanted to get our relationship back on an even keel it was up to her. She had to make the running to me. I'd had enough of pandering to her irrational whims and tantrums.

I ran up the stairs quickly, before I could change my mind, let myself out of the front door and started walking fast. I needed to clear my head and headed straight for the best place to do that. The bench on the top of Primrose Hill. I called Chard once I was settled up there, the big view and fresh air making me feel calmer.

'I'm afraid I've left Theo in your kitchen,' I said.

'Already?' he said, sounding surprised. 'Didn't the two of you sort things out down there?'

'I couldn't even get her to start talking about it, Chard,' I said. 'She just thinks we're all "fuckwits" and won't budge an inch. I'm afraid I can't take any more of her outrageous behaviour and I want to ask you a massive favour.'

'Anything, babe,' he said quietly, and I knew he meant it.

'Could Theo stay with you for a bit?' I said. 'I really need to concentrate on the business for a bit. Running after her with all this emotional rollercoastering, it's getting away from me and I need to catch up. Would that be all right? Just for a while, until we've both calmed down and can talk things through properly. It's all too raw now. She seems very at home at your place, I must say – although if she is going to stay, I think you would need to have a word with her about the way she speaks to Stravko. She was treating him like some kind of serf.'

'I'd be delighted to have her,' he said, with an enthusiasm that took me by surprise. 'If you think she'd want to hang here after that hard time I gave her just now . . .'

'I think she would do it just to spite me,' I said bitterly. 'But I'm sure she would love a break from me too. I'm sure she'll forgive you very quickly. It's really me she's mad at. You just got the crossfire.'

'Well, you know, Lullabelle, I'd love to have her here, because she's so amazing with my parents. She reads to my mum, does her nails, plays cards with dad. They adore her, she's like the grandchild they've never had – and it's really amazing for me to have some help with all that. It gets pretty lonely sometimes.'

'She does your mother's nails?' I said, incredulous.

'Fingers and toes,' said Chard. 'It's a proper little girls' dorm up there. Those were Nancy's knickers she was wearing last night. And her coat.'

He chuckled affectionately.

'I didn't think anything else could shock me today,' I said. 'But I am truly amazed – mainly to find out that she's actually been doing something useful with her time.'

'Cool. I'll go down and ask her if she wants to stay here – hold on.'

I heard the sound of his boots clattering down the stairs and him calling Theo's name.

'Hey, Theo, baby,' I could hear him saying, a few moments later. 'Are you still mad at old Deathbreath, or do you want to hang here for a while? Like move in for a bit? Your mum reckons you two need a break from each other and we'd love to have you here. What do you say?'

'Great,' said Theo. It was muffled, but it sounded as though she might have been crying again. I felt a physical pain in my heart, but I had to be strong.

'Just one thing from this end, baby girl . . .' Chard was saying. 'You've got to be cool – especially to Stravko. Respect and all that. If you're rude to him it's situation all over, OK?'

'OK,' she replied, and Chard came back on the line.

'She's cool,' he said. 'Want me to give her a message?'

'Tell her I love her,' I said, tears stinging my eyes all over again.

'Your mum says she loves you,' said Chard.

And I distinctly heard Theo blowing a raspberry as I ended the call.

I sat there for a few minutes, not even noticing London spread out before me any more, feeling so miserable that my relationship with Theo had reached this new low. I remembered all the times we'd sat up here when she was tiny, her eating a Marmite sandwich while I pointed out all the landmarks according to a strict order. She'd stamp her foot if I mixed them up.

No Mummy, she'd say. It's Centrepoint and *then* Big Ben . . . She'd always been very particular and liable to kick off if things weren't just so. So she hadn't changed that much, in some ways, I thought.

I sighed deeply, hurting all over again at the impasse we'd reached, but determined to tough it out. I knew she was in good hands with Chard, and found a grain of comfort in the news that she was helping him with his parents like that. She wasn't an entirely selfish creature.

It was horrible to think she wouldn't be coming home that night, but I was sure I'd done the right thing. I needed a break from the drama, so I could get some perspective and start to work out how to put things right – and she needed time to think about her behaviour without constantly being irritated just by seeing me, which seemed to be the effect I had on her these days.

Determined to hold on to my resolve, I forced myself to my feet and started back down the hill. It wasn't going to be easy, but when my shop sign came into view, my spirits immediately lifted a little. That was where I needed to put my energy for a while. A bit of hard work would get me through this difficult time.

And then as I opened the latch on the garden gate, two things Chard had said suddenly came back into my mind. He'd said I was 'a beautiful woman' and that Marc was 'clearly very attracted' to me.

I didn't know which one I found more weird.

Theo

Here I am living at Chateau Deathbreath. Welcome to the Hotel Halitosis . . .

Just when you think things can't get any more twisted your psychotic Mudda throws you out of the house. Fine by me. I've got a lovely big bedroom here with my own bathroom a view right into the treetops and everyone leaves me alone. Except ODD who wants to play cards 24 seven but that's OK. We're playing for money now and I'm ahead. It helps if he has a little sherry before we play. He gets reckless.

I've got everything I need. Called Shelley and sussed out when Mad Mudda was going to be out for a while and then nipped over to get my essential stuff which turned out to be not much.

Went light on the clothes as I'm going to buy a whole new wardrobe to mark this new start in my life. Also new toothbrush pants etc. Got my laptop out that was the main thing. Going to miss the new mothership computer but I think it's time D Breath updated his equipment he he he.

It was weird being in Mudda's madhouse not living there and I was glad to get out again. I won't miss the smell of stinky old clothes that's for sure. And that's just her bedroom.

Other weird things which have happened: I have been phoned by two men. Well I'd hardly call one of them a man but he is allegedly male: Marc Grave-Robber Thorssen. Didn't know it was him calling as obviously his number isn't on my phone or I wouldn't have answered. Felt violated by that.

Hi Theo! He said, sounding like a Blue Peter presenter.

Me: Who is it?

Him: It's Marc!

Me: Uh?

Him: Marc? Tattie's brother . . .

Me: Eeurugiugough?

Him: How are you?

Me: Dead.

Him: Ha ha ha. Anyway listen as you know Tattie's finishing her degree show on Thursday and I'm organising surprise drinks for her to celebrate. You will come won't you?

Me: Eeeeeuuuurrrrgh . . . Text me the shit.

Then I hung up.

Unbelievable. How could he – king creep – phone me? But I will have to go to the drinks for Tats. Everything else in my life is pure Twilight Zone and I sometimes think Tattie is the only speck of normality left. And I couldn't hurt her. It would be like kicking a puppy. It's not her fault her brother is the pervert love child of a rugby shirt and a deck shoe.

The other call was much more interesting. Paul Beaney. Yep. Mr Oxford Street himself wants me to go and see him at his office which is – funnily enough – in Oxford Street. It's over the flagship so I guess I know where that is. Like in my sleep.

He said he was interested in what I was saying about 'the brand' as he called it – fucking hate that word – at the party and he wants to talk to me some more. Sensible fellow.

I told him to get his ears candled ready and hung up.

Actually there's something else. Not even sure I can get my fingers to type the next fascinating fact. I actually had a third phone call from a man today. It was my fa . . . Hang on try again. Fath . . . Nearly. Father. Phew said it.

In a weak moment a few weeks ago I stoooooopidly gave him my real number when he asked for it in an email. It was at a delicate point in my negotiations for more $$$£££ and I thought I better give him the real one in case he checked it. I never thought he'd actually ring me on it. But he did.

He's coming to London and he wants to see me. Those heinous American slappers who were in the shop that time only bloody well told him they had been 'hanging out' with me when they were over here and it was 'so cool' and I'm 'so adorable' and now he wants in on the action.

Just when I thought things were getting relatively chilled. This. There is only one thing I can possibly do about it.

Nothing.

17
Loulou

The first few days without Theo at home were very difficult. Although she'd been out a lot during the day and mostly up in her room with the door closed even when she was there, there was still a distinctly different atmosphere in the house.

Although I didn't physically see much of her before, there would be signs of fellow human habitation. Another mug in the sink – a lot less ice cream in the freezer. A copy of *Grazia* left open on the kitchen table with arrows pointing towards clothes she liked. Spectacles and goatees scribbled on to celebrities she didn't. Now when I got up each morning, everything in the house was exactly as I had left it and I found it creepy.

I kept feeling as though I'd lost something – left my handbag somewhere. I remembered the same sensation when Theo had first gone to school, after spending her toddler years in the shop with me, and just as I had then, I got through it by buckling down to work.

Fortunately she had finished getting the computer system and website all set up before her abrupt departure and it worked really well. With a bit of help from Shelley – and the odd panic call to Keith – I was able to keep on top of it and it was already turning into an important new avenue of sales.

At her own suggestion Shelley was doing an extra day a week

to take photos of particularly tempting items of new stock and put them on the website, and we were already getting online customers from as far afield as Tokyo and Seattle. I found it amazing that anyone would buy a piece of vintage clothing without trying it on – or smelling it – but it didn't seem to deter them.

If that side of the business kept growing at the pace it was, I reckoned I'd soon need Shelley even another day, just to package up the goods, which had to be done in the Loulou Land style.

Along with those developments, I'd also received large consignments from my Paris and Edinburgh-based scouts – which I'd been able to preview using the wonders of Skype, thanks to Theo, rather than getting on a train or a plane, as I used to. So I had a nice lot to do, and getting back into it felt like putting on a pair of comfy old slippers to me.

I kept busy in the evenings too, seeing a lot of Keith – but always at his place, Claridges bar, or one of our other regular spots outside my immediate neighbourhood. I just didn't feel comfortable going up Regent's Park Road in case I bumped into Theo. My daily walks up Primrose Hill were out of the question and I had even taken to parking my car round the corner in Gloucester Avenue, so I could scuttle off to it without going any nearer Chard's place.

It felt incredibly weird to be actively avoiding my own daughter, but I really believed our relationship was balanced on a precipice and getting the next move right was essential. We couldn't see each other until we were both ready and it would have to be in a neutral context. I couldn't allow myself to think what might happen if we got it wrong again.

I did keep in touch with her at one remove, sending regular emails and texts saying 'I'm always here for you, Theo, when you're ready. You know I love you xxx' and things like that, which she didn't reply to. But that didn't surprise me. Theo sometimes didn't reply when you were talking to her in the same room.

The situation would have been intolerable if I hadn't had regular updates from Chard on his morning visits, which continued as normal.

'So how is my truly appalling beloved only child?' I asked him, as we sat outside on a gloriously sunny mid-July morning, when she'd been at his place just over a week. He didn't answer immediately and I sank my nose into the beautiful bunch of pink roses he'd handed me on arrival.

'Mmm, these smell so good,' I said. 'Thanks so much, Chardie. Go on, tell me. Is she behaving herself?'

'Hard to say,' he replied, taking his ciggie out of his mouth for a moment to take a sip of his mint tea and then adding three more teaspoons of sugar. He stirred it slowly and continued, the wretched cigarette back in his mouth and wagging at me as he spoke.

'I don't see that much of her. She's still being very good to the olds – they love having her in the house – and she's much better with Strav. She's even shown him how to make coffee properly, which has done us all a big favour and she did it quite tactfully for her. Got him to teach her how to make Bulgarian coffee first – you know, that powdery gear like they have in Greece and Turkey? Then he showed her how to read fortunes in the grinds. They use them like tea leaves. It was a gas. She told me I was going to make a lot of money and have a long happy marriage.'

He laughed, spluttering a bit as the cough kicked in. I really would have to talk to him about his smoking one day.

'What did Stravko see in Theo's grinds?' I asked.

'Lots of men,' said Chard, looking up at me from behind his shades. 'All very different from each other, but all dark-haired.'

'Well, that would be good,' I said, with sarcastic enthusiasm. 'If unlikely. Mind you, I suppose you, Strav and the Air Marshal makes three more men than she's used to having around her on a daily basis, so that's got to be good. Maybe daily exposure to testosterone and Y chromosome pheromones will normalise her a bit.'

'Not sure how much of that the Air Marshal's pumping out these days,' said Chard. 'Although he's definitely got more of a twinkle going on since Theo's been with us. If he had a step there would be a spring in it.'

'But you said you don't see much of her,' I pressed him.

'She goes out for a few hours most days,' said Chard. 'Morning or afternoon. No idea where. Don't ask. Apart from that she plays cards with Dad and hangs out with Nancy, reading to her and trying on her clothes, and I don't like to get in the way when that's going on. It's too precious golden for the crumblies, so I leave them to it. Apart from that she's in her room with the door closed. I only really see her in the kitchen. She really does make great coffee. And you make great mint tea, of course . . .'

I smiled at him. That was my Chardie, always the gentlemen.

'Well, I'm glad we're good at something,' I said. 'But that sounds exactly like what she used to do when she was here – apart from so much time hanging out with your parents, of course. That is a very welcome new addition.'

'Actually,' said Chard, looking at me over the top of his shades again. 'She's been visiting my parents for a while. A few weeks.'

'A few weeks! I had no idea . . .'

'Yeah, she just turned up one day and it kinda became a regular gig. So sweet for me, Loulska. Beyond.'

I shook my head in disbelief.

'She's so contradictory,' I spluttered. 'Vile to her own mother, but gorgeous to your folks. Don't get me wrong, I'm really delighted she's nice to someone, especially them, but you'd think she would have mentioned it to me – actually, Chard, why didn't *you* mention it to me?'

He took a long sip of his tea and smacked his lips. It was clearly at the nirvana point of sweetness and temperature. Chard was very particular about his mint tea.

'I didn't want to blow it,' he said. 'It was so pure and right, I just wanted to let it hang there. And knowing Babycakes – Theo – if she knew you knew, she would have stopped coming. Sorry, babe, didn't mean to be sneaky, but couldn't risk it.'

It was my turn to roll my eyes, but I could see his point. Chard was nothing short of a saint with his parents and I knew how much it would have meant to him to have Theo involved. When I looked at him again, he was smiling, with a tender faraway look in his eyes.

'What?' I asked.

'Oh,' he said, chuckling quietly, with the odd wheeze mixed in. 'The other night we watched *Grease* together – all of us. It was crazy. Theo and Stravko were dancing. Mum and Dad were clapping along and Dogbreath was howling to all the songs. I had to lock him in the laundry in the end.'

I sat in stunned silence for a moment, taking it in. It was an adorable picture, but at the same time, it made me feel so left out I could have burst into tears. *Grease* had always been Theo's favourite musical and we'd watched it together so many times, we'd both known practically every word of the dialogue as well as all the songs.

I knew Chard hadn't meant to hurt me, but hearing about that cosy family night was like a kick in the stomach. I felt like an exile from my own life and didn't know how to respond, so I was very relieved when at just that moment, I heard the familiar sound of the wrought iron gate opening. Saved by a customer.

I sprang to my feet, delighted to have an excuse to get up, but when I turned round and saw who the customer was, I nearly sat straight down again. It was Marc Thorssen. I was still holding the roses, which made me feel even more awkward.

'Hi Loulou,' he said, like it was the most normal thing for him to turn up at my shop. 'Nice flowers.'

'Hi Marc!' I squeaked. 'Theo's not here.'

He laughed.

'I didn't come to see Theo. I came to see your shop – and you.'

I couldn't believe how relaxed he was. I was mortified.

'Hi Ritchie,' he was saying, leaning around me to raise his hand at Chard in a friendly greeting, as I stood there, frozen with embarrassment, although not quite sure why. 'Those were some great mixes you were pushing out at that party the other week.'

'Glad you enjoyed them,' said Ritchie. 'You were certainly throwing some wild shapes with Loulou. You two were magic. I loved it. Really gave me something to work with.'

Marc laughed and patted me on the shoulder. I stiffened like one of my shop mannequins under his touch.

'Yeah,' he was saying. 'She's an amazing dancer, isn't she?'

I turned to look at him and he was smiling broadly at me.

'We'll have to do it again some time,' he said.

I was so distressed by this point I think I might have whimpered. And it got worse.

'Maybe at the Big Chill?' he continued. 'I think we're all going to be there, aren't we?'

Then I really did have to sit down. I don't think I did it very elegantly.

'Yeah,' said Ritchie, going into one of his nod-athons. 'I'm doing a set on the decks. I was going to go acoustic, but I had such a good time with Luke that night, he's coming down and we're going to DJ together. Main stage. You two can start the dancing.'

He stood up, gathering his ciggies and lighter, and clapped Marc on the shoulder as he sauntered past.

'Catch you later, guys,' he said, as though it were the most normal thing in the world to leave me alone to chat with a child. A child who looked like he had just walked out of a Ralph Lauren ad, but more attractive. 'Better get back to my clan.'

Which includes Theo, I thought with alarm, but I knew Chard wouldn't say anything to her about Marc turning up. He was fantastic in that regard, almost incapable of gossip. Partly because he couldn't remember anything very long, but mainly a natural sensitivity.

I watched him walk off down the street in something of a daze and then realised with a start that Marc had sat down opposite me. Suddenly he came into my focus, studying me with those extraordinary eyes, a small smile playing around his mouth.

'Would you like some tea?' I said, like Hyacinth Bucket on autopilot.

He glanced down at the table.

'Would you have to get up to get another glass for it?'

I nodded.

'No, then,' he said and the edges of his mouth lifted a little more.

I felt physically sick. He reached across the table and picked up my glass.

'I'll have some of yours,' he said and as he lifted it to his lips, his eyes didn't leave mine for a moment. He took a slow sip and I stared back at him, frozen, like a terrified rabbit.

I swallowed and felt my throat go up and down like a yoyo. Gulp. What a giveaway. Treacherous body. Marc's smile broadened as he saw it, and as he put the glass down again, he slid further down in the chair, his legs wide. Then he put his arms behind his head.

With his pale pink polo shirt pulled taut across his chest, slouchy old chinos rolled up to reveal just a hint of hairy ankle, feet in bright green Havaianas stretched out towards me, I couldn't take my eyes off him. I don't know how any woman with a pulse could have, but apart from the unbridled sexuality, I was just plain astounded at his confidence. It was outrageous.

Breaking the moment, he ran a hand through his hair, so it stood up like a field of ripe wheat. He and Chard could have a hair raking competition, I thought, watching transfixed. What was that all about?

'So here I am back at Loulou Land,' said Marc, glancing round at the terrace and the shop window. 'Is this a normal Thursday morning for you? Drinking tea in the sun? With a big bouquet of roses in your lap?'

I nodded. I was still holding them. What an idiot.

'Pretty much,' I said, putting the flowers on the ground by my feet. Chard – Ritchie – comes most mornings. And he brings me flowers sometimes. Sometimes cupcakes and stuff. He's very generous. He leaves if I get, er, busy.'

'So I saw,' said Marc, his eyes crinkling with mischief. 'Are pink roses your favourites?'

I nodded like a shy child. His questions were making me feel naked. It got worse.

'So, where is Theo?' he asked brightly.

I stopped mid-breath, completely thrown by him mentioning her – and also because I wasn't sure how to answer. But then as I looked at Marc's kind face, eyes narrowed, waiting for an answer, I felt I wanted to tell him the truth, just as I had that night in Lauren's garden.

'She's staying at Chard's place for a while. He lives just round the corner. We had a big falling out . . .' I paused for a moment. 'She was angry with me after the party. For dancing with you.'

He just carried on looking at me, a slightly more serious expression in his eyes, but he didn't say anything.

'She thought it was . . . inappropriate,' I added.

'Did you?' he asked.

'No,' I said quietly. 'I thought it was wonderful.'

He stood up, grinning broadly as he put out his hand to me.

'Are you going to show me round this shop then?' he said.

Theo

It must be the new knickers. It's the only explanation. Or it could be my new hair colour – I've gone brunette, looks amazing – but I think it's the pants. I'm only wearing those retro ones from Topshop which are frilly gathered cotton like something Bridget Bardot would have worn in 1959. Or maybe it's the new toothbrush? And I've changed my shampoo.

Whatever it is my life has changed. It's actually got better.

I don't think it's living at Chard's that has made the difference although at least I'm away from the accusing gaze of Mad Mudda. The slightly teary eyes under the fringe were getting me down. Like a miserable dog looking at you under a curtain.

I don't completely hate her anymore though. It's not her fault she's old and tragic. Well she could help the tragic part but I've decided not to hate her for it. I even asked Chard if she was OK the other day and he said she was fine but she'd be a lot better if I made it up with her.

I said there's a time for everything and this isn't the time. I might not hate her but I'm still not talking to her. I haven't forgiven her for that appalling lapse of taste at that stupid goddam party – which is what I mean by tragic.

Oh yes that party. Two more things about that.

1. The goodie bag was crap. I only got it when I went back to Mudda's to get my stuff the other day. And it was C.R.A.P. It had

a dreary scarf a yawny cocktail ring and three T-shirts in it. Three crappy West Wind T-shirts. That was it. But in some ways that was good because when I went to see Paul Weeny Beaney the other day I was able to use them to show him how rubbish they are.

I took a really good T-shirt Mad Mudda brought back from Australia years ago with me and showed him the difference. Thick and stretchy looks better than flimsy and floppy. And then I told him a lot of other stuff about everything.

He said what I had to say was so interesting we should 'have lunch and discuss it more'. I told him lunch was for wimps and walked out. I've been having an 80s film season and pinched that line from *Wall Street*. He got the ref and ran out after me to the lift laughing.

So instead of lunch we did what I like to do – a reccie of all the chain store flagships on Oxford Street. All of them except Topshop which was a drag because it's probably the best. But he refused to go there. Cunch of bunts he said. Or something like that. But I got him into all the others though. He put on a pair of really enormous dark glasses – because he wanted to be incognito in 'the competition' – but of course they just made everyone look at him wondering who the celebrity was so I bought him a Union Jack hat at a tourist stall and made him wear it. Beaney's Beanie he called it.

And I made him take his jacket off. I said it was because even if he didn't mind looking like a banker I really didn't want to be seen walking around with one. Actually I just wanted to check the label and it was Brioni like I thought. Nice.

He was quite obedient really and seemed to listen to my expert opinion on all the 'offers' as he kept calling them although he didn't like it when I said the shoes in New Look were better than his. Even though they clearly are.

When we got back to Oxford Circus I told him I was going home and he said he would be in touch because he wants me to be a consultant for the 'merch' and the 'brand' and he will have 'one of his people' call me about money.

I told him if he was going to continue using that embarrassing 90s jargon not to bother but if he could switch to normal vocabulary I'd be happy to talk to his *staff* about sorting out the *clothes* for his *shop.*

I left him standing there shaking his head. We'll see. It was quite amusing doing the shops with him but I'm still not entirely convinced he's not an A hole. Think there could be lurking arseholey tendencies. We'll see.

Oh yes the other thing about that party at his (rather arseholey . . .) house.

2. Tattie met a boy at it. As in really *met.* And several times since. Seven times in one night she said. Sounds exhausting but does prove what I said about her huge arse being a man magnet.

He's the brother of someone we both went to school with – which is seriously creepy verging on incest – but the whole thing is actually great for me because it meant I didn't have to go to that stupid drinks her stupid brother was stupidly putting on for her. The boy was going to be there so I could use the best gal pal/boyfriend gooseberry manoeuvre. Checkmate.

Freedom.

18
Loulou

I didn't take Marc's hand when he held it out to me. I had that much self-control left, even though I couldn't help noticing how nice his nails were. I glanced down. Even his toenails were beautiful. Holy Mary Mother of God.

But standing up again felt good. Being back on my own two crazy towering shoes grounded me somehow and I led the way into the shop, as its proud proprietor, not some tragic perimenopausal matron having one final hormonal surge in the company of an impossibly virile young man. Or at least I hoped it wasn't obvious.

'So, this is my shop . . .' I said, stepping back from him as far as I could without disappearing into a rail of clothes, and clinging on to Chard's bouquet like some kind of shield. 'Of course you've been before, but I was doing the display that night so you didn't see it at its best.'

He looked round appreciatively. Thinking I'd better keep busy, I grabbed the nearest dress and held it up.

'This is the kind of thing I'm known for,' I said. 'It's an early 1970s Pucci caftan. Beautiful fabric, in perfect condition and as wearable now as when it was made. I only put this out this morning, but it won't last until the end of the week in this weather. In fact, if I check my website it might even have sold overnight.'

I glanced at the price tag, as though I didn't already know how much it was.

'I'll get £800 for this little slip of silk jersey, can you believe it? But it's what people want and, as I said, it's in unusually good condition. Probably never worn.'

He was doing a good job of looking interested.

'Where do you get something like that?' he asked.

I laughed. The classic question from someone who knew nothing about the vintage business.

'Now that is a state secret,' I said. 'I get my stuff from all over the world, which is a lot easier now I have discovered Skype. I have loyal scouts in New York, Paris, LA, all the key places. I've worked with some of them for thirty years.'

Those last two words seemed to hang in the air after I said them. A small detail of my business that reminded us both that my shop had been open longer than he'd been alive. For a moment our eyes locked and the tension I'd felt on the terrace filled the space between us again. The stark reminder of our age difference should have cooled things down, I thought, but it seemed to have the opposite effect. That was weird.

'Anyway, you've come to see the menswear,' I said, as briskly as I could muster, determined to get control of the situation again.

Marc was an essential ally for me in my campaign to get Theo leading a more normal life for a girl of her age, so I just had to get over this silly business – which I might have been imagining anyway – without being unkind to him. Or making a fool of myself.

'And I really need to put these in water, so come through to the back here,' I said, leading the way and realising, as I took the first step, that taking Marc into the smaller space of the back room was not actually the greatest idea. Especially as he seemed all too keen to follow me in there.

'This whole rail is menswear,' I said, trying to assume my professional lady boutique owner persona again, but when I glanced over my shoulder at him, Marc really did seem set on distracting me.

He was leaning against the wall, his arms folded, biceps popping out prettily, his mouth curled in a smile that should have had an X rating.

'So, what do you think would look good on me, Loulou?' he asked, faux-innocently.

What was I supposed to say? I wondered. Everything, but preferably nothing. Just take all your clothes off right now you gorgeous young stud. That's what I wanted to say. Or better still, let me take them off for you, nice and slowly . . .

But I didn't say that. Instead I mustered all my self-control, sending up a prayer to every shrivelled-up old nun who had ever taught me, to help me to be good. Hail Mary, full of grace, I said in my head, grabbing a white linen suit – 1970s Saint Laurent – off the rail and thrusting it at him.

'Here,' I said. 'The trousers might be too long, but they can always be shortened. Try it on anyway.'

Marc's smile just broadened, letting me know he wasn't taken in for a moment by my *Are You Being Served?* pantomime.

'Here?' he asked, raising one eyebrow.

'Follow me, Marc,' I said, shaking my head and smiling, in some kind of acknowledgement of what he was doing, which I hoped might defuse it a bit.

I thrust the suit into his arms, making sure my hands touched him nowhere more intimate than his elbows and that the flowers were in between us too. But even that was enough to send forks of electricity shooting up my arms and down to where they had no business going.

Then the shop bell tinkled. A customer! A precious wonderful customer at the perfect moment, to stop me doing something I would deeply regret.

'In there,' I said firmly to Marc, pointing at the smaller changing room. 'I better go and see who's come in.'

And when I got into the main part of the shop, not one, but three young and attractive young women were standing there. The perfect antidote. Saved.

'Hello,' I said with sincere enthusiasm and they all grinned excitedly back at me. 'Let me know if you need any help with anything, or just browse as much as you want. Try on anything you fancy. Feel free.'

They nodded and giggled; clearly a trip to my shop was a big deal for them. They would never know how pleased I was they were there.

'Actually,' I said. 'Would you like some iced tea? It's so hot out there and I've got some in the fridge . . .'

And it might keep you here a bit longer, I thought. They were clearly thrilled to be asked and I was delighted for a reason to go out to the kitchen where I could recover myself and finally do something with Chard's beautiful flowers. Except, I didn't only do the flowers and get the tea, did I? No. I also checked my hair and re-did my lipstick in the mirror back there.

What are you doing, Elizabeth Mary Theresa Landers? I asked myself as I looked at my reflection. A well-preserved but definitely middle-aged face gazed back at me. Just making myself look nice for the girls, I tried to kid myself. Giving them the best possible Loulou Land experience, so they would keep coming back and would tell all their friends how lovely I was. Yeah, right. And as I spritzed some Mitsouko down my cleavage, I had to acknowledge that perhaps there was a little more to it than that.

I put my head in my hands and physically tried to shake some sense into it, then picked up the tray and headed back into the shop.

The tallest of the girls, a very slim brunette, was twirling in front of my big mirror in a floor-length backless 1930s evening dress in beautiful eau-de-nil silk. She had just the right kind of body for it, long and lean, with a completely flat stomach and practically no breasts. It looked great on her.

Meanwhile, her pretty blonde friend had taken off her trousers and was trying on a pair of gold 1950s beauty queen stilettos with her T-shirt barely covering her knickers. She had good legs. All round I was delighted with the scenario which would greet Marc when he eventually emerged. It would definitely stop him flirting with an old trout like me.

'How are you all doing?' I asked cheerily, feeling confident things would now be more normal.

They turned and smiled at me, but as I smiled back their expressions changed. The brunette's eyes opened wide and the blonde had gone bright red. I looked over my shoulder to see Marc standing in the doorway wearing the white linen suit – and nothing else.

'What do you think, Loulou?' he asked, stretching out his arms, so the front of the jacket opened wider, revealing a muscled chest and stomach with a line of dark hair heading south from his navel. 'Do you think the trousers are too long?'

The girls were now fully giggling, the blonde pulling down her T-shirt in a way guaranteed to attract attention to her legs, the brunette turning sideways to Marc so he could get the full effect of her slender figure – and perky nipples – in the dress. He waved cheerily at them.

'Looking great, girls,' he said. 'How do you like this suit on me?'

'You look amazing,' said the brunette, now recovered enough to pout. She turned her slim brown bare back to Marc and smouldered at him in the mirror. 'What do you think of this dress?'

'It looks great – and I love those shoes on you,' he said to the blonde, who promptly let go of the bottom of her T-shirt. 'Nice legs,' he added, as she was clearly expecting.

Far from diluting the sexual tension in my shop, the girls' arrival had just sent it through the roof. Marc's eyes were flashing with amusement as he turned his attention back to me.

'Really, Loulou,' he said. 'Is this the suit for me? Because I do actually really want a suit. I thought it would be fun to wear one to the Big Chill. Everyone goes really crazy with their clothes – men in dresses, that kind of thing – so I thought I'd like to look super-smooth. What do you reckon?'

Another reminder of that forthcoming event – and his presence at it – threw me into even more confusion. Every time I managed to forget about that damn festival something would bring it all back again. I could only take comfort from the fact that there would be thirty thousand people there apart from us, so I might be able to avoid him in the crowd.

But then I started to wonder whether Theo would be one of them now. Maybe she wouldn't come with us after all that had happened. I desperately hoped she would and realised that it gave me a deadline to sort things out with her. I worked it out in my head. Two weeks! That was all there was until that craziness kicked off. With all that swirling through my mind, I strained to snap it back to attention.

'It looks really great on you, Marc,' I said, because it did. 'It's actually a perfect fit. I don't think it needs any alterations, but try some others on anyway to be sure. Just go and help yourself, you know where they are. Now, let me pour the tea for these gorgeous young things.'

Emphasis on 'young'. Hoping I'd put him in his place for a bit, I busied around with the tea glasses and took the drinks to the girls who were now all in the big changing room together, clothes everywhere, in a state of advanced hysteria.

'Who *is* he?' asked the blonde, as I passed the tea in to them. 'He's absolutely gorgeous.'

'He's a friend of my daughter's,' I said. 'His sister is her best friend, you know how it is . . .'

'Is he single?' asked the brunette, who was manoeuvring herself into a skintight red satin 1950s fishtail frock, which I couldn't help noticing did nothing for her flat chest.

I didn't answer immediately. I knew he was, but I couldn't bring myself to say it to this rather pushy girl.

'You better ask him,' I said and left them to it.

They scurried in and out a lot, giggling and shrieking in various stages of undress, but Marc didn't make another appearance. I thought I heard the curtain of his changing room swish a few times, but left him to it, keeping myself busy checking website activity on the laptop behind the counter.

He finally emerged at a moment when all three girls were back in the changing room. He put the white suit on the counter.

'Did you have fun in there?' I asked him.

'Yeah,' he said. 'It was great. I tried on loads of things, but I didn't want to come out and bother you when you had real customers.'

'Would you like this suit, Marc?' I asked, putting my hand on the jacket. 'As a present. I meant what I said at the party. I would love to give you something as a thank you for being so nice to Theo and if you wore that suit to the Big Chill and told everyone where you got it, it would be a great promotion for the shop.'

'I'd love the suit, Loulou,' he said. 'But I couldn't possibly let you give it to me. Either I buy it, or I don't take it.'

I was disappointed to be losing my potential advantage. If he'd taken the suit as a present it would have put him in a subservient position to me and we both knew it. It was irritating, but I couldn't help respecting him for understanding that.

'How about if I give you thirty per cent off?' I said. 'That's what I give Tattie. It's my official friends and family discount.'

He considered it for a moment, then nodded and I started folding the suit up in tissue paper. Just as I was handing him the carrier bag, the girls came out of the changing room back in their own clothes.

'Oh, are you leaving too?' said the brunette, walking over and leaning on the counter next to Marc, very close to him. She put the eau de nil dress down and glanced briefly at me. 'I'm going to take that,' she said, then turned her attention fully back to Marc.

'We were wondering if you'd like to come and have a drink with us,' she said, with a toss of her hair. 'We thought we'd go round to The Engineer and then on to – who knows where?'

Brazen little tart, I thought, as I busied myself with her credit card and folding the dress. For a moment I was tempted just to stuff it into a carrier bag – a Tesco carrier bag – but business sense won out and I packed it into a box, the works. It was £300, which was a lot for a first-time customer, especially such a young one.

'Oh, that's really nice of you,' said Marc. 'But I've just started seeing someone and I'm not sure what she'd think if she knew I was going out carousing with three beautiful women.'

I was glad I was bent over, tying a bow on the box, at the moment he spoke, because I wasn't sure I could have hidden my surprise. He was seeing someone? Not that it was any of my business, but he'd told me at the party that he was single. That had happened quickly. I stood up and slid the girl's boxed-up dress into a carrier bag.

'Oh, that's a shame,' I heard one of the other girls saying in a simpering giggly voice I found particularly irritating. 'I mean for us – not for her. Is she someone special?'

'Very special,' said Marc and as I glanced at him, he held my gaze as he spoke again. 'Very special indeed.'

I was so freaked out, I dropped the carrier bag, which gave me a welcome reason to duck down behind the counter again and recover myself. What was he up to? Was he playing with me like a cat with a mouse, just for the fun of it, or was I imagining the whole thing? I really didn't know – and I couldn't decide which was worse – but either way, it was doing my head in.

Fortunately for me, just as the girls were leaving the shop – with a bit more last-minute simpering and pouting at Marc – another customer came in, a particularly demanding regular, who always expected a lot of personal attention from me.

While I was trying to look after her, the phone kept ringing and I was too genuinely busy to give him any more attention. So without me having to be rude, he got the message it was time to go. But not without one more parting shot.

'Thanks for the suit, Loulou,' he said, coming over to where I was kneeling on the floor, frantically trying to find a chunky gold 1970s pendant I had stored in the bottom drawer of an old draper's cupboard, which I knew would be the clinching piece to persuade the customer to buy the Pucci caftan. It would anchor it down on her voluminous breasts.

I was so preoccupied with finding the necklace before she got bored and went off the idea, I didn't notice what was going on and the next thing I knew, Marc had squatted down next to me.

I turned to look at him in surprise, and he put one finger gently under my chin and tilted it towards him, so I was looking up into those beautiful dark-rimmed eyes. In the tight skirt and particularly ridiculous platform shoes I was wearing, I couldn't move easily without falling over and I felt captive in his gaze. And it wasn't an unpleasant sensation, which made it worse.

But just as I was about to say something to break the dangerous spell, he leaned forwards and planted his lips firmly on mine, keeping them there just long enough for a fireball of lust to tear through my body.

I was so surprised, I felt quite dizzy and put my hand out to the edge of the drawer to steady myself, which was a good thing because it separated us before anything more disastrous could happen. Then the customer started calling out to me from the changing room that she really wasn't sure about the caftan and the spell was mercifully broken.

'See you at the Big Chill,' he said, getting to his feet, the customary mischievous expression back in his eyes. 'I'll be the one in the white suit.'

Theo

So far not too a-holey. Weeny Beaney actually did ring me like he said he would the day after our chain store massacre and I'm going into the boardroom for a meeting with his design team next week.

That would be B-O-R-E-D room? I said.

Him: Ha ha ha yeah and I'm the Chairman of the Bored.

Me: Alright dollface come on and bore me.

Him: OK Iggy.

I was quite amused.

Right after that someone else rang saying she was head of 'HR' for West Wind and needed my bank details for payments. She also told me I'd have to invoice the accounts dept on the first of each month for my 'consultancy fee'.

Me: Can you just remind me how much that is again?

She: £800.

Me: !!!!!

She: Plus expenses of course. Keep the receipts for any samples you buy and claim those on a separate invoice.

I wasn't exactly sure what an invoice was but I did understand that I would be getting paid £800 a month to go shopping. With that and the monthly hush money from Rob the Knob that's £24 000 a year. That's enough to get my own flat but I'm not going to. I'm really enjoying living at Chard's place it's all so easy. And I'd miss the staff.

I'd miss the olds as well now. Nancy has given me that leopard-skin coat and the matching hat. I gave her a pair of my Top Shop skinny jeans in return which are more like boyfriend cut on her tiny little pipecleaner legs. Seeing them when we were putting the jeans on made me want to cry. They're all wizened like Twiglets with the veins all sticking out. I had to pretend I was having a sneezing fit until I recovered.

Later we watched *Giant* so I could show her Liz Taylor working a rolled up belted jean and she totally got it. She wears them sitting on the bed with a pair of genius black patent stilettos I found in her wardrobe. Deathbreath loves it. Says he's been trying to get her to wear jeans for years. Shame she has bigger feet than me.

Talking of feet. Still haven't spoken to Mudda. I just can't make my mind up about it all. Sometimes I think of things I want to ask her – like how to do an invoice – and my hand is on my phone before I remember I'm not speaking to her. This morning I actually had to think for a moment to remember why not.

Then it came flooding back. Like a tsunami of raw sewage. Her gazing up at Captain Chino like Scarlett O'Hara copping off with Rhett Butler – in public – and the little chip of ice in my heart froze right up again.

I have allowed Deathbreath to give her my new phone number though. I'm not a total monster. She can have my number. I just won't tell her why I had to change it. Don't think she would like to know just how serious old Knobhead is about coming over to see us.

19
Loulou

I hardly slept a wink the night after Marc's visit to the shop – and that kiss. Surely, I told myself, staring at the ceiling as the first light of dawn started to seep in through the crack between my curtains, surely after that there was no mistaking his intentions? Unless he was some kind of psychopath who liked to tease tragic old lonely single women with his enthralling gorgeousness.

But you don't kiss someone lingeringly on the lips while gazing deep into their eyes as a light social gesture. So maybe what Chard had said to Theo that time in his kitchen was true: Marc was attracted to me and wanted to take it further. The really terrifying thing was that I wanted to as well. I'd stopped even trying to lie to myself about that.

A couple of hours earlier, when I'd got up to make myself some camomile tea in the desperate hope it would help me sleep, I'd finally allowed myself to accept that I had a fully fledged crush on Marc Thorssen. I was more attracted to him than I had been to anyone for years. And it wasn't just his glorious youth and beauty.

I liked his style. I liked the way he dressed, his perfect manners and general demeanour, and beyond that, I was in awe of his relaxed confidence. He was at ease with himself to an extent I found quite amazing. On top of all that, he seemed to be a really nice, decent and thoughtful person. What was not to like? Even his bloody toenails were beautiful. I couldn't pretend anymore. I wanted to kiss him again. I wanted to kiss him properly. Goddammit, I wanted to go to bed with him. Badly.

At the very moment I acknowledged these inappropriate feelings, I had to crash the shutters down on them. It didn't matter how much either – or both of us – wanted it, we couldn't possibly act on our urges. The way Theo had reacted to us just dancing together, I could barely imagine what her response would be if she found out there was more to it than that. Even what had happened so far was potentially disastrous in that regard.

And it wasn't just her disapproval I feared. While it did seem – incredibly – that Marc was attracted to me, I could imagine all too well how grotesque a liaison between us would seem to the outside world.

The numbers kept going round in my head as I lay there on top of the rumpled bedclothes: at twenty-four he was even less than half my age. Forget being old enough to be his mother, I could practically be his bloody grandmother. I would look ridiculous – and worse, tragic. A female version of the man in *Death in Venice*.

But then, like one of those devil/angel temptation sequences in old movies, up popped the image of Samantha from *Sex and the City*. Nothing tragic about her. She would have had Marc there and then in my changing room, if not already under the rose arbour in Lauren's garden.

I'd read the newspaper articles about the real-life cougars, sexually confident older women who got their no-strings kicks with permanently potent young stud muffins, but I really didn't aspire to join their ranks. That wasn't how I saw Marc, as hard meat, the means to a sexual end. I wasn't attracted to him because he was young and gorgeous, but despite it.

And while the cougars may have been helping to even out the ancient inequality between men and women in this regard, I really didn't want to be a female Chard. While I understood what had started it, his relentless pursuit of firm young flesh was leading him to a lonely and childless late middle age and was looking sadder every day.

But then – devil again – I thought of the younger man/older women couples who'd made a proper go of it. There was Sam Taylor-Wood with that really young actor and Demi Moore seemed to be happily married to her boy-man, Ashton thingy. See – said the angel on my shoulder – you can't even remember their names because you are so *old*.

So it went on. The devil popping up to suggest I slept with Marc just the one time to get it out of my system and the angel stepping in, appalled, reminding me that it wouldn't make any difference to Theo if it were just once, a full dirty weekend at Babington House, or an ongoing affair. If she found out, the damage would be irreparable. And even if she didn't find out, I'd have to live with keeping it a secret from her, which could almost be worse.

With the early summer sun now fully up, I wondered if she would feel any differently if it were a twenty-four-year-old she didn't know. She did seem to have some kind of weird problem with Marc in particular, which I'd never been able to understand, but the general concept of younger men wasn't the point, because it was very specifically him I was . . . falling in love with.

I sat bolt upright in bed as that idea arrived unannounced into my head. I wanted to scream like Munch's painting. Noooooooo! It was nonsense. Just a strong attraction. A flirtation made more maddeningly intense precisely because of its hopeless inappropriateness. And by the fact that I had been alone for so many years with just a few long-distance affairs to satisfy my physical and romantic needs. Maybe I deserved one last hot fling?

And then right after the devil had thrown that one at me, the angel played her trump card, delivering to my brain an unsmiling image of Marc's mother. She'd probably have a very simple reaction to the news I was dating her son. She'd hire a hit man.

So forget it, I told the devil firmly, there was going to be no more time wasted on this nonsense. Marc – *Marc!* – might be my soulmate, the yin to my yang and the tick to my tock, the Morecambe to my Wise, or more like the Ant to my Dec (he probably wouldn't know who Morecambe and Wise were), but there was no way it was going any further. End of story.

Firm in my resolution, I had finally gone back to sleep and was pleased to find it was still solid when I got up two hours later. That kiss had been a moment of madness on his part – probably the effect of the hot day and those half-naked girls in the shop – and I wasn't going to think about Marc Thorssen any more. *Finito*. *Basta*. End of story.

Over the days that followed, I managed to keep it together. Whenever thoughts of Marc drifted into my head, I pushed them away again, with a crisp reminder to myself that anything that could prevent a full reconciliation with Theo was off-limits. And I was glad that he didn't drop by again, phone the shop, or make any contact with me. It helped me keep my head on straight. But at night, it was harder to control my feelings. Wildly inappropriate dreams about him would wake me up and I'd find it hard to go back to sleep afterwards.

So I was feeling somewhat frail one morning the following week when Chard reached into his pocket, while we were having our tea ceremony out on the shop terrace, and handed me a piece of paper with Theo's new phone number and email address on it. Especially as it was in his writing. She hadn't even bothered to write it down for me herself. She could have texted it to me, I thought, tears springing into my eyes. Or emailed it.

'Why has she got a new number and email address?' I asked him, blinking fast to recover myself.

'Says she lost her phone,' said Chard. 'It looks like the same one to me, but what's the point in arguing details with Theo?'

'Quite,' I said, looking down at the wretched piece of paper. 'But tell me one thing: did she ask you to give me this – or are you doing it off your own bat?'

'Don't ask me that,' said Chard.

'Come on,' I replied. 'I need to know how bad it is.'

Chard looked at me steadily for a moment – well, I think that was what he was doing, it was hard to tell through the mirrored shades and the pall of smoke – before he answered.

'OK,' he said, heavily. 'She gave me the new details and I asked her if she had given them to you and she said, no. So I told her I was going to give it to you and she didn't object.'

'She didn't object?' I repeated. 'So I imagine she used the word "whatever". Am I right?'

'Something like that,' said Chard. 'She held her fingers up in a W shape . . .'

'Oh, well, at least she's allowed me to have the bloody number,' I said, my treacherous eyes flooding again. 'But as she won't reply to any of the messages or texts I will leave on it, perhaps you can tell me how's she doing?'

'She's doing well, Loobie Lou,' he said quietly, the head starting to nod. 'She'll come round to you again, I'm sure of it. She certainly seems a lot happier than she was. Not so snarky all the time. A lot more laughter. More like she used to be. Girlish *joie de vivre* and all that.'

'Must be getting away from me,' I said bitterly and then I couldn't hold back the tears any more. They weren't the painful hacking kind, but the really sad ones that just trickle unstoppably down your cheeks.

'Oh, baby girl,' said Chard, in such a caring tone, it just made me cry more.

He lumbered to his feet and came over, crouching by my chair and putting both his arms around me in a tight hold. It was a surprisingly physical gesture from Chard and I was very touched by it, as I soaked his chambray shoulder with my tears. Behind the fag ash he smelled of vetiver. It was rather a pleasant mixture. Even in my misery I registered that this was probably the closest I'd ever been to him physically in all our years of friendship, apart from dancing, and it felt like a very comforting place to be.

'I don't know how much more of this I can take, Chard,' I said, resting the weight of my forehead against him, while he stroked my head. 'It's nearly two weeks since she moved in with you and I really thought she would be ready to make up with me by now. But nothing. I just don't know what to do.'

'Well, you might have been sending the texts to the lost phone,' he said, with undeniable logic, pulling back and wiping my face dry with the cuff of his shirt. 'Oops, I've made it a bit smeary with the make-up there. I better leave that to you. Specialist stuff.'

He patted me on the shoulder and after a quick look over the top of his shades to make sure I wasn't crying anymore, he kissed me on the top of the head and went back to his side of the table, immediately firing up another Camel. I didn't tell him he already had one burning in the ashtray. The ritual of tapping the end of the fresh gasper and firing up the flame-thrower Zippo was a big part of Chard's smoking enjoyment. I was determined to raise the subject of cutting down with him, but this wasn't the moment.

'I really don't think she's happier because she's away from you, Loubie,' he said, blowing out a plume of smoke and stretching his long guitarist's arms behind his head.

'I think it's more that she's away from herself. She had painted herself into a corner with you, a downward spiral of bad behaviour and then guilt, which made her feel bad, and that would make her lash out and behave badly again. Guilt is the killer. People turn it back on the person they feel guilty about and make them into the baddie, so it was OK to do them wrong in the first place. But deep down inside they always know it's really them. Toxic stuff.'

He took another big drag on the ciggie, before continuing.

'So I think perhaps staying with me has given Theo a break from feeling she's a crap person. She's so great with my parents and I think that's making her feel better about herself. They absolutely adore her, so she's getting lots of positive feedback – and good behaviour breeds good behaviour, just as guilt breeds bad.'

I leaned forward and stubbed out the forgotten cigarette, considering what he'd said. There was a lot of wisdom in it, quite a staggering amount really, so much I needed to chew it over in my head for a bit.

I picked up the teapot and waved it at Chard.

'I'm going to be put some fresh hot water in this,' I said, knowing he wouldn't notice it was still half full.

I leaned on the shop's kitchen counter as the kettle boiled, taking quick breaths and blowing them out noisily through my nose as my yoga teacher had taught me. She said it got stale energy out of your body, and that seemed like something I badly needed to do. Not to mention Chard's bloody smoke.

As I did it, I thought through what he'd said about Theo being stuck in a downward spiral of bad behaviour. He was spot on. It had first started to get really bad when she'd suddenly arrived back from Manchester. Since then – apart from the brief happy spell when we were doing the website together – Theo and I had been stuck in some kind of stalemate where we were just existing together in a state of tension from one big row to the next. Maybe this separation would break the pattern and we really could have a fresh start.

For a moment my spirits rose, but then, as I poured the boiling water over the mint leaves I remembered the additional complication that I just didn't feel able to tell Chard about. Which was that I was now dealing with a big old load of guilt myself. Guilt about my increasingly confusing feelings for Marc Thorssen.

This latest upset about Theo brought it all flooding back into my mind, like a nausea-inducing theme park ride I couldn't get off. For a moment, standing frozen in the kitchen with the full teapot in my hand, I wondered if I should confide in Chard about it. Surely – given his own preference for inter-generational romance – he would understand?

But in a way that made him exactly the wrong person to discuss it with. He'd already made it clear he didn't see anything wrong with a flirtation between me and Marc and he'd probably just tell me to go for it. Not helpful.

Even apart from that I didn't feel comfortable with the idea of talking it over with him. Although he talked about his girly conquests in general terms – mostly to amuse me with his self-deprecating humour – he never went into detail and I'd certainly never discussed any of my sexual liaisons with him. It seemed to go outside the boundaries of our friendship somehow, so when I went back out to re-join him on the terrace, I'd already decided to say nothing.

But when he left, after another half hour of blessedly general chat, I was still feeling all jangled up and jumpy about Marc. With the genie out of the bottle again, I had to talk to somebody about it, but who? Keith would enjoy the gossipy scandal aspect of it far too much to give me any sensible advice – and would also be completely overexcited at the prospect of hearing about what such a beautiful young specimen looked like naked.

'Lools,' he'd enthuse, 'you've got to root him, because I can't . . .'

So who else? Shelley would probably have some interesting insights into it, but it would compromise the boss/employee balance way too much for me to be pouring out the details of my sordid – and not forgetting, theoretical – love life to her.

Rachel and Lauren would get every complicated angle of the age aspect, but they were too close to the whole scene for comfort. Also I didn't know whether Lauren had the kind of marriage where she told her husband everything – and I couldn't risk giving horrid Paul Beaney that satisfaction.

Then, as I cleared up the tea glasses and Chard's ashtray – which he'd nicked from the Paris Ritz and given to me years before – inspiration struck. My sister. She was always the one I could trust to be fully interested and totally honest. Telling Shelley I had to sort something out in the private showroom, I ran upstairs to call her.

'About bloody time,' she said. 'So how did it go then?'

'What?' I said stupidly.

'Your matchmaking party! It was nearly two weeks ago and you never rang to tell us about it. I texted you and you never got back to me. I'm gagging to hear how it went.'

'Oh, Jane,' I said, my vowels flattening like they had been run over by a Boddington's beer truck. 'I'm so sorry. I should have rung you sooner, but it's all been really mad here. The party went brilliantly, thanks. It was a great night apart from anything else and we had a really good crowd of lovely young ones. It was ace. Thanks to you.'

'Oh, that's grand,' said Jane. 'But what about Theo? Did she meet anyone?'

My heart sank. I didn't know where to start with it all, but I had rung my sister up to confide, so I did.

'No,' I said, flatly. 'Theo didn't meet anyone, in fact she hated the party and left early. She's furious with me. Not speaking, the whole catastrophe. That's why I'm ringing actually. I need to talk to someone about it.'

'Talk to me,' said Jane.

'Well, Theo didn't meet somebody at the party – but I did.'

'That's great!' she said. 'We've had a few of those too, with our group, the older ones meeting up as well, it's a whole other angle on it. Go on, then, who is he?'

'He's the twenty-four-year-old brother of Theo's best friend,' I said.

For a moment she was silent. Then she roared with laughter.

'You dirty bugger,' she said. 'Is he gorgeous?'

'Drop-dead gorgeous,' I said, feeling slightly hysterical.

'Have you, you know, done him?'

'No,' I said, outraged.

'Why the hell not?' said Jane.

'Are you serious?' I said.

'Why wouldn't I be? Are you single? Yes. Is he single? Presumably. Are you both heterosexual? Yes. Have you taken a vow of chastity? Not as far as I know, although sometimes I wonder. So what's the bloody problem?'

'Like I said, he's Theo's best friend's brother. I'm old enough to be his grandmother, Jane. Nearly.'

'So what? None of that matters any more – you've seen *Sex and the City* . . .'

'Yes, and Demi Moore and Vivienne Westwood,' I said, my voice tightening with a kind of panic. This was not the reaction I had been expecting from her. 'But don't you think it's a bit tacky?'

'No. I'm dead jealous.' She laughed again.

'But Theo hates it, that's why we've fallen out. She's living with Chard . . .'

'Oh, that girl,' said Jane crossly. 'She just doesn't want you to be happy. Does she fancy him, is that the problem?'

'No – she hates him actually.'

'Hmm,' said Jane. 'Well that might mean she secretly fancies him. Like punching the boy you like in the playground at infants school, remember? It could be that.'

I considered what she was saying for a moment.

'I really don't think that's it, Jane. She only saw us dancing together and she completely freaked out . . .'

'What was the track?'

'The Bee Gees . . .'

'Ooh, how lovely. Which one?'

'Yeah,' I agreed, sighing at the memory. 'It was lovely. *More Than a Woman* . . .'

'Oh, that's my favourite.' She hummed a few bars. 'Is he a good dancer, then?'

'An absolute dream,' I said, with all sincerity, my stomach turning over at the memory.

'So what are you waiting for, chuck? Great dancers don't come along very often – and you know what it means . . .'

More raucous laughter. I put my head in my hands. This wasn't helping at all. I was more confused than ever.

'Anyway,' I said, trying to snap out of it. 'That's enough about all that. I'll get over it. Tell me, what's going on with you?'

'Well,' she said, sounding excited. 'I was going to call you today actually, because I've got some really exciting news.'

She paused for a moment and then squealed. 'Our Becky's getting engaged! We're having the party next month. My baby is going to be a bride!'

'Oh, Jane, I'm so happy. That is the most wonderful news. Who's the bloke? Is it the engineer you told me about?'

'No,' she said. 'He's a, er, ceramicist. Very talented.'

She said it with a determined enthusiasm I could tell she had been working on.

'Oh, that sounds more interesting,' I said, with all sincerity. 'So did she meet him at your last matchmaking party?'

She started to laugh again. Her deepest chesty chuckle.

'No,' she said. 'She met him in a bar in Leeds . . .'

Theo

I'm happy. H-A-P-P-Y. Me! I'm never happy but now I am. Pray why? Because I'm having an interesting time. I'm doing stuff. I'm hanging out with people who do stuff and I'm helping them do it. And they like me.

And I like it.

I was a bit nervous meeting the West Wind design team and under all the fake friendliness they did seem a bit suspicious of me – who is this KID he's brought in now? kind of thing. They are clearly all totally terrified of Weeny Beaney and if he'd said I was the Tooth Fairy they would all have nodded and smiled at me.

So he introduced me and said I was doing an 'internship' – which is not what the HR lady told me but tever – and that I had some 'interesting contributions' to make as a bang-on West Wind customer with a 'truly fresh eye' on retail.

Then another new thing happened: I shut the fuck up. I just listened to what they had to say about 'second autumn winter' – as they all wankily called it – and then only when Paul asked me did I make my comments. And I said it quite tactfully. For me.

Of course I was thinking that the 'knitwear offer' (ie JUMPERS and CARDIES) looked like it was made from geriatric dog's pubes but I didn't say that. I just said I thought they could be bolder and perhaps look at some old pictures of Princess Di wearing jumpers with sheep on them. But make the sheep two-headed mutants with scary crystal eyes and stuff like that.

And then I got out the pictures of her I had ripped off the internet and photoshopped to show what I meant and they all went Oooo! Then I showed them I had shoulder pads sewn into my T-shirt and they all went Ooo Ooo Oooooo!

I wonged the shoulder pads out of Mudda's workroom ages ago. She used to have them taken out to make the heinous 80s cack slightly less vomitous and there was a big bag that the seamstress had brought back so I snuck a few. Knew they'd be useful one day. She leaves them in the 80s crud now.

Anyway then they all started going on about how I wasn't carrying a handbag and I said 'Bags are for wimps' and Paul looked at me and grinned.

Then I told them my whole theory about pockets and about how women are going to be so over bags in about 10 seconds time and we want pockets in everything like men have. And Paul said 'bags are for wimps' could be a great slogan because it was anti selling. Whatever the fuck that means but everyone was smiling so hard it was like a dentures convention.

So that was good but it got better. On Wednesday we all went up to Manchester together on a 'market research' mission. It was absolutely brilliant. There was me and Paul plus three design bods and two from marketing and they were all the most excellent laugh.

We went up on the train first class and stayed at a really nice hotel. And of course because it was Manchester I totally knew my way around and was able to show them all the cool places. We had a really hilarious dinner in this mad old Chinese place all the art students go to which used to be me gag spew. Luckily they have fucked off for the summer or I wouldn't have gone near the place. Bad memories of hateful course I never should have been on.

Being back in Madchester made me think about all that which I mostly block out. Bloody Mudda signed me up for a course I have no interest in and was then surprised I chucked it in. And ever since she's acted like I did something wrong. Uh?

First she assumed I wanted to be a wanky fashion designer, when I despise pretentious gits who go to St Martins and think fashion is 'art'. Fashion is clothes. I love clothes. I hate fashion. She's never been able to understand that. And she's never bothered to try. So when I said big fat no to that the next thing is I'm up in Manchester doing illustration because she says so. Whatthefuck? Illustration? Peter Rabbit? No thanks.

It's not that I don't like Manchester. Of course I like it – but why would I want to go to college somewhere I've known all my life? The whole point is to go somewhere new isn't it? Glasgow would have been good but I didn't get a say in it. Oh look Theo, isn't it wonderful you've got into Manchester! Frankly no.

OK maybe I didn't make much of an effort to apply anywhere else so that's why she did it all but it was still wrong and that's why I quit. And that's why I'm furious that she still seems to think I messed up when it was all her fault.

Well actually all that's not the only reason. There's another one I keep locked inside my head. In a nuclear proof safe. Which was that a bunch of lower life forms – posing as female students – ganged up against me there. They said I'd only got on the course because my mum pulled strings and called me Miss Primrose Hill and The London Snob.

I knew at least one of them was from Essex so I told them to get fucked back to Bluewater or whatever pond they came from and then they spread a rumour on Facebook that I was shagging the head of the illustration department.

And being illustration students they illustrated it with pictures of me. Photoshopped on to a picture of him. Photoshopped on to some hideous porno shot. So it looked like I was fucking him. And I mean really looked like it. Even I did a double take when I saw it.

And there was the morning I had to go round the whole art college taking that picture off every noticeboard where it had been put up. Poster size. Which was the same day the Dept Head called me into his office. I thought to be nice. But actually it was to make that picture happen in real life. Which was also the day I headed over to Manchester Piccadilly Station and took the next train back to London and the first available taxi to Regent's Park Road.

I never told Mudda or anyone about that. Not even Tattie knows. It was so horrible I just want to forget it forever and so when Weaney first said it was Manchester we were going to on this mission I nearly said forget it. Then I thought NO I'm bloody going and on my terms and I'm going to claim back my share of that city. Fooking right.

So there I was back in Manchester and able to enjoy it because I was there doing stuff I like. That I've chosen. And that she doesn't know about. The last thing I want is her saying Oh how marvellous you're working in FASHION I must call my best friend Wankface at wherever and interfere with it all and take over. No thanks. This is my thing.

So after twenty-five courses of Chinese the others all wanted to go out clubbing. I told them where was good but I didn't want to go because I hate clubs and Weanie said he's too old for all that so instead I took him on a walking tour. I showed him all the old buildings I love and we ended up in this brilliantly rubbish pub near Old Trafford drinking pints of Boddies. He's a good laugh for an old git.

Weanie asked me if I had noticed that none of the West Wind women had brought handbags on the trip with them. I had of course but made like I hadn't.

Me: Oh really? Is that right?

Weanie: You bloody well know it is you little minx. It shows I was right about you. You're an influencer. Other people follow you. Even older women. Do you know what that's worth?

Me: You tell me. You're the one who gives a shit about money. And while we're on the subject give me some for the jukebox.

When I came back – I put on the Stone Roses to celebrate

reclaiming my second home city – he did ask me one slightly odd question.

Weanie: Does your mother know you are up here with us?

Me: Of course not.

Weanie: Why 'of course'?

Me: Because I don't like her knowing what I do. This is my thing. I don't want her sticking her oar in and giving me 'expert' fashion advice from her centuries in the 'business'.

Weanie: Good. Let's keep it that way.

Me: Why do you care?

Weanie: I'm a Scorpio. I like secrets.

Me: Oh, for fuck's sake. Up until ten seconds ago I thought you were quite sensible. Just don't ask me what sign I am.

Weanie: What sign are you?

Me: No Entry.

He thought that was pretty funny and said perhaps he was actually 'One Way'. His way. Ha ha ha. I'm a Scorpio as well of course but no way I was going to tell him that. It's my rising sign too. Load of cobblers but interesting that we do seem to see things the same way. Oooooh spooky.

There was only one dodgy moment on the whole trip. I was coming out of the Selfridges up there with two of the design blokes who are my favourites and my Auntie Jane came right around the corner. Smack into us. Couldn't avoid her.

Shit. I just so don't want Mudda to know what I'm doing. Like I said it's my thing and it's private and I don't want her sticking her nose in and using words like 'merch'. So I introduced Ajay and Tony and said they were friends of mine and I was just showing them around Manchester as we were passing through.

They were really good about not saying anything. I pinched them both quite hard on the backs of their arms and they got the message. We had a good old laugh about it later but at the time Auntie Jane looked just like Mudda. All wounded and tragic. Gaaaaaa.

'Why didn't you ring us?' she said whole doggie in the window eyes thing going on. Makes me glad I've got Knobhead's eyes. 'Don't you want to come and see everyone? Becky's just got engaged – she'd love to see you.'

Me: 'Sorry Auntie Jane I didn't know I was coming until we got here. It was all spur of the moment and we're going back to London right now. In fact we're going to miss the coach if we don't get a spurt on. That's great about Becky. Give her my love. Give everyone my love . . .'

And then I legged it practically dragging the guys with me. They were cool.

So that was one small low point. The other more recent one was Deathbreath this morning. He knocked on my bedroom door – which he never does – and said he needed to talk to me.

I said I'd meet him in the kitchen thinking I would have Strav for cover but when I got down there Strav was nowhere and ODD not in sight either. When DB shut the kitchen door I knew it was serious.

He lit up one of his vile ciggies and looked at me like a snake charmer all narrow eyes and nodding blowing smoke all over the place. Put me right off my latte.

Me: Wassup Deathbreath?

DB: Do you like living here Theo?

Uh-oo I thought. That's no good. He called me Theo. He always calls me Baby or Angel or Honeychild and other folkloric 1970s names. It was going to be bad.

Me: Sure. I love it. You're the bomb.

Thought he would appreciate a bit of 21st century young person lingo.

DB: Well you can stick around a bit longer but there are some conditions.

Me: Which are . . .?

DB: Next weekend we are all going to the Big Chill and you are coming. No arguments.

I squirmed in my seat. Nooooooooooooooooooooo. I couldn't think of anything to say that wasn't an argument so I put my fist in my mouth. I could see he was trying not to laugh.

DB: That's good baby girl. Keep it there and listen up. At the Big Chill we are celebrating your mum's birthday. This is non-negotiable and you will be taking part. With grace.

Me: [strangulation noises]

DB: Hang on in there nearly finished. So everyone can have a good time at the festival – especially Loulou – you have to end this ridiculous stand-off with her. You started it so you have to make the first move to reconciliation.

Me [spluttering like exploding coffee machine]: I STARTED IT? SHE BLOODY STARTED IT! She's the one who was banging a bloke young enough to be her grandson in public! My best friend's brother – it was like incest. Vileness. All I did was be publicly humiliated! How do you get I started it out of that?

DB [takes dramatic drag on cigarette ends up having coughing fit sounds like Chernobyl going up face as red as Man U home strip]: Stop it Theo. I won't have it! This is my house. My rules. If you want to stay – start playing by them. Your call.

Me [silent as have never seen Deathbreath this cross before and scared he might drop dead at any moment].

DB [still coughing and cross but no longer red in face]: It's simple Theo. If you want to carry on living here – go and see your mother today. Say you're sorry. Make it up with her and explain that you just want to stay here a little longer to get your head together. Today. Got it?

Me: Traitor.

DB [coolly and calmly more like normal but a bit terrifyingly serious for him]: Listen Babycakes. Don't call me a traitor I'm trying to help you here. I know what's at stake. You've only got one mother – one parent, to all intents and purposes – and you don't want to fall out with her you really don't. I know what I'm talking about. When I was your age I was a total arsehole to my parents. I was just like you. A spoiled little shit who was cross with everything. Christ only knows what makes us like that. Born with all the advantages and we come out kicking and screaming but we do seem to be similar in that way. I think it's some kind of creative hang-up makes us oversensitive to life and we lash out – or maybe we're just little shits – but either way I don't want to see you waste the time I did being horrible to the people I love the most. My folks.

Me: Uh? But you're amazing to your parents. They live with you. You have breakfast with them every day. You give your dad baths. You're a rock star. You don't have to do all that but you do.

DB [shaking head probably for wider dissemination of toxic smoke]: Why do you think I'm good to them now? Because I was horribly bad to them when I was young and I so regret it. When my brother died I didn't even go to the funeral. I was on tour and way too self-important to come home for that. The big rock star. The big a-hole.

Me: Your brother? You have a brother?

DB: I *had* a brother. Wonderboy. He died. Car smash. I was so jealous of him I couldn't forgive him. He even got that over on me. I was furious he died before me and got all the attention. Like I say I was a shit. But I've learned not to be one. It took me a long time and I don't want to see you go through all that. It's just a waste of everything. It doesn't help.

Me: What was his name?

DB: David. He was older than me. His picture is by my mum's bed. In school uniform.

Me: In the cap? I thought that was you.

DB: Yeah? Well it's poor dead Dave. So that's the story. You need to make it up to your mum. And if you want to live here you need to do it today. Meeting over.

And that was it. He kissed me on the top of my head that way he does and shambled off. And I do want to carry on living here so I will have to go and see Mudda. Gfkahgkasdhfkdhflksdhfklasdhfklsdhf.

Sad about his brother though. Poor Nancy. That's really horrible. And I have heard her raving on about someone called David. I thought it was a boyfriend who had got killed in the war and it was actually her son. Shit.

I'll go up there in a minute and give her a foot massage and think about this new pile of poop I've got to deal with.

One hour later: Nancy's having a nice nap after her massage. I read her a saucy bit from *Polo* too. She loves it.

While I was working on Nancy's gnarled old toes I thought over DB's conditions and reckon it's worth it to stay here. I love living here.

And if there is any chance of Rob the Knob making a live appearance in my life I would rather have Mudda on side. Tho I'm hoping now he doesn't have my phone number or email address and I wouldn't accept him as a friend on Facebook or a contact on LinkedIn and blocked him on Twitter he might put his plans on hold.

Must also admit thinking about him – the vileness – does make me less angry with her even if she did puke me out beyond belief frotting off with Captain Chino that night.

At least I haven't had to endure any more surprise calls from him since I changed my phone number. That was such a good move but I feel a bit bad not giving the new one to Tattie though. I really ought to ring her and see how her degree show went but I don't want to risk her giving the number to her cringesome brother again.

It's not Tattie's fault her brudda did that embarrassing thing with Mudda but that – combined with her having that big love action going on – is making me feel suffocated. I need a breather from that whole scene. Very Scorpio of me ha ha ha. Ha ha.

But I'll have to see them all at the Big Chill next week aaaaaaagggggh. NEXT WEEK. Don'tthinkaboutit don'tthinkaboutit.

Looking on el bright side: One good thing about being forced to go round to Muddaville is I can pick up some more of my stuff while

I'm there. I need some of my key accessories as the final touches to my new stylee. I'm going on another market research mission with my West Wind buddies on Tuesday. To Milan.

Happy Theo. Ciao baby.

20

Loulou

When Theo walked into the shop on Saturday morning I had a fairly good idea Chard had put her up to it. For one thing he didn't come by for his own visit – which was very unusual as Saturday was the prime hot chick meat market in Loulou Land. He very rarely missed one, especially in nice weather. Maximum firm young skin on display.

I also wasn't entirely convinced by her rushed declaration that she was sorry she had been so mean and wanted to make up with me, either. It didn't quite ring true, but I was so pleased to see her I didn't care if Chard had sent her round at gunpoint. I had my baby back in body, if not entirely in spirit, and that was something.

The shop was absolutely packed, so I asked Shelley to do her best while I went upstairs with Theo. I just needed to be with my daughter. To talk to her and to look at her. I was biased, of course, but I did think she was looking particularly amazing.

She'd dyed her hair – usually a mix of dirty blonde and highlights – very dark brown, just the right side of black, and it really suited her. Her father and I were both dark, so Theo's lighter hair had always seemed like some kind of weird genetic anomaly and now she looked more herself somehow. I loved how she was dressed too, it was a lot less trashy than before.

She had on a pair of wide grey slubby linen pants with pleats at the waist and turn-ups, worn with loafers and a boat-neck Breton-style T-shirt tucked in and belted. Her hair was up in a big messy French pleat, with a wide black jersey headband around the hairline. And she was wearing no jewellery apart from a man's watch. As I'd known her to wear earrings, necklace and bangles – and belt – in matching pink fluoro plastic, 'less is more' was a big improvement.

'You look wonderful, darling,' I said, as we settled at the kitchen table. 'Very chic.'

'Thanks,' she said.

'So,' I started, pouring iced tea for both of us, but before I could say anything more she interrupted me.

'Isn't there any Diet Coke?' she said, looking at the glass of tea as though it were a pot of stale urine.

Some things don't change, I thought.

'It's in the fridge,' I replied in as even a tone as possible, determined not to get riled and slip back into our old ways. 'Help yourself.'

I had to stop myself tapping my nails on the kitchen table as she busied about getting a glass and ice and a slice of bloody lemon – her preferred lime not being available; she did ask. I just didn't feel up to making light conversation as she meticulously constructed her drink. I needed her opposite me. I wanted to look deep into those conker-brown eyes to see how she really was and I also had some curly questions to ask her. It all had to be treated with great delicacy and I hadn't had any warning she was coming, so I'd have to busk it.

'Are you going to sit down any time soon, Theo?' I asked, in what I hoped was a cheerful, teasing way, as she started banging cupboard doors.

'Mmm,' she said. 'I was just looking to see if you had any Cheddars, or has Keith been over recently?'

'I think there's some in the cupboard with the pasta,' I said, ignoring her slightly barbed remark.

She finally sat down opposite me, plonking a bowl of crisps down between us.

'Found these instead,' she said, pushing a handful into her mouth. 'Yum. Salt and vinegar, my favourite.'

'So how are you, darling?' I asked, scrutinising her face. She still wasn't making eye contact.

'I'm good,' she said, smiling, with her eyes resting on mine for the merest instant, before going back to the crisps. 'Really good. It's fun round at Chard's. You should come over.'

'He tells me you're a great help with his parents. That's lovely.'

'They're brilliant, I love them,' she said, sounding sincere. 'Nancy is hilarious and I play cards all the time with Old Daddy Deathbreath. Rummy mostly. I'm up £7.40 at the moment.'

'You play cards with who?'

'Oh, you know, the Air Marshal, Deathbreath's dad . . .'

'Deathbreath?'

She had the grace to look a bit sheepish.

'Chard,' she said. 'It's my new name for him. The cigarettes make his breath stink.'

I had to laugh, but still it seemed a bit harsh.

'Does he know you call him that? I asked.

'Yeah, it kinda slipped out . . .'

'Doesn't he mind?'

'He seems to think it's funny.'

I shook my head indulgently. If I hadn't seen him be firm with her, I'd think she had one over on Chard to an unhealthy degree, but on balance I'd decided they were pretty evenly matched. He knew when to be tough with her – and was able to do it without the onslaught of conflicting emotions which made me so useless when I tried it.

'So what else have you been up to?' I asked, still forcing myself to keep my tone bright and casual.

'Oh,' she shrugged. 'You know. This and that. The usual.'

'Well, what is that exactly, Theo?' I asked, but quickly pulled myself up before I sounded too testy. I couldn't blow this. 'Have you seen Tattie? How did her degree show go?'

'I haven't been in touch with her much recently. She's got a big deal boyfriend scene going on and I'm happy for her, but I didn't want to be the inadequately depilated fruit, you know?'

'That's great news,' I said cheerfully. 'About the boyfriend. I'm delighted to hear Tattie has a chap at last. Where did she meet him?'

Even as I said it, I could have bitten off my own tongue and swallowed it. Theo's face told me the answer. She'd met him at the party. *That* party. Oh well, there wasn't any point trying to keep up my cheery chit-chat mode any more, I might as well get stuck into it. I sighed deeply and launched in.

'I take it from your expression that she met him at the party where I danced with her brother . . . Am I right?'

'Something like that,' said Theo, finally looking me straight in the eye, chewing slightly manically on a mouthful of crisps.

'Look,' I said, my heart starting to beat faster with something approaching panic. 'I know you were upset with me for dancing with Marc that night, but can we please leave that behind now? It was just something that happened. I like to dance, he likes to dance, we happened to be next to each other on the dance floor and it happened . . . and then Chard deliberately played soppy songs to make us carry on dancing in that style, because he thought it was fun and it *was* fun. So can we move on? Forget it happened?'

'OK,' said Theo, clearly as keen as I was not to talk about it any more. 'I'm sorry I reacted so badly, Mum. It just freaked me out. I'm sorry. It was just weird, OK?'

And as I looked at her, something very like tears seemed to fill her eyes and I saw her as the vulnerable little thing she really was under all that cheek and bluster.

'Oh Theo,' I said and rushed round the table to put my arms round her. For once she didn't shake me off. She hugged me back.

'I'm sorry, Mum,' she said. 'I was too hard on you, but it freaked me out. I'm not used to seeing you cosying up with men – apart from Chard and Keith and they don't count – and it was weirder because it was Tattie's brother and I really hated that party anyway. So I'm sorry, please forgive me.'

I held her face, so loved, so familiar, in my hands and looked deep into her eyes. She meant it. I could tell. I kissed her forehead and after squeezing her hands one more time, went back to my seat.

'All over,' I said, mentally reminding myself it was, in every way. 'Let's move on, but I do have something else to ask you about . . .'

'What?' said Theo, wariness creeping back into her face.

'Your Auntie Jane rang me last week,' I started.

'Yeah,' said Theo, interrupting me before I could say any more. 'I know. I saw her in Manchester. I bumped into her.'

'That's what she said, but what were you doing there? And why didn't you tell her you were going up?'

'Oh, it all just happened on the spur of the moment, some friends were going and they asked me to go with them because I know my way round and – well, I wasn't speaking to you at the time, remember? So I didn't feel like speaking to Auntie Jane either . . .'

She had the grace to look a little ashamed.

'Fair enough,' I said. 'But if you could give her a ring sometime soon, I would really appreciate it. She is your auntie and she loves you dearly. You hurt her feelings. And you've got a good excuse to ring – your cousin Becky just got engaged.'

'Yes, she mentioned that . . .'

'Well, you don't sound very excited. She's the first of your generation – it's a big deal to us. Jane's having a party to celebrate. She'd love us both to go up for it. Any chance you might come?'

A horrified look crossed Theo's face. Another party – and with family. Clearly her idea of a total nightmare, but to her credit, she forced herself to look more positive.

'OK,' she said nodding, in a way that reminded me of Chard; she must have picked it up living there. 'I'll come. Providing I haven't already got anything on that night, of course, but in theory I'll come.'

She'd built in a let-out clause, of course, but I was impressed that she'd even agreed to come in principle. Whatever Chard was doing over at his place, it seemed to be working. I needed to do my bit too.

'I promise I won't dance with anyone younger than I am, OK?' I said.

She laughed.

'And I promise not to lock myself in the loo, or storm out,' she said

I squeezed her hand across the table, delighted we seemed to have reached an understanding. But before I could relax too much, she had another bombshell to drop.

'Well, it's been great seeing you, Mum,' she said, draining her Diet Coke. 'I'm glad we've sorted things out, but it looks like you're pretty busy in the shop and I've got a lot to do today too, so I'd better be off. I'm just going to get some stuff from my room and I'll see you on the way out.'

She stood up, took her glass over to the sink and rinsed it out.

'What do you mean, get some stuff?' I asked as she turned to walk out of the kitchen.

'From my room,' she said. 'There's some bits and pieces I need to take back to Chard's.'

I just stared at her.

'Do you mean you're not moving back here?'

She looked surprised.

'I'm staying at Chard's . . .' she said, as though it was obvious. 'I will keep in touch with you now, I'll come round and see you, but I'm staying there for the time being. He needs me, Mum.'

And I don't? I thought, looking at her with what I knew was an expression of deep hurt on my face. I couldn't help it. I'd assumed that now we'd patched things up, she'd be coming home, and she wasn't. Body blow.

I took a breath and forced myself to deal with it then and there. I had wanted her to leave home, after all. It was about time. I'd just expected it to be a bit further away and with people of her own age. Not with my pal round the corner.

'OK, darling,' I made myself say. 'I understand. But whenever you do want to move back here, you know you can. It will always be your home.'

She smiled at me, clearly relieved I wasn't going to make another scene, and came round the table to give me a big hug.

'Love you, Mudda,' she said and then she was gone.

Mudda? I thought. What was that supposed to be? My version of Deathbreath presumably. The lovingly insulting nickname.

Oh well, that was my Theo. Always a bit of grit in the oyster. I just wondered when the pearl would start to form.

After that confusing morning, I was happy to immerse myself in the busy shop again – although it did cross my mind that having commented on how frantic we were, it would have been nice if Theo had offered to help out. Oh well. I couldn't expect everything to be perfect overnight. It was a big step forward that she was even speaking to me.

But what was that she'd said about having a lot to do herself that morning? Like what? Paint Chard's mother's nails? Play cards with his dad? Make coffee with the housekeeper?

She was such a funny girl the way she liked to be so cloak and dagger about things. Perhaps if I told her how much she reminded me of her father in that way, she'd start to be a bit more open about her activities, I thought, taking over from Shelley at the till so she could go and pin up a dress which needed shortening for a customer.

Especially if she knew that his Man of Enigma act turned out to be largely a cover for all the affairs he was having and the plans he was making to move halfway around the world without taking us with him.

I was looking at the list of what had sold that morning and it made pleasant reading, but at the same time I was cringing all over as I remembered how, when I'd first met Rob, I'd thought it so dashing and romantic the way he would mysteriously come and go like some kind of dandy highwayman. It wasn't so fabulous once we had a baby, but I just used to tell myself that was the way he was. What an idiot I'd been.

Of course, before the days of mobile phones – and even answering machines – it was easier for someone to live like that. But I had felt such a fool when I found out what he'd really been up to. Keeping up several relationships at one time spreads a guy pretty thin.

Luckily the shop was too busy for me to be able to wallow in such pointless and negative reveries for long and I threw myself into the Saturday whirl with pleasure. As my head snapped round on reflex to smile at a new customer for about the nine hundredth time, I was delighted to see it was Tatiana, accompanied by a strapping young chap I assumed was the new boyfriend.

'Tattie!' I said, genuinely delighted to see her. I rushed out from behind the counter to give her a hug.

'Hi, Loulou,' she said.

'How lovely to see you,' I said. 'I was just asking Theo how you were . . . And who is this you have with you?'

'Oh, Oscar, come and meet Loulou. Loulou – this is Oscar.'

'Hi, Oscar,' I said, shaking the large paw that was held out to me. He looked like a nice bloke. Ruddy cheeks, broad shoulders, good firm handshake, a rugby sort of a fellow. Not drop-dead handsome, but a very healthy young specimen, the kind any mother would be delighted to meet. I, in particular, would have been ecstatic, but that was another story.

'How do you do?' said Oscar, with perfect vowels I was sure Tattie's mother would approve of. Provided he wasn't from a family of penniless aristos. She'd have no truck with that crew.

'So, are you looking for anything in particular, Tattie? Ooh I nearly forgot – how did your degree presentation go?'

'It went really well, thanks. Loulou. And that's why I'm here, really – I'm looking for Theo. She hasn't answered any of my texts or emails for ages and I was quite worried about her. Is she OK? I want to tell her about my degree – and I need to thank her . . .'

'Oh,' I said. 'You too, huh? Oh dear. I'm afraid Theo's had one of her little turns. A particularly bad one, actually. Until this morning she wasn't even talking to me. She's staying with her godfather at the moment – you know, Ritchie? And she's changed her mobile number and email address and not told anyone, but I have the new ones. I'll give them to you.'

I scribbled them down and just as I was about to hand the piece of paper to her, I hesitated.

'Or you could just pop over and see her,' I added. 'Ritchie only lives round the corner in Chalcot Square. I'll put the address on here. Just turn left out of the gate here, then take the first turning on the left and walk along to the square. It's two minutes away.'

Tattie took the piece of paper I'd scribbled the address on and put it in her bag. She was such a lovely girl, I thought. Naughty naughty Theo for freezing her out too. It wasn't Tattie's fault her brother had danced with me.

'Great,' she said. 'We'll do that, if you think Ritchie wouldn't mind . . .'

'He'd be delighted,' I said. 'But before you go, Tattie, tell me about your degree – what did you get?'

'I got a 2:1,' she said, beaming. 'Which was much better than I was expecting – and it's all thanks to Theo, because I got a first for my practical project, which was creating my own magazine, and Theo helped me so much with that. Without her I might have failed. I was so stuck and she made it so easy for me.'

I hugged her. I was ecstatic Theo had done something useful with her time. If this was the kind of thing she got up to when she was off on her mystery projects – helping friends with their degrees and godfathers with elderly parents – I was more than delighted. If still at a loss as to why she couldn't tell me about it.

But at the same time, it cut me like a knife that she could help a friend get a first for a project, but had never finished a degree herself. Why was she determined to throw her talent away?

'I'm thrilled for you, Tattie,' I said and meant it. 'And your mum must be so pleased with you. I'd like you to choose something from the shop as a graduation present from me and Theo. Have a look round, see what you fancy.'

Her dear face lit up.

'Thank you, Loulou!' she said. 'That would be amazing. Are you sure?'

'Of course I'm sure,' I said. 'I remember you from your first day at school, so your degree is a big deal for all of us. Go and have a look at the rails and if you need any help just ask me or Shelley.'

She glanced at Oscar, clearly wanting to make sure he didn't mind hanging around while she tried on clothes. It was too early in the relationship to be making assumptions like that.

'Can I get you some tea or coffee, Oscar?' I said. 'I've got the Saturday papers here, so you can sit outside with them, if you want to, and I'll come and get you when Tatiana is ready to show you something.'

Tattie gave me a grin which told me I'd called the situation right, and Oscar shuffled contentedly outside with the *Telegraph* sports section. Then she spent a happy half hour or so trying on dresses, but was so self-conscious about her ample rear end, we couldn't convince her she looked nice in anything. It was such a shame.

She might not have had a model figure, like Theo did, but she had a lovely face, that amazing thick auburn hair, and the generally glowing gorgeousness of youth, enhanced all the more by the attentions of the young man sitting outside. Shelley always said she could tell who was getting lots of sex by the bloom of their skin, which made me glad I never revealed very much of mine. Working on that theory it would be like dried-up old crêpe paper.

I was beginning to think I would have to move Tattie on to

failsafe accessories if we were ever going to find anything for her, when Shelley appeared from the back room waving a glorious 1950s negligee. It was made from gorgeous beige chiffon trimmed all round the edge and cuffs with maribou. It was perfect on Tattie and her cheeks flushed all over again when she looked at herself in the mirror wearing it over the matching nightdress.

'Shall I go and tell your boyfriend to come in and see it, before you decide?' asked Shelley, after we had all cooed over how gorgeous Tattie looked.

'No!' she said, blushing and giggling. 'I've decided – and he'll see it later.'

We all laughed and I took great pleasure in packing it up for her with loads of tissue paper and ribbon, in one of my best boxes. Once it was ready, she hugged me again, brought Oscar in to say goodbye and then they left.

But a couple of minutes later she suddenly appeared back in the shop, brandishing an envelope.

'Sorry, Loulou,' she said. 'I forgot to give you this. Marc asked me to drop it off. He said it's something you needed . . .'

'Oh,' I squeaked, trying not to sound surprised her brother was sending me notes. 'Fine. Great. Please thank him. Very helpful . . .'

I stuffed it into my skirt pocket – glad the 1950s dirndl I was wearing actually had one – and waved her off. The minute she'd left the shop I shot out to the loo in the back to see what it was. Pathetic, I knew, but I just couldn't open that envelope in the shop. I had no earthly idea what it could be and didn't trust myself not to shriek or faint if it was something too surprising.

It was a mobile number. Presumably his. And a brief note, in bold handwriting, fountain pen: *'Text me yours. We'll need them at The Big Chill.'*

And to my very great shame, I immediately did.

Theo

Io amo Milano. Io amo men in Brioni suits on sit-up bicycles smoking cigars. Io amo Bagutta a fabulous old restaurant with 1930s murals all over the ceiling. Io amo old ladies with hair the colour of roasted carrots in tight skirts and high high heels. Io amo very strong macchiatos standing up at the bar with the local dudes. Amo amas amat.

There were just four of us on this trip. Me, Weanie, Tony the designer and Nicolle the head marketing lady. I'm not wild about her but Tony is hilarious and Weanie has made it clear I am part of the team now so she doesn't dare diss me off – although she did piss me off by arriving at the airport carrying a ridic Mulberry bag covered in enormous brass fittings like a plumbers' warehouse. Tony was funny.

Oooh missus he said to Nicolle. Winking at me. Nice arm candy. But didn't you know that handbags are so like over?

Nicolle: Handbags are a crucial part of our business.

Tony: Not with the new pocketed range of clothes I'm working on.

Nicolle: You can charge a much higher margin on a handbag than a pair of pants. Even in our market. It's seen as an investment purchase.

Tony: But we're going to shift a much bigger volume of units when the customers get the hang of hands-free living as demonstrated by young Theo here. They're going to buy whole new wardrobes with lots of lovely pockets so they won't need to carry horrid big heavy bags any more. Have you been to the chiropractor recently Nicolle?

I waggled my hands at her from where they were thrust into the trouser pockets. I had deepened them myself using Nancy's sewing machine with Velcro at the top to keep my passport safe. I had my money on the other side in a specially designed inner slot like those change pockets on old Levis.

Tony had thought it was genius when I'd showed him the week before and was already making the samples for his version. I loved how quickly things moved at West Wind. If Weanie approved it the range would be in the shops in a few weeks. Fast fashion. 21st century chainstore style.

Nicolle was narrowing her eyes at me rather alarmingly when Weanie hoved into view back from his research mission round the retail thrills of Terminal 5. Suddenly she was all smiley again. Snake lady.

Anyway she can go fug herself. I had a genius time in Milano.

We stayed at this fab hotel called the Principe and Weanie knew all the great places to eat and although it was boiling blinking hot and – he told me – absolutely not the time to be in Milan I bloody loved it.

We were there deliberately at the Wrong Time because he is trying to set up some deal with one of the really big Italian clothing factories. And the wrong time was exactly the right time because he was having all these shifty meetings with people he didn't want other people to know about. They were all off safely in Sardinia and Croatia he said. He brought the rest of us along to check out the shops and general groove but I think really to keep him company between undercover rendezvous.

The idea is to get them to make a special 'tailoring' (clothes for people with boring jobs) line for him at a screwed-down price because his order would be so massive. It would still be more expensive than the normal West Wind gear but *prima qualita*.

So not like your normal sweatshop shit then? said I.

Bang on said Weanie.

Va bene said me.

I love Italian. *Che bella lingua*. My shoe size is *trente otto*. Key words in that town. Especially when Beanie insisted on buying me a pair of ridiculous high heels in Sergio Rossi. I kept saying I don't want them. I don't wear heels. Have you seen how long my legs are recently?

But he kind of hissed in my ear to shut up because he wanted them as samples to copy so I did shut up and then pretended to let him buy me five pairs of shoes.

It was hilarious because the sales girl clearly thought I was some kind of ho out on an asset-stripping mission with my sugar daddy trick. He certainly looked the part in his suit and shades so I got into character parading around in the puttanesca heels copping poses and lifting up my trouser legs to show him my shapely calves.

Then I waltzed out of there on those crazy heels which make me taller than him and I had to hold on to his arm to walk and it's all cobbles in those streets so I had to keep holding on to it. But when we got near to where we were meeting the others he suddenly stopped at the corner and grabbed me by the tops of my arms and said I think you better put your own shoes on now Theo.

His voice was all gruff when he said it and he was standing really close to me and holding my arms so tight it was quite sore. I could feel my heart beating really fast so I did what I was told quick smart. Unusually for me.

Weanie can be quite scary sometimes.

When we got back to the hotel I was in my room watching some crazy game show on Italian TV which seemed to be all about the women contestants taking their clothes off and there was a knock on the door and our driver was standing there with two enormous Sergio Rossi carrier bags.

For you Mees Theo.

No for Mr Beaney.

No Meeester Beaney say for you.

So I took them. Maybe he didn't want to carry them through customs in case people thought he was a crossdresser.

Then my phone went blip and the text said:

> Wear the snakeskin ones to dinner tonight.

I was just sticking my tongue out at the phone when it went blip again:

> And that's an order.

So I did.

21
Loulou

All the way to Herefordshire in Keith's car on Friday morning, I kept turning my mobile on and off and on and off again. I was so regretting texting Marc my number I didn't know what to do with myself. Why had I done that? What if he texted me? What if he didn't? What if I had the phone turned off in case he rang and Theo was trying to text me and I didn't get the message and she couldn't find us at the camp site and had nowhere to sleep?

She was making her own way to the festival – typically. Chard said she'd been away for three nights on one of her secret missions and he had no idea where, but she had seemed very excited about it before she left. Another Theo mystery, but at least it wasn't just me she liked to keep in the dark about her activities. I found a small grain of comfort in that.

'What are you doing, Loulou?' said Keith eventually, as I turned the phone on and off yet again. 'You can't leave that bloody phone alone. It's driving me nuts. I don't suppose there's any signal out here anyway, but there'll be plenty at the site. They've put up extra masts this year. It was on the website. So will you stop fiddling with that thing for a minute and talk to me?'

'Sorry, I'm just worried how Theo's going to find us,' I babbled, which was sort of partly true kind of.

'She knows we're in the family camping area and she's going to call me when she arrives at the gates,' said Keith, turning to give me a scrutinising look. 'Why are you so jumpy?'

'Oh, I don't know,' I lied.

I knew exactly why. The reason had dark blond hair, golden eyes with mesmerising dark rings round the irises and a stomach like an ironing board. And might very well be wearing a killer white YSL suit.

'It's just I've never been to one of these things before,' I continued, partly truthfully. 'It's all a bit daunting. I haven't been camping since I was at school – and I hated it then – I'm dreading the loos, and I'm forty-nine on Saturday. Lumped together, it's all making me feel a bit anxious.'

Keith punched me on the upper arm.

'Relax, you big banana,' he said. 'It's called the Big CHILL. Geddit? Chill. That's what you're supposed to do. Hang out, lie back and let it all flow over you. The whole point of this weekend is that you don't have to do anything except be you and be adored by all of us. Just wallow in it. I've taken care of everything for your comfort. Apart from that what will be will be. Or not. Whatever.'

Which was exactly what I was worried about. Whatever would be would be and what would that be exactly? And what if it wasn't? But I couldn't say anything. In the meantime, I decided to leave the phone turned off. That was the safest thing to do. Then Theo could ring Keith and Marc couldn't ring me. Perhaps I'd turn it on once a day just to check, so I knew what was going on. Maybe once in the morning and once at night. Maybe I'd throw it down one of the vile lavvies.

'I'm going to put the iPod on,' said Keith. 'It might calm you down. Shame I haven't got any new age whale music on it. I've never seen anyone so nervy about going away for a weekend to be worshipped by her friends. I'll have to get you drunk as soon as possible.'

I didn't think he'd have to try very hard. Even before we got there all my negative preconceptions about festivals were being confirmed as we sat for ages in a long queue waiting to get into the car park.

Then we had to yomp up a big hill with our luggage, with people scuttling up and down all around us with trolleys and wheelbarrows piled with gear and small children. It was like a refugee camp. Not my idea of a relaxed experience at all and I wasn't making it any easier for myself by wearing heels. I was determined not to take them off until the last possible moment, but walking up what seemed like the lower slopes of Snowdon in them was practically impossible, even for me.

Once we had handed over our tickets and been fitted with humiliating little hospital wristband things and were allowed inside the ugly chain link fence, the first thing I saw – although I smelled them sooner – were the portaloos. There was a truck with a big tank on it next to them and a huge pipe making loud pumping noises . . . Aaaarrrgggh, it didn't bear thinking about.

At that point I just wanted to go home, but after shouting happily down his phone for a few minutes, Keith snapped it shut and, grabbing my hand, set off determinedly along one of the fenced-off pathways that criss-crossed the huge field. It was already covered in tents, with baggage-laden people wandering around rather desperately looking for spots still left to claim.

'Blimey,' I said. 'So many people. So many tents up already. It started yesterday didn't it? We're late. Is there going to be room for us? And where is all our camping gear anyway? We've only got hand luggage. What on earth are we going to sleep in?'

'Don't you worry about any of that, darling,' said Keith, grinning excitedly as he scanned the horizon. 'Aha!' he added, stepping over the rope fence and turning round to help me over. 'I see it. We're on our way . . .'

I had no idea where we were on our way to, but he was striding forth with great confidence, weaving through the narrow gaps between other people's tents, which was more than a little challenging for me with my shoes and the guy ropes, and carrying a weekend bag. I nearly went flying several times.

'What exactly are we aiming at?' I asked, getting a bit testy, as I manoeuvred my way through a tented mini-kingdom someone had created complete with rugs and Moroccan lanterns.

'See that flag?' said Keith, happily. 'The one with the platform shoe on it? That's where we're going.'

I followed his pointing finger and high above all the tents I could see a triangular flag waving in the light summer breeze. It was painted with the image of one of my favourite Balenciaga shoes and the words 'Camp Loulou'.

'That marks our camp,' said Keith proudly. 'So we'll always be able to find it. I was going to call it Loulou Land, but I thought people might try to come shopping.'

From that moment all my ill humour disappeared and once we got to it, Camp Loulou was truly fabulous. It consisted of five of the nylon tipis Keith had shown me pictures of, plus two large normal tents, all pitched in a circle around a central area covered by two enormous gazebos, and furnished with folding tables and chairs, and two bright pink inflatable plastic sofas.

The whole zone was roped off with colourful bunting strung at knee level between all the tents, presumably to keep other people out. More bunting decorated the gazebos and someone had drawn beautiful flowers and hippy-style patterns over the tents with marker pens. When I looked closely at them I could see that my name was incorporated repeatedly in the design.

'Wow!' was all I could say.

'Do you like it?' asked Keith, modestly.

'I love it,' I said, giving him a hug. He picked me up and clasped me to his chest, spinning me round, laughing.

'I'm so pleased you like it. I'll show you our tent,' he said, leading me towards one of the non-tipi ones.

It had a big 'room' in the front and three sleeping pods, with zip 'doors', at the back. Two of them were all set up with double air beds and cosy-looking sleeping bags, proper pillows and fluffy white towels; the other was zipped shut.

'Those are our bedrooms,' he said.

'What's the middle one?' I asked.

'Have a look,' said Keith, smiling.

I opened it to find a dress rail complete with padded coat hangers, plus some kind of collapsible camping storage unit with shelves made of nylon fabric.

'All right?' he said. 'I couldn't get the electricity and plumbing sorted, but at least you'll be able to hang your clothes up.'

Tears pricked my eyes. I knew Keith loved organising things – especially when it involved having a drink and a good time – but this was something special even by his standards.

'This is really wonderful, Keith,' I said, hugging him. 'Will you show me the rest of the compound?'

The other proper tent was a storage centre, mainly for alcohol as far as I could tell, with one bedroom in it set up for Theo. The tipis were the guest rooms – although he still wouldn't tell me who was going to be in them.

'You'll just have to wait and see,' he said, emerging from the storage tent with a bottle of pre-mixed gin and It and a big bowl of his beloved Cheddars.

He cut slices of lemon on the table under the gazebo, adding ice cubes from a kitsch old plastic pineapple ice bucket, and we settled on folding chairs in the midday sun, holding hands and toasting each other.

'Thank you, Keith,' I said, raising my glass to him. 'Thank you for doing this for me. I'm sorry I was so churlish about it. It's amazing and I can already tell I'm going to have a great time, but I don't understand how our tents were all up ready like this. How did you do that? And how the hell did you get *ice*?'

'Easy,' said Keith, taking a big slurp of his drink and pausing to stuff in another big handful of Cheddars before continuing. 'One of my nephews is over here from Australia on his gap year, so I got him and his mate to come down yesterday and set it all up – according to meticulous plans supplied by me – in return for free tickets to the festival. I bought them tents as well and gave them a bit of drinking money. They're good kids. My nephew did the graffiti on the tents – probably while his friend did all the real work, if I know Matt. And supplying fresh ice just before we arrived was part of the gig. Remember that text I sent from the car park? That was the ice alert.'

He smiled with satisfaction and I leaned over and kissed him on the cheek.

'You are simply amazing Keith McNamara,' I said, meaning it. 'Have you ever thought of having an alternative career as an events organiser?'

'Nope,' he said. 'I love my boring job and the nice secure salary it gives me, thank you very much. Doing stuff like this is my hobby and I'd hate it to become stressful homework.'

His phone bleeped.

'Ooh,' he said, squinting to read the text without putting his specs on. 'First lot of arrivals. You wait here – I'm going to bring them in.'

He raced off and I sat back in the chair, eyes closed, the gin starting to hum pleasantly in my system, enjoying the feeling of the sun on my face. I kicked off my shoes and wiggled my toes in the grass, feeling a very particular kind of peace settling into me. I sat outside on my terrace with Chard most mornings in summer, getting my vitamin D fix, but there was something different about being outside in the country. I could feel the city tension leaving my system. It was delicious.

My reverie was broken when somebody putting up a tent nearby suddenly swore loudly and everyone within earshot cheered. I joined in and as I opened my eyes I suddenly noticed that across the valley, right in my line of vision, was that bloody great castle Theo had shown me on the website, like something out of a fairy story. Grey stone battlements and turrets, the lot. It looked like Rapunzel might let down her hair at any moment.

I couldn't believe I hadn't noticed it before, but I'd been so busy looking down at my feet to make sure I didn't trip up, exploring Keith's compound, and worrying about the loos, I hadn't taken in the setting at all. It was glorious. I stood up and did a 360° reccie, realising that apart from the acres of tents, the castle was the only man-made structure in sight. Just green fields, trees and a big blue sky. Wow, indeed.

I had just gone into the tent to start unpacking my stuff when I heard a lot of excited squealing outside.

'Where's the birthday girl?' said a familiar American accent. 'Come out come out wherever you are . . .'

'Here!' I said, emerging to find Lauren, Rachel and Fiona standing outside.

'Hurray!' I said, as hugs and kisses were excitedly exchanged. 'Practically the whole party committee. How lovely.'

'And Natalie's coming later,' said Fiona, with her usual lack of tact.

'No more guest list revelations!' ordered Keith.

'Oops, sorry,' said Fiona. 'Will this help you forgive me?'

And she moved a bag on the top of the trolley she had dragged up to the camp, to reveal a wine carton.

'Veuve,' she said. 'Shall we crack one?'

'Bloody oath,' said Keith, tossing back the last of his gin, before heading off into his storage tent. 'I'll get the flutes.'

Lauren caught my eye.

'Did he say flutes?' she said.

'Yep,' I replied. 'Keith never entertains in anything but the highest style. Would you like to see your sleeping quarters?'

I showed them the nearest tipi, which was fitted out to the same standard as our tent, right down to rugs on the floor and lantern torches on each side of the blow-up beds.

'What are these?' said Rachel, picking up some kind of small gold strap thing with a plastic blob on it. There were two on each bed. There had been one on mine as well, I remembered. In my excitement, I'd forgotten to ask Keith what it was.

'I think it's a head torch,' said Fiona. 'We have them at pony club camp, but these are very glamorous versions.'

'What the hell is a head torch?' said Lauren.

Fiona put it round her forehead and fiddled with the plastic knob at the front. A beam of light came on.

'It's for going to the loo in the night,' she said. 'Hands free.'

We all got completely overexcited, Lauren put hers on and I rushed off to get mine.

'We're ready for our close-ups, Keith!' I said, as he appeared with a tray of plastic champagne glasses, and he made us pose next to one of the tipis for what promised to be the first of many team photos.

A couple of glasses of bubbly and several photo opportunities later, his phone bleeped again.

'Next arrivals,' he said.

'Before you disappear,' said Lauren. 'Have you done a sleeping placement for the tents? I would prefer to be next to my husband if possible . . .'

'Is Paul coming then?' I asked as brightly as I could, although my heart had sunk at the mere mention of his name. I'd been thrilled when Lauren had turned up on her own. I thought it meant the party was going to be just the committee girls, plus me, Keith and Theo, with Chard nearby in his yurt, and had been delighted at the prospect.

'Yeah,' she said. 'He's coming later. He's been away for work and he's coming here straight from Heathrow.'

'Oh, that's great,' I said, trying to mean it.

Maybe Paul would be nicer off his own turf, I thought. Some people were like that. But it definitely added another level of stress to the stupid Marc thing. I'd really have to avoid him at all costs now, because if even the most casual contact was scrutinised by Paul's hostile eye, I knew it would make me super self-conscious and gauche.

'Well, you two will need a tent to yourselves if you've been apart for a few nights,' said Rachel and we all made lewd noises.

'Yeah, right,' said Lauren, sarcastically. 'I better hand out the ear-plugs now . . .'

'And I think Bill is coming with Natalie,' continued Rachel. 'So they'll need their own digs and Fiona and I can have a girls' dorm. Which tipi do you fancy Lauren? Any preferences?'

They chose their billets and then we all unpacked with lots of running in and out of each other's tents and showing off gadgets and outfits. Everyone had feature wellies, with my purple platform ones getting the biggest laugh and leading to another group photo. We were just setting it up on an auto timer when Keith appeared with Natalie and Bill.

I ran over to greet them and as I was hugging Natalie, two more people popped out from behind a neighbouring tent – my sister Jane and her husband Martin. I shrieked with delight.

'Surprise!' said Keith, beaming with excitement.

'Janie!' I cried, throwing myself at her. 'What a lovely surprise. I had no idea.'

'Hello, Lizzie, love,' she said, kissing me warmly on one cheek. None of that two-cheek kissy-kissy malarkey for her, that was a poncey southern pretension. 'Although I'll have to try and remember to call you Loulou, won't I?'

'Call me whatever you like,' I said. 'I'm just so glad you and Martin are here.'

'And Becky's here too, with her fella – the husband-to-be – so you'll be able to tell me what you think of him.'

'Oh, that's fantastic,' I said. 'Are they staying here with us?'

'No, they're camping over on the other side, where all the young people are, but they're going to meet up with us for your birthday celebrations tomorrow.'

Keith opened another bottle of champagne and after everyone had been introduced and had sorted out their tents, we gathered under the gazebo drinking and chatting. As I looked around at the crowd I felt incredibly lucky to have such great pals. I stood behind Keith's chair and put my arms around his neck, leaning round to kiss him on the cheek.

'Thank you, Keith,' I said. 'You really are the most wonderful friend.'

'Love you, sweetheart,' he said, reaching up to squeeze one of my hands. 'You know I'd do anything for you. Even though you do your best to make it hard for me.'

I pretended to cuff him round the head and he grabbed my hand and pulled me forward, so we both fell on to the grass, which led to some extended play-wrestling, with him eventually pinning me down and threatening to kiss me.

'Tongues, Loulou,' he was saying, leering down at me, as I thrashed around and squealed in protest. 'Brace yourself, girl. I'm going to do tongues.'

He never did, but it always made me absolutely hysterical – and then, according to our usual pattern, I made my escape by tickling him under the arms, until he collapsed on the grass next to me, giggling like a baby. We'd always carried on like that and it never occurred to me that it might seem peculiar, but when I stood up again, Lauren and Natalie were looking at me with amused, quizzical expressions.

'Don't take any notice,' I said, slightly embarrassed. 'We're only fooling around. Keith is basically a supersized lion cub.'

'Right,' said Lauren, smiling, with one eyebrow ironically raised. 'Glad you explained that.'

'Don't worry,' said Keith, getting to his feet. 'You'll all get a go. In fact, according to my schedule, Lauren . . . you're next.'

And he lunged at her. She jumped out of the way and the two of them charged off, Keith in pursuit, round and round the gazebo. Everyone was laughing, but I couldn't help thinking how much Theo would have hated it if she'd been there.

She'd always loathed it when Keith and I got physical with each other – so maybe it wasn't surprising she'd reacted badly to me dancing with Marc that time. As she'd admitted that afternoon in the kitchen the weekend before, when we'd made up, she just didn't feel comfortable seeing me interacting that way with any man. I could see her side of it, but that didn't make it right. We were both going to have to get over our hang-ups about all that.

But when on earth she was going to turn up? I knew it would be when she felt like it and not one moment sooner, but I hoped it would be soon. I wouldn't be able to relax completely until I knew she had arrived. Then I wondered who else was coming, as one of the Camp Loulou tipis was still unaccounted for. I was running through possible candidates in my head when Keith's phone went again.

'Theo?' I asked. 'Paul?'

He shook his head, winked, and set off for the entrance again, while the rest of us finished off the champagne.

'So you're the sister who had the great matchmaking idea,' said Lauren to Jane as she filled her glass.

'Well, it wasn't all my idea,' said Jane. 'There was a group of us.'

'Has it been successful for your lot?' said Fiona. 'Because none of our daughters met anyone suitable at our party. We all had a great time, but it was a hopeless flop on the matchmaking front.'

'Don't mind Fiona,' said Rachel, poking her with a finger. 'She likes to speak her mind, but it was a bit disappointing.'

'Yeah,' agreed Natalie. 'One of Freya's male friends met a lovely girl – and didn't Theo's friend meet someone?'

I nodded.

'Yes, he's lovely,' I said. 'Perfect for Tattie. Exactly the kind of young man mothers dream of, but that would just be too easy for my daughter, wouldn't it?'

They all laughed.

'Our lot just seem to be hopeless cases,' said Rachel. 'It was really annoying. So have you lot had better luck?'

'I've got loads of weddings this summer,' said Jane, glancing quickly over at me. I'd already started giggling and she knew what I was thinking.

'What's cracking you up, Loulou?' said Lauren. 'What's the joke?'

'Jane's got a lovely wedding coming up later in the year, haven't you, big sis?'

'Yes, Lizzie. I have, thanks,' said Jane, going pink.

All the committee girls turned to look at her.

'Go on, tell us,' said Fiona.

'Well, my own daughter's getting married,' said Jane, now really red and giving me furious looks.

'That's fantastic,' said Lauren. 'So the matchmaking party thing really did work out for you. Congratulations. Wow. All your hard work paid off.'

I was now snorting into my champagne flute.

'Go on, Jane,' I spluttered out. 'Tell them where she met him, then.'

'Oh, all right,' said Jane. 'If it will stop you laughing at us. She met him in a bloody bar. In Leeds.'

Lauren, Natalie, Fiona and Rachel were silent for a moment and then they all burst out laughing too.

'So you went through all that effort with the matchmaking parties,' said Rachel. 'And she met him in a bar?'

'In Leeds!' I chipped in.

They turned and looked at me blankly.

'What's the big deal about Leeds?' said Lauren. 'Isn't it meant to be a cool place?'

'If you're from *Yorkshire*,' chipped in Jane's husband, Martin. 'Which is on the wrong side of the Pennines.'

'We're from Manchester,' I added. 'Lancashire. West side of the Pennines.'

Lauren still looked bewildered.

'Don't worry, Lauren,' said Fiona. 'It's only to do with a war that happened five hundred years ago.'

'Oh, OK,' said Lauren. 'Crazy English stuff, I get it.'

After Martin had explained the War of the Roses in some detail, with me chipping in that it wasn't originally a film with Meryl Streep and Danny de Vito – we sat sipping our drinks for a bit, until Rachel suddenly piped up again.

'Does that mean we don't have to do another party then?' she said.

We all glanced at each other, wanting to see how the others felt.

'Well, I loved the *party* aspect of the party,' said Lauren. 'And it was great to get to know all you guys, but I'm quite happy to leave the matchmaking side up to fate . . .'

'Agreed,' said Fiona, clinking her glass against Lauren's. 'It was a monstrous bore chasing them all for money and most of the other mothers were ghastly . . .'

'Hurray!' said Rachel. 'No more horrible rude people who can't be bothered to RSVP. I'm delighted to jack it all in – as long as we can all stay friends.'

'Me too,' said Natalie.

'Me three,' I added. 'I think I might just send Theo up to Leeds.'

We were happily drinking a toast to the relief of giving up matchmaking – Fiona had opened another bottle – when an odd-looking figure stumbled into the compound, tripping over the bunting.

I'd been so caught up in our conversation I'd forgotten we were expecting someone – and this didn't seem like anyone I knew. He looked like some kind of weird Orthodox priest, with a long beard, wearing a large black cowboy hat and very dark shades, a cigarette dangling from his lip.

'Holy shit,' he was saying. 'Nearly set fire to my goddamn beard . . .'

I was a little alarmed that this weirdo seemed to be heading straight for me, especially as he was now tugging on his facial hair in a most peculiar way. It wasn't until he was right in front of me and holding the beard in one hand that I realised who it was.

'Chard!' I squealed.

He chuckled and bent down to kiss me on both cheeks. Definitely a southerner.

'Did my disguise work then?'

'Too bloody right,' I said. 'I thought you were Charles Manson's scarier brother. That's one freaky chin rug.'

He greeted everyone, giving my sister a particularly warm hug and sat down, rubbing his jaw where the false beard had been.

'Itchy bastard, too,' he said. 'Yeah, it's pretty extreme. Theo got it for me, because as I'm actually playing this gig, I've got to check out how cool the crowd are before I go out and about in real time, if you get my drift. I've got my yurt set up over in the artists' VIP area just in case, but I'd much rather stay here. I just hope no arsehole Ickieologists start hitting on me when I'm trying to big chill out and enjoy your birthday.'

I had looked over at Lauren before I could stop myself. It was just an instant reaction because there was going to be a card-carrying Ickieologist staying right there in the compound – who happened to be her husband. I was really starting to resent Paul Beaney. He had a unique way of ruining everything. But fortunately his wife was as cool as he was crass.

'Don't worry, Ritchie,' she said. 'I've told Paul to leave you alone about all that stuff. He really is a proper fan, that's the problem, but he'll calm down, I promise.'

'Oh, that's fine, babe,' said Chard, smiling at her. 'Sweet of you to say it, but I do understand. I was the same when I met Robert de Niro. Made a total tit of myself going on about *Mean Streets* – I was even doing bits of dialogue, what a twat – until he told me he hadn't seen the film since he made it and couldn't remember anything about it, not even his character's name.'

He laughed heartily, with it turning into his usual hacking cough, and once again I marvelled at Ritchie's natural graciousness. He'd gone out of his way to make Lauren feel OK about her ghastly husband. He didn't have to do that, but he had. What a lovely lovely man he was.

I felt quite teary for a moment, moved by my good fortune at having such amazing friends, but with a twinge of disappointment that the one key person who still hadn't turned up was my own bloody daughter. Oh well.

'Anyone feeling peckish?' said Keith after we'd finished the third bottle of Veuve and the entire supply of Cheddars.

After a rousing chorus of yes – it was nearly three, so it was hardly surprising we were all ravening – he told us to get ourselves together, it was time to set off for the festival proper, where there was loads of great stuff to eat.

'What do you mean the "festival proper"?' I asked him, as we went into our tent to gather our bits and pieces. 'Aren't we already at it?'

'This is just the campsite, Loulou,' he said. 'You ain't seen nothing yet . . .'

'Gosh,' I said. 'That sounds exciting, but do we have to walk a long way to get there?'

'Yes,' said Keith, looking pointedly at my feet. 'Over rough ground and through mud.'

My heart sank. Did I really need to wear flat shoes? I'd been scoping women's feet as we walked in and it had all been Havaianas, Birkenstocks, Hunter wellies, Ugg boots and even vile Crocs. Foulness. I just couldn't countenance the idea, so decided to let myself in gently with a pair of red Korkeaze platform sandals. They gave height, if not elegance, and the block shape of the sole made them like flat shoes, just raised about four inches off the ground.

Plus, they looked spot-on with what I was wearing: a really nutty full-skirted 1950s sundress, strapless and tight-waisted, in a fabulous print of multi-coloured sombreros, suns and cactuses on a bright yellow background. My earrings were big shiny red cherries, with a brooch to match.

As I sorted a few essentials from my handbag to put into the flower-embroidered straw basket I was going to take with me – cash, lipstick, tissues for loo emergencies, scent, anti-bacterial hand gel – I came to my phone.

I sat on the edge of the blow-up bed looking down at it. Was there any point in taking it if I wasn't going to turn it on? Not really. But my phone was also my camera and what if I missed some fabulous photo opportunity? As a compromise I threw it into the basket, but didn't turn it on.

Theo

The Big Thrill

It's a good job I enjoy keeping secrets and lying. Otherwise it might have thrown me sideways with 180° turn plus twist and pike to bump into Mudda at the Big Chill – walking along arm in arm with Weanie Beaney's teenie weenie wife. She's a skinny mini blondie that one. Must have been quite beautiful when she was young.

Seeing the two of them just boom like that when a few hours before I had said goodbye to her husband at Heathrow airport after three brilliant days with his team in Milan was a bit of a brain stir fry. I was still wearing the shoes he bought me too. Mudda's eyes nearly popped.

You're wearing heels Theo!

Yeah I said. Because no one else is. Not even you.

She had on the most terrible clompers like two house bricks strapped to her feet and probably the worst outfit I've ever seen her in – and that's saying something. She looked like she was starring in an am dram production of *Grease*. As the ugly one.

Anyway it was freakie deakie bumping into them like that because I reallyreallyreallyreally want to keep my West Wind connection secret from Mudda so she can't ruin it and try and take it over and own it and start telling me I should 'ask Yohji' and shit like that. So it was just weird seeing Mrs West Wind live in concert.

But at least I know she doesn't know I'm working for them.

Weanie was firm on that. Wifey has nothing to do with West Wind now he told me. Except spending the profits he said. Luckily he wants to keep me working there a secret as much as I do. He cornered me in the business class lounge at Milan airport and gave me strict orders to keep to our cone of silence pact and I told him: Suits me big boy.

He seems to like the game of it and I certainly do but he hadn't mentioned that his wife was coming to El Chillos with my Mudda and he knew I was because I moaned about it the whole time we were in Milan. Sneaky bugger.

Anyway Mudda was thrilled to see me and I had promised Chard to be nice to her so I did my best.

Mudda: Why didn't you ring Keith to let us know you were here?

Me: Was I supposed to?

Mud: Well how would you know how to find the compound?

Me: What compound?

Mud: In the family camp site – where we are all sleeping. Keith's created the most amazing little zone for us. You've got a lovely room in a tent all of your own.

Me: Oh I'm sharing with my friend Stew – in the party campsite.

Mudda got a bit vinegar faced at that info so I called Fatty Stew over and he charmed her out of it – he's gifted with old people – then we agreed to tag along with them for a meal which thrilled Fatty as there's nothing he likes better than a free feed.

Turned out to be a whole great big posse of old folks on the loose including my Auntie Jane and Uncle Martin and Deathbreath looking hilarious in the joke shop beard I'd got for him. I introduced him to Stew as my Uncle Deathbreath and he didn't have any idea who he really was behind the acrylic fuzz. Mind you he might not have had any idea anyway but it was still funny.

It was even better when we all sat down on the grass to eat under these big trees and DB couldn't get the food into his mouth through the beard and got pumpkin risotto all over it.

I was laughing so much I was lying on my back waving my legs in the air. Which was a relief in those shoes because they were starting to bloody kill me but totally worth it because I knew they were ace hot with my high-cut cut offs. Offs offs. Ha ha.

And that was the position I was in when I heard everyone going 'Hey!' and 'At last!' and 'Here he is!' and I opened my eyes to look straight up at Weanie Beaney standing there like the Godfather in his black suit and shades.

Shit.

22

Loulou

How was I supposed to know that the copse of lovely big oak trees to the far side of the main stage was a well-known meeting point at the Big Chill?

I'd never been to the Big Chill before, or any other flipping festival for that matter and it had just seemed like a nice place for us all to sit down in a big group and eat our curry, burgers, risotto, falafel, pies, sausage and mash, burritos, fish and chips, laksa and all the other United Nations of nosh we were having. I was so excited by the amazing variety, I turned on my phone to take a picture of the spread so I could put it on Twitter.

It was great to have Theo with us at last – especially as she hadn't actually been in touch, we'd bumped into her completely by chance, casually strutting down the main festival field. I'd thought it was rather amazing in such a big crowd, but with her endless legs in crazily skimpy jean cut-offs – and wearing the most fabulous pair of snakeskin heels – she was having the full Girl From Ipanema effect on the male half of the Big Chill crowd, so we couldn't really have missed her.

But while I was delighted to see her, I was also extremely alarmed that even among such a huge mass of people you could just run into someone like that. I'd been relying on the anonymity of the mob to avoid Marc. I certainly couldn't keep him out of my head.

However hard I tried to push the thoughts away, he was always lurking somewhere in my mind. Whether I was having a laugh with my sister and brother-in-law, or talking seriously to Rachel about her latest problems with Cassandra, who looked like she might have to go back into rehab, there was always part of my brain worrying about whether I was going to see him. Or not see him.

Between that, eating my vegetable curry, and trying not to mind that Theo had casually announced that she wasn't going to stay in Camp Loulou, but with her friend Stew, a sweet young man who was following in her glorious wake like a chunky little tug boat, I was quite distracted. Even so I did become aware of a unusually high volume of text action going on around me. Lauren, Keith, Stew and Jane were all hammering at their phones. It wasn't very relaxing.

Then Chard started effing and blinding because he couldn't eat with his false beard on and had managed to cover it with risotto. It was pretty funny and Theo went a bit over the top waving her legs in the air in dead fly mode, which had every man for miles staring at us. One in particular, I noticed.

Paul Beaney. Wearing a black linen suit, dark glasses and a mean expression, looming up like a storm cloud.

I glanced round to see if anyone else had noticed him and saw heading towards us from the opposite direction, but much further away, another man in a suit. A bright white suit. With Marc Thorssen inside it. My stomach did a bungee jump.

It was just too much and there was only one thing I could do. After hastily telling Rachel I had to go to the loo in a hurry – 'Too much bubbly for my old bladder . . .' I jumped to my feet and legged it away from them all up the hill.

As I jogged, which wasn't easy on grass, at quite a steep gradient, in those shoes, I heard a welcoming cry go up as they all spotted Paul – which I hoped would have the happy result of no-one noticing which direction I had gone in. I didn't hear the same for Marc's arrival, but possibly because I was already too far away.

I made for a gap I could see at the top right-hand side of the main field. I had no idea where it would take me but it looked like somewhere I could lose myself. As I went, now at a fast walk, I was planning how I could explain my safari as looking for a remote set of loos that were likely to be less vile than any near the main stage – a tip Fiona had given me, courtesy of her daughter, Phoebe, a seasoned festival-goer.

The gap turned out to lead to a track up through a kind of service area to another festival field beyond and as I passed through it my phone rang. Shit. I'd forgotten it was still on from taking the photo of the food. I rummaged in my basket and found it just as it stopped ringing. Missed call: Marc.

As I stood frozen, staring at the screen, the voicemail symbol popped up, and then a text message came through, quickly followed by two more. I immediately deleted the voicemail without listening to it. Whatever Marc had to say it was better I didn't hear it. I just didn't trust myself enough to be strong.

I clicked on to the texts page to find they were from Keith, Theo and Marc, in that order.

Keith:

> Rachel says you've gone to the lavs. Good luck. Paul's just arrived. We're going to find the fancy dress tent. Call me so we can meet up.

Theo:

> Have decided to stay at Camp Loulou see you later xxx

Marc:

> I'm following you.

There was so much to take in, I just stood there gormlessly looking down at the phone. Fancy dress tent? What on earth was that? And if they weren't under the trees any more, how would I ever find them?

Theo was staying at Camp Loulou after all – great! And she'd sent me three kisses, even greater.

Following me?! What did that mean? How could he follow me? He didn't know where I was . . . did he?

I turned round and coming up the hill towards me, fast, was a figure in white. It could only be him and when he saw me looking, he waved. So this is how the fox feels, I thought. What was I supposed do? Try and run away from him? He was twenty-five years younger, super-fit, male and wearing flat shoes – I didn't have a chance. So I waited for him.

I'd have to see him sooner or later over the weekend, I reasoned, and perhaps if I got it over with now – away from the offputting scrutiny of Theo, Keith and horrid Paul Beaney – and told him he had to stop treating me as anything more intimate than a friend's mum, I could relax and just enjoy myself for the rest of the festival.

In what felt like just moments he was right in front of me, puffing a bit from the exertion and grinning. His cheeks were pink from running in the August heat, which made his golden-brown eyes even more striking than usual. My stomach bungee-jumped again. Wretched organ.

'If I didn't know better, Loulou Landers,' he said, his head on one side in that way of his. 'I would have thought you were running away from me.'

'I was,' I said. There was no point pretending. The only way to deal with this ridiculous situation was to confront it, deal with it and move on. I was the adult and it was up to me to take charge.

He laughed, like it was a great joke, tucked my arm through his and before I could protest, or start my speech, we had set off up the hill.

'OK,' he said. 'Now we're up here, let's go and see what the Crouch Enders are up to in the mind, body and spirit area. That's always a laugh. We can have our auras read and I'll buy you a wheatgrass shot. That'll make you sit up straight.'

So instead of taking charge of the situation, I found myself being led along while Marc happily chatted on, completely at ease, as always.

As we walked and he talked, I noticed he was having the same effect on the passing crowd as Theo had earlier. Except in his case it was the female element who were affected. Every woman's gaze lingered on the vision in the killer white suit – with his auntie on his arm. It was cringe-making for me, but he seemed oblivious. He was probably used to it.

'So what do you think of The Big Chill so far?' he was asking. 'You probably haven't had a chance to take it all in yet. There's another two huge fields over beyond the main stage with loads of crazy things in them and there's all this up here and the art walk. It's massive. How's your camp? Phoebe said your friend Keith was laying on a big production number in your honour. Our area is pretty sordid, as you can imagine. Tattie told me Theo is going to be over with us too, which is great, but I thought she was going to be with you . . .'

'She just texted me about that,' I said, finally recovering myself enough to speak. 'It seems she is going to be staying with us after all.'

'She probably heard how luxe it is over there. Is it true there are five tipis?'

I nodded. 'And two huge tents and gazebos and bunting and tables and blow-up sofas and ice buckets . . . It is pretty amazing.'

'I can't wait to see it,' he said, smiling broadly.

I opened my mouth to protest. There was no way I could let him anywhere near Camp Loulou. I absolutely had to put a stop to this nonsense immediately, but before I could get a word out we had come to a juice stall and he was already busy talking to a young man with blond dreadlocks and a huge gold ring through his septum.

'Two beetroot and apple juices, please,' said Marc. 'And double wheatgrass shots on the side.'

As the man made the drinks and Marc groped around in his pocket for the change to pay for them, I managed to gather my wits a bit. I quickly pulled a twenty-pound note out of my wallet.

'I'll get these,' I said, handing over the cash and then turning to meet Marc's eye, with what I hoped was a commanding expression. I was determined to regain control of the situation – and myself.

That familiar mischievous look was back in his eye.

'Thanks,' he said. 'I'll get the next round.'

Once again, I had failed to get the upper hand and the imbalance of power continued as the white rasta handed the change and the cardboard tray of drinks directly to Marc, ignoring me.

'We need to find somewhere to sit,' he said, indicating for me to follow him. 'Can't risk grass stains on the YSL, can I?'

I trailed behind as he headed away from the stalls selling dreamcatchers and wind chimes, and tents offering massage, reiki and crystal healing, towards a quieter area beneath some trees, where I could see there were some low stools made from rough-hewn tree trunks. Marc sat down and patted the one next to him. I lowered myself onto it and he handed me a small paper cup of wheatgrass juice.

'Have you had this before?' he asked, holding his own beaker up as if making a toast.

'Yes,' I said. 'Fairly regularly since about 1980.'

He laughed.

'Well, you know how foul it is then. Down the hatch!'

He tossed it back in one and I did the same, quickly grabbing my beetroot juice to wash the bitter taste away.

'I better be careful with this stuff,' said Marc, gingerly raising his cup of deep red juice towards his lips. 'Really don't want to get it on the suit. How do you think it looks, by the way?'

He did that thing when he fixed my eyes with his and held the gaze slightly too long.

'It looks great, Marc,' I said. 'The pink polo shirt and the Converse are perfect with it. That's why every goddamn woman here is staring at you, and we have to have a little talk . . .'

'Yes,' he said, nodding. 'Why did you run away when you saw me coming just now?'

'You know why,' I said. 'The last time I saw you, you kissed me – on the lips. Then you sent your mobile phone number to me via your sister. I think it's all getting a little inappropriate and I didn't want to see you again for the first time after all that, with other people watching. Particularly Theo.'

'If you think things are getting "inappropriate", as you put it,' he said, looking at me over the rim of his juice. 'Why did you text me your number? You could have just ignored me.'

I looked down at my hands. I didn't have an answer – not for him and not for myself.

'I don't know,' I said quietly.

'I think I do,' said Marc.

He put his paper cup on the ground, reached over and did the same with mine, and then took my hand and held it in both of his. I didn't take it away, but carried on looking down at my feet. My ridiculous feet, in those stupid shoes. I felt like a clown sitting there in that outfit. It was going in the shop the moment I got home. Or on a bonfire.

'You sent me your number because you wanted to see me, just as much as I wanted to see you,' he said.

I sighed deeply. He was absolutely right, of course, but there was no way I was going to admit that. Despite my hopelessly weak attempts so far, I was still determined to take charge of this potentially disastrous situation. I looked up at him and gently removed my hand from his grasp. As I settled it back in my lap, I could feel it glowing from the memory of his touch. I had to be strong.

'I shouldn't have sent you my number, Marc,' I said. 'It was a moment of weakness. I was flattered by your attention, as I was by your kiss and by you dancing with me that time. I can't imagine why a young man like you is even interested in talking to me, but it seems you are and it affected my judgement. Will you do me a favour and wipe my number from your phone?'

'No,' said Marc, looking more serious than normal.

'OK, that's up to you,' I said. 'But I'm going to take yours off mine, because we have to set some ground rules here. The thing is, I like you very much – too much.'

I paused, took a deep breath, and then forced myself to continue.

'I'm very attracted to you,' I said. 'But why wouldn't I be? You're a ridiculously handsome young dude in your prime and you have the confidence of a prince. I'd have to be made of Playdough not to find you attractive, but all that's irrelevant. I am more than twenty-five years older than you, your sister is my daughter's best friend, and Theo has already reacted so badly to our little dancing session, she has moved out of my house and is living with her godfather. However gorgeous you are, my relationship with my daughter is more important. Sorry.'

He winced slightly.

'Theo moved out because we danced together?' he said.

I nodded.

'She's a sensitive, highly strung girl,' I said. 'As you know. Her father left when she was very young, which you also know. She's not used to seeing me with men in that, er, way and it freaked her out. My relationship with her has been fraught for some time, we've just got it back on something like an even keel, and I just can't risk damaging it any more by indulging in a flirtation with you, however much I would like to. Do you understand?'

'Yes,' he said, looking at me steadily. 'I understand that you are allowing Theo to limit your life. You're a beautiful, sexy woman, Loulou. Who cares how old you are? I don't. It's just a number. If you are attracted to me – and I'm thrilled to hear you say you are – you have every right to act upon it. The person who needs to grow up in this scenario is Theo.'

I was so surprised that for a moment I just gazed back at him. And not just because he had said I was beautiful and sexy. Gosh, did he really think so? I batted that thought out of my head as soon as it came in, treacherous brain, and considered the rest of his statement. Should I be outraged by what he had just said about Theo? No, because I knew there was an element of truth in it, but still, I had to stand my ground.

'It's not just Theo,' I said. 'You and I might appear to have some weird connection that bypasses our age difference, but to the rest of the world I would just look grotesque. It's fine for you to be experimenting with random age groups, but not for me. I'm forty-nine tomorrow, for god's sake!'

I felt the dreaded number hanging in the air between us. There, I'd said it, he knew. The full catastrophe. I half expected him to recoil in horror, making the sign of the cross with his fingers as he staggered back, but he didn't even blink. He just picked up his juice, finished it in one gulp and then gestured at mine with a raised eyebrow. I nodded and he sculled that one too.

'OK,' he said, wiping his mouth on the back of his hand and then after a moment's thought, rubbing his hand on the grass. 'Oops, got to watch the suit. What can I say, Loulou? I don't give a toss how old you are, I would love to take things further with you – a lot further – but you've made yourself clear and I know when to back off.'

'Thank you,' I said quietly, feeling like I could finally breathe out.

For a few moments we just sat there silently, the sunshine filtering down on us through the leaves, the various competing noises of the festival a strangely relaxing aural backdrop. Despite the awkward conversation we'd just had, I realised I felt quite content sitting there. It was all so weird.

Eventually I turned to look at him, only to find he had turned his head towards me at exactly the same moment. Once again we held each other's gaze a few beats longer than you normally would. Danger. I had to get away while I still had things the way they needed to be between us. I rubbed my face with my hands to try and break the spell.

'So, how do you want to play the rest of the weekend?' said Marc taking my cue and sitting up straight. 'Do you want me to leave?'

'No,' I said, instantly feeling awful. 'Of course not. We can both still have a good time here. It's big enough for the both of us – and we don't have to ignore each other. Just treat me like your sister's best friend's mother, that's all.'

'If that's you want, that's what I'll do, and I'll stay out of your way as much as I can,' he said, standing up, adjusting the collar of the suit and copping a stance. 'Quite John Travolta, don't you think?'

'Don't start . . .' I said, amused despite all my better judgement.

He put his hand out to pull me to my feet. I held both mine up in refusal and stood up unaided. Lucky I had those stupid shoes on, I thought. In my normal footwear, it might have taken a crane.

'How shall we choreograph the re-entry then?' he asked. 'Do you know where your posse are?'

'Keith said something about a fancy dress tent?'

Marc laughed.

'Oh, that would be pretty funny with your crowd. It's usually in the far field. Go back to those trees where you were sitting and keep going west.'

I looked at him blankly.

'That way?' he said laughing and pointing off to my right. 'Where the afternoon sun is headed? I'll go up the hill here and look at the art trail, so you won't run into me down there. No-one will see us together.'

'Thanks, Marc,' I said. 'Thanks for understanding.'

'I understand, all right,' he said. 'It doesn't mean I agree, but I'll do as you ask. Bye Loulou. Bye Mrs Landers.'

He leaned forward, clasping my upper arms and kissed me on the cheek, his lips lingering far longer than a social kiss. I closed my eyes. I could enjoy this one last contact, no harm in that. Then all too soon he was gone.

I opened my eyes and turned to watch the white-suited figure heading up and across the field between the stalls, every female head turning to look.

I squared my shoulders and headed off in the other direction, mentally congratulating myself for saving what could have been a horrendous situation. It had all worked out perfectly. He'd been really understanding and I was confident it was fully sorted.

So how come I felt like crying?

Theo

Had to find a secret place to write this. It's not like I can sit on the loo here and do it. They're not exactly conducive to hanging around. Strictly a hit and run scenario. So I just kept walking uphill until I found this area that feels like it's miles from everything and everyone and got the phone out.

I was gazing into space thinking when I noticed this bloke walking past wearing the most genius white suit. I was checking out the tailoring when he suddenly starts walking backwards and then sits down on the tree stump next to me. It was the creature Marc. Tattie's brother.

Of course he'd turned up earlier back under the trees in that suit but at that particular moment I'd been more interested in the black suit that had arrived at the same time so I'd zoned him out.

Do I even need to mention that cup of chino had ruined that beautiful bit of 'tailoring' (Weanie Beaney wanky word alert NEE NAR NEE NAR) by putting it over a PINK POLO SHIRT?

It had looked so good from the back and I wanted to puke when I was reminded of the full travesty of his outfit. And on the feet. Those horrendous 'wacky' yellow Converse of his. Puhlease.

That's one thing you have to give Weanie credit for. He works a suit like an Italian. Wears it like a man. More about him later.

Anyway Marc starts chatting to me.

So Theo . . .

So what?

Are you having a good time?

Do I look like I am?

It's always hard to tell with you.

What's that supposed to mean?

What it sounds like. It's hard to tell if you're having a good time because you hardly ever smile.

Why do you care?

I've known you since you were four Theo. You're my sister's best friend – and I really like your mum – so I would have thought we might have got on and been friends too.

I couldn't believe my ears. 'I really like your mum'! How creepy is that? I couldn't let it go.

What do you mean you 'really like' my mum?

I like her! She's . . . amazing.

How do you know?

I've chatted with her a bit.

Yeah – and danced with her like some tragic pervert gigolo.

You seriously need to get over that. She's a great dancer and I love dancing properly. Not many girls our age like doing it.

Old women do though. Ha ha ha.

Oh Theo. Give it a rest. This aggro pose of yours – it's getting pretty lame and I don't think it's the real you. Tattie says it isn't.

Tever.

He pretended to box with me when I said that and I batted him off but without too much actual violence.

Then we sat there in silence for a bit. I thought about telling him to clear off because I had stuff to do but in some wacko way talking to him about that weirdness of him dancing with my mum that time made me feel a little less insane about it. Made it human again. So I just sat there and waited to see what else he had to say. I was going to let him speak first. He did.

So are you staying with all of us in the party camp site tonight or not?

Looks like it.

I heard you were – then I heard you were staying with your mum after all.

Well I'm not.

Isn't it her birthday tomorrow?

Yes. Have you got her a card?

Ha ha. Very funny. Have you?

Not exactly.

I heard Keith has made an amazing camp for her with five tipis and all kinds of luxury and you've got your own tent.

Yeah I heard that too.

But you're not going to stay there.

I said no didn't I?

All right keep your shorts on. What there is of them. They're kind of just a waistband with leg holes really aren't they?

I play-cuffed him harder this time. Maybe he wasn't so heinous. At least he made an effort to talk and not just in pre-digested ready-meal just-add-water and microwave for 30 seconds platitudes like most of the stinking bores I'd have to endure later over at the 'party camp'. I let out a big sigh at the prospect.

Him: What?

Me: You tell me what – what's the crowd like at your camp?

Him: The usual mix. Tattie of course and her new fifth limb Oscar. He's all right actually I quite like him and I'm just so glad she's finally got a bloke. Then there is her other new best friend Phoebe who's a bit chalet girl does Glastonbury but nice. And Ariadne of course and loads of Tattie's other friends from college – like Stew and all that crowd you already know. Lot of black hair dye and white shoes – and then a few of my friends from school and uni. You'll think you hate them but you might actually enjoy talking to some of them if you try it. Bit older. Pretty bright. Really scarily bright some of them. Won't put up with any crap from you.

Me: Hey!

Him: Hey yourself. So are you going to give it a try? Coming out with us all tonight and having a good time . . .

Me: OK.

Him: Good. Well catch you later. I'll leave you and your phone to do whatever you're doing and see you in the dance tent.

Me: I won't dance with you. You might try and twirl me.

Him: Good. I'm not going to ask you.

Then off he went. Considering how much I thought I hated him perhaps he was OK after all. It wasn't his fault he had absolutely no style. And I had to hang out with his lame crowd because there was noooooo way I was going back to Camp Mudda now even though I had texted her I was. Here's why.

After Weanie arrived earlier – which is why I'd immediately texted Mudda I was staying with her – we all went straight over to the dress-up tent and it was a total gas.

It was this marquee full of really crappy vintage gear – Mudda would be horrified but she was off somewhere on a Mad Mudda Mission so it didn't matter – and fancy dress costumes. You could hire stuff to wear for the weekend or just play dressing up and there was a catwalk outside you could parade on when you'd got your look together. Pretty funny.

All Mudda's ancient old friends and relations were carrying on like a gang of toddlers and I had such a laugh kitting Deathbreath out with a better disguise. He'd set fire to the beard in the end it was annoying him so much and it went up like a flame thrower. Luckily my cousin Becky had just arrived with her new bloke who was wearing big work boots and he jumped up and down on it before it set light to the whole field.

Deathbreath was a bit disappointed because he was just about to wee on it.

After that he had to go beard commando between where we had been sitting under the trees and the dress-up tent which was bloody miles away. Loads of people recognised him and just pointed like idiots. You could hear this creepy hum of Ritchie Ickies Ritchie Ickies Ritchie Ickies hubbub hubbub through the crowd. I can see why he doesn't go out much.

He had to sign a few autographs which he didn't mind but then a couple of psycho Ickie-arsehole-ologists tried to physically drag him off to have a drink with them. It was like a mugging. Poor Deathbreath. I hissed at them like a vampire but it didn't help.

Weanie saved us. He pretended to be DB's security and he looked the part in his suit and shades and he put his phone thing in his ear like the CIA which was funny. Plus he is one of the scariest fucking people I have ever seen so the wankers left us alone. He just walked in front of Deathbreath looking really menacing. It was genius. Plus he is a big Ickies wanker himself so he loved it.

When we got to the dress up place I put Deathbreath in this slinky fluorescent lime green flared nylon catsuit thing and a bright pink afro wig. Funniest thing I've ever seen. Sadly he refused to wear it for the rest of the festival but I did get him to do a turn on the catwalk outside with huge star-shaped purple shades on so no one recognised him.

'Get up, get on up . . .' we all sang along to the sound system and DB got into the groove doing this really hilarious funkadelic dancing. He's so lanky he looked some kind of mad old ostrich in Lycra but at the same time kind of great. I heard Lauren say to Rachel she thought DB was 'seriously hot ' which was weird. And slightly creepy.

DB's DJ friend Luke from the hell party was there too and he led the sing-along doing the bass line and then Weanie was being the drums. Take it to the bridge Deathbreath! I called out. It was quite cool and people were starting to gather to watch so DB had to rush inside the tent again before anyone realised it was him.

I laughed so much I very nearly pee peed myself and had to run up to some loos way at the back of the field near the Big Top. That girl Phoebe who seems to know everyone had told me to do that. Scope out the far flung toilies.

When I came out Weanie was waiting for me looking like Don Corleone in his black suit. Pretending to queue.

Nice shoes he said.

Nice fancy dress I said.

Anyone would think you worked in fashion he said.

Anyone would think you were a grown-up I said.

Then he made me go for a walk with him. Right round the back of the Big Top. We sat down on the grass and looked at each other.

Me: So what's your name?

Weanie: I'm not sure any more.

Me: Why's that?

Weanie: Because the only thing in my head is your face.

And then he kissed me.

Like a sex machine.

23
Loulou

The smell of frying bacon woke me up the next morning. I unzipped my 'bedroom' and peeped out of the front of the tent to see Keith happily tending a camping stove, wearing just his underpants – grey Calvin Klein trunks, of course – and a frilly apron.

'Happy birthday, Loulou darling!' he sang out.

His stamina amazed me. We hadn't crawled back to the tents until well past two the night before, after frequent forays to the vodka bar and various others, taking it all in as the festival changed from day to night and the whole energy shifted. In my case I hadn't so much hit the cocktails as seriously assaulted them, keen to dull any lingering thoughts of Marc and rather frenetically determined to have a good time. Not helped by the fact that Keith kept pointing out attractive young men for me to hit on.

'You told us all after the matchmaking party that you've decided to go after the young blood now, so this is like an all-you-can-eat smorgasbord for you,' he'd said, greatly to the amusement of the others, who'd enthusiastically joined in.

'Yeah, go on, girlfriend,' Lauren had chipped in. 'You're single, godammit. Grab yourself an early birthday present. Look at that one by the bar in the tight plaid shirt. Woof woof!'

And of course with dear Mr Beaney in tow, looking even more grumpy than usual, I'd had to go along with it, pretending to salivate over young blades I couldn't have cared less about.

Adding to my distress I'd seen a flash of white in the distance several times during the evening and been convinced it was the one young man in the place who did stir my blood. But it never was, so he was clearly keeping his promise to stay out of my way. So why did that make me so miserable?

He was doing exactly what I wanted, but I still felt wretched every time I thought about him. Which was way too often. I'd been so sure having that 'little talk' with him would enable me to move on from the whole sorry episode, but it hadn't.

'A full English?' enquired Keith happily as I blinked out at the daylight. 'And your tea will be ready in a moment.'

I went over to see what he had on offer. The works. Even a tea-pot and a nice big china mug, just the way I liked it.

He put one of his enormous arms around my shoulder and gave me a hug.

'How does it feel to be forty-nine then?' he asked. 'Have you mutated into a shrivelled-up old lady over night? No. So enjoy it. Today is all about you.'

I tried to be pleased about that. I knew Keith had gone to enormous lengths to put all this together for me, but it felt like a bit of a responsibility to live up to all the attention, especially with the hangover which was really beginning to bite around my temples. I'd just have to do my best.

He kissed the top of my head.

'I always forget how tiny you are without your President Sarkozy elevator shoes on,' he said.

'So do I,' I said. 'I feel too low down. I'm going to put some on.'

I went back to the tent, pulled a caftan worthy of Margot Ledbetter over my head, swiped on some lipstick, shook my bob into place and slid my feet into a pair of rubber wedge flip-flops, which made me at least four inches taller. Then, mug of tea in hand, Loulou Landers, forty-nine, felt ready to face the world.

By the time I'd come back from the loo and the shower block – which was built from hardboard and open to the sky, as Theo had told me, but better than nothing – I was feeling much better and looking forward to some nice greasy bacon.

'Happy birthday Loulou!' went up a big cry as I stepped over the bunting back into our camp.

Everyone was up and sitting around in various states of undress, eating Keith's brekkie. They all came over and hugged me, and it was only once I was sitting down and holding a second mug of tea that I noticed a huge pile of brightly wrapped presents on the central table.

'Wow!' I said. 'Is that really all for me? Can I open them now?'

'You better,' said Keith. 'I want to see what you've got.'

It was only when I reached for the first package – splendidly wrapped with a big purple bow – that I realised that Theo wasn't there.

'I'll just get Theo up to join in,' I said and as I spoke, I saw Keith and Rachel exchange a look.

'What?' I said.

'She's not here,' said Rachel. 'Ritchie went to wake her up so she could greet you with the rest of us, but she's not there.'

I turned immediately to Chard. He shrugged and looked unhappy.

'I don't know, babe. She told me yesterday afternoon she was staying here, but I guess she ended up going back with the young crew after all.'

'Remember when we bumped into a whole crowd of them at that bar near the lake?' said Keith. 'It was just before we went to watch that guy singing Joni Mitchell in drag . . . Tattie and Ariadne and Phoebe and that guy Stew and loads of others I don't know the names of, were all there. I think she was with them. They all went off to the dance tent.'

My memory of the evening was too fuzzy to remember much

detail and my hungover brain not up to processing much new information, but I couldn't help minding that she wasn't there on my birthday morning after she'd texted me to say she would be.

Of course, I was thrilled to think of Theo cavorting around the festival with a crowd of young people. The dance tent! It was everything I wanted for her, but because she'd specifically told me she was going to stay at Camp Loulou after all, I just couldn't help being disappointed she hadn't.

'I'll just go and check my phone,' I said.

I went off into my tent and as I sat down on the edge of my mattress, Chard came in through the front door.

'Hey, Loubie Lou,' he said, sitting down next to me and putting his arm around my shoulder. 'Don't let it get you down. I'm sure she just went back with her mates rather than walk back here on her own. Did you see those crazy shoes she had on? Even wilder than yours. They probably had to carry her.'

I nodded, feeling comforted. Darling Chard. He always knew the right thing to say and it did make me feel slightly better about it – she'd just gone with the flow, which was what this festival thing seemed to be all about – but I fired up my phone anyway. It would be nice to know if she'd bothered to leave a message.

There were three texts and the most recent one was from Theo:

> Happy Birthday! You are incredibly old.
> Sorry ended up back here after all. Was
> easier. See you later. Get Keith to text me
> with plans. xxx

That was OK, then, and I could see by the time on the message – 2.49 am – that she'd left it the night before, which was very thoughtful. Feeling much happier, I opened the next one without thinking.

> Sorry. Just did a drink 'n' text. Bad idea.
> Please delete it along with my number.

It wasn't signed but I knew it was from Marc, because his name had popped up on the phone when I scrolled to the text – I hadn't wiped his number like I'd said I was going to. And this meant that the third text was from him too and he'd sent it before this one. Shit. I knew I should just press delete without looking, but I was desperate to read it. What had he said which he later regretted?

I glanced at Chard, who was looking at me with fond concern.

'OK?' he said, squeezing my shoulder and then taking his arm away.

'Yeah,' I said, nodding and smiling, although I knew I'd stiffened and that was why he'd instinctively moved away from me. 'Nice happy birthday text from Theo. You were right. She just went back with her mates like you said. We'll catch up with her later.'

He patted me on the back in his well-meaning awkward way.

'Cool,' he said, lumbering to his feet. 'You can come and open your presents then.'

I knew I should just turn off my phone, get up and go with him, but I was simply longing to read that first text from Marc. I looked down at the phone and then up again. Chard was still waiting for me. I knew it was wrong, but I was so desperate for him to just get out of the goddam tent so I could read Marc's text, I was itchy with irritation.

Chard was looking a bit uncomfortable too, but then he seemed to make a decision and sat down next to me on the inflatable mattress again. It was all I could do not to groan with frustration. What kind of a friend was I? A crap one. A crap one, behaving like a teenage girl and an immature one too, but even knowing that I didn't seem able to help it.

I started to get to my feet, thinking if I could at least get him out of the tent, I could find an excuse to bob right back in again so I could read the text, before re-joining everybody, but he put a restraining hand on my arm.

'Hang on a moment, Loulou,' he said. 'I think I'd like to give you my present in here.'

I sat down again, momentarily distracted from my obsession with Marc's text by Chard's odd demeanour. He seemed strangely nervous.

'Great,' I said, trying to sound more excited than I felt. 'I'm happy to accept presents anywhere.'

Chard was leaning back on the mattress awkwardly groping around in his jeans pocket, his sunglasses falling off his head. I took them off before he crushed them.

'Where the hell is it?' he was muttering to himself, before producing a very small box, which he handed to me.

I looked down, rather astonished. It was unmistakably a jewellery box. A very nice navy kid leather one too. Vintage. I glanced back at Chard, too surprised to say anything.

'Go on,' he said, smiling shyly, his pale blue eyes looking deep into mine. With no shades and no wreaths of smoke, it made a nice change to be able to see them for once. 'Open it.'

I did and found a spectacular pair of antique drop earrings, with multicoloured dangling gems.

'Wow,' I said. 'These are really beautiful.'

I was gobsmacked. Chard was very generous by nature, always bringing me cute little gifts to the shop, but never anything like this. I looked back up at him. He was grinning.

'Do you like them?' he asked.

'I love them,' I said. 'They're gorgeous. Are those yellow diamonds, Chard?'

He nodded. 'Yes, and the pink ones are Burmese rubies, the dude in the shop told me. The blues and greens are things I've never heard of, but Theo said she's seen them all in the Natural History Museum.'

I smiled fondly.

'Yes,' I said. 'She always loved the gem collections in there. It was one of her special places, as a child. Did she help you choose these?'

He nodded.

'She told me which shop we had to go to and then I chose them. They reminded me of all the colours sitting on your terrace with you. Put them on.'

I fumbled a bit with my clumsy hangover fingers and he reached up and took them from me.

'Can I?' he asked and very carefully and tenderly looped the earrings through the holes in my lobes.

'Nice,' he said, touching the stones gently with his fingers. 'Yellow for the sun, blue for the sky, green for the tea, dark red for your . . .'

But before he could say any more, we heard the unmistakable tones of Keith yelling through the tent door.

'What are you doing in there, girlfriend?' he was saying. 'We're all waiting for you to open these bloody presents out here . . .'

Then he started a chorus of 'Why are we waiting?' which the other campers enthusiastically joined in.

'Coming!' I shouted back, quite relieved that the moment had been broken. I had felt a little awkward at the generosity of his present – and of course, I did still want to read that wretched text.

'Thanks, Chard,' I said, standing up and then turning round to reach down and kiss him on the cheek. 'That is the most beautiful present. It was incredibly generous of you. Thank you so much.'

He was blinking up at me, looking a bit bewildered, when Keith came bursting through the main door of the tent.

'What's going on in here?' he asked. 'Your fans are waiting, Miss Loulou . . . Come on, Ritchie,' he added, peering round me and into my little sleeping chamber, where Chard was still sitting on the mattress.

'Very cosy,' said Keith, giving me an arch look. 'Hope I'm not breaking anything up.'

I rolled my eyes at him as Chard lumbered out.

'Chard was just giving my present,' I said, holding my hands up to my ears. 'Aren't they gorgeous?'

'Oh my GOD,' shrieked Keith, bending down from his great height for a better look. 'Serious jewels. I am loving those.'

Chard grinned happily, as Keith patted him on the back.

'Excellent gift choice for a straight boy,' he was saying, as he practically pushed him out of the tent. Then he turned round to me.

'I'll be there in one second,' I said. 'Just need a moment. Girly thing.'

It was a cheap shot, but I knew any reference to unmentionable female things, however vague, was guaranteed to give me a moment's space from Keith.

'OK, darls,' he said. 'You know where to find us, but please don't be too long.'

'I won't,' I said. 'I'm dying to open my presents. Can you rack me up another tea? Head is a bit thick this morning . . .'

And can you please just GO!

'Oh forget tea,' said Keith. 'We're already on the hard stuff . . .'

And with one last peal of laughter, he was finally gone.

Alone at last, I crouched in my little bedroom, so desperate to read the text my fingers were slipping all over the phone and I nearly dropped it. Terrified I'd delete the thing before I could see what it said, I forced myself to slow down and take some deep breaths.

Finally it came up again and with a sense of thrilled foreboding I tapped the screen to read it:

> Staying away from you is so hard. I can see you from where I'm writing this. You're with your friends and you're laughing. You light up that group like a firework display. I'm with my friends and they are boring me witless. No I don't want any drugs. No I don't think that girl has great tits. No I don't think this track is wicked. No I don't want to dance. Why did you make me back off like this Loulou? Your reason is rubbish. It's nobody's business except ours. We are

humans not ages. You said you were going to delete my number. Well now you have it again. Marc x

I stared down at it in disbelief. I didn't know you could send such a long text, but the length wasn't really the issue, it was the content. I felt stunned. I'd known he was attracted to me for some weird reason, but this seemed like a declaration of something deeper than that.

For the first time I allowed myself to acknowledge the idea that he might really be keen on me. That he might have feelings for me which were something more than just an amusing novelty flirtation, which is what I'd thought it was for him. Not just the 'older woman' box to tick on his sexual CV. File under MILF.

For a moment I just sat with the thought. Marc *liked* me. Really liked me. Blimey. Did it make any difference to the situation? No. I'd still look like a craven old crone feeding on young flesh. Then I realised it did make a difference – it made sticking to my resolution even harder. It had been bad enough dealing with my own deeper feelings for him. Knowing it was reciprocated didn't help at all.

I put my head in my hands. He'd sent the second text to cancel the first, but it had failed. I knew and now I could never unknow. For a moment I wondered if I should reply, saying something mean like, 'Have deleted both texts and your number. Please don't ever contact me again.' But decided it wouldn't help either. Any contact at all was just prolonging the agony for both of us. I just had to ignore it.

After that bumpy start, though, my 'special day', as Keith would keep calling it, quickly improved. Chard had to go off – accompanied by a real minder this time – to check everything was in place for his appearance later, which was a shame, but the rest of us had great fun sampling Keith's 'morning cocktails'. Which seemed to be any kind of hard liquor with fruit or vegetable juice added.

'You've got several food groups in that one drink,' he was telling

Jane as she happily slugged back a potent concoction of tequila and V8, with a celery stick stirrer. 'And ice is one of your five a day.'

We were just starting to sort out the fancy dress they had picked up the day before when Theo arrived at the camp. She was rosy-cheeked and looking prettier than ever, and gave me what felt like a very loving hug. I was also thrilled to see she was carrying a holdall which looked like it had her clothes in it. Maybe she would be staying after all.

'Happy Birthday, Mudda,' she said and I didn't even let the latest insulting nickname bother me. Chard had told me she'd got the idea from Stravko's pronunciation, so it didn't seem so bad.

'I'm going to spend the whole day with you, if you can stand it,' she said.

I was thrilled and amazed and even more surprised by the present she had for me. Two pairs of fabulous Sergio Rossi shoes. They weren't quite my usual style, being more your crazy high stiletto than the crazy high platform arrangement I favoured – mainly because they gave you more height with less agony – but they were divine.

'Hot dog!' I said, strapping on a pair of gold sandals and strutting around the camp.

'Whoa, lady!' said Fiona.

'Give us a go!' said Jane.

'And me!' said Keith.

'Love dem shoes!' said Lauren, coming out of her tipi. 'But don't let Paul see you in them – he's a full-on shoe fetishist. Gets all hot and bothered around high heels, don't you, honey? Shame for him I won't wear them . . .'

She laughed heartily and I looked over at Paul, who was sitting at the far end of the gazebo. He looked even grumpier than usual and scowled as she spoke. Not a morning person, clearly.

'Thanks, Theo,' I said. 'They're amazing. Were the ones you were wearing yesterday Sergio Rossi as well?'

'Yeah,' she said casually, as though buying three pairs of £400 shoes was quite normal.

'I don't want to pry, but is there any particular reason you are suddenly buying luxury designer shoes in bulk?'

'Oh, I got them from a project I'm doing,' she said casually. 'You know I was helping Tattie? That kind of thing.'

I knew there was no point in trying to get more detail out of Ms Mystery, so I left it there. I was just thrilled she was involved in any kind of project with anyone.

'Great,' I said. 'Lucky me. And I see you're still wearing yours. Aren't they a bit uncomfortable all day on rough ground?'

'Yep,' she said. 'Agony, but you've always told me you have to suffer for style. These shoes got me into all kinds of trouble yesterday. I ended up sleeping with three other people in a two-man bivouac last night because of those shoes, instead of here in my own luxury tent. Can I see it, by the way?'

Keith gave her a tour of the camp and as she walked past Paul I saw him give her a blatant once-over. Head to high-heeled toe, with a lot of lingering in between. What a monstrous creep. I did understand that my daughter was extreme eye candy for middle-aged men, especially wearing tiny hotpants as she was, but I did think he could restrain himself in front of her mother – and his own wife.

It looked like Theo had caught him at it too. As she passed she gave him a playful clip around the ear. I would have liked to have given him a real one.

Theo

That showed him. Oh his face when I walked into that camp. And gave Mudda the shoes he had bought me. Thunder. So funny. And I wasn't at all surprised to hear shortly after that Weanie was leaving the Big Chill imminently. Some terrible crisis with the business apparently. Yeah right. A crisis in killer heels. Called Theo. About to take up residence in a tent just a few metres from him. I knew he wouldn't be able to stand it.

That kiss was amazing. Just about blew my head off if you really want to know. Nuclear. But I wasn't so keen when he assumed a kiss meant a shag behind a tent in public at a festival with his wife in residence. No thanks.

Me: Why now?

Him: When else?

Me: We were in the same hotel for three nights last week.

Him: Too obvious.

Me: Are you turned on by the danger Weanie?

Him: Of course. And those shoes. Eeeeuuurrgh . . .

He sort of growled and made another lunge but I was too quick for him. Zup. I was up and standing with my hands on my hips looking down at him. Not as easy as it sounds in those shoes and with the pulse rate I had going. Felt quite dizzy. I put one foot on his chest to balance myself. In those shorts he must have had quite a view.

Have a good look I said. That's all you're getting.

And I strutted off. Working the shoes to the max of course. Suffer Weanie. Suffer.

As I walked away I weighed up which would be maximum punishment for him. Me staying at the camp with my mum and Keith and everyone including him and his WIFE that night. Or me not staying there. In the end I decided I couldn't be bothered with the hassle of having to act cool around him so I just hung with my crowd all night and then crammed into Stew's tent with him and two other girls I didn't even know.

But today was Mudda's birthday and I had promised Chard I'd do the right thing so I did. Which was very much the wrong thing for old Weanie ha ha. So he's pissing off back to London. And his wife too. I'm glad because I'd rather not be reminded. And Mudda seems madda about her so that's all a bit shit too.

But what I really hope is that all this wifey wifey family cack isn't going to stop me working for West Wind. I would be really gutted to lose that now but if the whole thing was actually a game plan to get Weanie's weenie into my shorts then the only thing he can fuck is right off out of it.

Oh Weanie I thought you loved me for my brain boo hoo hoo. Ha ha ha. Never mind. I'll go and work for Topshop and tell them all West Wind's plans for the next three months.

Anyway haven't got time to write much more now. Have snuck away from Camp Loulou to this internet caff thingy where you can charge your mobile and use computers but there's a long queue and you only get ten minutes. Plus I've just spotted Tattie and Marc going past. I'm going to catch up with them and see what they're doing later. I've got strict instructions from Keith to hurry back for all the birthday activities but I'm going to find out what the Young People are up to long term first. Amazing but I might actually want to hang with them again.

Ended up having quite a laugh with them last night. Even with

Marco Polo Shirt. Well it was more general interface than laugh with him as he was being a bit odd and spent a lot of time hanging around outside on his own looking moody while we all DANCED. Yes even me. I like dancing in high heels. Makes it into more of a dangerous sport. Gives it an edge that makes it more interesting and plus I had to do something to stop thinking about that kiss with Weanie.

Aaaaaggggh . . . It's sending me mad. I want another one. Badly. I know I shouldn't because of the not small matter of the wife detail – plus messing up the work thing – but my head and my shorts seem to be on different settings about it. Head says no no no shorts say more more bigger faster now.

As well as liking dancing another discovery I made last night was this: I might have a very small amount of something called a conscience because after that chat we had up the hill I was feeling a bit bad how rude I've been to Marco Polo over the years. So when he didn't come back into the dance tent for ages I went out to see what he was doing. He was just leaning against this big wooden pole thing gazing off into the distance holding his phone.

Hey Polo man. I said. You're doing well. Looks like my grumpy lessons are working. Can you frown a bit more though? I could only give your frown a six right now. I'd like to see it get up to an eight before the end of the evening.

Hey Theo. Having fun?

I think I might be. Is that what this is?

He laughed.

I reckon it is Theo. It's what young folk like us are supposed to do.

So why aren't you doing it then?

Not in the mood. I'm missing someone.

Your old girlfriend who was shagging your mate? Tattie told me about that slapper.

No it's not her. Thank you for reminding me about that charming little episode with the woman I thought was the love of my life . . . but it's someone else. Doesn't matter.

Well it clearly does.

He looked a bit sick for a moment. I really hoped he wasn't going to cry.

I don't know what it is Theo but the women I like just don't seem to like me.

Have you ever thought it might be the polo shirts?

Oh fuck off.

Ha ha ha. Just a suggestion. Anyway I'll leave you to it. You carry on practising your misery and I'll keep trying this fun malarkey.

It's a deal.

Anyway so he's all right I think. In small doses. Very small. But the funny thing is although I can see he is monstrously good looking in a hilariously obvious way and women practically fall over having multiple orgasms every time they see him I couldn't kiss him. And it's not just his terrible clothes. I find him about as sexy as a cuddly toy.

But I can't think about much else than kissing Weanie again and he's really old and quite ugly. How weird is that?

24
Loulou

Theo turning up at Camp Loulou meant more to me than all my presents, splendid though they were – especially Chard's – but then I had another lovely birthday surprise – from Paul, of all people. Just as we were getting ready to head for the festival proper, he came stumping out of their tipi shouting for Lauren, who was right in front of him, and saying they had to go back to London immediately. Hurrah!

It seemed he'd just had a text from his second-in-command telling him there had been some kind of a disaster with a cargo ship with most of the autumn ranges on it and he had to rush back to town to crisis-manage.

It really took all my self-control not to look thrilled, although I didn't have to act when he made it clear he expected Lauren to go with him. She had to drive so he could spend the whole journey shouting down his phone. How lovely.

'Do you really have to go?' I asked her. Paul had disappeared off somewhere, after ordering her to get on with the packing. That man really was a prime pig.

'It's a pain in the ass,' said Lauren. 'But it's what you get when you're married to the "big man" and it's kind of normal to me. I grew up with shit like this – my dad was the big man too, remember.'

'But can't they send a driver for him?' I persisted.

'Sure they could, they could send a fricking helicopter, but he's pissed off, so he doesn't want me to have a good time here without him. He was really looking forward to this in his own little way – spending a weekend with Ritchie? Are you kidding? Dream come true for him. And all those beautiful young things to look at . . .'

I wondered if she'd noticed him scoping Theo too.

'Is that something Paul likes to do?' I asked tentatively.

'Haven't you seen him?' she said. 'He just about gave your daughter an X-ray earlier and didn't you notice how overexcited he was back at the matchmaking party? He didn't know which way to look first. I thought he was going to go into meltdown. He just loves them young, my old man.'

I was horrified.

'Doesn't that bother you?'

'I'm used to it, and again – Daddy dearest. Hollywood runs on a constant turnover of fresh firm flesh. It's like the fuel that keeps the whole city going, so in a funny way it makes sense that I would choose a guy like Paul who was wired like that.'

She was so open about it, I was quite taken aback – but it was exactly that straightforward quality that I loved in Lauren. It was so refreshing after the British approach of talking around emotional subjects, so you had to be able to read the invisible subtitles to know what someone really thought and felt. She just came out and said it.

I wanted to make the most of her company for the short remaining time I had her, so I made myself comfortable on the blow-up bed while she packed. There was also a slightly less than admirable part of me which wanted to know more grisly details about the man I already disliked so heartily and I knew Lauren wouldn't mind direct questions, so I plunged in.

'Does he ever act on it, or does he just look?' I asked.

'Oh, he has his little flings. He gets crushes like a girl, it's pathetic, but I know what they are and I live with it. He has his little fumble, gets a bit obsessed and then he's home to mama when it all gets complicated. Usually around the time when the phone starts to ring at home, but the person always hangs up when I answer . . .'

'You're amazing,' I said. 'I couldn't live with that.'

'I'm the mother of his children, Loulou, and we built the business together – it's like our fourth child – so we're welded into a solid unit by all that. And it would cost him *so* much money to leave me . . .'

She laughed.

'But you're not involved with the business any more, are you?' I said.

'No, he edged me out years ago. That's where he meets his little pussies. But it suits me. I don't want to work. I have my painting classes and my yoga and my houses and my kids and I'm very happy with my life.'

I lay there taking it all in. It sounded like the traditional aristocratic set-up that Princess Diana had so much trouble living with. I knew I wouldn't have been able to handle it. I'd much rather be in my own situation. Single, sexless, but independent, busy and making my own living.

'Can I ask you two more questions?' I said after a while.

'Sure,' said Lauren, clearly amused by my interest.

'Okay, number one: do you ever have affairs?'

'Mmm, maybe I do, maybe I don't . . . that's all I'm saying to that one.'

'So that's a yes, then. Right, question two: do you love him?'

She paused, holding a T-shirt in her hands, and smiled to herself.

'Of course I do,' she said. 'He's a selfish shit, but when I look at Paul, I still see the amazingly ambitious, wildly aggressive young guy I met when I was twenty-two. The council estate kid from Ruislip who wanted the good life and didn't care whose head he had to stomp on to get it. For a girl like me, born into the privilege he craved, and growing up with lots of spoiled, unhappy rich kids who just pissed it all away, his hunger and ambition seemed very exciting and attractive to me. It still does.'

I stood up and gave her a hug. So far, Lauren was the best thing to come out of that whole crazy match-making party lark.

I was sad to wave her off, but after they'd gone there wasn't a moment to spare in my 'birthday schedule', as Keith kept referring to it, to the general hilarity of the group. It was fun and treats all the way.

One of his more amusing stunts was a group foot massage – 'in homage to Loulou's commitment to the killer shoe . . .' – up in the Mind, Body and Spirit area. We must have looked pretty hilarious sitting there in the flamenco dresses – men and women – which Keith and Theo had chosen as our group fancy dress theme.

Watching my brother-in-law Martin, who owned a motorway maintenance company, dressed in a flouncy red-and-white polyester polka-dot dress, having his feet tenderly rubbed by a young man with a tattooed shaved head, wearing dhoti trousers and toe rings, was so funny it distracted me from remembering the last time I'd been up in that part of the festival – and who with. Especially when Keith handed his camera to a passing stranger to take a group photo of the event and Martin pulled his skirt up over his head.

'I don't want my picture on bloody Facebook wearing a bloody frock!' he said. 'I'm copping enough flack from the lads for even coming to a festival. One of them asked me if I wanted him to get some ecstasy tablets to bring with us.'

'Did you?' said Keith and we all cracked up.

Despite such distractions I was aware there was a lot of whispering going on and I had a fairly good idea Keith had some kind of big surprise set up for me later in the day. I didn't want to know what it was, so I was trying to keep my ears closed, but I had picked up that it was going to happen under the trees where we'd eaten lunch the day before.

Early in the afternoon Keith disappeared off somewhere and Jane and Rachel frogmarched me off towards the far side of the festival site – their arms linking mine on each side – on some rather spurious mission. I knew I was being got out of the way and just went with it.

'This is lovely,' I said, amused by their determined casualness. 'Am I allowed to know where we're going?

'Theo told me there's a charity shop over here,' said Jane. 'I thought you might find some stock in there.'

She laughed heartily, still finding it unbelievable after all these years that I made my living selling old clothes so, partly to amuse her, I spent a very happy forty-five minutes meticulously rootling through the rails. Like my fashion designer clients, I didn't get down to the grassroots of my trade much any more and I still had the taste for it.

I'd found such amazing things in stinky Oxfam shops over the years there was always the tantalising sense of promise, and this pop-up shop was for St Michael's Hospice, which I'd always found to be one of the better sources. Every charity had its own character, I'd learned over the years, attracting particular kinds of donors. Well-bred ladies seemed to give to this one.

'Oh, the smell . . .' Jane was saying. 'I've a mind to go and buy some joss sticks so these poor lasses won't have to stand in this terrible stink all day. Oooh . . . look at this! I had one like this in the Eighties.'

She held up a purple-and-black polka-dot one-shoulder polyester party dress with a puffball skirt.

'It might have been this one, actually . . .'

'You should get it for Becky,' I said. 'All that's back. She'd love it.'

Rachel was following me around the stall, which was delightfully disorganised, just the way I liked it, watching fascinated as I ran my hands along the rails and snatched occasional things out. I could find possible treasures just by feeling along the fabrics. The warm crunch of good tweed, the cool creamy feel of silk, the weight of crêpe de chine sang out to me from among the acrylic and viscose. I really could do it with my eyes closed.

'What have you found, Loulou?' she kept asking, as I pulled items out and piled them over my left arm.

'We'll have a proper look in a minute,' I said. 'This is just the first run-through. You take hold of this lot, would you? While I do this last couple of rails.'

Once I'd finished my first reccie – and Rachel resembled an overworked cricket umpire – we headed for the changing room. Not to try things on, I explained to her, but as a quiet place to examine what we had.

It was occupied and as we were waiting outside the curtain swished open and there was Jane, resplendent in the purple polka-dot dress.

'It fits!' she cried out.

'It looks great,' I added.

She turned round and looked at herself in the mirror. Then she pulled the bodice up towards her nose and sniffed.

'Doesn't smell too nasty . . .'

'And I'll give you a few squirts of my scent,' I said, getting my travel spray out of my bag and holding it up. 'This can cover any amount of mustiness. It's much better than Febreze.'

'I'm going to get this frock,' said Jane, squirting Mitsouko around liberally. 'It's cleaner than that awful flamenco dress. I've spent the whole morning trying not to think about the armpits on that thing. This one hasn't got any to worry about . . .'

She rushed off to pay and came back to watch me going through the pile of clothes. It was a battle to stop Rachel trying everything on, but fifteen minutes later I had an edited pile of five garments – plus the hilarious outfits Rachel and I were now also wearing.

I'd found Eighties treasures for us too, just as over-the-top as Jane's and we were all delighted to be out of the tatty flamenco gear – plus looking forward to surprising the rest of the crowd with our new looks. I'd also found a really funny New Romantics-style shirt for Keith.

As I was gathering up my carrier bags, I saw Rachel glance at her watch and was aware of a bit of semaphore going on over my head.

'Well, I don't know about you two,' said Jane, in theatrically casual tones. 'But I'm ready for a nice cup of tea and some refreshments. Shall we head for the main field where the best food is?'

'Oh that *is* a good idea,' said Rachel, equally artificially. 'Perhaps something sweet to toy with . . .'

I could tell the two of them were trying not to giggle and I was beginning to wonder what on earth Keith was cooking up for me.

Theo

Shit. I'm missing Weanie. How can that be? I'm sitting here under the trees remembering how I felt when I looked up YESTERDAY – cannot believe it was only yesterday – and saw him standing there in his suit looking like George Clooney's very ugly younger half-brother. The one whose mother was a gorilla. And a plain one.

I'm also thinking how much I would like to see his great ape face when Mudda sees what Keith has set up here. That would be funny. Actually I'm looking forward to seeing Mudda's face.

Where has she got to? Everyone's here now. The whole gang. Family/friends/'the young'. I know Auntie Jane and Rachel are herding Mudda up here and I wish they'd hurry up about it. The only usual suspect I can't see round this table is Polo Mint. I'll have to ask Tattie where's he got to. Seeing as how he 'admires' Mudda I'm surprised he hasn't come to pay his respects to the great ancient. Maybe he's off somewhere practising his frown for me ha ha ha.

Oop, here she comes. I like the blindfold. Nice touch BFG. Big Fat Gayer.

Holy man-made fibres – what is she wearing?

25
Loulou

Rachel and Jane stopped just before we turned the corner into the main field and put a blindfold on me, which I thought was going a bit far.

'Bloody hell!' I said. 'I did figure out you were all up to something, but this is getting a bit extreme.'

'Don't worry,' said Jane patting my arm. 'You're going to love it – and I mean *really* love it.'

And they both cracked up again, which made me even more alarmed. It was odd walking through the crowd blindfolded, aware of people laughing and saying things like 'Look at her!' I knew they were staring and pointing at me, even though I couldn't see them, but I could stay vaguely oriented by the gradient of the slope. Once it got steeper I knew we were heading up toward the trees and finally, we came to a stop.

I heard a great cry go up.

'Here she is!'

'Hey, Loubie Lou!'

'It's the birthday girl!'

'Mudda!'

Rachel and Jane let go of my arms and I felt a very large hand take hold of mine.

'Hello, Keith,' I said laughing. 'What on earth have you come up with this time?'

'Ready?' he asked.

'You tell me,' I replied and he untied the blindfold.

I blinked into the light and saw there was a long table stretching up the slope, covered with starched white cloths and laid with lovely old china tea sets. All along it, sitting on the kind of gold chairs they have at couture shows, was everyone I knew who was at the Big Chill. I shook my head with my mouth hanging open. It was amazing.

People from the general crowd were gathered round watching and I realised there was a red silk rope cordoning the area off, with an enormous security guard at the opening and another at each corner. Still blinking and trying to take it all in I noticed that everyone round the table had changed their clothes. There wasn't a flamenco dress in sight. The women were all done up in party dresses and the men were wearing various versions of black tie.

I turned to look at Jane and Rachel, who were grinning at me in delight.

'It's so lucky we changed!' I said.

They both laughed heartily.

'Do you really think that was an accident?' said Rachel.

'We knew you'd find outfits for us there,' said Jane. 'Mind you, I found my own, but taking you there was Theo's idea – clever girl, isn't she? She found her own frock in there too . . .'

I looked over to the table, to see my daughter in a glorious gold lame 1960s cocktail dress, her hair piled up on top of her head, her mouth painted with red lipstick, which was a new look for her and great with her new dark hair. She waved at me. I waved back.

'Do you like it?' asked Keith, leading me through the gap in the silk rope and up to the far end of the table, where there was a bigger gold chair, rather like a throne.

'I love it,' I said, squeezing his hand and reaching up to kiss him on the cheek. 'It's amazing.'

'You're here, birthday queen,' he said, ushering me into the throne. 'You've got me on one side and Ritchie on the other, OK?'

'Perfect,' I said, turning to smile at Chard as I sat down.

'Great dress,' he said, leaning over to kiss me on the cheek.

'It would be nothing without the earrings,' I answered, which made him grin. I sat back to take it all in. With all of Camp Loulou, plus Theo, Becky and her fiancé, Tattie and Oscar, Stew, Phoebe, Ariadne and various other young people I recognised from their gang, there were about twenty of us. They all smiled back at me.

Then I noticed Keith looking towards the trees to our right and at a signal from him, a procession of waiters appeared, walking towards the table carrying plates of cucumber sandwiches, teapots, cake stands with scones and iced fancies on them – the full afternoon tea.

It took a couple of moments before I registered something distinctive about the waiters. They were all young men. They were all preternaturally gorgeous – and they were all bare-chested beneath open white shirts and jeans. It was like being waited on by a platoon of Abercrombie & Fitch salesboys – clearly not an accidental affect.

The crowd which had gathered around the perimeter of the silk rope cheered – well, the female element of it did. Some of them wolf-whistling and making lewd comments.

I turned to Keith, my eyes popping.

'Where did you get them?'

He laughed heartily.

'Never you mind, the big thing is do you like them?

'How could I not?' I asked. 'They're gorgeous . . .'

But wanting to add: Why now? Why me? Although I knew damn well why. And then that made me think of the one other person I would be even more mortified to have at this event – Marc. All of the young camping crowd were round the table, but he was nowhere to be seen. I was so relieved I nearly crossed myself, but at the same time it made me sad that he was following my instructions so obediently he was missing out on the fun. Determinedly I put him out of my mind. I had enough to deal with.

Keith squeezed my hand, grinning.

'The boys are your special birthday present from me. Now I know you've got a taste for them young, I thought I'd spoil you for choice . . .'

'Thanks,' I said, mustering all my strength to stay looking delighted. I was appalled.

I looked round the table. Everyone was tucking in to the food and looking like they were having a lovely time, but they weren't in shock like I was. They'd all been in on it and that's what was so mortifying. Everyone there knew Keith had set this up because of my newly revealed fetish for younger men and they clearly all thought it was a hoot.

Even Martin seemed to be enjoying himself, piling a scone high with jam and cream, although he must have been so far outside his comfort zone it was almost another planet. Jane, Rachel, Fiona and Natalie seemed to be loving it, and Stew and Theo were giggling together like ten-year-olds. He was definitely getting off on the waiters, even if I wasn't. And then it got worse.

After another signal from Keith, the love gods started to bring out trays of champagne glasses. This time, minus the white shirts.

As a bare-chested young man reached past me smiling, his bare nipple nearly grazing my face, to put a glass on the table, I wondered if I was having my first hot flush. A wave of fiery embarrassment washed over my body and I so wished Lauren were there. I was sure she would have understood. But that would have meant Paul being there too. A thought almost too awful to contemplate. If he had been witness to this toyboy parade, I think I might have just dropped dead on the spot.

Once it had been filled with champagne by another half-naked pin-up boy, I grabbed my glass and gulped it down in one. As I banged the empty flute back down on the table – harder than

I meant to in my anxiety – I felt a gentle touch on my hand. I looked left to see Chard proffering his own glass of bubbly.

'Do you need this, Loubie?' he said, quietly.

I nodded, taking it from him and necking the contents. He reached under the table and patted my knee, as he would his dog. He knew how I was feeling. I didn't know how he knew – considering the female version of this event would have been all his erotic dreams come true – but I knew Chard knew. He didn't need to say anything; when I turned back it was all there in his eyes, which I was close enough to see through his shades.

Then I realised something else. Chard's hand was still on my knee, where he'd patted it. I wouldn't have thought twice if it had been Keith, but ongoing physical contact like that was so out of character for Chard, I could only assume it was because he understood quite how freaked out I was feeling, and it was his way of offering ongoing support.

Then that made me worry that my distress might be painfully obvious to anyone who looked at me, so I quickly I turned back to Keith, with what I hoped was an amazed and delighted expression on my face.

'However did you get all this together?' I asked him as brightly as I could muster.

'You know I love organising things, Loulou,' he said. 'And this was a *really* fun challenge. You should have seen the casting.'

'But how on earth did you set it up with The Big Chill? You must have needed their permission to do this in the main area . . .'

'Easy, darls,' he said, leaning in to whisper. 'My company insures this event, so I made sure they got an especially good deal on the premium this year.'

He winked at me.

'You see,' he added. 'Insurance isn't all boring, as I keep telling you.'

I kissed him on the cheek again. Although I was deeply mortified by the half-naked stud element – and the additional weirdness of Chard's hand still being on my knee – I did appreciate the rest of the set-up and was determined to keep up a jolly front for Keith. The champagne – and I'd had two more glasses in quick succession – was a big help, and I needed it because the torture wasn't over yet.

Keith must have signalled again, although in my now pleasantly tipsy state I hadn't noticed, because all the man-child waiters suddenly disappeared behind the trees again. Then two of them came out carrying a tray with an enormous birthday cake on it. And now they were just wearing underpants. Tight grey trunks, like the ones Keith had been wearing at breakfast.

The watching crowd – which had been growing steadily – whooped loudly, with even more catcalls and dirty remarks. I closed my eyes for a moment to collect myself and when I opened them again, the cake was right in front of me, alight with candles, and everyone was singing 'Happy Birthday'.

And as I stood up and leaned forward on automatic pilot to blow out the candles – all forty-nine of them – I saw that beyond them on the very top of the cake was a marzipan model of a large cat. Rampant. A cougar.

It was as though everyone else noticed it at the same time. I heard the word go round the table – and then into the mass assembled around the silk rope.

'Go Samantha!' called out a female voice from the crowd, inspiring raucous laughter all round.

'Give them one from me!' shouted out another and I felt Chard's hand, which he'd had to take off my knee when I stood up, settle on my waist. He gave it a squeeze followed by a couple of pats. A big demonstration of support from him. What a friend.

I didn't even dare to turn and glance at him, in case I burst into tears, and forced myself instead to look at all the smiling faces round the table and remind myself they were all there for me and on my side. The silly business with the cougar cake and the nearly naked boys was just a joke.

'That's hilaaaarious. I'm always Samantha when I do the *Sex and the City* quiz . . .' Stew was saying to Theo, which clearly reminded her what had prompted this whole event.

'Hey, Tattie,' she called across the table, in one of those sudden lulls in the conversation, so everyone heard. 'Where's your brother? Shouldn't he be dirty-dancing with my mum at this point?'

'Yeah! Bring him on!' added Keith and everyone laughed, totally oblivious to how I was feeling. Although, alongside the utter humiliation of the cougar cake, it did seem a massive leap forward that Theo was now able to joke about that night. Then I did turn to Chard. He was the only person who would have understood how I was feeling.

'It's all good, Loubs,' he was saying, in full nodding mode. 'Go with it, it's all good.'

'At least she's joking about it, eh, Chard?' I said.

He carried on nodding.

'Massive,' he said. 'And don't get hung up on this young guy thing, I know it's not really your bag, or you'd have an army of them already. Keith's done this for himself as much as for you. More so.'

I smiled at him with heartfelt gratitude. He so got it. But then I was distracted by Tattie's voice ringing out.

'I don't know where Marc is . . .' she was saying. 'He definitely knew about this, I told him myself. I was sure he was going to come. It's really weird he's not here.'

Not to me, I thought. He was probably sitting somewhere on his own, knowing what he was missing out on, thanks to me. I hoped he'd picked up some beautiful young woman to take his mind off it. That was what he needed. Thinking about Marc again made me feel even lower and I was actually quite relieved to be distracted by the boys coming round again with slices of the cake.

'They're not going to take anything else off, are they?' I asked

Keith. Trying not to notice the bulging crotches that kept appearing at just below eye level.

Keith laughed.

'Well, I did consider having a naked boy jump out of the cake and give you a lap dance, but thought that was going a bit far, even for me.'

I silently promised the Virgin Mary and all the saints I would say a hundred novenas in thanks.

'Mind you,' added Keith, leaning in to my ear. 'I think they look sexier with the trunks on . . .'

Finally, the cake eaten, the last champagne poured and swallowed, it was over. The watching crowd quickly dispersed and as I stood up to go and mingle with the pals who had been sitting at the other end of the table, Chard also got to his feet and put his hand on my shoulder.

'Cool, babe?' he asked, resting it there for a moment.

'Yeah,' I said, nodding at him in his own style. 'All cool. Positively chilly.'

Then feeling a sudden rush of affection for him – increased by lingering guilt at how I'd wanted him to clear off out of my tent so I could read Marc's text earlier that day – I threw my arms around his neck and hugged him hard.

'Thanks for being such a good friend, Chard,' I said, breathing in the now familiar combo of ciggies and vetiver. 'I don't know what I'd do without you. Sometimes I think you're the only person who really understands me.'

He looked shyly delighted at the compliment. People were always telling him he was a musical genius and a living national treasure, which I knew bored him beyond endurance, and I realised that a genuine expression of appreciation would have meant a lot to him.

'Likewise, Loubs. Big time,' he said, squeezing me back – and not letting go. I felt awkward for a moment. What was he doing?

But then I just surrendered to it. It was a bit odd, but nice odd. He rested his head on top of mine and I leant my face against his chest as he shifted his weight slowly from foot to foot, rocking me gently, like a baby.

I don't know how long we stayed like that, but with the strangely ambient cacophony of festival noises, the warmth of his body and the rocking, I felt so relaxed I almost could have gone to sleep. My reverie was broken by a gruff voice saying: 'Are you ready, Mr Ritchie?'

I felt Chard lift his head and nod at whoever had spoken, then he gently pulled away from me and taking both my hands in his, looked deep into my eyes, over the top of his shades.

'I've got to go and get ready for my set, Loubie Lou,' he said. 'I'd rather stay right here, but I've got a job to do. I'm coming on at nine, main stage. Don't be late – OK? And then there's the usual drinks backstage after. Keith's got all the passes.'

I smiled up at him, blinking as though I had just come out of a yoga meditation. I felt quite befuddled. He leaned down and gave me a big kiss on my right cheek. Then after pulling away for a moment, he came back and gave me one on the other side, still not letting go of my hands.

'Go on, then,' I said, taking my hands out of his and putting them on his chest, jokingly pretending to push him away. 'Off you go. Don't keep the roadies waiting.'

Then as I looked at my hands on his jacket, I realised what he was wearing.

'Hey,' I said, fingering the lapel. 'Isn't this the tux you bought from me about five thousand years ago?'

'The very one,' he said, clearly pleased I'd noticed.

'Wow, that's 1930s Savile Row. I sold it to you in 1979 – and it still looks amazing.'

'I bought it the first time I ever came to your shop, Lulabelle,' he said, shooting the cuffs and adjusting the collar. 'Best jacket I own.'

I laughed.

'Tell my sister that,' I said. 'And break a leg, or whatever you say to DJs, with your set. I can't wait. I know it's going to be brilliant.'

He blew me a kiss and ambled off, his usual cowboy boots and jeans cladding the bandy legs below the dinner jacket. I heard the words 'Ickies, Ritchie' start to hum through the crowd, as he went, and was relieved to see the huge security guard, who had been manning the silk rope, was at his side. Didn't want him getting mobbed.

I stood for a moment, watching him go. What had made Chard suddenly loosen up on physical contact, so he was more like laid-back touchy-feely Aussie Keith, than the uptight English public schoolboy who lurked beneath that rock star persona?

And just as suddenly it seemed Theo was fine about me dancing with Marc – or fine enough to joke about it at least. So many things were changing, so quickly. But all for the better. The Big Chill seemed to be living up to its name.

Four hours – and several more bottles of champagne in the bar down by the lake – later the entire tea party crew was gathered again, centre middle in front of the main stage, waiting for Chard's set to begin. Along with what looked like just about everyone else who was at the Big Chill.

I hadn't been in a crowd so big for years. When I went to see The Ickies I always stood at the side of the stage with the band's wives and I'd forgotten what fun it was to be down among the heaving bodies.

When Chard finally took to the stage – a suitably superstar twenty minutes late – the crowd went nuts. I was delighted to see he was still wearing the dinner jacket, now over a vintage western shirt, also from my shop, and black leather pants, his favourite electric guitar slung over his shoulder. What a dude. He may not have been far off being eligible for a bus pass, but his stage presence was completely undiminished.

'Hello, Big Chill!' he said, in the classic tradition. 'All right?'

'YEEEEEAAAAAHHHH!' we all yelled.

Theo was so excited and proud of her godfather she was literally jumping up and down – quite a feat considering she still had those crazy heels on.

'I'm Ritchie Meredith,' Chard was saying, completely unnecessarily, and the crowd was screaming again. 'I normally play with a band called Icarus High . . .'

More screaming.

'But, tonight I'm doing something a bit different. So please welcome my friend Luke Ma who's taught me everything I know about spinning sounds . . .'

The crowd politely applauded the unknown DJ as he walked on to the stage and, at a nod from Chard, cued the first track, which was a simple drum beat, boosting the sense of anticipation.

'And now,' said Chard. 'I want to dedicate this entire set to my best friend – a very special lady called Loulou Landers. It's her birthday today. Happy Birthday Loulou! I love you, baby.'

The excited crowd cheered and I was so amazed I just stood there with my mouth hanging open, while our little gang went bananas all round me.

Keith, Stew and Martin were pointing at me and telling everyone within sight that I was the Loulou in question and hordes of total strangers were grinning and waving and giving me the thumbs-up. It was pretty special.

'Now everybody,' Chard was saying, playing a few familiar sounding notes on his guitar. 'I want you all to help me wish her a happy birthday. On three. One, two three: Happy Birthday to you . . .'

It's quite something to have thirty thousand people singing you 'Happy Birthday' – especially accompanied by one of the world's greatest rock guitarists giving it some musical flourishes – and I stood there just gawping like an idiot, until Jane came and put her arms round me.

'Oh, you silly bugger,' she shouted in my ear. 'How amazing is this?'

'Totally!' I shouted back.

He finished it off with three cheers and while the crowd was still whooping and yelling, Chard glanced over his shoulder at Luke and the unmistakeable opening bass riff of one the Ickies' most iconic songs rang out and Chard started playing along, his great long arms flying around like windmills. We all went wild.

Towards the end of the number Chard headed back to the turntables, pushed his guitar round behind his back and after putting on his headphones, seamlessly blended the Ickies track with what I recognised as one of his favourite old blues numbers.

And so it went on, Chard's and Luke's heads nodding in perfect time just as they had at the matchmaking party. I found it as hilarious as I had then, the gnarled old rocker and the sharp young Shoreditch blade in perfect agreement about the sounds. Whenever the mood took him, Chard would come out from behind the decks again and play along. The crowd seemed to love it.

After a while the tempo of the songs got slower and Chard came back to centre stage, now carrying an acoustic guitar, and climbed on to a stool a roadie had set up. As the track on the turntable faded he started playing, with no introduction, a piece I'd never heard before, with no words, just the guitar. It was absolutely beautiful and there was an awed hush over the crowd as they listened.

I gazed up at my friend, that so-familiar head bent down over his instrument in complete concentration, oblivious to anything except the lump of wood he was holding and the magic he could make with it. When he finished, there was a pause and then the crowd went crazy with applause. Chard looked down at us all, smiling.

'Oh, you're all still here are you? Did you like that? Good. It's for the new album. I'm still working on the words, but it's for someone special. Do you think she'll like it?'

The crowd roared back its agreement. I didn't know he had a big thing going on with anyone, but whoever she was, she was very lucky to have that written for her. It managed to be a love song even without words. I hoped she would appreciate it. And him. Picturing one of the spoiled young lovelies he normally went for, I felt a sudden lurch of protectiveness, mixed with some kind of resentment. She'd better not hurt my Chard, or she'd have me to answer to. Yessir.

After that he played some more new material, mixed in with some classic Ickies tracks which sounded amazing played acoustically, then the roadie came over with his electric guitar and Chard jumped to his feet, ramping up the energy, before signalling to Luke to come back in with the decks again and they embarked on a mix of tracks you just had to move to.

By the time the first claps of 'Car Wash' rang out, it seemed everyone was getting on down, with Theo happily dancing with me, Jane, Keith and Stew. I was so happy. I didn't know when Theo had last danced with me – but when she was a child an after-dinner disco had been one of our treasured nightly rituals, so it was the best birthday present I could have had.

Every track they played made you want to keep dancing, until I began to feel quite dizzy from it, and as the sun began to set, the atmosphere got even more intense. The whole crowd was grooving together like one rhythmic organism and I was completely lost in the beats, when suddenly I noticed a familiar figure not far off. Wearing an unmistakable white suit.

Feeling like my feet were in charge and my brain had absolutely no say in it, I found myself moving inexorably towards him, and just as I reached his side Marc did a spin and saw me. He came to an abrupt stop and first a delighted smile, then a cautious frown crossed his face.

Then, as I grabbed his hand, the opening bars of *Time After Time* came flowing out of Chard's sound system, and we were off, perfectly in synch like the first time.

Everyone at the Big Chill already knew I was a tragic old cougar, I told myself, as he pulled me back in to his arms after an extravagant double twirl, so I might as well act like one.

Theo

It's going to take me nearly five hours to get back to London on this goat train but I don't care. I had to get away from there.

I'd had enough of camping enough of vomity portaloos enough of Stew wittering on enough of Tattie being surgically attached to that human rugby ball she calls her boyfriend and enough of grass. So tedious to walk on. Gimme some proper hard London pavements. And most of all I'd REALLY had enough of my tragic MOTHER cracking on to the Polo Mint child in PUBLIC. Again.

It was the again-ness that was the thing. We'd talked about it and stuff and that boys-on-toast cougar birthday tea was really funny but that doesn't mean I want to see her ACTING OUT on her perverted impulses. That's what she doesn't get. We can talk about it but that doesn't make it OK to DO it. Different.

It ruined Chard's genius set for me and I was having such a good time until I looked round and saw them at it AGAIN.

Those quite cool friends of the Polo's had turned up and we were all getting down on it in a really funny way and it was even OK when I realised that he was with them because I don't hate him any more. But then a bit later I did a twirl and there was Mudda bumping and grinding with him again and it was growwwwwwtesssskkkk.

So I made the funniest of Polo's yooni pals come and dance with me right down by the stage where we couldn't see them so

I could at least catch the end of Chard's set without feeling physically ill.

When it was over I went straight back to Keith's camp and went to bed. Well not straight to bed. That friend of Polo's insisted on walking with me. Whatsisname? Oh yeah Dylan. Freakishly terrible name but he is really funny if you close your eyes while he's talking. Although I do rather like his beard. It looks a bit like the one I got for Deathbreath but it's actually real. Proper pubey.

I was glad he was there to take my mind off things because I was majorly pissed off to miss Deathbreath's post-gig backstage party. It would have been brilliant but there was no way I was risking Mudda being there publicly tonguing the Mint or worse. I felt really bad letting Deathbreath down but it was her fault.

Me and Dylan were still talking under the gazebo when I heard all the olds coming back laughing like tragic drunks – I could hear Auntie Jane miles away swearing as she kept tripping over guy ropes – and I made him scarper and jumped into bed before they saw me. Got that zip down just in time.

I heard Uncle Martin saying: Should we check if Theo's here?

BFG: No she's either asleep or she's back with her own friends. Or maybe she's with Loulou – wherever *she* is. It must be something good to make her miss Ritchie's party ha ha ha.

Ha ha ha WHAT THE FUCK? She hadn't come back with them – and she'd missed Deathbreath's party too? Then where the hell was she? That was something really NOT to think about. The possibilities too too terrible. I zipped my sleeping bag shut right round over my head to try and block it out.

So after all that trauma I got up really early this morning and snuck off. Leaving a note for the BFG and his Teeth. Not for HER.

I hitched a ride into the nearest town which is about the size of my nipple and got the first train to London which goes via Birmingham and possibly John O'Groats and I've got to change three times but I don't care because it's taking me away from there. And her.

And closer to Weanie who has sent me rather a lot of texts saying how much he misses me. And how he needs me to come into the office as soon as I get back because they are going to do a whole new special range called Made in Britain which will actually have to be made in Britain because all the stuff made by foetuses in Bangladesh is being held to ransom by Somalian pirates or some such nonsense.

I thought he'd made the whole work crisis up just so he could leave the Big Chill and not camp next to me with wifey in residence. I'll be disappointed if it's a real crisis.

Either way he says we've got to do this new range to go in store in September and he can't do it without me.

Too right he can't.

26
Loulou

It felt so right to be dancing with Marc again I didn't care how wrong it actually was. It didn't bother me if everyone at the Big Chill was pointing at us and laughing. Look at the tragic old cougar and her toyboy! In fact, I thought they were more likely to be saying what great dancers we were.

Lost in the rhythm and the moment – and the not inconsiderable amount of champagne I had consumed that afternoon – I completely forgot about everyone else I knew who was there and the energy of our dancing seemed to move us naturally through the crowd until we weren't near any of them anyway and I couldn't have cared less. Like the song Chard played near the end of his set, with me resting in Marc's arms, my head on his shoulder, *Nothing Else Matters*.

I didn't even care if Theo saw me in that compromising position. She'd made a joke about me dancing with Marc at Keith's terrible tea, so I was hoping she was over that silliness now. And after the gross humiliation I'd felt at that well-meant birthday 'treat', it seemed a fair recompense to spend a blissful hour or so getting down with the most compatible dancing partner I'd ever had.

And it was all about the dancing. We didn't try to talk. It wasn't possible over the volume and I didn't want to anyway. Physically being together was enough. We said everything we needed to say with our bodies.

After two encores, Chard's set was finally over and the masses started to disperse. Without saying a word, Marc put his arm around my waist and led me away from the stage and up the hill. At that point I would have followed him anywhere.

'Aren't we going to your tree stumps?' I asked him, as we went past the turning to that spot.

'No,' said Marc. 'I want to show you somewhere better than that.'

We carried on walking uphill until we left the lights of the festival behind and he got a small torch out of his pocket to light our way. We felt so far away from it all by then, I wondered if we'd actually left the Big Chill site, but finally we stopped.

'Here we are,' he said quietly and as I was still taking in that we were under a small stand of oak trees, the torch went out and he seemed to disappear from my side.

'Marc?' I said into the darkness, my eyes not yet adjusted, and then I felt his hand reach out and find mine. He pulled me down and I tumbled onto what I realised was a hammock strung between the trees.

I couldn't help laughing, but at the same time I realised I was now lying down in Marc's arms and even in the dark I could see that his face was right next to mine. I could feel his breath against my cheek and while I was still taking in the situation his lips were already on mine.

His hand came up and held my cheek as he pressed his lips down more firmly and then slid his tongue into my mouth. Immediately mine was pressing back against it and as they twined together, I felt like I was falling backwards in space. My body felt super-alive as if an electric current had just passed through it, but at the same time my brain kicked in. Dancing was one thing – this was quite another.

I pulled away and sat up in the hammock – which wasn't easy. I nearly fell out.

'Hey,' said Marc, half sitting up himself and grabbing my arm to steady me. 'What's the matter?'

'It's all going too fast, Marc,' I said.

I heard him sigh, but he swung his legs over the edge of the hammock and sat up next to me. I don't know whether it was the evening chill, shock or simple lust, but I began to shiver and he immediately took off the white jacket and draped it round my shoulders, leaving his arm resting across my back.

For a while we just sat there, and it was almost physically painful how comfortable and right it felt to be there with his arm around me – and how much I wanted to resume what we'd just been doing and take it further.

In the end, after everything that had happened earlier in the day, it proved too much for me and hard as I tried to stop them, tears started rolling down my cheeks.

'Hey, Loulou,' said Marc. 'Don't cry. What's wrong?'

'Oh, you know what's wrong,' I said, taking the handkerchief he had just pulled out of his pocket. Even in my distress I registered amazement that a man of his age would be carrying an ironed cotton hankie at all, let alone at a festival.

'Spell it out,' he said. 'Seems I'm a little dense on the subject.'

I felt so awkward talking about it, but I owed him an explanation. I'd danced with him like a shameless ho in front of twenty-nine thousand nine hundred and seventy-five strangers – and about twenty-five people I knew – yet now we were completely alone in a field, in the pitch dark, I couldn't let him kiss me, no matter how much I wanted him to. I owed myself an explanation too.

'It's just the same old shit,' I said. 'The age difference. I feel so vulnerable even being attracted to you and I can't let myself give in to it.'

'You did while we were dancing,' he said.

'I know,' I said. 'And I loved it. Like I love just sitting here with you like this, but anything more than this freaks me out. It makes me feel so exposed to shame and mockery.'

'Tell me about the tea party,' he said.

I sat up straight and turned to him in surprise. How did he know how relevant that was to the way I was feeling now? He'd nailed it.

'Tell me what you know about it, first,' I replied.

'I know there were practically naked young studs serving . . .'

I groaned.

'It was terrible, Marc,' I said. 'It summed up everything that makes me feel confused about you.'

'So why did they put it on then? Wasn't it supposed to be your big birthday treat? They must have thought that was your thing . . .'

'That's the whole problem,' I said, frustrated. 'Because I made a big joke about dancing with you at that party, saying I was getting into hard young meat – to try and cover up how I really felt – Keith thinks I am actually into younger guys in a pervy, sexy way. So he thought I'd love all those half-naked boys, that it would be the most wonderful treat for me.'

I groaned at the memory.

'The cake had a marzipan cougar on the top,' I whispered, finding it hard even to frame the words.

To my surprise Marc burst out laughing.

'What you mean like cougars in *Sex and the City*? Middle-aged women who pursue hot young guys for sex? Oh, that is hilarious.'

'It's not,' I said. 'It was so humiliating. With Chard – Ritchie – being there and everything, a big crowd gathered to watch and they all started calling me Samantha. I thought I was going to die.'

Marc was laughing so much he fell back down on to the hammock, which made it swing precariously and I found myself lying down next to him again, our feet still on the ground, our heads side by side on the woven string netting. And I found I was laughing too.

'Ahaha, Samantha,' Marc was gasping. 'Oh that's so funny. I can't think of anyone less like her than you. It's hilarious.'

After we finally recovered ourselves we just lay there for a very still moment staring into each other's eyes and he gently put out his hand and stroked my cheek.

'I think you're definitely more of a Carrie,' he said. 'Although when I did the quiz on Facebook, I was Miranda. I wasn't sure how I felt about that.'

'You took the *Sex and the City* quiz on Facebook?' I asked him, secretly thrilled I even knew what it was. A few months earlier I wouldn't have had a clue.

'Anything rather than get on with the essay I was supposed to be handing in the next day. In the Disney quiz I was Mickey Mouse. I so wanted to be Goofy.'

That set us off again.

When we'd recovered from the kind of manic laughter that comes only after previous tension, Marc swung his legs back into the hammock and put out his hand to me.

'Come and lie back down, Loulou,' he said. 'I won't kiss you, but it's so much more comfortable. And let's just enjoy this time up here in our own little secret world where it doesn't matter what anyone else thinks.'

So I did and it was nothing short of blissful, lying there with him in the dark, pleasantly aware of the music from the festival still audible in the distance, but not so loud that we couldn't hear the breeze rustling the leaves of the trees overhead.

I sighed with pleasure and he kissed the top of my head.

'Oops,' he said. 'Broke the kissing promise. How about if I just promise not to kiss you on the lips?'

'OK,' I said.

He kissed the side of my head. Then my ear and then started nuzzling my neck. In an instant my body was alight and I only just managed to collect myself as I was about to hook my leg over his hip.

'Um, Marc,' I said, lying flat again. 'Can we just lie here?'

'Sorry,' he said. 'I keep thinking I can contain myself and then I can't. You smell so good.'

He put his nose against my neck and breathed deeply.

'Mmm . . . Delicious.'

'Not helping,' I said.

He chuckled and settled himself back next to me again. As we were lying there, a bright light suddenly appeared in the sky passing slowly overhead, getting smaller as it went.

'What the hell is that?' I asked him. 'Is it a UFO?'

Mark raised his head and looked in the direction where it had come from.

'No,' he said. 'It's a flying lantern. Look, there's more coming.'

I lifted my head to see and sure enough another light was coming up the hill towards us, followed closely by another.

'What are they?' I said.

'They're Chinese paper lanterns. You light a wick inside them and the warm air from the flame lifts them up and carries them away. Beautiful, aren't they?'

'They're gorgeous,' I said, transfixed.

We lay in the hammock, completely still, watching the golden lights float overhead, climbing higher and higher in the sky and becoming smaller with every moment, until they disappeared from sight over the Malvern Hills.

Mark found my hand and held it in his and we watched as two lanterns appeared, floating close together, drifting apart a bit on the air currents and then coming back towards each other.

'Those two are like us,' he said, after a while.

I didn't say anything. Nothing I could think of seemed up to the moment.

'Two independent spirits, quietly going their own way, but inexorably drawn together . . .'

I didn't dare to look at him. The urge to kiss him again was so strong, I knew I wouldn't be able to resist it. So I watched the Marc and Loulou lanterns as they floated higher into the night sky and then just before they disappeared from view, they clearly bumped together.

Marc laughed softly.

'Told you,' he said, squeezing my hand.

I poked him playfully in the chest with my finger, pulling my hand away sharply after it made contact with the hard muscle there. I could sense his head was turned towards me and it took all my self-control not to turn my own head and consume him.

Perhaps, I thought, staring determinedly upwards, perhaps one kiss would be enough, but I knew I was kidding myself. The small taste I'd already had had set me off like a string of firecrackers, sexual excitement snapping through my body.

So maybe one night of hot loving would do it? Do it all, eat him alive, get it out of my system and move on. It was so tempting. I wanted him so badly. But what if it had the other effect? What if it just made me fall really properly in love with him? Even more than I already was.

And what about him? It wasn't just my feelings that were at stake. His young heart was probably much more tender and vulnerable than the shrivelled-up old walnut in my chest. He'd already been badly hurt by a girlfriend, he didn't need me messing with his emotions to satisfy my carnal needs. That really would make me a ghastly predatory cougar.

I desperately wanted simply to exist in that delicious moment, to abandon myself to the relatively innocent pleasure of lying there with him, side by side with that vital male body and knowing he wanted to be there just as much as I did, but my brain couldn't shut down. I was relieved when he spoke.

'Tell me something else about the tea party . . .' he said.

'What?'

'How did Theo react? Was she appalled?'

'No, that was the strange thing. She wasn't. She seemed to think it was really funny and she even asked your sister where you were – and made a joke that you should be slow dancing with me.'

'That's good,' he said. 'I'm glad about that.'

'You don't seem very surprised.'

'Well, I kept my promise about Theo,' he said. 'The one I made the night of the party. You remember, in the garden, under the rose bower, in the rain . . .'

We were both silent for a moment, remembering. Whatever there was between us, it was clear to me now it was already well in train back then. Probably from the night in the shop when I nearly fell off my ladder. Marc squeezed my hand very gently. I wasn't imagining it. He knew it too.

'Anyway,' he said. 'I think I've finally convinced her I'm not a total arsehole and I introduced her to some of my uni friends and I think she quite liked them. Especially Dylan.'

'Who's Dylan?'

'Interesting bloke. Super bright. Spent his gap year in Afghanistan working for an aid project. His dad is that banker who got done for massive fraud a few years ago. He's in prison. Dylan hates him so much he's changed his name by deed poll. His real name is Rupert.'

I laughed.

'He sounds perfect for Theo,' I said. 'They've got a lot in common on the dad front. Is he good-looking?'

'Is he good-looking?' repeated Marc, sounding bemused. 'I don't know, but probably not. He's more what you would call "interesting" looking. Big nose, crazy long beard . . . but with his brain, it doesn't matter.'

'You're right. It was a dreadful question to ask, I'm sorry. I'm afraid that's one of the less attractive aspects of the industry I'm in. It makes you over-concerned with the hopelessly superficial . . . and Marc – thank you. Thank you for keeping your promise about Theo. She's been so much more relaxed since we've been here and I had no idea it was down to you.'

As I spoke, another less pleasant thought occurred to me. Had us dancing together publicly again destroyed the improvement? With the dawning of that harsh reality, I suddenly started to find the hammock really uncomfortable and the air increasingly damp. It felt like our golden moment was over.

'It's getting cold, Marc,' I said. 'It's been gorgeous, but I think we should go now.'

'OK,' he said, 'I'll walk you home.'

I felt every year of my age as I staggered up from the hammock and tried to get my aching old limbs back into working mode. Clearly unaffected, Marc flicked up the collar of his polo shirt against the chill, fired up the flashlight, and we set off back down the hill, arms around each other, not caring who saw us. There were plenty of people around still, but we didn't see anyone we knew and no-one looked twice at us. Probably too dark to see how ridiculous we looked, I thought.

When we got near the bottom of the main festival area, by the main stage, Marc stopped.

'Is your camp that way?' he asked pointing off to the left.

I nodded.

'Where's yours?' I asked.

He pointed in the other direction.

'You really don't have to walk me home, Marc,' I said.

'I do,' he replied. 'But I've got a better idea. Come and stay in my tent. I won't molest you. I'll keep all my clothes on and I'll be in a separate sleeping bag, but I just want to have this one night with you. I'm not ready to be separated yet.'

'But aren't you in the party camp with the others?' I asked, imagining crawling out of Marc's tent to see all of them in the morning. Hi Tattie!

'Near, but not in it,' he said, shaking his head. 'I've got my own little separate billet on the other side of the same camping area. It all gets a bit much with that crew, the giggling and the shrieking. I like to have my own space. And if I'm really honest, I was secretly hoping I might get to spend one night in it with you this weekend.'

He dropped his head as he spoke, in an uncharacteristic moment of shyness. I was so surprised, I laughed – and made a snap decision. It was my forty-ninth birthday and an exceptionally gorgeous and lovely twenty-four-year-old man wanted me to spend the night with him.

I could do that or wake up alone, sharing a tent with my best gay friend. Was there really a choice?

'Your place,' I said.

Theo

I'm writing this on the mainframe back at Mudda's madhouse. It's great to be back on the big pooter again – nearly crippled my fingers trying to keep this up on my phone – but weirdo to be back here. Especially considering how furious I was with slut Mudda for her excruciating repeat paedo performance with Marco Polo Mint but no choice because when I got to Chard's place this afternoon there was no-one there and I don't have a key.

Chard's never given me one because someone is always in because of the ancients and I had forgotten Strav was taking them to the seaside. Brighton I think. Don't know when I'll get back in there because Deathbreath's going straight from the Chill to meet up with the rest of The Ickies somewhere.

They're starting work on another 'album' which really seems like a waste of the world's dwindling resources to me. You've delighted us enough I told him ha ha ha. He said that was a good name for the album silly old sod.

Anyway so I slid round to Mudda's. I'll just have to deal with it.

Weanie offered to put me up in a hotel when I told him I was homeless. Yeah right. I knew what that meant. He'd be round to collect the rent in arse dollars. No thanks. I do want to kiss him again. Badly. But only in the right circs. Like when it's my idea.

But the one great thing about being here is I can work on looks for the new collezione as they say in Milan on this big fat Mac which means I can do much more interesting things. I've been looking at pictures of the Taliban. Dylan was wearing an Afghan gilet thing at the Big Chill and there's potential there. I like those rolled-up hats they wear too.

I'm seeing them in fluoro in deliberately really bad acrylic knit which would be easy to get made in the UK ha ha ha with sewn-on patch peace sign Stars and Stripes badges etc which would be original 70s old stock. I know exactly where to source those in bulk because I had to input Mudda's tedious database into this computer myself by hand like a Victorian slave clerk.

I'm thinking Afghaninam which is what Dylan calls it. Doesn't matter if some 13-year-old just thinks it's a cool hat to wear to vandalise the bus shelter. As I keep telling Weanie if you start with a serious proper idea it is SUBCONSCIOUSLY (big word oo er) imparted to the customer without them knowing and they will choose the Afghaninam hat over the dumbass hat just instinctively.

Like when you see an old lady on the bus and she's carrying a market stall rip-off of a Marc Jacobs bag and the only thing she knows about any Jacobs is cream crackers. The thing that made her think it was a nicer bag than any of the others down the market was the ghost essence of the fashion genius thought still in it. That's what I call Theo's Theorem of Fashion Bullshit.

Weanie loves all that.

And apart from getting back on the computer mothership and having a roof over my head I am very very very very glad I came here before Mudda gets back later because I have averted a major disaster.

I hacked into her email – the password of 'theo88' was so obvious it seemed rude not to – and found a recently arrived scroll from loser_dad@knobhead.com:

> hi Loulou
>
> I found this email address on your website. I have tried

calling the shop and even when I get an answer your PA won't give me your cell number. I would appreciate it if you could let me have that.

The problem is I can't get through to my daughter. Her cell just rings out and all the emails I send bounce right back. This has been going on for a couple of weeks now and I'm getting anxious. Is she OK?

As she will have told you, I am coming over to visit Theo later this month and I need to make arrangements with her. I have taken a yacht in Croatia which she will enjoy sharing with us.

I know you are still unreasonably hostile to me, but I do have a legal right to be in touch with my daughter and so I expect you to reply as soon as possible to this and to have her contact me.

Please also tell her I have now stopped her allowance and it won't be reinstated until I hear from her.

Rob

Rob Clarksonne, Photographer

President, Rob Clarksonne Institute of Photography, Malibu, California, USA

I just looked at the screen in speechless horror. I wasn't sure which bit of it made my lunch rise most quickly. 'My daughter' was up there and as for being trapped on a boat with him 'which she will enjoy' give me the most enormous break. Outrageous! I hate boats.

And who was 'us' exactly. Him and his ego? As for the Rob Clarksonne Institute of Onanism it was probably a box of tissues and a large mirror.

But of course the most utterly terrible section was the words *'I am coming over to visit her later this month . . .'*

I'd been relying on my complete radio silence to put paid to that ridiculous idea but in the light of the words 'allowance' and 'stopped' I would have to take action.

I immediately replied to him – as Mudda, of course:

> Rob
> I have been away for the weekend and have just received your email.
>
> Theo is travelling at the moment and has only very occasional access to the internet. Her mobile phone doesn't work in the remote areas of Afghanistan where she is working on an aid project.
>
> She hadn't told me about your visit, but as she will be away until the New Year, I'm afraid she won't be here to see you.
>
> As for stopping Theo's allowance I understand she is relying on it for her travels, so stopping it could leave her safety seriously compromised and I ask you to reinstate payments immediately.
> Loulou

I pressed send and once it was gone, I deleted it and Knob's original email from the system. Delete. Delete. Clear deleted items. Zap. That ought to sort that out. Close call. Fancy footwork on the cash I thought ha ha ha.

To cover all bases I gritted my teeth and sent Mudda a non-rude text asking if I could stay back at her place for a bit so she didn't freak out when she got home and think I was a burglar and club me to death with a shoe.

I probably could have got into Chard's house via the cleaner on Monday morning I realised but it was better to stay where I was so I could check her email every morning before she did. Delete. Delete. Delete. Of course this also meant two annoying things:

a) I would have to set an alarm to get up before her every day chiz chiz chiz.

b) I would have to be pretend nice to her and not say anything about the second public Polo Mint malfunction.

Bloody annoying. So then I got onto Google and researched how difficult it would be to change my surname. Not difficult at all it turns out just like Dylan told me. It's always fugged the buck out of me to have my father's name with that cringetastic pretendy spelling of his real name Clarkson and I've had enough.

But change it to what? Theo Landers? No way. It would yoke me to all that heavy clanking weight of Loulou Landers 'Style Icon' and associated Zombieland. Also the suffocating family ties. Had enough of that this weekend. Cousin Becky got me in a corner at one point – quite hard outdoors at a festival – and gave me a really hard time about all that. How hurt her mum had been when she'd bumped into me in Manfridges that time and why was I so horrible to Auntie Lizzie? Who? Oh yeah, Mudda. 'Loulou'. Her name is as fake as Daddy dearest's. And they wonder why I get stroppy with her.

Becky: What are you so angry about all the time Theo?

Me: What have you got?

I watched that reference fly over her head like one of those balloon lantern things that people were letting off later. When I saw them I wished I could grab hold of one of them and just float away. Which is pretty much what I did this morning.

So what name shall I have then? Now I think about it Mum had wanted to change it to Landers when I was a kid but Knobhedde called the lawyers in. That's his default response to anything which requires discussion. Pathetic. And so obvious and corny oh I live in LA speak to my lawyer. If he's not calling his lawyer he's probably calling his agent or his shrink or his chakra realigner. He's probably got RSI from speed dialling. On his knob.

But now I'm over 18 it's up to me what I'm called. Dylan changed both his names because he hates his dad so much. He tried to legally adopt himself too but they wouldn't let him do that ha ha ha.

I wonder if Deathbreath would mind if I was Theo Meredith? I think it's got a ring to it. I like the Th and the beginning and the th at the end. Th th th.

Theo Beaney not so good at all.

27
Loulou

I didn't get any sleep that night. But not because we were having hot and heavy sex. In a very small tent in a very crowded campsite? We couldn't even talk much because you could hear every word anyone nearby said, which meant they could also hear us. We had to whisper.

I had my own sleeping bag – although Marc did mention that they unzipped all the way round – and I got into it still wearing the hideous polyester satin dress I'd bought in the charity shop. It was so uncomfortable. Somehow it simultaneously had no warmth and made me feel sweaty. Plus it was scratchy, but I wasn't taking it off. I wasn't wearing much underneath.

I wouldn't let him get into his sleeping bag in the YSL suit, though. It was already really wrecked from more than twenty-four hours of festival frolics. Neither could I quite cover my eyes as he disrobed.

It was pretty dark, but not dark enough. He'd put a lantern torch on the ground and it was throwing out just enough light to torture me. Especially when he took the trousers off. I was glad to see he was wearing old-style boxer shorts. No tight jersey trunks for him.

'I'll keep my shirt and shorts on,' he said, turning round and smiling down at me in his most wicked way.

'You better,' I said, putting my hands over my eyes.

He climbed into his sleeping bag and for a moment or two we lay there like two kippers in a basket, as my dad would have said, and then I got an uncontrollable fit of the giggles. Marc joined in.

'Why are we laughing?' he asked me, between snorts.

'It's just so bonkers,' I whispered after someone in another tent called out for us to shut up. 'We're like two little kids having a sleepover.'

'Do you want to cuddle my teddy?' said Marc and that just set me off again.

I was sure I had eye make-up all over my face. I didn't know when I had last gone so long without looking in a mirror. I couldn't even remember if I'd used waterproof mascara and a tentative touch to my cheeks suggested I hadn't. I was going to look like Marilyn Manson in the morning.

'Marc,' I said. 'Can you reach that hankie of yours?'

That was a mistake. He leaned over to reach into his trouser pocket and after handing it to me he stayed sitting up and pulled off his polo shirt. The torch was still on and I had a floodlit view of the most glorious chest, back and stomach. Not a perfect gym body. Nothing as obvious as that. More of a school games physique, mellowing into glorious manhood, with a little bit of hair here and there to make it more interesting. Much more attractive than those waxed and spray-tanned toy boys Keith had paraded past me.

'Not fair, Marc,' I said.

'I was hot,' he said. 'Aren't you a bit uncomfortable in that kit you've got on?'

'It's unbearable,' I said truthfully. 'Like trying to sleep in a crisp packet.'

'Well, take it off then,' he said in a low quiet voice. The sort of voice it's very hard to say no to. Well, that's what I told myself.

I sat up and pulled the dress over my head, making no attempt to preserve my modesty with the sleeping bag. It was nothing more than he'd see if we were sitting on the same beach in the South of

France, I told myself in further self-deceit. And perhaps it would break the tension a bit if I behaved as if I were innocently sharing a tent as somewhere to sleep, as I would with Keith, Jane or Lauren. Yeah, right. Wrong.

Marc lay on his side, head on one hand, the sleeping bag low round his waist and looked at me. Completely shameless lingering looks. Who was I kidding? I knew I had good boobs and I wanted him to look at me like that. Forever.

I lay down again and we carried on gazing at each other. Then, very slowly, he reached out and ran his fingers softly down my bare shoulder and onto my breast. As he grazed my nipple, I gasped involuntarily. It was like a small electric shock. Then he took his hand away and picked up mine, placing it on his shoulder and moving it down in exactly the same arc on his body. His soft golden skin was so silky beneath my fingers that when I reached his chest, I just couldn't take my hand away again.

I let out a wobbly sigh.

'Come here,' he said, putting out his arms. I rolled over and sank into them with my back to his chest. He enclosed me and nuzzled my neck with his nose.

'Mmm, that smell,' he said.

I couldn't speak. What was I doing? Exactly what I'd promised myself I wouldn't do, but it was so heavenly. So delicious.

'Listen, Loulou,' he said in that low tone which I found so mesmerising. 'If you stay here I'm going to kiss you and I'm going to stroke you and lick you and possibly bite you just a little bit, but I'm not taking this sleeping bag off, OK? We made a deal, you've told me your reasons and I'll respect that, but I can't lie in this tent with you and not kiss you.'

I didn't answer. Instead I turned over, propped myself up on one elbow, leaned over and kissed him so deeply he couldn't say another word.

Marc kept his promise. We 'made out' as Americans call it,

snogged as I used to say. We explored each other and relished every millimetre of each other's bodies – but only above the waist. It was bonkers really. Like some kind of religious sect which could only make love in sleeping bags, but it worked.

There were so many times I wanted to rip the damn things off and jump on him, but some tiny shred of my dignity remained intact and the ridiculous proximity of our tent and the next one – less than two feet – was a very useful device to stop us going any further. It was hard enough to keep the noise down as it was.

I don't know what time it was when we finally lay still again. It was exhausting wanting someone so badly and restraining yourself, and I was physically spent. For what felt like ages we just lay there breathing in harmony, our faces millimetres apart, until I realised that Marc had fallen asleep. The carefree, casual sleep of the young.

I gazed at his unlined face, so close to mine, and wondered yet again what the hell I thought I was doing. Then I rolled over on to my side of the impossibly thin foam mattress, so I wouldn't wake him up with my sighing.

I closed my eyes, but it was useless. My body was exhausted, but my brain was racing. I lay there for what felt like hours, with it all turning round and round in my head, until I began to feel quite demented. I shouldn't have done this. I should have gone back to Camp Loulou. I couldn't have not done it. It was perfect. Perhaps I would be out of his system now. Perhaps he'd be out of mine. Some bloody hope.

I turned to look at Marc again, his sculpted lips very slightly parted, eyes flickering behind the closed lids. I wondered what he was dreaming about. And as I looked at those beautiful features, which were becoming dangerously familiar to me, I suddenly realised I could see them much more clearly than I could even a few minutes before. Dawn was breaking. I had to leave. And quickly.

Very carefully, I extracted myself from the sleeping bag and inched down to the end of the mattress. There wasn't room to stand up in the tent, so I kneeled down next to the entrance and put the ridiculous dress back on.

Then I grabbed my bag to see if I could find something to leave him a note with. The only piece of paper in it was a receipt from the cash machine. It would have to do, but I had no pen, so I took out my lipstick, rubbed it over my lips and planted a big smacker on the paper. That was the best I could manage. Then in a moment of inspiration, I grabbed my bottle of scent and sprayed the paper.

As I crawled up the side of the mattress and tucked the note underneath the torch, I looked down at Marc's sleeping head, desperately wanting to give him one last kiss, but I didn't want to risk waking him. I knew he'd pull me back into bed and I absolutely had to get back to Camp Loulou before any of that crew woke up.

I stepped outside the tent nervously but it was quite amazing walking back alone through the sleeping festival in the pre-dawn light. Well, there were some people up. There was one bloke doing tai chi down by the lake and a few going to and from the loos, but most looked like they were doing the walk of shame like me and we smiled conspiratorially at each other as we passed. One young guy gave me a big wink and I blew him a kiss.

I stole back into Camp Loulou and unzipped the tent as quietly as I could, happy that I knew from many shared holidays that Keith was a very heavy sleeper.

I glanced at my watch as I lay down gratefully on the blow-up mattress, which felt like untold luxury after Marc's terrible bit of foam, and saw it was already five forty-five. For a moment the image of his sleeping face came into my head and I wondered how he'd feel when he woke up and found I'd gone. I hoped he'd find my perfumed note and understand.

Then I grabbed my phone to send him a text, which was, I realised, what his generation would have done in the first place. There were quite a few new ones in the inbox, I noticed, from Jane, Keith and – unusually – Chard, but I was too tired to read them. And too concerned about getting the tone right in my message to Marc.

After fumbling around a bit I pressed send:

> Morning. Had to be back in my camp before they woke up. Sorry to leave without saying goodbye. You look so beautiful sleeping. L xxx

Was that enough, I wondered? Was it too much? Did I need to add something about calling him later, or should I be saying thanks for everything, it was amazing, but never call me again? I just didn't know. I was way too tired and confused to know anything. So I left it at that, pressed send, pulled on my sleep mask and finally fell asleep, only to have restless dreams full of him.

What felt like a very short time later I was woken by the sound of everyone else at Camp Loulou greeting the morning and each other. I desperately wanted to go back to sleep, but didn't get the chance, as the zip around the entrance to my 'room' was briskly unzipped and Jane came in carrying two mugs of builders' brew. Jane was the only person I knew who made tea stronger than I did.

'Morning campers,' she said in her jolliest tones.

I knew better than even to try and argue my case for more sleep with her – Jane was very much a morning person – so I pushed up my sleep mask and silently took the mug she was holding out.

'So where were *you* last night, Miss Lizzie Landers?' she said, getting comfortable on the edge of the mattress. 'We all went back-stage for the party after Ritchie's set – and it was bloody brilliant, I must say – but you never showed up. No one knew where you were. Ritchie was a bit disappointed actually, especially as Theo wasn't there either, but you'd just disappeared. Did you cop off with one of them lads from the tea party?'

I stared at her in horror. Not at the crack about the toyboys, but at the terrible realisation that I'd been so wrapped up in my little fantasy world with Marc, I'd completely forgotten about Chard's party. My oldest, bestest, most loyal and lovely friend – abandoned. And Theo hadn't gone either? What was going on? I put my hand over my mouth and then onto my forehead, as if I was taking my own temperature.

'Oh Lizzie,' I said. 'How could I have done that? I feel dreadful.'

'Well, we were a bit worried about you, but I just tried to make a joke of it, saying you'd gone off with one of the waiters . . .'

I groaned audibly. I knew I should be grateful she'd covered my back like that, but the joke about me and young men was getting a bit thin. Especially as although Chard knew I wasn't really a career cougar, there was more than a grain of truth in it in this instance. Or more like a bloody great boulder. Another wave of shame washed over me. I closed my eyes to try and block it out. It didn't work. I'd have to make it up to Chard and big time. I always went to his backstage parties – and I knew what a big deal they were to him.

He'd told me years ago how hard it was to come down after a big show, with all the adrenaline and weird love from total strangers. It had nearly sent him nuts in the first big blast of his career and he'd had to learn to deal with it.

He believed not getting grounded properly after a gig was what made a lot of superstars and divas go bonkers and turn to drugs and other self-destructive outlets. That was when he most needed people who knew him in 'real time', he'd told me. People like me. He called it 'decompressing' and I should have been there to help him do it last night. I'd really let him down.

'I feel so awful about Chard,' I said to Jane. 'How could I have been so rude and thoughtless after that beautiful dedication? I better go and find him to apologise. Is he up yet?'

'He didn't stay here last night,' said Lizzie. 'He's moved to his yurt over in the VIP area. Security thought it was a better idea after the gig being such a massive hit with the crowd, plus he's going off to start the new album with the Ickies this morning, so he asked me to say goodbye to you.'

'What about all his stuff?'

'Oh, one of his people came for that yesterday. You know how they look after him . . .'

Of course they did. I'd forgotten, I realised. I was so used to seeing Chard in our funny little Primrose Hill bubble of mint tea, cupcakes and chats, I'd forgotten what his real life was like. I treated him like some loveable old dog I occasionally threw a bone to, but for loads of people – I couldn't imagine how many – he was integral to their livelihoods. He was more than a man to them, he was like a deity who scattered munificence in his wake. No wonder they looked after him so assiduously – and no wonder he needed real friends who saw him as person, not a human cash dispenser.

I rubbed my eyes and shook my head, feeling really disgusted with myself. It was bad enough being a tragic old cradle-snatcher, but letting Chard down was really unforgiveable. I couldn't have got through that tea without him – but where was I when he needed me? In a hammock with Marc. I shook my head in shame.

And it was even worse if Theo hadn't been there either.

'Did you say Theo wasn't at the party either?' I asked Jane, hoping I might have heard her wrong, but no such luck.

'No sign of her,' she said. 'We kept texting both of you, but neither of you replied. I kept telling Ritchie there must be something wrong with the phone reception. That cheered him up a bit and then someone brought some gorgeous young things along and that cheered him up even more. He looked like he was copping off with one of them. She was really gorgeous – looked like a model. Might be another reason he went back to the yurt last night, eh?'

'Thanks for covering my arse,' I said flatly. 'Our collective arses.'

I took a big drink of tea, which just made me feel queasy. So much to take in on so little sleep. What a mess. And I also felt a completely irrational twinge of annoyance about Chard and the bimbo. I was quite glad I hadn't been there to see that. I didn't mind him constantly trying to pick up women in my shop, but I wouldn't want to see him actually getting it on with one.

I didn't quite understand why, but it seemed to breach our non-sexual code of friendship somehow. Yet he hadn't minded seeing me getting cosy with Marc at the matchmaking party . . . Marc – eeugh. A fresh onslaught of remorse washed over me. It was all I could do not to dive inside the sleeping bag, but Jane hadn't finished with me yet.

'So, where were you last night, little sister?' she said. 'Rachel said she thought she saw you dancing with that young lad again – Tattie's brother. The one you told me about from the party. So were you?'

I blew out my breath like a trombonist. The truth was almost as bad as her joke about me picking up one of the waiters.

'Yes,' I said. 'I did dance with him and afterwards I went off with him. Not like that . . .' She pulled a lewd face and I threw my sleep mask at her. 'We just went up the hill to this quiet spot . . .'

'Did he kiss you?'

'Jane! This is like being back at the youth club.'

'Well, did he?'

'Yes,' I said and then, despite everything, despite all my shame and regret, I couldn't help exploding into giggles. I threw myself down on the mattress and buried my head in the pillow. Jane slapped me on the bum.

'You dirty girl!' she said, sounding delighted. 'Was he a good kisser?'

I raised my head and nodded. I was behaving like a fouteen-year-old.

'A fantastic kisser,' I said with all sincerity, then sanity returned. I put my hand on Jane's arm.

'But I don't want everyone to know, Jane. I did kiss him, but that was it and it was just the heat of the moment and my birthday and all that. I'm not really one of those terrible cougars . . . He's a lovely lovely boy. I'm very fond of him, but I know how bad it would look.'

'I'm just so bloody jealous,' said Jane. 'Did you, you know, cop a feel?'

'Jane!' I said again.

'Well, did you?'

'A feel of what, exactly?'

'Him. His chest, his bum. His bits . . .'

I just stared at her in amazement.

'You old perve,' I said.

'What's wrong with it?' she said. 'Do you think Martin doesn't like looking at young women? And I thought that horrible bloke Paul was going to eat your Theo alive, the way he was looking at her yesterday. It was disgusting.'

'Oh, you noticed that too, did you?'

'Yeah, I don't like him. I'd keep him her away from her. He's not a nice man.'

'I couldn't agree more,' I said. 'And such a lovely wife.'

'Yeah, funny that. Anyway, your young fella . . . You were telling me.'

'I wasn't actually, but I am fascinated to discover that you've turned into a female Benny Hill in your old age. What's brought this on?'

'Have you seen *Twilight*?'

'Oh, not you as well. Theo got obsessed with all that.'

'Well, the young man in that is gorgeous and that one on *Glee* with the mohican and Zac Efron . . . Becky brought round a film with him in it and he's got his shirt off in the first scene. I don't see anything wrong with it. Young bodies are beautiful. Why shouldn't I like looking at them? So come on, dish . . .'

'All right, we had a bit of a snog and yes he is gorgeous and I can't imagine what he sees in me, but he's so lovely, Jane . . .'

I sighed and realised too late that my face had probably turned into something like a dreamy teen gazing at a poster of a boy band.

'Oh no,' she said, suddenly looking concerned. 'You're not falling for him, are you?'

'No . . .' I said, unconvincingly.

'Well, that would be a bad idea,' she said, gathering up the tea mugs. 'Having a snog and a bit of a bunk-up with a hot young bod is one thing, but falling in love with a youngster would be really sad. So watch yourself.'

'I will,' I said, glad to be reminded of it. 'And Jane, please don't go talking to Keith about this. I know he thinks it's hilarious that I like young blokes, but I want to move on from that now. It was just a funny thing that happened. I'm really not on the hunt for young hunks as a genre. It was a one-off.'

'I know,' she said. 'I understand that. I might like looking at Zac Efron's hairy armpits in a film, but I've never liked that male stripper thing. I don't think women coming down to men's lowest level is the answer, but it was all just a bit of fun yesterday. Keith would do anything for you and he honestly thought you'd love it. Anyway, I promise I'll keep my beak shut about last night and you just use that lovely glow you've got today to attract some gorgeous fella nearer your own age. Or older. A fling is fine, but a real relationship is what you really need, Lizzie Landers.'

I nodded.

'Yes, Auntie Jane,' I said.

'Oh shut up – and get your lazy arse out of that bed. We're going down to the festival proper for breakfast before we pack up.'

It took me a while – and the rest of Jane's turbo-charged cuppa – to compose myself, but eventually I managed to haul myself up off the mattress, into a caftan and out of the tent.

It wasn't the prospect of breakfast that got me up – the very idea made me retch – I wanted to find out what was going on with Theo and why she hadn't been at Chard's party either. I was really hoping it was for a positive reason, perhaps involving one of Marc's friends. After what he'd told me the night before, I was quite optimistic, almost excited.

'Here she is,' called out Keith in his perma-cheery tones, as I emerged into the daylight, blinking. 'The former birthday girl, now more like the creature from the black lagoon.'

I groaned and went back into the tent to get my sunglasses.

'Take two,' said Keith, when I came out again. 'Action! Ready for breakfast, darls?'

'No,' I said, shaking my head. 'And possibly not ever again. You lot go on without me and I'll get myself sorted out here.'

'But I want to hear what you got up to last night, you naughty, naughty girl,' he said, coming over and putting his arm round me. I winced as he gave me an affectionate full-body squeeze. In my condition, it felt like an assault.

'I'll tell you in the car,' I said, wondering what on earth I was going to tell him. I needed time to work that out. Still not quite with it, I finally registered that the camp seemed very quiet. I looked around for the rest of the gang, but there didn't seem to be anyone else there apart from Jane, who was just emerging from Theo's tent.

'Where is everyone?' I said.

'They've gone ahead,' said Keith. 'Me and Jane were waiting for you.'

'Has Theo gone for breakfast?' I asked.

'She's not here, Loulou,' he said, but not in the playful kind of way I would have expected, quite seriously.

'Oh, that's good,' I said, determined to stay upbeat about it. The last time I'd seen Theo, she'd been dancing with me and before that, making jokes about me and Marc, so I really didn't think there was a problem. I wasn't going to let there be a problem. 'It means she stayed at the kids' camp again. Brilliant. That's where I want her to be, with people her own age.'

Jane came over.

'She's gone home, love,' she said. 'She left this note. We realised she wasn't here a few minutes ago and I just found this on the floor in her tent. We didn't see it before.'

She handed me a piece of cardboard which had clearly been torn off one of Keith's wine carriers. It was addressed to him too.

> Hi Keith. I've gone back to London already so I won't need a lift. Thanks for the tent and everything. See you later. Theo xxx

I could almost feel the cogs in my hangover-befuddled brain straining to connect. It was a perfectly civil note, nothing agro, considerate even, but just odd that it was addressed to Keith – and with no mention of me.

'Hmm,' I said, at a loss for anything more sensible to say. 'So she's gone home on her own. She hasn't given a reason, but that's Theo, eh? Nice of her to let you know though, wasn't it Keith?'

'Yes,' he said. 'Very thoughtful – for her – and are those the words "thank you" I see on there? Amazing.'

'Maybe it's something to do with one of those boys from the other campsite,' I said, still not willing to let go of the idea. 'Maybe she's gone home with them. More fun than being in a car with the olds?'

Jane nodded, looking happier.

'She was dancing with one of them,' she said. 'Lad with a big black beard. Looked a right weirdo to me, but they were having a good laugh, by the look of it.'

I beamed at her, delighted.

'Great,' I said. 'That's just what I wanted to happen and, come to think of it, I've got quite a few texts I haven't read from last night, so maybe one of them is from her telling me about it. You go off to breakfast and I'll stay here to pack, and do all that. I'm not at all hungry.'

'Okay, darls,' said Keith, giving me another loving-but-painful squeeze, clearly relieved I wasn't upset by Theo's vanishing act. 'You look just about ready to hurl. We'll leave you to it.'

They walked off, arm in arm, and I was glad to have some time to myself. After several attempts and burned fingers, I managed to get Keith's camping stove lit and put the kettle on to boil, then I settled down with my phone, to see what it might have to relay to me.

It wasn't very edifying. Nothing from Theo, nothing from Marc – a relief – several from Keith and Jane along the 'where the hell are you?' lines, sent from Chard's party – and then a great stream of them from him, which made me feel really ashamed:

> Hey Loulska where r u? Keith still has your pass so maybe u can't get past security. I'll send Mickey down.
>
> Loulou – if you can't get past security ask for Mickey.
>
> Loulou – I've been down to the gate but the security boneheads said they haven't seen you. Ask for MICKEY.
>
> MICKEY
>
> The party's no good without you.
>
> ??????
>
> Just text me to tell me you're OK.

It was the last one that made me feel really terrible. I knew exactly how he would have been feeling when he'd sent that, because I'd been through it so many times with Theo. The tipping point when you go over from being confused, irritated and annoyed, into fully, stomach-churningly anxious.

I had to answer that one immediately and didn't even pause to wonder what I would say. I just told him how I felt:

> Hey Chard. I'm so so sorry I missed your party. Furious with myself. Just got all your

texts this morning. Must have been out of range last night. I got into a situation and I just couldn't make it. Too much to go into on here. Will tell you when I see you. I loved your set – your dedication and singing Happy Birthday meant so much. And your gorgeous present. Feel so bad I let you down after all that. Hope you can forgive me. Your totally devoted (but quite crap) friend Loulou xxxxxxx

Pressing send didn't make me feel any better. I'd let him down horribly – and for a reason I wasn't at all proud of.

Then I had another thought, which made me feel even grubbier: I was glad Chard had gone away for a while to record with the band, as it gave me some breathing space before I had to apologise to him in person.

A crap friend indeed.

Theo

First Wednesday ABC (After Big Chill)

It was getting so hard monitoring Mudda's email I had to make knobhead.com a blocked sender. Don't know why I didn't do that right away because the time difference between here and LA meant if he got straight down to it when he woke up the eem would land early afternoon in London just when Mudda was likely to be exploring her new discovery the interweb. So I just blocked him.

It was a close call because it was only with split second timing yesterday that I managed to head off a very cross eem from him threatening legal action if she didn't enable him to be in touch with me wherever I am at all times.

He has a RIGHT to know where I am apparently and is foaming at the mouth that she's allowed me to go off somewhere as dangerous as Afghaninam without his permission.

I almost replied to that one myself: I'M OVER 18 DICKHEAD. I CAN DO WHATEVER I LIKE.

The problem is though that as long as I'm getting money from him he does slightly own me. In his opinion. I reckon he owes it to me for services not rendered. Of being a parent. Or even human. I'm greatly relieved I've got him to turn the cash flow back on again but I can see that as long as I have to manoeuvre myself to continue getting it I am a slave to the system.

Dylan believes we are all slaves to the system. I told him to go and start a union. He said he was going to start an onion instead. He makes me laugh.

Anyway with the possibility of ongoing $$$£££ bollocks with Knobbeheadde it's a good thing I've got my West Wind gig going on. But even apart from the filthy lucre I'm having such a good time there. I really really love it.

I took all my West-Ham-Afghaninam ideas in yesterday and STORY BOARDED it for Weanie and the team and they went mad for it. Even Nicolle the snotty marketing woman was smiling.

This is really interesting she was saying. We can really take this somewhere. Mixing the vintage trims in with the new-make is a really strong recycling message and with the collection actually made in Britain as well we can really sell an ethical story.

Yeah and loads of shit acrylic hats ha ha ha.

But I am really happy they liked it and then it was even better because I got to actually work on making it into a collection. Me and the two proper designers Tony and Ajay went into their studio and spent the whole day developing it as a team because Weanie says it has to be ready to go into production at the end of the week. It's already bloody Wednesday.

He kept popping in 'to see how we were getting on' but I knew he only wanted to see me. Then he sent me a text from his office on the top floor asking – or more like ordering – me to go for lunch with him and I texted back:

Lunch is for wimps. Remember?

He loved that.

So we just kept on working right through today. We had Chinese food delivered for dinner and we were still there after eleven at night. By then we were on to making the toiles for the samples using all this amazing computer equipment they have. You design the clothes on it and then the same pooter makes the pattern and cuts out the toiles. Does all the sizes automatically too. That's called GRADING.

But we still had to sew it together ourselves. All the sample machinists had gone home so I did it. The guys were quite amazed I knew how to use a sewing machine but that was one good thing Mudda taught me. She used to do a lot of her own alterations and the sewing machine was always on the kitchen table so I just learned. I'm always surprised when other people can't do it. I can't drive but I can change a bobbin.

So then I was the fit model and I didn't care because Ajay and Tone are big screamers so I was standing there in just my knickers and a bit of calico falling off my hips while they were farting about at the back trying to make it curve round my arse a certain way and I hear the lift go and there in the doorway is Weanie.

Weanie standing there in his beige linen Brioni suit with a silk hankie in the pocket his black-rimmed specs and a big cigar in his gob staring at me and my tits. My nipples went hard the traitors. That made him smile.

Hey boys I said looking right back at Weanie. The pizza delivery is here.

They looked round the sides of me and cracked up when they saw who it was. I made like I'd had my arms across my chest the whole time so they wouldn't know what just happened and then I casually reached over and grabbed my T-shirt. Nothing else though. Just my T-shirt and my frilly knickers. I do like to torture Weanie. He deserves it.

So we showed him what we'd done and he loved it – with a few of his usual boring moans about costs which meant we had to lose some of the cool detail but the boys kept saying That's High Street Theo – but mostly he was super impressed.

Then he said he had come in specially to make us all to go home and that he would give me a lift because it wasn't much out of his way and he had the driver downstairs.

Of course the guys know exactly where I live because of them being fashionheads and worshipping Mudda and the shop. And as they know as well as I do that the day will never dawn when Primrose Hill is on the way to Fitzrovia from Oxford Street I saw them exchange a look. I was hoping it wasn't that obvious but it clearly is. Shit. But also – so what?

I know they respect what I deliver in terms of ideas for the clothes so if they've figured out that the boss is also slipping me the tongue occasionally I'll just have to live with it. And so will they.

I didn't have much time to think about it then because Weanie had me out of there so fast I barely had time to put my shorts on. Then he opens the door to his ridic big Bentley and I get in but he goes round the front and has a word with his driver before he gets in the back.

We set up off along Upper Regent Street and Weanie's hand is holding mine and he's staring at me with his eyes all narrowed like a gangster while he sucks on that big cigar. Until I took it off him.

I took a big draw blowing out the smoke like Deathbreath showed me once and then I have another puff and blow and Weanie was looking thrilled.

I think it's really sexy when women smoke cigars he said.

Do you? I said and then I opened my window and threw it out.

He was so furious it was brilliantly funny.

That was a Cuban Monte Cristo you just threw out of the window! If you don't like it why did you bloody smoke it?

Because I might be planning to kiss you and now you won't taste so vile.

That had him smiling again and he had his tongue down my throat in a flash. He really is the most monumentally great kisser and I was lost in it until I realised we were well into Regent's Park and the driver had pulled over in a nice dark spot.

I pulled myself out of his grip which wasn't that easy. It was like snogging one of those multi-armed Indian gods. His hands were everywhere at once.

What? He said all croaky when I finally got out of his clutches.

Did you tell your driver to come this way and stop?

Errrrr . . .

So that's errrr . . . meaning yes. Well no thanks Ganesha. I'm not into dogging.

And I got out of the car.

Theo! Come back . . .

I heard him call after me but I was already running. Lucky I had my shorts and flats on and I know that park so well I could have jogged through it blindfolded which is pretty much what I had to do in the dark because I knew once I was under the trees he wouldn't follow me. Might get his suit creased.

I ran all the way home and was really exhausted and sweaty when I got here. I had a nice long bath but when I got into bed I still couldn't sleep. I couldn't stop thinking about Weanie.

Weanie and his wicked wicked kissing.

28
Loulou

There were two unexpected deliveries to the shop that Thursday. Mid-morning I did a double take when a young man with a long bushy black beard walked in, wearing full traditional Afghan dress, with the long waistcoat and baggy trousers, and the rolled-up hat. It looked rather elegant.

'Hi,' he said shyly, in tones that were clearly more Kensington than Kabul. 'Is, er, Theo here?'

Of course, I knew exactly who he was. It had to be Marc's friend Dylan, but I decided to play it cool. I didn't want to put him off – and I didn't trust myself to say Marc's name. So I told him she'd gone out early that morning and I had no idea where she was, or when she would be back, but could I give her a message?

He fumbled in his bag and produced a scruffy brown paper bag, which he handed to me. I looked down and saw it had 'To Theo, slave of the system' written on it in felt tip.

'Could you give that to her?' he said.

'Sure,' I said, absolutely thrilled that a young man was calling on my daughter, even if he did have an alarming beard. 'Who shall I say dropped it off?'

'Dylan,' he said.

'Oh, of course,' I said, in my best 1950s hostess tones. 'You're Tattie Thorssen's brother's friend, aren't you?'

'Yes,' he said. 'I'm at uni with Marc Thorssen.'

'And you were at the Big Chill too.'

'Yes, that's where I, um, met your daughter.'

He seemed to go a bit pink behind his beard. What a sweetie.

'Tell me, Dylan. Are those Afghan clothes you're wearing?'

He said they were and we had such an interesting conversation about how he'd been dressing like that since he'd worked out there on the aid project, I thought about asking him if he would like to have some mint tea with me, but sense prevailed. If this delightful young chap was trying to make friends with Theo, the worst thing I could do – as far as she was concerned – would be to appear to be taking an interest in him, so I thanked him for the parcel and he took the hint and left.

The next delivery was a huge bunch of beautiful old-fashioned garden roses, in various shades of pink, which arrived just after lunch. They were my absolutely favourite flowers, which made me wonder for a moment if they might be from Chard. He always got me old roses when he could.

He brought me flowers most weeks and sometimes sent them via a florist when he was away, but I certainly didn't feel like I deserved anything from him after my dreadful no-show at his Big Chill party.

He'd sent a characteristically gracious reply to my apology text – 'Don't sweat it babe xxx' – but I hadn't heard from him since. It wasn't surprising while he was recording, but it still niggled away at the back of my mind, as unfinished business.

So assuming they weren't from him, I was sure they'd be from a designer, someone on a magazine I'd helped out with a last-minute clothing loan, or a grateful bride. But when I opened the card I had to sit down.

I need to see you. Desperately. Your call.

That was it. No name, no number, but I didn't need it, I knew exactly who the bouquet was from. Marc. What I didn't know was what to do about it.

The terrible thing was I felt like I desperately needed to see him too. I hadn't stopped thinking about him since I'd left the Big Chill. I'd slept all the way home in the car – much to Keith's annoyance, because I'd managed to drop off before he could grill me about the night before – and as I drifted in and out of slightly psychedelic dreams, Mark's face, lips and voice had been the only thing in my head.

I had been so crazed with raging sex hormones and lack of sleep I probably would have rung him the moment I got home and told him to come over right away, but as we were driving over the Hammersmith flyover I'd had a text from Theo asking if it was all right to stay back at my place for a while.

I was delighted, of course, and amazed, that she was asking me rather than telling me – or just being there when I got back – and replied to that effect, the delighted part. But there was a little tiny part of me which was irritated. The part which was desperate to see Marc again and now couldn't invite him over. I was shocked at myself, but I couldn't help it. That was the truth.

Even his roses were making me feel nervous with Theo in the house. It wasn't madly out of the ordinary for me to get lovely flowers, but I was paranoid that this time she would somehow connect them with Marc. Maybe it was because we had been so close for so long, but she could be almost spookily insightful sometimes – and what would I say if she asked me who they were from? I'd have to lie, outright. And apart from the collective conspiracies of Santa and the Tooth Fairy, I'd never deliberately lied to my daughter and I didn't want to start.

I sat behind the counter turning the card over in my fingers and then, after reading it one more time, I went into the back room and reluctantly put it through the shredder, but even that didn't stop me obsessing on it.

The message had been in his own writing – that bold script, in fountain pen. Such style for one so young. When I'd been his age young men didn't send you flowers, let alone with hand-written messages on gilt-edged cards. But then, the men I'd gone out with in my twenties hadn't been the scions of major bankers. Which had the unfortunate effect of reminding me of Marc's mother.

I could all too clearly imagine how she would react to the news that her son was romantically pursuing someone she clearly considered a ghastly déclassé purveyor of second-hand tat, was her age and – gasp – Northern. Crime upon crime. But the age would be the worst thing, I had no illusions about that.

No, it was all ridiculous and I had to stop thinking about him. But then I walked back into the shop, which was heavy with the scent of the roses, and every cell in my body seemed to throb with the physical memory of him. Surely, if nothing else, I had to thank him for the flowers. That was just good manners. My hand was on my phone before I allowed my brain to stop it.

He answered immediately.

'Loulou,' he said in that soft deep voice. My innards did a triple somersault. 'You called me . . .'

'Thanks for the flowers, Marc,' I said, my voice coming out almost as husky as his, with emotion – and a fair amount of lust. 'They're absolutely gorgeous and you remembered pink roses are my favourites. Thank you so much. The whole shop smells of them.'

'You're welcome,' he said. 'And thank you for falling perfectly into my trap. I just couldn't hold out any longer. So I thought I would try and make you call me and then it would be your fault. Result.'

I laughed, glancing at the clock. Theo had been out on one of her mystery missions since quite early that morning and of course I had no idea when she might be thinking of coming back. If only she could do me the courtesy of giving me some clue of her schedule, I thought yet again, my life would be so much easier.

'I can't talk for long,' I said. 'Theo is back living with me again and she could walk in at any moment.'

'When can I see you?' he said.

'It's not so much when,' I said, 'as where? You can't come here, I can't come to your house . . .'

And – I thought – I really don't want to do that hotel room thing with you. That had been pretty much the entire scenario of my love life since Rob had left and for reasons I really couldn't understand, what I felt for Marc didn't seem like one of those liaisons of convenience.

Apart from anything, I didn't want to see him just to have sex. In fact, that was the thing I was still determined not to do with him no matter how much I wanted to. I was convinced that was the key to holding on to my self-respect in the whole wacky scenario. So I needed to see him in a neutral setting, but where? I couldn't have dinner with him, or even drinks. We'd look ridiculous at best. At worst I'd be asked who was going to taste the wine – me or my son? I couldn't go there.

'Well, what are you doing tomorrow?' he asked me.

'I'm going down to Brighton to look at the stock of a vintage shop which is closing down.'

'That's perfect!' said Marc. 'I'm going to be in Brighton too. I'm working at the Jack Wills store down there all this week. I volunteered because I thought it would make a change. Take my mind off you . . . Why don't we have lunch in Brighton? I get an hour off.'

Lunch would be much less fraught with romantic implications, I thought. And in Brighton we'd be a lot less likely to run into anyone I knew.

'OK,' I said. 'Great.'

It did seem like an ideal arrangement, but as the day went on I felt more and more twitchy about it. Maybe I should just book a suite at the Haymarket Hotel instead, for one never-to-be-repeated sexfest weekend, so I could sate myself and get over him once and for all. But would I?

I knew that's what my sister Jane thought I should do. She'd told me very clearly: grab the sex and run – and definitely don't allow any other feelings to develop. As I seemed to be doing exactly the opposite of that, I couldn't call her to ask for advice, as I normally would.

I sat behind the counter fiddling with trays of jewellery, making them look worse, not better, desperate for something to take my mind off Marc. Customers drifted in and out, but they were all the happy browser variety who were best left alone. Normally I was delighted when they came in because I could get on with other things and still make money, but that afternoon any kind of distraction would have been welcome.

I walked around twitching already perfect displays and trying to look serene and style icon-ish, while my brain darted about constantly wondering who I could talk to about Marc. And realising, as I had before, there wasn't anybody. For someone who thought she had a lot of friends, I felt decidedly lonely.

Then, after an unusually long empty spell, when a very beautiful young woman – clearly a model – came in, it finally struck me that the particular person I was missing was Chard. This was the fourth day back in the shop without his morning visit, and I was surprised at what a big hole his absence left.

There were days when he came ambling over that it felt like a bit of a nuisance having to stop what I was doing to hang out with him, but now I appreciated it was often the best part of my day. Sometimes we didn't even chat. We just sat there together, enjoying our tea in mutually contented silence, feeling passively validated by the other's unconditional approval.

What would he say about my predicament if he were there? He was a world expert in dating people much younger than himself, but was he in it solely for the flesh? Or did he feel a heart and head connection with the young women he pursued, as I did with

Marc? Because that was the thing that was confusing me so much. I absolutely knew it wasn't just his young hotness that made me so attracted to Marc. I would have been just as drawn to him if he'd been my own age. More so, in fact – because then I wouldn't have had a single doubt about him.

It was so ironic, because to find a man you clicked with who was also gorgeous should have been a dream scenario, but because he was so young, it had become a nightmare. There was no getting away from it: the age difference between me and Marc was simply impossible. So why couldn't I stop myself thinking about him?

After listening to all of that, what would Chard tell me to do? I really didn't know on which side of my internal debate he would fall. And anyway, perhaps he wasn't the person to ask. His love life was as hopeless as mine, consisting of nothing more than serial short-lived affairs. But then, as I turned the shop sign to closed, I decided not to waste time pondering what he might think anymore. I'd bloody well ask him.

As I picked up the phone and dialled his mobile, I felt quite shy. Although he was as permanently attached to his various mobile phones as anyone else, Chard and I hardly ever communicated that way for some reason; our friendship existed almost entirely out on my terrace, or in the shop.

Even the recent flurry of texts had been an anomaly – and thinking about them reminded me that I did have another very good reason to call him. I really did need to apologise properly about the party. A text wasn't enough – and neither was it right to wait until he came back. I owed him more than that.

Still, I felt almost nervous as the phone started to ring – a feeling which disappeared when I heard the warmth in his voice on answering.

'Loulabella Fantanella!' he said. 'To what do I owe this unusual telephonic pleasure?'

'I miss you,' I said honestly.

'That's nice,' said Chard. 'I miss you too. Big time. I hope you're keeping my seat polished.'

'I am,' I laughed. 'And your tea glass. I hope I'm not interrupting your session . . .'

'The phone would have been off if I'd been in the studio, but what's really on your mind, Loulou? You don't normally call me. We're strictly face-to-facers, so I know something's up – is Theo OK?'

'Yes,' I said. 'And she's staying with me, because there's no-one at your place.'

He chuckled. 'That worked out then,' he said. 'I never did get round to giving her a key . . . Funny that.'

'Thanks, Chard,' I said. 'I did rather assume that it wasn't entirely her own choice, but it is great to have her back. I hardly ever see her, of course, but it's just so nice to know she's here again.'

I paused for a moment, wondering how on earth I could broach the things I really wanted to say. They were both awkward – and not unconnected.

'So how's it going with the band and everything? Is the album coming together?' I babbled, knowing it sounded lame as I said it. I never talked to him about that kind of stuff. It was one of the reasons he liked me.

'Come on, Loulou,' he said. 'This is me here. Let's drop the small talk, OK? What's really going on?'

'Oh, Chardie,' I said. 'I'm embarrassed to talk to you about it, but you're the only one who would really understand . . .'

'So it's the young guy, is it?' he said.

I half-laughed, half-gasped, temporarily mute with surprise and equally divided between relief that I didn't have to explain, and horror that it was so obvious.

'How on earth did you know?'

'I've got eyes in my head, Loulou. You can see into the audience from a festival stage before night falls, you know. It's not like a darkened theatre. I saw you dancing with him again and then when you didn't come to my party, I figured that's where you were . . . Eventually.'

'Oh, Chard,' I said, quickly leaping in. 'I'm *so* sorry about your party. A text wasn't enough to tell you how sorry I was, but I was so ashamed of the reason. It was unbelievably rude and awful of me after you'd got the entire Big Chill to sing me 'Happy Birthday' and everything . . .'

'It's OK, babe,' he said. 'I was disappointed, I'm not going to lie to you – especially as Theo didn't come either . . . But then I got over myself and figured out you were probably both gallivanting with hot young dudes and that's got to be good. It's what festivals are all about.'

'I'm still sorry, Chard.'

'Forget it, really,' he said and I could tell he meant it. 'I missed you both, but I still had a great time. There were a lot of other people there . . .'

'Yes,' I said, feeling confident our friendship was safely back on its normal footing, so it was safe to start teasing him again. Rude not to, really. 'Jane said you'd made some lovely new friends . . . Blonde friends, were they, Chard? Tall? Slender? Not much to say?'

He chuckled, softly. 'What's an old rock star to do, Loulou? It can get mighty lonesome in a yurt on your own in the wee small hours . . .'

I laughed and was about to get stuck into some more intensive ribbing, when he spoke again.

'But now you're not sure about the scene with Mr Young Dude – am I right?'

'You are one hundred per cent right,' I answered, too surprised at how accurately he'd read the situation to ask him how he'd known.

'So, what's the problem? He's messing you around? Hot and cold kind of shit?'

'No,' I said, intensely relieved to be able to talk about it with someone I trusted. 'He's pretty committed, I think. That's a large part of what's freaking me out, but mainly it's the age thing, Chard. He's less than half my age . . .'

He was chuckling again. 'So I see why you rang me. The world expert in cradle-snatching.'

'Yes,' I said firmly. 'But it's so different for women. Nobody looks twice at you with a twenty-year-old model – it's almost in your job description – but I couldn't possibly go out in public with Marc. I'd feel ridiculous.'

'So stay in with him,' said Chard.

I didn't say anything.

'Ask me all the other things you want to about this,' he continued. 'I can tell you're holding back, Loulou, so don't. I know we don't normally talk about this stuff, it's always been kind of off-piste for us, but it seems like time for us to start. So what do you want to know?'

'OK,' I said firmly. 'Number one: with your baby women, is it just about the firm young flesh, or do you feel some kind of deeper connection with them?'

'I could never sleep with a woman I didn't feel a connection with, Loulou,' he said. 'I'm not a stud bull; it takes more than the scent of fertility to turn me on, but it doesn't mean I'm looking for a deep and meaningful with them. It's a passing pleasure, like a holiday, a great meal, a really good bottle of wine. Sweet at the time and then moving on, file it as a happy memory. No ties, no baggage, no hard feelings.'

He paused for a moment before continuing.

'And the thing is, babes, it's easier for me to find that casual scene with a chick young enough not to be frantically looking for a baby papa or husband. It's quite pragmatic – the bloom of youth is an added bonus, it's not all that motivates me.'

'Wow,' I said. 'I'm quite surprised. I'd always assumed it was the nubile young body thing when older guys go after younger women. That's quite comforting.'

'For some guys it might be – and the whole status symbol model bullshit. I just like pretty women.'

'But don't you ever want something deeper?' I asked, tentatively. This really was territory we didn't go into. 'A proper ongoing relationship?'

He sighed, which was unusual for him. 'Of course I do, baby,' he said quietly. 'I'm just waiting for the right one. As long as it takes.'

'But what about that song you played at the Big Chill? That beautiful instrumental you said was for somebody special . . .'

'It is,' he said. 'Like I say, I'm waiting for her. It's all in the timing.'

'Wow,' I said, feeling slightly miffed that he clearly wasn't going to tell me anything more about this mystery woman. 'Sounds intriguing. I really hope it works out for you.'

'Oh, I think it will,' he said, and I could hear the smile in his voice. 'I'm biding my time. But back to the here and now – what are you going to do about Little Lord Fauntleroy?'

'I don't know,' I wailed. 'That's why I called you. What do you think I should do? Shoot, shag, or marry?'

'Definitely shoot,' said Chard, laughing and coughing heartily. 'Good-looking little fucker, but seriously, you can't decide about stuff like this in a considered way. It's not a rational part of your head that you're dealing with here. This is heart and gonad territory, Loulou. Brain stem, not frontal lobes. Just see him again as soon as possible – alone – and then you'll just know. And don't let what anyone else would think come into it. Not even Theo. What she doesn't know won't hurt her.'

'But I couldn't be dishonest with Theo,' I protested. 'Not even by omission.'

'Well, your subconscious will have all that in the mix. Don't try and logic this, just trust your instinct in the moment.'

'I think I know what you mean,' I said. 'Like when I'm dancing with him, I don't think about the next move, I don't know what I'm going to do and then I've already done it – and it was always exactly the right thing.'

'Bingo,' said Chard. I was fairly certain he was nodding as he spoke. 'It's the same when I'm working. I can't order my brain "write a song now" like programming a dishwasher. I just have to let it unfold, noodling around with the guys, scribbling words, stuff just comes. Or it doesn't. And then it does.'

'Thanks, Chard,' I said. 'You've really made me feel better. I was going crazy trying to think it through. But just one thing, though – you won't say anything to Theo about him, will you?'

'Do you think I'm crazy?' he said, laugh/coughing again. 'It was fun having her to stay for a while and my parents loved it, but I don't want her as a permanent housemate. Can't afford the coffee.'

We said our goodbyes and I put the phone down with a satisfied feeling that I had asked exactly the right person for advice about my Marc dilemma. But as I climbed the stairs back up to the flat, I found myself wondering who on earth the woman Chard was waiting for could be.

And what was so flipping special about her.

Theo

Fly-day

Another brilliant day in the design studio. I got there really early because I had something I wanted to work on before the machinists came in at nine and the design team rolled in whenever after that.

I was trying to make a knitwear pattern from a real Afghan roll-up hat that Dylan had dropped over to the shop yesterday. I'd texted him to ask if I could borrow it and he'd got right on to it. Shame I wasn't there to see him. I found it on the kitchen table when I went down this morning so I presume Mum took delivery of it. I hope she didn't talk to him.

Anyway he'd put an onion inside the hat and a note, saying: Dear Theo you are now a member of an onion.

Ha ha ha.

So about eight thirty-five this morning I'm swearing at the bloody hat and realising I am going to have to unpick it somehow to work out how it's constructed when I hear someone laughing behind me. It was Weanie.

You're in early Theo.

Yeah. I'm keen.

I'm impressed.

He came over and sat on the edge of the table next to me. Crotchily.

What are you doing?

I'm trying to make a knitwear pattern for this bloody hat and I'm thinking it would work better in woven after all. It won't sit right in knitted but it will be hard to do it in a trashy enough fluoro if it's woven.

Weanie picked up the Afghan hat and rubbed the material between his finger and thumb.

Do it in a fleece-lined sweatshirting he said.

I just looked at him.

Wow. I said. That's brilliant. That would be brilliantly cheesy and right. Why didn't I think of that?

Because you haven't been doing this shit for thirty-plus years like I have. But you're good Theo. You're really really good. And I'm sorry about last night.

That surprised me.

Cool. I said. Forget about it.

I won't be able to do that. You know exactly what you do to me and I'm not going to let it go. But I won't set you up like that again. OK?

OK.

Then he leaned down and put his head very close to mine speaking very quietly right into my ear. It tickled.

I'll do it nicely. He said. I'll be a gentleman. But I am going to have you Theo. I always get what I want.

And then the machinists started to arrive and Nicolle the marketing lady came bustling in all hot and bothered saying she had been looking for Weanie everywhere and he was needed right away for the meeting and she gave me a very funny look.

I waved at her cheerfully and got back to my pattern which was really easy now I was making it in sweatshirting. And when it was finished I took a photo of the pattern on the screen with my camera with all the West Wind copyright shit around it and texted it to Dylan with a message:

Your hat is now a slave to the system.

29
Loulou

I set off for Brighton on Friday morning feeling equally nervous and excited. I'd even faffed over what to wear – that was how immature I was being about the whole thing. Part of me wanted to dress down, to try and fit in with his cool young scene, but the better part of me knew that would be fully tragic.

Marc liked me despite – or maybe even because of – the way I dressed, so I was got up very much as myself in my wide-pant Riviera mode, with my towering platform espadrilles and my embroidered basket bag. I was going to the seaside, I told myself, finishing off my outfit with a 1950s US Navy sailor's hat. Plus I had business to do down there. I had to look like Loulou Landers, vintage queen.

The work part of my trip went brilliantly. The shop had some superb pieces, but rather than just cherry-picking the best bits, I did a great deal by buying it all, right down to the last headscarf and clip-on earring, as one job lot.

I actually needed some cheaper stock like that for a new website I was setting up, which Shelley was going to run for me. It was a kind of diffusion label, called Loulou Too, aimed at younger customers who couldn't afford our big-ticket stuff, who we then hoped to recruit as lifelong Loulou Land customers. Anything left would go to charity.

I felt very buoyed up as I made my way from the North Lanes

down towards the seafront. My father's blood roared triumphantly in my veins when I did a deal like that. Sweet for me, because I was going to make a tidy profit, but also good for the woman who was closing the shop and had unloaded everything in one easy go, for a fair price. Clever her, for offering it to me first. Clever me, for taking it.

But as I walked along mulling those pleasant thoughts, I realised that away from the Primrose Hill/West End nexus of my life, even in funky Brighton, my outfit made me stand out from the crowd more than I was used to. By the time I could see the Jack Wills shop hoarding further down the street, I was beginning to wonder if the sailor hat was a mistake.

I ducked into a branch of Jigsaw a few doors up and, under the pretence of trying on some cardigans, considered my reflection. The light in the changing rooms was terrible. I looked old, lizardy and over-made-up. The foundation that had seemed so smooth and flattering in my bathroom mirror was flaking and my lipstick was creasing into the little lines round my lips.

I stuffed the stupid sailor hat into my bag and seriously considered buying a plain navy cardigan to wear over the red-and-white striped 1940s blouse which normally made me feel so cheerful.

Determinedly reapplying my lipstick in the shop mirror brought my ancient old face into sharper focus and I wondered if I shouldn't just head straight back to the station and the safety of my rarefied little pocket of London. This arrangement with Marc was as ill-advised as our little adventure at the Big Chill had been. I should bail out now. Send him an apologetic text from the train home. But I just couldn't.

Knowing he was just a few yards along the road was more than my willpower could handle and I picked up my silly handbag, handed the dull cardigans back to the salesgirl and headed for Jack Wills. Telling myself that, apart from any other attraction, it would be interesting to check out a retail phenomenon I'd heard a lot about – much of it vitriolic contempt from Theo – but hadn't seen myself.

Yeah, sure, Loulou. It was essential professional research.

I was actually quite impressed by the Jack Wills shop. It was in a grand old building complete with all the original Victorian features, which set off the retro-modern styling of the clothes: a determinedly English take on the Polo Ralph Lauren and Abercrombie & Fitch groove thang. Classic athletic wear rendered cool and sexy – but only if worn on hard young bodies.

The ground-floor womenswear area was staffed by exactly the kind of young filly Marc should have been snogging in his tent at the Big Chill rather than me. Tiny, lissom bodies, with tracksuit pants rolled over at the waist to reveal taut brown stomachs and tight grey marle T-shirts highlighting the brand logo in appliqué – and pert little breasts. They all had tumbling long hair and startlingly white teeth.

The irony was Theo would have fitted in perfectly. She'd look amazing in all these clothes, but they were the focus of her greatest scorn, representing what she considered the pathetic herd aesthetic of her class and generation. Individuality was the quality Theo valued above all others – and although she'd hate even to countenance the idea, I strongly suspected it was the result of growing up with me, in my shop.

I paused to look at an antique table featuring baskets of frilly cotton knickers I thought would really look cute on Theo. I picked a pair up and one of the willowy girls came over.

'Can I help you with anything?' she asked sweetly.

Was I imagining the merest twinge of patronising kindness in her tone? Can I help you – Auntie?

'I'm just wondering what size to get for my daughter,' I said, truthfully – and also to buy myself admission to the store. 'She's about your size. Maybe a little smaller.'

I couldn't resist it. The girl's smile hardened very slightly and she disappeared off to the stock room to find me the lilac gingham style in a size eight. I drifted round taking it all in. Crossed vintage oars on the walls, old team photos, the whole shebang. Not original, but well done. If I were Theo's age, I wondered, would I shop there? Probably not. My arse would have looked enormous in the tracksuit pants.

The girl came back with the knickers and I said I would take them, but wanted to have a look upstairs first. Which gave me my passport to go up to menswear, where I knew Marc would be. My heart rate quickened as I walked up the wooden stairs. I could still cut and run, I told myself, but my feet kept going until I emerged into a space as big as the ground floor, with no-one in it.

I wandered through fingering the rugby shirts and zipped hoodies, not sure if I was relieved or disappointed that he seemed to have forgotten our arrangement. But then I walked through an arch into a room at the front of the building and there he was, standing by an old billiard table folding stacks of T-shirts. My espadrilles didn't make any noise on the floorboards and he didn't look up until I was standing across the table from him.

His face lit up when he saw me.

'Loulou!' he said. 'I thought you'd forgotten me.'

In a moment he was round the table, pulling me into his arms. I stepped back in alarm, my head swivelling up to the ceiling.

'There might be CCTV in here . . .' I said.

He laughed and turned his embrace into a hug, with a kiss on each cheek.

'You look great,' he said, giving me the once-over and then cupping one of my buttocks with his hand and squeezing. 'You feel pretty good too.'

I stepped back out of his reach and looked him over. Slouchy worn-in jeans – probably fresh off the rail – leather slide sandals and his preferred pink polo shirt, collar up, erect nipples clearly visible through it. It took all my self-control not to tweak them.

'So what do you think of the shop then, oh fashion retail guru?'

'It's great,' I said. 'The brand styling is spot on and I like the clothes too, more than I expected. They look terrific on you – and on the girls downstairs. It's a very confident offer.'

'I'll show you round,' he said. 'Amy – the store manager – really wants to meet you. She was really excited when I told her you were coming in . . .'

'You told her?' I asked, horrified.

'Yeah. I said you were coming in to see the shop and to take me out to lunch – I told her you were Tattie's best friend's mum. She was seriously impressed I knew you. And that's all I told her, OK?'

'OK,' I said, relieved he had set me up in the auntie role, but simultaneously hating it. I didn't want to be somebody's friend's mum. I wanted to be fabulous me, but that was the scenario I was in. Lump it or leave, I told myself.

I was duly introduced to Amy and all the other members of staff, who seemed sincerely excited to meet me, even the snotty one who'd helped me with Theo's knickers. Most of them had been to my shop and they cooed over everything I was wearing asking where it was all from. I played to the gallery, showing them my hat and explaining I'd taken it off because I felt people had been looking at me weirdly.

Then Marc put it on and looked so outrageously, camply gorgeous in it, I could only pray that my feelings about him weren't plastered across my tragic old face. But I don't think any of the girls would have noticed anyway, they were all too busy gazing at him themselves – as was the other male assistant.

Eventually Marc announced I was taking him out for lunch and I played up to my part.

'I'll buy him an ice-cream if he's good,' I said. 'He's been very kind to my daughter and I owe him a big thank you.'

'Can I have chips?' said Marc, getting into character.

'Only if you eat your peas first,' I said and we walked out, a careful distance apart, him still wearing the sailor hat, me with my basket over the arm nearer to him, Maggie Thatcher body-armour style.

'So where am I taking you for your after-school treat?' I asked him, once we were outside.

'Just follow me,' he said, leading me across the road and into one of the narrow alleys that give Brighton its character.

'You've learned your way around quickly,' I said, as we stepped from that passage, across a road and into another.

'You bet I have,' said Marc, suddenly taking my arm and pulling me to the right, where another, narrower alley led off. Halfway along he stopped, gently pushed me against the wall and started to kiss me.

He kissed me so hard and so sweetly I forgot everything. Forgot I was leaning against a dingy wall in Brighton. Forgot I was forty-nine and more than old enough to be his mother. Forgot he was my daughter's best friend's brother. Forgot his mother was a terrifying harpy. All that existed was my mouth and Marc's – and something lower that was practically pinning me to the wall.

And that was when reality suddenly hit me. I pulled away from him like I'd had an electric shock. It was bad enough having a crush on a man – almost a boy – half my age, but practically humping him up against a wall in a dank alley was seriously tacky. Especially as he still had the sailor hat on, which was the final detail tipping the scenario into the grotesque.

I propped myself against the wall opposite him, trying to gather myself. He was blinking like I'd just woken him up.

'What's the matter Loulou?' he said. 'Are you all right?'

'Yes, well – no. It's no good, Marc. I can't do this . . .'

Chard had been right, I thought. Just as he'd said I would, I'd known instinctively in that moment that anything more than friendship between me and Marc had to stop.

'I'm sorry,' he said, coming closer and reaching for my hands. I pulled away, putting the safe distance back between us.

'Let's go and have lunch, Marc,' I said. 'This isn't right. And give me that stupid hat.'

I snatched it off his head quite roughly and stuffed it in my bag. He looked quite bewildered – and I realised it was the only the second time I'd ever seen him uncertain.

'I'm really sorry, Loulou,' he said. 'I didn't mean to insult you. I just . . . I just can't help it. I'm so attracted to you and after that night in the tent, sorry, I was just too keyed up . . . I thought you felt the same.'

'It's OK, Marc,' I said. 'I do, but I don't. Not like this. It's not your fault. I probably shouldn't have come today. I'm very confused. Let's just go and have lunch, OK?'

'Can I still have the ice-cream?' he said, the mischief back in his eyes.

He'd recovered quickly, I thought, flicking him on his upper arm. I couldn't be cross with him, although I did feel tainted by what had just happened. I might have been half-crazed with lust for him, but not enough to behave like that. It brought everything that was wrong about us together all too clearly to the front of my mind.

'So where would you like to have your chicken nuggets?' I asked him, trying to keep things light.

'That Jamie Oliver place is just along here and across the road. I believe he does a nice line in turkey twizzlers.'

'Lead the way,' I said and followed him out of the alley.

As we stepped out into the street, I couldn't see immediately for the bright sunlight and walked straight into a man pushing a wheelchair.

'I'm so sorry,' I said, steadying myself on its armrest.

'Loulou, my dear,' said a familiar voice and as I blinked my eyes into focus, I realised it was Chard's dad, the Air Marshal, sitting in the chair, being pushed by Stravko.

'Oh!' I said astonished and then remembered that Chard had sent his parents down to Brighton for a change and some sea air while he was away at the Big Chill and then recording the album.

'Hello, Mrs Landers,' said Stravko, turning his head to look at me and then rather pointedly at Marc, who was standing next to me smiling. Shit shit shit.

'Hi, Strav,' I said in a slightly over-jolly tone. 'Hi, Ralph.'

I leaned down to give him a kiss.

'What are you doing here, Loulou?' he asked.

'Business – I'm buying stock from a dress shop that's closing – and I'm taking young Marc here out to lunch. He's Tattie's brother. You know, Theo's best friend?'

'Ah, Theo, that darling girl. Is she with you? Is this her young man?'

I cringed a million cringes. It was a perfectly valid question.

'I don't know,' I said, laughing like a character from a 1920s play. Played by a particularly bad actress. 'Are you, Marc? She wouldn't tell me if you were . . .'

'How do you do, Sir?' said Marc, leaning down to shake Ralph's hand. 'Marc Thorssen. No, I'm not Theo's young man. I'd have to join a very long queue for that privilege.'

The ninety-year-old Air Marshal smiled up at him, clearly recognising a fellow traveller.

'Ralph Meredith,' he said. 'Good to see you.'

There were nearly seventy years between the two of them, but they had a lot in common, I realised, as Marc then turned to shake Stravko's hand. Beautiful manners for one thing.

'So are you enjoying yourself?' I asked Chard Senior. 'How's Nancy?'

'Oh, she's stuck back at the hotel, poor old girl, but they are looking after her beautifully and she loves looking out of the window at the sea. We all do. We're enjoying ourselves enormously, aren't we, Strav? But it is a bit dull without Theo around. I miss my cards. Do you play cards, young man?'

'I love a game of poker . . .' said Marc.

'Oh good, so do I, and Theo can't play that. We stick to rummy and she usually beats me, but we can have a game of poker this afternoon, if you would care to. Although I better warn you, I'll probably thrash you. Seven card stud is my game.'

He chuckled happily and Marc joined in.

'I can't wait,' he said.

'Marc has to go back to work shortly,' I said quickly.

'That's true,' he said. 'But I'd love to have a game of cards when I finish, Mr Meredith. What hotel are you staying at?'

I was amazed and pretty appalled, but it gave me an idea.

'What are you doing now?' I asked Stravko.

'We go back to hotel, we have lunch,' he answered.

'Well, why don't we all have lunch together?' I said. 'We were just going to that restaurant across the street there.'

So we did and it was a great success. Marc and Ralph got on so well, I found myself talking mainly to Strav. I found his observations about Britain very amusing, but I couldn't help being a little distracted as I tried to catch on to what the other two were talking about.

As far as I could tell, listening with half an ear, it seemed to range very quickly from the Air Force to Iraq, to cricket and then *Strictly Come Dancing*, about which they both had very strong opinions.

Considering Marc's prowess on the dance floor I shouldn't have been surprised and I was sure Ralph and Nancy used to cut a dash at the mess ball, but what I couldn't get over was how two men with such a huge gap in ages could find so much common ground and chat so easily.

At one point Ralph was slapping Marc on the back and saying: 'Good man! Good man!'

I just shook my head and laughed. It was adorable seeing them together, but this whole age range thing was doing my brain in. Every time I thought I had it straight something happened to mix me up all over again.

Theo

Splatterday afternoon

I worked really hard again with Ajay and Tony yesterday because we had to have all the samples and patterns ready to go up to the factory. We could actually email the patterns over to them which I thought was beyond brilliant but the samples had to go there in real life.

They were supposed to go on Friday but Nicolle turned up late in the afternoon with a message from Weanie to say it was OK for the samples to go in the morning.

Then while she was still there looking at what we'd done and being really nice about it all I got a text from him.

> I'm driving the samples up to Leicester
> myself tomorrow and you're coming with
> me. Be outside Kings Cross station at 8 am.
> Wearing the Sergio Rossi shoes.

I curled my lip at the screen. Nobody tells me what to wear. But then I remembered how I'd felt stalking around the Big Chill in those shoes and my cut-offs with everyone looking at me. It had turned me on in some weird way. Made me feel powerful.

I could remember very clearly standing over Weanie with my foot on his chest him staring up at me his eyes wild. I could have killed him then with one of those heels in his eye King Harold stylee. Maybe

I should have. Would have stopped him trying to boss me around. But I was having too fun much in the studio to think about all that. I'd decide in the morning.

The boys made me model all the samples for Nicolle and Ajay was putting all these really funny tracks on the iPod and I was copping poses to make them laugh. Then Nicolle disappeared and came back with a bottle of champagne and four glasses.

So we got into that and then we were all dancing and she went and got another one.

Where are you getting the bubbles? Said Ajay.

I've got a secret supply she said. Boner's office.

They all laughed and I didn't get the joke. Tony put me out of my misery.

Boner is what we call Paul he said.

I call him Weanie.

They all fell about.

How did you meet Weanie Boner? asked Nicolle.

More laughing. But I could tell they were all dying to know. I saw a bit of eye-catching going on.

My mum is friends with his wife I said. They do yoga together I think. Old lady stuff. We went to a party at their house and I told Weanie that West Wind did the best handbags on Oxford Street.

Ajay punched the air. He was in charge of accessories.

But the worst knitwear.

Oh that's OK said Tony. The girl who did that shit has already left.

But how did you end up coming to work here? said Nicolle.

Her eyes were beadier than usual. It was making me feel uncomfortable and to my great relief before I could cobble together an answer her phone started ringing and after glancing down at it she stood up and ran out of the room with it glued to her ear.

I was relieved to get out of that tricky moment but the party mood was gone which was a shame. Ajay stood up and took the glasses out to the kitchen to wash them.

I guess I'll be going then I said. I stood up and put my jacket on and Tony came over and hugged me.

Thanks for all your work Theo. We couldn't have done this without you. You bring such fresh ideas. And you're great on the sample machines . . .

I loved it I said. I hope I can come in and do more with you guys.

Well we've got to start thinking about first winter on Monday. Bring your ideas in.

I grinned at him.

See you then I said and headed for the door but before I got through it he stopped me.

And Theo. Don't take any notice of Nicolle. She really rates you and what you bring to the team but she's jealous. She used to be Paul's mistress and she's still in love with him. It's sad.

I just looked at him and nodded. I got the implication. She used to be his mistress and now you are. I couldn't be bothered to protest that I wasn't because I didn't know how long that was going to be true.

And I think that's why I ended up standing outside Leicester station at 12 noon today wearing a pair of stupidly high-heeled shoes. I needed to know how far I was going to go with this thing. I had to push it to the limit.

But I wasn't going to drive up there with him. I don't take orders and I couldn't be bothered to endure two hours of his Ganesha groping at high speed on the M1. Plus I don't like cars much. They make me nervous. I'm an inner city public transport girl.

So I texted him at 7.55 saying:

> I'm going by train. I'll be outside Leicester
> Station at noon. Haven't decided which
> shoes I'll wear yet.

He replied telling me he would decide nearer the time whether to meet me or not. I knew he was trying to play me at my own games but he's just not as good at it as I am. I knew he'd come.

He wasn't in his usual car. So when a low sporty thing pulled up and the door was flung open I was surprised but relieved to see he was at the wheel. No sleazy driver pulling over into laybys. That was one less of his eight arms to fend off.

Good you were here he said.

I changed my mind at half past seven this morning. I've never been to Leicester.

He smiled looking straight ahead not at me clearly pleased he was getting his own way. Also I was wearing crazy spike heels which I'd seen him check out as I got into the car. Not the ones he'd bought me though. They were knackered by the end of the BC but I'd bought another great pair. From New Look ha ha ha. He got nothing for nothing from me.

We went straight to the factory which was really interesting. I got to talk through the samples with the production manager bloke and he showed me the whole computerised set-up. It was pretty amazing. Weanie let me do all that bit which I was very pleased about.

Then he put the screws on the poor guy about schedules and delivery dates. It was quite scary seeing him in Weanie Boner Big Boy mode looming over him like Tony Soprano. The production bloke was practically backed up against the wall. I hated Weanie for it. And I wanted to shag him right there. He has that effect on me.

So that was that and then Weanie said he would take me home. Or I could break my rule and have lunch with him. He'd booked somewhere really nice he said out in the country.

I told him the lunch is for wimps thing only applied during the week and in the city. Plus I was really starving and a bit hungover from the champagne the night before. Couldn't see any harm in a bacon sarnie and a couple of puddings. On Weanie's bill. Maybe three puddings.

We drove for ages out into the country and then turned into this drive like something off a Jane Austen bonnet drama so I figured it was going to be one of those country house hotel jobs. It was. Very

very Pemberley. I didn't bother saying that to him. Would have gone over his head so fast it might have scalped him.

We walked in and I expected to be shown into some fabulous dining room looking over the ha ha with serfs gambolling in the meadows but the man on the front desk came out saying Ah Mr Beaney welcome back and all that caper and then he said: I'll show you to your room, Sir.

Uh? I said. I thought we were having lunch . . .

We are. In a private room.

A private room with a bloody great four poster bed in it. There was a table set up with loads of silver cutlery in the window looking over the garden and it was all dandy but the main thing in that room was the bloody bed.

Subtle much? I said as we sat down and the waiter bloke waved our napkins around like flags.

Weanie just laughed.

Well it's better than Pret a Manger isn't it?

It's beautiful but Pret doesn't have a bloody great bed in it.

I thought you might want a nap after your busy morning.

He was chuckling away to himself. He was in charge and he knew it.

Then the food came. Shazam. I didn't get to look at a menu or anything normal. A waiter just arrived with trays of nosh and champagne and I knocked it back because I thought it would get rid of the headache from the night before and because I was nervous. The bastard had done it. He'd got me on my back foot.

Finally the puddings came. There were six different ones in tiny little portions. He must have been able to see my greed gland throbbing.

I remembered you like your sweets he said.

After the waiter left he got up and locked the door. Then he picked the tray of desserts up and put it on a low coffee table number in front of the huge sofa and sat down. He patted the seat next to him and like a hungry dog I was over there in a moment my tongue hanging out for some of the chocolate mousse. My favourite.

What are you going to try first? said Weanie.

Anything chocolate I said reaching for a spoon.

But before I could get hold of it he'd scooped up a spoon of the mousse and was holding it up to my face. Like a tiny baby I opened my mouth and in went the spoon.

Do you want some more? he asked.

I nodded and he fed me again.

More?

I nodded again and this time he held the spoon up tantalisingly.

Come and get it he said. And he put the spoon in his own mouth.

So I did. I kneeled on the sofa put my hands round his face and sucked that chocolate mousse right out of there.

30
Loulou

That Saturday morning was nutsy busy in the shop and I was delighted because it stopped me thinking about the many layers of weirdness from the day before. I'd walked back to Brighton station after lunch – uphill all the way in my platform wedges – to try and clear my head, but it hadn't really helped.

Marc had said a cheery collective goodbye to us all while we were having coffee after lunch, because he had to get back to work, and his parting words were to Ralph, about their cards fixture later. I was just included in the general dazzling smile and wave. Why did that bug me so much?

Maybe because our 'date' had started with me assuming the role of his auntie, moved quickly to frotting up against a wall like a street whore, and ended with him arranging to play poker with a 90-year-old Air Marshal in a grand hotel on the seafront.

Whatever the reason, it seemed I didn't have the sense of 'closure' about him I had hoped for and rather than feeling illuminated by Chard's predicted flash of insight, I realised I was as confused about Marc as ever.

It was very disappointing and I was delighted to be back in the familiar surroundings of my shop, where I felt more grounded than anywhere else.

Shelley couldn't work that Saturday and as I'd known better than to rely on Theo's help – lucky as she'd left home before I even got up that morning – I'd organised an alternative shop assistant: Keith.

His light chatter and permanent readiness for a laugh turned out to be exactly the therapy I needed and he loved the novelty of working in the shop. He was good at it too. He was so charming and so clearly relished women's company that customers of all ages adored him.

'Well, Miss Loulou,' he said, as we sat down for a welcome break – regular English breakfast, no mint nonsense for Keith – during the lunchtime lull. 'Now I understand the point of your old nana knicker shop a bit more. It's fun playing dress-ups with human dollies isn't it?'

'It is to me,' I said.

'Well, as I was given a sound thrashing the time my dad found me playing with my sister's Barbies, this feels like something I've been waiting my whole life to do.'

'Do you like it better than insurance then?' I asked.

'No,' he said. 'I couldn't imagine liking anything better than lovely insurance, but this is good for a new hobby.'

'Well, I hope it doesn't replace organising amazing birthday treats for your friends.'

He grinned.

'Did you love it?'

'I really loved it,' I said, crossing my fingers behind my back for a moment. It wasn't really a lie, not entirely. I had loved being at the Big Chill with all my pals, I'd adored Camp Loulou – it was just the toyboy waiter aspect of the tea party I'd found hard to take.

Then, as I thought about all that, the image of Marc taking his shirt off in that tiny little tent flashed into my head. It was a glorious memory, which did nothing to alleviate my ongoing confusion about him. Cue stomach: triple somersault, back flip and roll.

'Next year I think we'll do Port Eliot Literary Festival . . .' Keith was saying, getting a faraway look in his eye, but I wasn't listening – I was too distracted by what I'd just seen through the shop window. Marc. Opening the garden gate and walking up the path. It was so odd to see him when I'd just been thinking about him half-naked, I felt slightly queasy.

'Loulou?' said Keith, in tones that suggested I had a funny look on my face. Then he turned round to see what I was staring at and burst out laughing.

'Oooh! Look who it is – teeny twinkletoes,' he said, springing up to the open the door.

'Hello Marc,' he said, ushering him in with an outstretched arm and a big smile. 'I'm Keith, Theo's godfather. It's great to meet you at last. I've seen you dancing but we've never met properly.'

Then he kissed him, very warmly on both cheeks, which I thought was a bit much, but Marc didn't seem to mind. I don't know why I was surprised. Nothing seemed to faze him.

'Hi, Loulou,' he called over to me, like it was the most normal thing in the world for him to pop in to my shop. 'You seem quiet at the moment, that's good. I know how busy you get and I was worried I'd be in the way on a Saturday.'

'Not at all,' said Keith, answering for me. 'You've arrived at the perfect time. I've been Loulou's acting assistant today, because Shelley's off and I've got to go in a minute, so you can take over.'

I just stared at him, speechless. I'd booked Keith to help for the whole day followed by dinner. I'd bought a chicken. What did he mean he was leaving?

'Hi Marc,' I said, before Keith could say anything else crazy.

Marc came round behind the counter and kissed me. Only on the cheeks but much more lingeringly than a social peck, and squeezing my bum slowly with a hand that Keith couldn't see, although I had a good idea he'd figure it out. He was beaming at me, so pleased with himself he'd engineered his own exit. Marc still had his hand on my arse.

'Oh, is that the time?' said Keith, looking at his watch with all the naturalness of Widow Twankey, his enormous pinkie finger daintily raised. 'I'd better be off. Have a good time, you two. I'll call you tomorrow, Loulou. Byeeee!'

And still grinning with glee he waved at us and left. I was so stunned I didn't know what to say. Marc did.

'Now I can say hello properly,' he said and pulling me into his arms, he kissed me again, this time on the mouth. And in it. To my shame, I didn't immediately resist. I was still in shock at what had happened and how quickly. I had to hand it to Keith. He really could think on his feet, but it was so uncalled for. I hadn't even got over my mixed feelings about the day before and here I was kissing Marc in public again – and worse. In my shop.

Then my sixth sense for approaching customers alerted me as two women came through the garden gate and I managed to pull away before they could have seen us.

And that was when I finally did have my Chard revelation. It was funny that it took the commercial setting to make the reality of the situation suddenly and instantly clear to me, but in that moment I finally knew my mind: if I couldn't kiss Marc in my shop, I couldn't kiss him at all. Full stop.

'So have I got the job?' he said, standing inappropriately close. 'I've got fashion retail experience . . .'

'If you want it,' I said, in what I hoped were measured tones. I still had to work out how I was going to explain myself to him, kindly. I wanted to stay friends if possible – and at that moment I really did need him in the shop. The first two customers were already in the shop and there were three more at the gate.

'I really would love some help this afternoon, Marc,' I added. 'But no more hanky panky. I'm at work here.'

He grinned.

'What time do you close?'

'Never you mind that,' I said firmly. 'We've got customers to see to – but if you're going to work here you need to change. I'm not having a Jack Wills billboard walking around in my shop. Go and choose a suit and a shirt. You know where they are.'

And it would give me some recovery time, I thought, going over to ask the three newest customers if they needed any help. As it turned out, they needed a lot; they were dressing themselves for an amateur dramatic group production of *Blithe Spirit*. I was delighted to oblige.

From then on I didn't want for distraction. The shop soon filled up to the normal Saturday mania and I was very grateful for Marc's help. In between rushing in and out with floaty bias-cut dresses suitable for Madame Arcati, I could see he was doing a great job.

As usual for a Saturday afternoon, there were loads of teens and young women in the shop, and they were clearly thrilled to be served by someone their own age – and looking totally gorgeous, in a blue 1960s mohair suit. They were particularly keen for his comments on how they looked in outfits which were only ever half done up, I noticed. Marc had to pull up a lot of zips and fasten a lot of catches.

He also got busy with the music, whipping the iPod Keith had set up for me out of the dock, putting his own in, and whacking up the volume. I normally played cruisey background music quite low, Ella Fitzgerald and stuff like that, but the Black-Eyed Peas at high decibels definitely charged the atmosphere. At one point when we passed each other in the back room he grabbed my hand and spun me into a double twirl. I had to laugh.

It did cross my mind a few times that Theo might come home at any moment and find Marc installed in the shop, and I knew I probably ought to be bothered about it, but I wasn't. Because – even with her own very particular moral code – there was no rational reason she could object to him being there. We weren't doing anything I would be ashamed of doing in front of her – and now I knew we never would, it felt great.

I almost hoped she would come in and be forced to deal with

it. Especially as it would give me grounds to remind her that if she helped me out occasionally, I wouldn't have to rely on the willingness of friends.

As it turned out, Theo didn't come in – but Rachel and Lauren did. I was thrilled to see them. It would give my Marc resolve exactly the test it needed.

'Hey girls,' I said. 'Great to see you. You can meet my new assistant . . .'

I went and got Marc, who was busy looking the other way while handing things to some giggling young customers through a not-quite-closed curtain in the big changing room, and brought him back into the main shop.

Rachel and Lauren squealed.

'It's your dancing partner,' said Rachel.

'This is Marc Thorssen,' I said, deliberately formally. 'Marc, these are my friends Lauren and Rachel. Marc is the brother of Theo's best friend, Tatiana. She was at the party at Lauren's place, and the Big Chill. Lots of gorgeous auburn hair? Has a lovely boyfriend called Oscar . . .'

They were nodding in recognition, while shamelessly looking Marc over. He smiled at them. I smiled to myself. It was perfect. I didn't feel an iota of shame or embarrassment about him. Paul Beaney could walk in and it wouldn't have bothered me. Re-sult.

'Hi girls,' he said, instantly winning points for not saying 'ladies'.

'You look great in that suit, Marc,' said Lauren. 'Like a young Michael Caine – but better looking. Much better looking . . .'

'He's certainly good for business in it,' I said. 'Marc's been working at Jack Wills in his uni vacation, so I drafted him in to help me here today. Shelley's got the weekend off.'

I mentally congratulated myself for thinking on my feet like Keith. He'd be proud of me.

'How do you like selling vintage, Marc?' said Lauren. 'Bit of a different market, I would think.'

'It's really fun,' he said. 'There's a more interesting mix of customers here and you have to be more creative with what you suggest to them. Can I help you with anything?'

'Well, maybe you can,' she replied. 'I'm going over to see my family in California and I want to take vintage pieces as gifts for my nieces, who are about your age, so you might be just the person to help me choose what they'd like.'

She smiled at me, showing her approval for my choice of helper. I beamed back, so happy I had finally found a way I could enjoy Marc's company without feeling weird about it. There was the small hurdle of explaining that to him, but my mind was made up just as Chard had told me it would be. No more physical stuff, no more confusion.

Lauren and Rachel left an hour later, both happily laden with purchases and we were so busy with other customers, it didn't seem like long after that it was finally time for me to lock the door and turn the sign to closed.

'I suppose I'd better take this suit off and turn back into a pumpkin,' said Marc.

'Well, you could let me give it to you, as your wages,' I said.

'No, I couldn't,' he said, laughing. 'I helped out as a friend – not an employee.'

And as he spoke I had an idea. A crazy idea, but brilliant at the same time.

'How much do they pay you at Jack Wills?' I asked him.

He told me.

'I pay more than that,' I said. 'How would you like to come and work here until you go back to college? As a properly paid employee. I have an assistant who works four days a week, but she's spending more and more of her time on the online business and we're just about to launch a whole new website selling cheaper stuff that she's running, so I really do need someone to help me in the shop. You were brilliant today, I'd love you to do it. And you can have that suit as your uniform.'

He looked a bit puzzled.

'Well, it sounds great, Loulou, I've really enjoyed today, but – well, wouldn't it be a bit odd working together considering the other thing we have going on between us?'

I took a deep breath.

'We need to talk about that, Marc,' I said. 'We need to sort all that out, so have dinner with me – here, tonight – and we'll talk about it.'

'That would be great,' he said. 'And speaking of food, that reminds me, I nearly forgot the whole reason I came here today – well, the reason I was using as a shameless excuse.'

He went behind the counter and picked up a scruffy Sainsburys bag he'd been carrying when he arrived. I'd forgotten about it.

'It's for Theo,' he said, handing it to me. 'My friend Dylan asked me to drop it off. I've no idea what it is.'

'It smells a bit funny,' I said, taking the bag and tentatively sniffing it.

'It's a string of onions,' he said. 'I had a look. Typical Dylan. It will have some deep mystical meaning only Theo will understand.'

'Are they close then?' I asked, instantly overexcited.

'Well, I know Dylan would like to be. But who knows about Theo? She's like a sphinx, but they talked a lot at the Big Chill and he really made her laugh.'

'That's a very good start with her,' I said. 'There's a note. Written on a luggage tag thing.'

'Read it,' said Marc.

'I couldn't do that,' I said. 'It wouldn't be right and Theo would somehow know I'd done it. I'll just put the bag in her bedroom and she'll see it when she gets back – whenever that is.'

'You don't mind that she might find me here?' said Marc, his eyes wide.

'No,' I said. 'Absolutely not.'

And with a completely clear conscience, I led him upstairs.

Theo

I'm back home now on my trusty old laptop. Need to get this down calmly so I can start to download it into my brain's hard drive. And then delete it.

So I kissed Weanie and sucked out the chocolate mousse and he kissed me back and without his driver in the front or thousands of happy festival goers milling around it all got hot and heavy pretty quickly. But after all that champagne I was really needing to make pee pee so I told him I'd be right back.

While I was in there I stood in front of the mirror staring at my face which is something I do when I'm drunk. It's like looking at a stranger in a weird kind of out of body experience and I find it interesting. Anyway while I was doing it I could hear Weanie talking. I thought he might be ordering up some more champagne or even better more chocolate mousse.

Then I go back out there and he says he's going to the loo now so I sit down and when he's gone I pick up his phone which he's left on the table. Why did I look at it? Because the screen was lit up which means he'd just used it and you wouldn't use your mobile to order room service would you?

Last call was to: WIFE.

That was how he had her listed in his phone book. Wife. It made me feel physically ill. To call her that like she didn't have a name just a function as related to him. And to be ringing her while I was in the loo and he was waiting for me to come back so he could get on with shagging me. That was it. Lucky I still had my clothes on. I just picked up my bag and walked out of that room not shutting the door so the noise wouldn't alert him.

I had no time to make a plan. It was quite scary. I couldn't steal his car because I can't drive and I couldn't order a cab because he'd be down looking for me before it made it all the way out Northanger Abbey but I remembered seeing bicycles lined up to the side of the house so I made for those.

There was a sign saying they were for guests' use so I jumped on one and pedalled like the clappers. Not down the main drive which was too obvious but down this other lane thing at the back which I thought was probably the tradesmen's entrance.

Whatever it was it got me back to the main road and there was a pub right opposite so I headed over there and asked the landlord to give me a number of a local cab firm. Forty minutes later I was back at Leicester station and an hour and a half after that I was back at Mudda's house. Phew.

I was heartily relieved the shop was already shut and crept upstairs so she wouldn't know I was here. I was feeling distinctly nauseous from the whole experience on top of a lot of champagne in the afternoon and I didn't feel up to telling her any lies and certainly not what had really just happened.

I could hear people in the kitchen as I tiptoed past. There was Keith's deafening honk and Mudda's mad cackle but it sounded like there was someone else male in there too. I was pretty sure Deathbreath wasn't back yet so it was a mystery man. Whoever it was I was glad he and Keith were giving me cover to sneak in.

Now I'm safely in my dear old bedroom and I've finally turned my phone on again. I'd killed it while I was waiting in the pub although he'd already rung a few times before I got to it. Now there were eight missed calls and four texts. I listened to the first message and it was so shouty and cross I deleted all the others without playing them.

Then I looked at the texts. The last one said could I just tell him I was OK as he was really worried and didn't know whether he could go back to London or not. So I thought fair enough he has got a point there and I sent him a reply:

Already back in London. Fuck off.

I know I did the right thing. It's the wife factor that made me see it. If I hadn't met her at the Big Chill and seen how much Mudda liked her I might have gone ahead. But she was a person now in my head not just a concept.

But even if I hadn't met her I think seeing the word WIFE on his phone like that would have been enough to puke me out. I'm not like the woman who ran off with Knobbeheadde when I was a baby and I don't want to be.

And I don't want anything to do with a man who would do that either. Weanie is actually as big a knobhead as Knobbeheadde when you think about it. The great suits are not enough to make up for that.

The only thing that's bugging me now is that I really want to carry on working for West Wind. And as I never actually did it with Weanie I don't see why I can't.

I slightly wish I hadn't put fuck off in that text now but that was to do with what happened in the hotel room. Work is a separate thing. And Tony did tell me to go in on Monday with my ideas for winter so I'm going to spend the rest of the weekend working on them anyway.

And the other thing I'm going to do is see Dylan.

When I got back I found a plastic bag on my bed with a big string of onions in it and a label saying 'Trades Onion Conference' with today's date and the address of a pub in Camden.

It says 'Opening Address by Dylan Bogart 8pm' and I'm going.

31
Loulou

I took Marc up to the kitchen and immediately put him to work grating carrots for a salad while I jointed the chicken. I thought if I kept us both busy it would give me some time to think through exactly what I was going to say to him. I opened a bottle of white wine, poured us both a glass and raised mine to him in a toast.

'To my new shop assistant,' I said.

'To my new boss,' he replied, with a look in his eye which told me he was totally on to the game I was playing.

As we pulled the meal together I managed to keep things light and chatty, and every time he brushed past me at the kitchen sink I felt more sure of my resolve. Chard had been absolutely right. It was as if a switch had been pulled in my head. I'd made up my mind and I wasn't going to budge, however gorgeous he was.

Finally, all the food prep was done and we just had to wait for the chicken to cook. I sat down at the table and indicated for Marc to take the chair opposite.

'Cheers,' I said.

'Likewise,' said Marc, his eyes narrowed, but with a hint of amusement in them. 'I know what you're doing, Loulou.'

I laughed.

'Good! That will make it easier. So, go on, tell me what I'm doing.'

'You're putting barriers between us. Emotional – the boss and employee thing – and physical. This table.'

He smacked it with his palms.

'Yes and no,' I said, putting down my glass. 'I am putting up a barrier, but only in one area. You see, working with you in the shop today it finally sank in that I really do want to get to know you better – but as a friend and only as a friend. The physical side of things between us has to stop, it's just not right. As gorgeous as you are, I will never feel comfortable about it. And the more we see of each other in a public setting like the shop, the easier it will be to resist it.'

'But why do you want to resist it, Loulou? We could go to bed right now and have an amazing time. Why won't you give in to that?'

'Because that would be it. We probably would have a great time, but afterwards I would feel bad about it and that would make me feel uncomfortable about you. I want to be friends with you, Marc.'

'Do you think a heterosexual man and a woman can ever really just be friends?' he said.

'Definitely,' I said. 'I've been friends with Chard – Ritchie – for over thirty years.'

Marc laughed, putting his head back and rubbing his scalp with his hands, which made his hair stand up in crazy peaks.

'What?' I said.

'Has there really never been anything physical between you in all that time?'

'No,' I said. 'I'm not his type. I'm about thirty years too old and I've never been a model.'

'Are you blind, Loulou?' said Marc leaning across the table towards me in a way which made it momentarily necessary for me to check my resolve again. It was still in place. Excellent.

'What do you mean?' I said.

'You really think Ritchie Meredith isn't attracted to you?'

'Of course he isn't,' I said, getting exasperated. 'Like I said, he only dates young women. No baggage. I'm an old lady to him more than it seems I am to you, weirdly, and anyway, it's just not about that between me and him. We're friends. That's it.'

Marc was shaking his head and rolling his eyes. Theo had competition.

'What?' I asked, starting to get irritated.

'Haven't you noticed the way he looks at you? He pretty much declared himself in front of 30 000 people at the Big Chill when he dedicated that set to you and I heard he risked being mobbed by Ickies fans camping in the public campsite to be with you on your birthday . . . All that and you really don't see it?'

'No,' I said, quite outraged. 'Chard is my friend. A very good friend. Probably my best friend. I see him every day. He's always there for me when I need him. He was incredibly good to me when Theo was younger. He's really good to me with Theo now . . .'

My words trailed away, as Marc nodded more and more enthusiastically at each statement.

'Oh stop it,' I said, having to laugh, but feeling a little unsettled. 'I really think you're reading it wrong, Marc. We're very close, but that's all there is to it.'

'I'm just telling it how I see it, Loulou,' said Marc. 'As an outsider I might see things you don't. I thought he was the reason you were reluctant to get it on with me actually. I thought maybe you two were already having a thing.'

'Well, we're not. We never have and we never will. We're just really good mates and I would like to be friends with you in the same way. I've got a long history of friendship with men – I've been close to Keith nearly as long as I have to Chard.'

'But he's gay, that's different,' said Marc.

'I suppose so, but you can ask him about that in a minute. He's on his way back here to have dinner with us.'

Between jointing the chicken, marinating the pieces with wedges of lemon, and scrubbing the new potatoes, I'd sent Keith a sneaky text, ordering him to come back for dinner, as previously arranged – using Marc as bait. I'd wanted him there in case my resolve crumbled and even though I was now sure it wouldn't, it still turned out to be a great plan.

Keith arrived in high spirits, revved up by the lark of it all and carrying two bottles of champagne.

We'd finished dinner and were well into the second bottle of fizz when the conversation came round to the subject of all of our love lives. Or rather, was wrenched there by Keith.

'So tell me, Marc,' he said, refilling all our glasses. 'How many girlfriends have you got on the go at the moment?'

'None, it seems,' he said, giving me a pointed look. 'I was seeing somebody – or thought I was – but it turns out she just wants to be friends . . .'

'Oh, that old chestnut,' said Keith. 'It just means they don't fancy you after all, doesn't it?'

Marc was laughing.

'Does it, Loulou?' he said.

'No!' I said. 'It could just as easily mean what it says. That however much someone is attracted to you sexually at the outset, they don't want to spoil a potentially lovely friendship with a bit of transient rumpy pumpy. Sex always complicates things. And meaningless sex is much easier to find than someone you really want to be friends with.'

'What do you think, Keith?' said Marc.

I was wriggling in my seat, desperate to change the subject.

'I don't know about heteros so much,' said Keith. 'You're all weird to me, but gay men? We do seem able to separate sex from other emotions more easily than you lot, but people you want to keep as long-term friends are definitely much harder to find than wham-bam-thank-you-Sams.'

'Ha!' I said, triumphantly, poking Marc on the upper arm.

'What?' said Keith.

'Oh, it's just that Loulou has recruited me to work in the shop so she'll stop wanting to shag me,' said Marc. 'She wants to, but she won't let herself. I keep trying, Keith, but she won't put out. That's right isn't it, Loulou?'

I just put my hands over my face and screamed silently. Keith shrieked with delight.

'Is that true Loulou?' he said.

'Pretty much,' I said, deciding it was easier just to give in and also hoping that talking about it openly would help Marc to understand I was serious.

'This gorgeous young stud muffin here wants to shag you and you said no?' he persisted. 'Are you insane?'

I nodded.

'Possibly,' I said. 'But while he is utterly gorgeous – you are utterly gorgeous, Marc – I do really like him as a person and if we did "shag", as you two so romantically put it, we wouldn't be able to be friends afterwards. It would all be too weird. So I'm choosing friendship over shagship. OK?'

'Well, in his case,' said Keith, relishing the turn the conversation had taken. 'I think that's a friendship I'd be prepared to risk for the sake of the whoopee. But I guess that's really a fundamental difference between men and women, whether gay, straight, or undecided.'

Marc was nodding in agreement.

'You might be right,' I said. 'Because I absolutely know I want the friendship with Marc more. It's the age gap. I just wouldn't feel comfortable. I know I joked about being a Samantha and cougaring after I first danced with Marc that time, but really I like him for himself, not for his age and his body. In fact, they are more of an inconvenience than anything. Why aren't you fifty, Marc? Even forty would be OK.'

'Sorry,' he said, lifting up his hands. 'I could have surgery, I suppose.'

'Oh, but think about his stamina . . .' said Keith, and he and Marc had a good laugh.

'Well, I wouldn't know about that,' I said, flicking Keith's ear. 'But, as I was saying, I want to be friends with Marc and he's coming to work for me, so we can get to know each other better in a neutral context. And now I would like to stop talking about him as if he wasn't here.'

'I don't mind,' said Marc. 'I love being the centre of attention. So many of my friends think I'm weird and boring because I don't take loads of drugs and have a different woman every night, so it's a nice change that anyone thinks I'm interesting enough to talk about.'

I looked at him for a moment.

'People think you're boring?' I said.

'Yeah,' he said. 'I live at home. I'm nice to my sister. I don't drink and drive. I don't even smoke cigarettes, let alone anything illegal. I study hard, I go to the gym, I row, I play the cello. I'm genuinely interested in international affairs. I'm a boring geek. Even my best friends think so. They call me the Mormon.'

He laughed, but I could see that behind the bravado, he minded. I marvelled at the yawning gap between the way we see ourselves and how others see us.

'I don't think you're boring at all,' I said, remembering him pushing me against that wall in Brighton. 'Far from it.'

'Thanks,' he said. 'I suppose it all goes back to what I was saying earlier about people seeing each other with a fresh eye, which reminds me – Keith, do you think Ritchie is in love with Loulou?'

'Shit, yeah,' said Keith, grinning.

'What?' I said, turning towards Keith in amazement. 'What are you talking about?'

'You and Ritchie.'

'What about me and Ritchie?'

'He adores you,' said Keith.

'Well, I adore him,' I said. 'Along with you, he's my best friend.

I see him every day, I don't know what I'd do without him. I've really missed him this week . . .'

I faded out as Keith and Marc started nodding at each other.

'Not you as well, Keith,' I said, dropping my head into my hands.

'I was telling her earlier he's in love with her,' said Marc. 'But she can't see it.'

'Everyone else can, darling,' said Keith, putting his arm round me and giving me a squeeze.

'But that's nuts,' I said. 'Chard only dates baggage-free dolly birds. I'm a geriatric to him in that regard.'

'He's just passing the time with them until you see sense,' said Keith.

'But he's never said anything,' I spluttered, feeling like my whole world was tipping over. It was a bit like finding out your best girlfriend was really a bloke in drag, or your dog was really a cat.

'He comes to see you every day,' said Marc, ticking it off on his fingers. 'He brings you flowers . . .'

'And cup cakes,' chipped in Keith.

'He helps you out with Theo. He's always there for you. He dedicates sets to you . . .'

'And buys you amazing earrings with real jewels.'

'Did he?' said Marc, directing the question entirely to Keith.

'Yeah,' said Keith. 'Real beaut ones. Serious big bucks.'

Marc pulled a goofy 'fancy that' kind of face and they grinned at each other. I felt like screaming. Especially as the bit about the earrings was making me feel distinctly queasy. That had taken me by surprise.

'Blokes don't do that stuff for fun, Loulou,' continued Marc. He's just waiting until you're ready. Barkus is willing and all that . . .'

'What's a Barkus?' said Keith. 'A kind of dog?'

'Never mind,' said Marc. 'It's a dopey Dickens thing. I told you I was a geek.'

'Stop it, you two!' I said, waving my hands around, the bit about Chard 'waiting' until I was ready ringing uncomfortably in my ears.

'Why have you never said anything about this to me before, Keith? You're always telling me to get a boyfriend, but you never mentioned Chard being an option.'

'We've all kind of been waiting for you to figure it out yourself,' he replied.

'Who is "we" exactly?'

'Your sister. Shelley. Lauren. Rachel . . .'

I was so freaked out, I got up and walked around the room and then, just for something to do, put the kettle on. I'd have some nice comforting mint tea, I thought automatically, then felt embarrassed by the association with Chard. It was like I'd caught myself out. I'd make some fresh ginger tea instead. My head was whirling.

'But Keith,' I said, turning around quickly from the kitchen counter. 'If you think I should be getting it on with Chard – who is ten years older than me – why on earth did you lay on that toyboy tea for me at the Big Chill and with him there? That was the opposite message. I thought you were telling me to jump aboard Marc here. My sister certainly thinks I should.'

'Hurray!' said Marc. 'Hurray for Loulou's sister! Shame you didn't listen to her.'

'Well, there was no harm you playing the field until you finally figured it out about Ritchie,' said Keith. 'He certainly has. You need to get yourself back in the saddle a bit. The toy boy tea was just a bit of fun for all of us – especially me. I got it on with one of them later.'

He roared with laughter. I brought the teapot over to the table with a plate of chocolate-covered orange peel and we all sat in silence for a bit, chewing. Marc spoke first.

'So what are you going to do, now you do know about Ritchie?' said Marc, quietly.

'Nothing,' I said. 'I don't even think it's true and even if I did – and I absolutely don't – I wouldn't do anything. Chard is my lovely, treasured friend and I'm not going to do anything that could spoil that.'

'Like with me, then?' said Marc, his head on one side, in that way of his. I noted with satisfaction that it no longer triggered a gymnastic display in my gonads. 'Just be friends? That seems to be your default setting, Loulou.'

'That's what I'm always telling her,' said Keith, holding up one giant palm for a high five. Marc obliged with a satisfying smack. 'She's got some kind of blockage and I don't mean the kind you can clear with senna. She can have lovers and she can have male friends, but never the twain shall meet. And do you know what the really funny thing is?'

He leaned across to the table to Marc, who mirrored him, one dark eyebrow still raised in expectation.

'Her daughter is exactly the same.'

Marc inclined his head in acknowledgement and then they both turned to look at me.

'Oh, hello! I'm still here am I?' I said, feeling really irritated now. 'I thought you were talking about one of your patients, Dr Freud. That's Keith Freud, by the way. The less well-known one.'

'Well, I'm sorry if it's hard to hear it, girlfriend,' said Keith. 'But that's how it is.'

'Is that right?' I said. 'Well, perhaps you might feel a little – how did you put it? – "blocked", if your husband upped and left you and your baby girl with absolutely no warning and ran off to another country with some brainless bimbo he didn't even stay with when he got there.'

'You know what, Loulou darling,' said Keith, taking my hand and holding it in both of his. 'I love you dearly – not in the way that Ritchie does, obviously . . .'

He and Marc had a good laugh about that. I sighed as loudly as I could.

'Anyway, I love you dearly,' he continued. 'But I'm getting a bit tired of hearing that particular country and western track. It's twenty years since that arsehole left, get over it. And I have to say I think you could do a lot worse than getting over it with Mr Meredith. He's one of life's true gentlemen, great-looking – in a straight, old, rock 'n' roll way – he's a legend, he's loaded and most importantly, he really loves you. What's not to like?'

'What? Apart from the minor detail that I could lose my best friend of thirty years' standing for the sake of a quick bunk-up? But even if he did feel like that – and he doesn't – it's not on the agenda anyway, because I just don't feel attracted to him like that. I adore Chard, but he doesn't stir my loins.'

There was a moment's pause and then we all started laughing, which turned hysterical in that group way, and had the blessed effect of breaking the tension and moving the conversation on.

Even so by the time they left an hour or so later, I felt completely drained. As we stood by the front door, Marc gave me a chaste kiss on the cheek, but squeezed my bum at the same time. I slapped his hand off.

'Behave yourself, employee!' I said and he laughed, chucking me on the cheek.

'Do I still stir your loins a little bit?' he said.

'You stir mine,' said Keith.

'Get along with you,' I said. 'Both of you. Terrible boys.'

They went off together laughing into the late summer night and I stood watching them go and breathing in the delicious warm air. Then I glanced at the cast-iron table and chairs where'd I'd spent so many happy hours with Chard. My adored *friend* Chard.

I went over and sat down in my chair, trying to remember what it felt like to be there with him sitting opposite. As comfortable and nurturing as wearing the cosiest sheepskin slippers, I decided. But wasn't that how friendship should feel? Surely it didn't signify anything more.

Then I remembered what I'd said about him not stirring me sexually. Was that really because I didn't think he was attractive, or because there had just never been the right circumstances for me to think of him in that way?

I was still married when we met and when I found myself suddenly single again, he was married; by the time that ended our platonic friendship was completely bedded in. Plus, I was so raw and ragged about what Rob had done to me, all I wanted from any man was friendship. I would have recoiled from anything else.

It wasn't that I couldn't appreciate he was a striking looking man. With his height, high cheekbones and thick shock of silver-streaked black hair, he would have stood out in a crowd, even if he hadn't been world famous. And on the few occasions he took his shades off, he had those amazing pale blue eyes.

I got up and sat down again on the other side of the table, in his chair, trying to imagine I was him looking at me and how that would feel, but I couldn't do it. The whole thing was nuts and I just hoped the seed Marc and Keith had planted in my head wasn't going to affect my precious friendship with Chard, just by being in there. I hoped I'd be able to forget it and move on.

After glancing in at the mess in the kitchen and deciding it could wait until the morning, I tramped up the stairs to bed, reflecting on all that happened since Marc had unexpectedly turned up that morning, and decided that things really couldn't get any weirder.

How wrong I was.

Theo

Manic Monday

Writing this on Mudda's laptop behind counter in shop. Why am I here on a Monday afternoon? It's freaky. I'll get to that. There's other stuff I need to download first.

Had a totally ace time with Dylan on Saturday night. He was waiting for me in the pub with a bag of cheese and onion crisps and when I'd eaten them he pinned the packet to my T-shirt saying it was my trades onion delegate's pass. I do like someone who can flog a running joke until it's screaming for mercy.

We talked about all kinds of stuff and then he said: Next item on agenda – Past Relationships.

I said: You first.

He told me he'd been in love with an Afghan girl while he was out there. Said he'd never seen her face under her burqa and they couldn't speak to each other because she would have to be killed for bringing shame on the family.

Me: If you couldn't see her or speak to her how did you know you were in love with her?

Dylan: It was a large part of the attraction.

Ha ha ha. I think he's almost as twisted as me.

Then he said it was my turn and I had to name and describe all my boyfriends.

I said: Pass. I don't do that shit.

He looked surprised and said: Oh. Name and describe all your girlfriends then.

Not that again I said I've already had that 'special conversation' with Tattie. And if I was lezborial I wouldn't do the girlfriend thing either. I just don't do any of that relationship caca. Really can't be bothered.

He said it was because of my dad leaving me when I was a baby and I told him to fuck off. Because he's probably right. I told him that too.

And something about talking about all that super personal stuff made me tell him the whole story of Weanie. The whole catastrophe including how powerful and turned on I felt standing over him in those shoes and everything. I told him because I knew he wouldn't judge me for it and he didn't. He seemed to find it interesting like David Attenborough watching a new kind of dung beetle.

But he did ask me if I was wearing the shoes right then because he felt like having a little lie down. I pulled his Afghan shawl over my head and told him he wasn't allowed to talk to me anymore. Just kidding obviously.

Then I asked him what he thought I should do about the work thing because I so wanted to go back in to the design studio to West Wind and he said I should.

What's he going to say? said Dylan. Get her off the premises she's fired because she wouldn't shag me?

He also told me to take my contract in with me because if he did tell me to leave it would be unfair dismissal and I would be able to sue him for breach of contract and Dylan would help me do it because he's doing law and he wants to specialise in employment law particularly with regard to the downtrodden worker.

I said I'd downtread Beanie in my scariest high heels if he tried any stunts like that and Dylan laughed. He also put his arm round me and kissed me on the cheek telling me I was a funny funny girl. Then I went to the loo because I didn't want him getting any ideas. Or to see I was blushing.

So I decided I would go in to the design studio today. I spent all of yesterday working on my ideas for deep midwinter as I call it. I can't stand those terms they use like 'second winter' they don't get me in the mood at all.

But just thinking the word midwinter makes me feel like a Tudor peasant in deep snow and I got into that mindset working with the same tacky market stall fabrics but introducing long full skirts and cloaky things all with my signature pockets. I even went down to the Victoria and Albert to look at the old clothes and get some ideas. I love all that. I was up most of last night working on it.

I'd even done a great thing with the Sergio Rossi shoes I knackered at the Big Chill sewing fluoro trainer shoe laces onto the straps and tying them round my ankles. They looked amazing in a really twisted way and I wore them into the studio on Monday morning.

Tony and Ajay seemed really pleased to see me. Even Nicolle was quite friendly and they loved what I'd done. It was interesting because Tony had gone riffing off with market stall fabrics too but in tailoring and it worked really well with what I'd done. And Ajay had some great ideas for accessories making my pockets into sort of bags on strings which was cheating but still cool and when I suggested using fluoro bootlaces as the straps they loved it.

We all got really revved up and spent the whole morning 'story-boarding' it to show to Beanie in the afternoon. There was a big ideas meeting in the boardroom and all the key people from the company would be at it they said.

I'd never been to one of those before and I felt really excited. Even though I knew that the man I would be presenting to was the one I'd been snogging in a hotel room less than forty eight hours previous.

The one I'd run out on.

And told to fuck off.

But I loved what we did in the studio so much I just couldn't process that he might not be thrilled to see me.

So off I went with the rest of the team up to the boardroom

which is right next to his office on the top floor with a massive table and loads of people I didn't know already sitting round it.

We sat down in our little clique chatting and fooling around as more peeps came in but still no sign of Boner as they were all calling him.

If only they knew I thought. He had quite one on him. Maybe that was why Nicolle came up with the nickname. But I shut those thoughts down right away.

Then the door from Weanie's office opened and in he stalked wearing a black suit and dark glasses and looking like a very very scary gangster. For a moment I remembered why I'd ended up in that hotel room with him but then I thought about his wife laughing with Mudda at the Chill and remembered just as clearly why I'd run out of it again.

He didn't notice me at first. There were a lot of people in there he seemed to need to shout at. Particularly the production team because there was some problem with the Leicester factory.

I didn't waste my fucking weekend going up there so those arseholes could work on a load of frilly fucking nighties for marks and fucking spencers he was yelling and he threw his shades down on the table in front of him.

That was when he saw me. It made him shut up which was one benefit then he really did go pale. I don't think I've ever seen that happen before.

Something made me look at Nicolle and she was looking from him to me and back like she was watching a Wimbledon final.

What's that student doing here? said Weanie looking at me and then at Tony.

That fucking work experience girl. HER. Next to you.

He picked up the sunglasses again and threw them at Tony.

They missed. Then something amazing happened. Tony came to my defence.

If you're talking about Theo he said. She's here because I told her to come. She put a lot of great ideas into the filler collection as you know and she's brought in some great looks for second winter. Like this . . .

He pulled up the storyboard with my Tudor market stall ideas on it and showed everyone.

I don't care what she's fucking done Weanie was yelling. I don't want fucking fashion students in my boardroom. Get her out of here.

Don't worry I said. I'm leaving and I stood up and walked out.

And when I got outside the room I took off the Sergio Rossi shoes and threw them at him through the open door.

Then I scarpered.

I was in Topshop when my phone rang.

Weanie: Where the fuck are you?

Me: TOPSHOP.

Weanie: What are you doing in that shit hole?

Me: Buying some new shoes.

Silence.

Weanie: You know that's just about the one place in London I can't come in and pull you out by your hair don't you?

Me: You got it baby.

And I hung up.

When I came out about half an hour later dressed head to toe in new clothes he was waiting for me. I walked straight past him but he followed then grabbed my arm and pulled me into a doorway. Somehow he'd managed to turn me so my back was pressed against the wall. He planted his hands on either side of my head pushed his body against mine and glared at me. I could feel his hard-on pressing against me.

Me: What?

Weanie: Don't fuck with me Theo.

Me: Or what?

Weanie: Or nothing. Just don't fuck with me.

Me: I don't want to do any kind of fucking with you. I thought I'd made that clear already. And if you don't understand what I'm saying I'll ask my mother to get your wife to explain it to you. OK?

And while he was spluttering and clearly wondering if anyone would notice if he strangled me right there quick as a snake I slithered down and escaped out from under his arms before he even realised it was happening and bolted off down Oxford Street. I knew he couldn't run after me. People might see him. Or he might have a cardiac arrest.

As soon as I thought he couldn't see me any more I stopped and hailed the first cab I saw. Home. Which is how I come to be sitting here watching Mudda busying around in the shop.

I needed to be with someone. I'm scared of Weanie. I've never seen anyone so angry and this is where I feel safest. I don't know if Chard's even back so I don't know if I could have gone there or not but I'm quite surprised how right it feels to be here. With Mudda. Mum.

Even though I did open the door to be welcomed by Polo Mint Marc. He's the new shop assistant it turns out. Shelley's in charge of online now and Marc's in the shop until he goes back to yooni. It's so sick it's almost funny but at least it means he's not shagging her although I did ask him to be sure.

Me: So is this you moving in? Are you going to be my step dad?

Marc: No. I like dancing with your mum Theo. I think she's amazing. But I'm strictly her employee. And her friend. OK?

Me: Just checking.

So that's cool. I can have a laugh with him. He is Tattie's brother after all. Plus he's Dylan's best friend so how could I not like him? And he's just told me Dylan is coming over to have lunch with him so I can go too and I'm happy about that.

Happier than I've been for a very long time.

So that's where I'm at. But – hang on a minute. What's going on? Mudda has just dropped the vase of flowers she was holding. Right on the floor. There's broken glass and flowers and water and shit everywhere and there's a man opening the door. She's screaming for Marc to come.

What the fuck?

32
Loulou

I've heard about people fainting with shock, but I'd never actually experienced anything like it myself until I looked up to see Rob opening the door to my shop. That being Rob – Theo's father. Rob who had walked out of that very same door twenty years before with no warning.

I hadn't seen him since. Even when he'd come back that Easter to lay claim to some of Theo's seven-year-old attention, Chard had helped me by handling all the collections and returns so I didn't have to see him. I'd known I wouldn't be able to cope with it and one of my conditions of that visit had been that he couldn't come within five hundred yards of the house. Chard had done it all from his place. What a friend.

And now here Rob was again. Twenty years older but still instantly recognisable as the handsome bastard who, it turned out, had been enjoying girlfriends all over London before he ran off to LA with one of them.

So after all that time, did he enter politely? Did he seek my permission to step over the threshold? No. He walked in shouting.

'I knew it!' he was yelling, pointing at Theo, who was practically crouching behind the counter she was so terrified. 'I knew she wasn't in Afghanistan! I knew you weren't giving her my messages! Well, I'll tell you what Loulou Landers you are going to be hearing from my lawyers!'

I screamed for Marc to come. I don't know what I thought he could do with this raving madman, but Theo and I needed someone on our side. He ran in.

'What's going on?' he said, his rower's shoulders immediately hunching up into defence mode. 'Who are you?' he said to Rob. 'What do you want?'

'I want my daughter,' said Rob, advancing on Theo, who was now actually hiding behind the counter.

'Hold on a minute, mate,' said Marc, grabbing his arm and pulling him back. 'You need to calm down a bit.'

Rob turned on Marc and attempted to leer down at him threateningly. He was a bit taller, but Marc was much better built.

'And who are you, little boy?' said Rob. 'The pool boy? The tennis coach?'

'Just calm down,' said Marc.

'Don't tell me what to do!' said Rob and while I watched in utter horror he pulled back his right arm and punched Marc in the face.

'Shelley!' I screamed, although I could hear her footsteps already running up the stairs from the basement. 'Quick! Call the police!'

Marc punched Rob back, getting him right on the jaw and as I launched myself at them, trying to grab hold of Rob's arms, I saw Theo crawl out under the counter and scuttle over to the door still on all fours. She caught my eye as she stood up and I nodded frenziedly at her, as if to say – Go! Go! And she ran off.

Shelley came bursting through the door from the house.

'Quick,' I said. 'Help me hold him back.'

She rushed over and we managed to get hold of one of Rob's arms each, although he was flailing like a madman.

'Get off me!' he was screaming. 'I'm going to sue you all for assault.'

'I don't think so,' said a voice from the door. 'There's three of them to testify against you and I can see Mr Thorssen has sustained a serious injury. The one who's going to be done for assault is you.'

It was Marc's friend Dylan. He rushed over and the two of them took over from me and Shelley and got Rob in an armlock. He wasn't going anywhere – except maybe Camden Police Station. Shelley was already on the phone to them.

'Who is this fuckwit?' asked Marc.

'My ex-husband,' I said, taking the opportunity to have a good look at him, the man who had done so much damage to my life. 'Theo's dad, unbelievably. He always did have a problem controlling his temper.'

'I just want to see my daughter,' he said, trying to pull himself out of their grip. 'I've been phoning and emailing for weeks and getting nothing and I knew that story you told me about her being in Afghanistan was all bullshit. So I came in to see for myself and I was right. You were lying to me all along.'

'What stories about Afghanistan?' I asked him, beginning to wonder whether he was seriously mentally ill.

'You told me she was in Afghanistan working on an aid project,' he said. 'I've got print-outs of all the emails with me in case you tried to make trouble. If your little thugs will let go of me, I'll show you.'

I went over and locked the shop door and put the keys in my pocket.

'Let go of him,' I said to the boys. 'But if you start off again, Rob, we'll tie you up next time. Show me these emails you're talking about.'

He opened the bag he'd been carrying and thrust a folder at me. It was a ring binder with printouts of emails, filed in date order. They were all from Theo. I didn't read them properly but even just glancing through I could see references to a photography course and needing money for it. I didn't know anything about a photography course. This was nearly as weird as the Afghanistan stuff he had been raving about.

'Shelley,' I said. 'Call the police back and tell them not to come – unless you want to press charges, Marc. Do you?'

He shook his head and touched the skin around his eye gingerly with his fingers.

'No, I reckon a black eye will make me look quite tough,' he said.

'Just make you even more handsome, you infuriatingly pretty little Mormon,' said Dylan.

I carried on flicking through the emails.

'The ones from you are at the back,' said Rob.

I flipped the pages over and sure enough there were emails from my address and signed 'Loulou' – but I hadn't seen any of them before.

'These are from my email address, but I didn't send them, Rob,' I said. 'And I've never had an email from you.'

'But I've been sending them for weeks, trying to find out where she is.'

'She's been here the whole time.'

'Well, why is somebody claiming she's in Afghanistan?' he said. 'It's insane.'

'I was in Afghanistan working on an aid project,' said Dylan cheerfully and as I turned to look at him, it all fell into place.

I looked back at Rob.

'I think Theo may have sent you those emails – allegedly from me,' I said.

I glanced down at them again.

'Had you told her you were coming over here?' I asked him.

'Of course I had,' he said, ever the arsehole. 'I told her months ago that I've leased a crewed yacht in Croatia and I've been trying to contact her so she can make arrangements to come with us.'

I glanced at Marc. He raised an eyebrow in a way that suggested that he was thinking the same thing I was.

'Yes,' I said. 'I'm fairly sure Theo sent these bogus emails to you. Tell me, did she ever mention that she'd lost her mobile phone a few weeks ago?'

'No,' said Rob. 'That was the other thing, I was leaving texts and messages on her phone and she never replied. I called here too.'

'That's true,' said Shelley. 'I spoke to him a couple of times, but I didn't pass on the message, Loulou. I thought it would only upset you and I wouldn't give him your mobile either. He was so bloody rude.'

'Oh, that was you, was it?' said Rob, turning furiously towards Shelley. 'Well, thanks a bunch. You were a fat lot of help. Nice staff you have, Loulou.'

'Don't start up again, Rob,' I said. 'Or we will get the police in.'

'Call them, I'm not worried. My lawyers will look after me and meanwhile they will be serving you with papers demanding that you let me see my daughter.'

'It's not up to Loulou,' said Dylan, walking over to Rob while rolling a cigarette. 'Or you. Neither of you have any legal rights over your daughter. She's over eighteen. It's up to her whether she sees you or not, mister, and from what she's told me, I don't think she wants to.'

'I don't know who you are, buddy boy,' said Rob, squaring up to Dylan, who didn't seem in the slightest bit worried. 'And I don't know what interest you have in this situation, but as long as she is living on my money and has my name, I am going to have a say in her life.'

'Ah,' said Dylan, looking up at Rob with one open eye, as he licked the edge of his ciggie paper. 'But that's just it, she doesn't have your name any more.'

'What do you mean?' I said, turning to him.

'She's changed it,' he said. 'I helped her do it. I changed mine as soon as I turned eighteen. It's so easy. You just hire a lawyer, show them your birth certificate and passport, sign a document, pay them £85 and you can be called whatever you like.'

'So what on earth is she called now?' I asked him, imagining Moon Unit Zappa or Apple Martin.

'Theo Meredith,' he said happily, putting the neatly rolled ciggie behind his ear.

That was when I started laughing. The whole thing was so

ludicrous, I just couldn't stop. From Rob's arrival and the subsequent barroom brawl, to Theo hacking into my email and making up ridiculous stories about Afghanistan and bogus photography courses, and then changing her bloody name, I just couldn't process it any other way.

One thing I did know though, was that I had to see my daughter as soon as possible – and I was fairly certain I knew where I'd find her. But before I went there I had one more thing to say.

I turned back to Rob and looked him up and down.

'You are a total fuckwit,' I said to him. 'Not for walking out on me – now I fully appreciate just how lucky I was to get rid of you – but for missing out on your daughter. She was a glorious child and now she's the most amazing young woman and you'll never know her. I hope all the shags you've had since you left us were worth missing that for, Rob.'

He looked at me angrily, but I could see in his eyes that I'd got to him. He did know what he'd missed and that was what had brought him back here now. But it was too late. Way way too late.

'I'm going now, Rob,' I said. 'I'm going to see my daughter. And as you're so keen on lawyers, just to let you know, you will be hearing from mine. I'm going to reinstate that restraining order – the one that made it an offence for you to come within five hundred yards of this building, or me. And if you don't want me to take things further, I suggest you start acting like it's already in place.'

I walked over, unlocked the shop door and stood with one arm extended to usher him out. He scowled at me, picked up his bag and stomped over.

'Oh, just one more thing before you go,' I said, touching his arm patronisingly as he stepped out of the door. 'Leave your business card with me. I'll give it to Theo and if she wants to be in touch with you she can call you. And if she doesn't . . .'

I shrugged and smiled at him, as sarcastically as I could.

'Fuck you,' he said and stormed off.

For a few moments I stood stock still until I saw him get into a black cab that was blessedly passing. Once it drove off, I went back into the shop and punched the air.

Marc, Dylan and Shelley all came over and hugged me, and we danced around in a crazy little victory jig.

'What a total fuckpig,' said Dylan, when we stopped, sounding almost impressed. 'I think he's actually worse than my dad. Shocking. I'm going outside to smoke this to recover.'

He headed out to the terrace and Shelley went with him, saying she needed a calming ciggie too. I felt a momentary pang as I saw them sit down at what I thought of as Chard's and my table, an all too familiar pall of smoke starting to form. I wondered what he'd say when he came back from recording the album and I told him the story, whenever that would be. I hoped it would be soon.

I was standing gazing out of the window, still in shock, when Marc came and put his arms round me. I laid my head on his shoulder and he gently stroked my hair. It felt completely asexual, safe and very comforting.

'Are you all right, Loulou?' he said quietly.

'Yes and no,' I said. 'Thank God you were here, Marc. You were amazing.'

I lifted my head and looked up at him.

'You really are a wonderful friend,' I said and he laughed.

'I hear you,' he said.

I gave him the kind of squeeze I would give Keith and then pulled away.

'And now,' I said. 'I'm going to find my daughter.'

'Where do you think she went?' said Marc.

'Oh, I think I know,' I said and set off along Regent's Park Road.

I could see Theo's legs stretched out from our bench well before I got to the top of Primrose Hill. I could also make out some even longer ones stretched out beside them and when I realised who they belonged to, my jog turned into a run. Chard.

'Theo! Chard!' I was calling out, puffing from exertion and starting to cry all at the same time.

I saw them both jump to their feet and it was Chard who made it to me first.

'Hey, Loulou, baby,' he said.

Then he picked me up in his arms and carried me to the top of the hill. As we went, him puffing and panting a bit, I buried my head in his neck, breathing in his familiar scent of vetiver, and stifling sobs. It was all too much.

He put me down carefully on the bench, in between him and Theo and we just clung on to each other in a mess of weeping, her head on my shoulder, her arms around my waist, and Chard's long arms around both of us.

'Oh, Mum,' said Theo eventually lifting her head to look at me. 'Did you get rid of him? I was so frightened. He's like a mad man.'

'He's gone,' I said. 'And he won't be coming back. Ever. I mean . . .'

I had to laugh, despite my tears. 'I did suggest he leave his card, so you can call him if you want to.'

She lifted her head to check I was joking and smiled, wiping the tears from her face.

'I love you, Mum,' she said. 'I'm sorry I've been such a beast to you. I've just been so confused about all kinds of stuff – I'll tell you sometime – and I can see things more clearly now. You've been everything to me to all these years and I've been so awful.'

Then she really started sobbing and I pulled her to me, just as I had when she was a little girl.

'It's all right darling, it's all fine. I love you too. I knew you didn't really mean any of those things. It's all fine.'

I kissed the top of her head and turned to look at Chard. He was smiling at me gently, his eyes full of affection, an unlit cigarette hanging off his lip, and I realised how familiar and precious that funny old smile was.

'Where did you spring from?' I said. 'I've missed you so much.'

'I got home late last night,' he said. 'I was going to come over to see you this morning, but I got held up with my parents and then Theo called me just now, so I came straight up here.'

I carried on looking at him. That was the role he'd been playing in my life for the last thirty years. Always there when I needed him. Always there when Theo needed him. Then I remembered something. I turned back to Theo.

'Do you know what finally got the message through to your father that you really don't want to have anything to do with him?' I said to Theo, who was now sitting up.

She shook her head.

'Light your heavy tar, Chard,' I said. 'You're going to need it.'

He smiled, raising his eyebrows and waggling it in his mouth. I waited another moment for him to light it, but when he didn't I decided to go on.

'Theo's changed her name, Chard,' I said.

'Yeah?' he said, taking the cigarette out of his mouth and throwing it into the litter bin near the bench. I watched in some astonishment, but I was too dazed by what had already gone on that afternoon to say anything.

'What to, baby?' he asked, leaning around me towards her.

Theo looked uncharacteristically bashful.

'Theo Meredith,' she said.

Chard blinked a few times and then leaned past me to plant a big kiss on Theo's cheek.

'Thanks, babe,' he said, starting to nod. 'That's beautiful. Really beautiful.'

We all sat there for a moment, just taking it all in. Rob was gone, Theo had Chard's name and it all felt so right.

'You know, Loulou,' said Chard eventually. 'I think it could get pretty confusing you and your daughter having different surnames.'

I looked at him, puzzled. We'd always had different surnames. I'd had mine and she'd had Rob's. I'd never used my married name.

'Wouldn't it make life simpler,' said Chard, taking my left hand in his and raising it to his lips. 'Wouldn't it be easier, if we all just had the same one? If you were Loulou Meredith.'

And he kissed me on my ring finger.

'Marry me, Loulou. Please.'

For a moment I just stared at him, bewildered.

'You want to get married?' I said moronically. 'To me?'

He nodded.

'Who else?' he said.

'I don't know, but there must be someone else . . .'

'Who?' said Chard.

I racked my brain. He hadn't appeared in the shop with a hot young thing on his arm for ages when I thought about it. Like, really ages.

'But what about the woman you dedicated that beautiful song to at the Big Chill?' I said. 'The special one you told me you are waiting for?'

'That woman was you, Loulou,' he said laughing and coughing. 'I thought you'd know that.'

'But how could I know? You've never mentioned it before.'

'I thought with all the flowers and the cupcakes and seeing you every bloody day, you'd get the idea. Do other men sit and gaze at you adoringly every morning?'

I blinked at him and then turned to look at Theo who was bending forward watching us intently.

'Did you know?' I asked her.

'Duh?' she said, in her most Valley Girl style. 'It couldn't have been more obvious if he'd hired an aeroplane to sky write it over this hill. "Deathbreath luvs Mudda OK".'

'I did consider that,' said Chard. 'Not quite that wording . . .'

I still couldn't take it in on top of everything else that had happened that day and it really didn't seem quite normal to be discussing a proposal of marriage with my daughter listening in and contributing. But then, I thought, what had ever been normal about my life with Theo? This was just the latest freak show.

'Go on then, Mum!' said Theo, poking me in the ribs. 'The man is waiting for an answer.'

I looked at her vacantly for a moment and then snapped my head back to Chard. He was smiling at me so sweetly my stomach did a funny little somersault. Oh my goodness. Chard. And me. The boys had been right. Crikey.

'But you only go out with very young women, Chard,' I said, finally finding the words to express what was really confusing me. 'We talked about it. The baggage-free ones.'

He reached up and tucked a piece of hair that was sticking to my lipstick behind my ear. Then he stroked his finger down my cheek.

'Only to pass the time until you made a move on me,' he said. 'String-free dalliances. And apart from that small aberration at the Big Chill, I haven't had one of those for a while, you might have noticed.'

'So why were you hanging around my shop all the time hoping to pick up girls?'

He rolled his eyes to Theo's standards.

'Maybe I was really hoping to pick up someone else? Like *you*,' he said, tapping me gently on the forehead. 'It was just a cover story.'

'But what about the baggage?' I said, my face tingling where he had touched it. 'What about my baggage?'

Chard laughed again.

'But I love your baggage,' he said, leaning forward to pat Theo on the leg. 'This baggage, sitting right here.'

'Mutual, Deathbreath,' she answered. 'Totally mutual, baby.'

I sat back and put my hands over my face. It was all too much.

When I took them off again and looked at Chard he had another unlit cigarette hanging out of his mouth. What was going on?

'Why aren't you smoking, Chard?' I asked.

'I've given up,' he said, taking the ciggie out of his mouth and flicking it up into the air.

'You've given up?' I asked, stupidly.

'I wasn't recording last week,' he said. 'That was a front. I was doing nicotine rehab. Cold turkey.'

'That's amazing,' I said. 'I really thought you were a lifer. I never thought you'd give up. It's fantastic, but whatever prompted you to suddenly do it after all these years?'

'I thought it would increase my chances of getting with you. You've been very long suffering of my filthy smoking all these years, but I knew you hated it really.'

'Wow,' said Theo, sounding uncharacteristically impressed. 'He must really love you.'

And I think that's when it really sank in. He loved me enough to give up smoking for me – but there was still one thing bothering me.

'How can I marry you Chard?' I said. 'We've never even kissed. It's not the eighteenth century. What if you think I'm an awful kisser?'

'Well, that can be easily remedied,' said Chard. 'Look away, Theo.'

Then he pulled me into his arms. Those long, lanky arms which I had spent so many years looking at, as they played guitar and picked up tea glasses on my terrace, but had hardly ever felt around me. Then, his lips touched mine for the very first time and it felt like a homecoming. Still quite nicotine flavoured, but delicious all the same. Very slow and confident. I felt quite dizzy.

'Have you finished yet?' said Theo, in a muffled voice.

'For now,' said Chard, kissing me lightly on the lips and settling me into the fold of his arm. I just gazed up at him, that so familiar face now inspiring an entirely new set of feelings. Lust well to the fore.

'So, Loulou, baby,' he said. 'What's it going to be? Will you marry me?'

'Yes,' I said, nodding repeatedly as I finally took in that there was nothing else I would rather do. 'Of course I will.'

'Woohoo!' yelled Theo, leaping to her feet and punching the air. 'Rock and roll!'

'You're pleased?' I asked.

'Ecstatic,' she said. 'Deathbreath will be my dad, ODD will be my granddad and Nancy will be my legal granny. I love it!'

I turned to Chard and smiled at him, resting my head on his shoulder where, I now understood, it had always belonged. And so we sat there saying nothing, on our bench, looking out over London. Together.

Theo

OMIGOD I am larfing. Well the part of me which isn't cringing a million cringes is laughing. I just found my old diary when I was looking for something else on this computer and it's hilarious.

What a prize little shit I was. I'd forgotten. I haven't read this for nearly a year because I don't need to write it all down any more. Now I just live it.

So what's happened since my last digital vomit? Pheweeee so much. When I typed that I had just run away from one scary man – Paul Beaney – only to be pursued to my very home by another. My ex-dad.

Oh lordie what a day that was. It ended up with Deathbreath proposing marriage to my mum in front of me up on Primrose Hill. Is that normal? No it isn't. Is it good? Hell yeah.

He's officially my dad now. Legal. Loving that. And not just because he's married my mum. He has actually really adopted me too so I am 100% his real actual daughter.

But I think I always really felt he was anyway. Right down to being ultra embarrassed to be seen with him in public. He wears chambray shirts. Ironed. How am I supposed to feel?

So with all that coming on top of a general hysteria about what had happened in the shop earlier – and in my case the previous encounter with another homicidal maniac – we were all pretty cranked up.

It was Deathbreath's idea to have a party.

My beautiful babes he said. We need to celebrate. It isn't every day I get the love of my life to agree to marry me and acquire myself a wonderful daughter. I'll get Stravko firing on the refreshments. You two round up the usual suspects.

So I left the love birds to it up on the hill – keen to escape any more geriatric heavy petting – and rushed back to the shop to get Marc and Dylan and Shelley and we went round to Deathbreath's place for a genius barbecue and then danced like crazy maniacs.

Keith the Teeth turned up with Mudda's friend Rachel and Stravko brought Nancy down to sit on the sofa and watch and it just all kicked off. It was so great.

Mudds was physically attached to DB for the entire night and didn't dance with Marc once – which was a good thing as it might have scuppered the wedding plans ha ha ha. Actually I don't think anything could have got between those two once they realised what they had thought was BFF was actually Tru Luv 4 Eva OK.

And it was OK because Captain Frappachino was getting on down big time with Shelley and Rachel and me. He is a freakishly great dancer. I can see how Mudda got sucked into that now. I even let him spin me strictly come quickly a few times but I was mainly waltzing around with Dylan and twirling ODD in his wheelchair.

The Air Marshal was so sweet. When he heard the news about Deathbreath and Mudda he smiled so much I thought his head might crack open. Then he wheeled over and gave me the biggest hug. You are the granddaughter Nancy and I have always dreamed of he said into my ear. I cried.

We all cried later when Chard got out his guitar and played that really beautiful acoustic number he'd done back at the Big Chill.

You might remember this he said. It's called For Loulou.

We all went aaaaaah because he had gone a bit pink and it was so sweet and even I was over vomiting at soppiness by then.

He'd put words to it and it was all stuff about silk and chiffon and peau de pêche and eau de nil mixed in with sunlight and smiling and tea and your hands pouring. It was amazing.

I looked over at Mudda and her face was glowing like one of Auntie Jane's luminous figurines of the Virgin Mary. She looked properly happy. Real sweet as Deathbreath would say.

At the end Dylan leaned in close to me and said: Your stepdad is a LEGEND. I nodded a lot as a tribute.

So now they're married – the wedding was in *Hello!* HEINOUS but I got over it – and happily playing Mr and Mrs Meredith together round at Deathbreath Towers and I live here over the shop with my own darling. Dylan.

He thinks it's brilliant that I've only lived in one house my entire life – apart from a few unhappy weeks in a student hall of residence in Manchester – and is obsessed that I must never leave it. Suits me. As long as he stays here with me I told him. He says he will. He bloody better.

He is my shining star.

He's still finishing his law yooni thing so I'm the breadwinner for both of us. I don't live off my ex-dad anymore and Dylan doesn't live off his. I earn our cash. I work for Topshop. In the design studio. I bloody love it.

I got the job because the day I ran away from Weanie the head designer Tony got up and walked too. Turned out he'd already been talking to the enemy and that was the final insult that convinced him to go. And he very kindly took me with him and Ajay. We have such a laugh.

So I'm happy at home and happy at work. I have a boyfriend and a father and two very crumbly grandparents as well as the totally cool mother I've always had but haven't always fully appreciated. I do now though.

I also have more chain store clothes than I will ever be able to wear. But weirdly I'm wearing more of my mum's vintage tat these days. Probably because she's helping me put together a range for Topshop inspired by her favourite ever pieces.

It's called Loulou For You and they are planning to use the two of us together in the ad campaign to show how different ages can wear the same vintage-inspired gear. It was all my idea of course but it has made me realise just what a genius my mum is.

So with all of that I think my life has finally started. And this diary can finally end.

Acknowledgements

The author would like to thank the following people:

Mel Pointer for letting me be a Saturday girl in her wonderful vintage shop The Wardrobe, High Street, Old Town, Hastings: wardrobe-dress-agency.co.uk. And for all the beautiful things I have bought there.

Fanny Dowling for her invaluable insights into the vintage clothing trade over the past thirty years.

Heartfelt thanks to the wonderful team at Penguin: Julie Gibbs, Ingrid Ohlsson, Erin Langlands, Tony Palmer, Kirby Armstrong, Daniel Ruffino, Louise Ryan and Sally Bateman. With particular respect to my editor Jocelyn Hungerford. Not only are they all brilliant at their jobs – you'd want to have dinner with them too. They're hilarious. (Can I keep that one, Jocelyn?)

To my lovely agents at Curtis Brown: Fiona Inglis in Sydney and Jonathan Lloyd in London.

My title committee: Barbie Boxall, Laline Paul, Victoria Killay, Alice Lutyens, Katy Watts, Lottie Watts and Glen Holmes. And most especially Josephine Fairley – who came up with it (with a little help from the late Malcolm McLaren).

And all my love always to my husband Radenko 'Popi' Popovic, without whom nothing would be possible.